CALL OF THE DRAGON KNIGHT

CALL OF THE DRAGON KNIGHT

TIMOTHY MCGOWEN

REVIEWS ARE IMPORTANT

Every review matters, get your voice heard.

Follow me on Amazon to get informed when my next book is released!

https://www.amazon.com/stores/Timothy-McGowen/author/B087QTTRJK

Join my Patreon for early Chapters!

https://www.patreon.com/TimothyMcGowen

Join my Facebook group and discuss the books

https://www.facebook.com/groups/234653175151521/

I dedicate this book to all those struggling with one thing or another. I hope this book is a light in the darkness for you.

CONTENTS

LEAVE A REVIEW &
CHECK OUT MY WEBSITE

Don't forget to leave a review!

Get an exclusive short story to read if you subscribe to my newsletter at https://authortimothymcgowen.com/

CHAPTER 1
ONE DAY LEFT

It always started with fire.

I knew I was dreaming before the acrid smell of smoke hit my nostrils. It was a dream I'd had many times before. Standing on a hilltop, away from most of the carnage, I watched as a dragon rider flew through the sky, the last of his kind—this I knew only in the same way you just know things in a dream.

I never see his face; he's always just too far away and never circles closer. I heard the endless battle, the rip of thunder through the sky, and the silence as the last Dragon Rider and his dragon fell to their deaths.

Staring up at the rafters of my small room, lying in my bed no more comfortable than any morning before, I listened to my heart as it tried to pound out of my chest. I could almost hear my father's voice echoing in my ears; he'd told me the tales of dragon riders, including the one about the last dragon rider ever to fly the skies of Vareth.

It had happened in one of the southern cities whose name I couldn't pronounce easily, so I never tried. I could almost hear his voice from the grave, "Kaelric, there are great adventures to be had if you're willing to just give the impossible a chance." He'd said that to me the night he died. I was out with friends when the fire came roaring through the town, killing so many that night.

I was an orphan, or at least I had been. I turned 25 a few weeks ago, and today was the final day of training before all those like me who'd turned 25 this year would participate in a ritual that would unlock our potential and allow us to become adventurers, meaning a life full of dungeon-diving, slaying wild monsters, and growing powerful enough to claim a class of our own.

I heard footsteps down the hall and knew it was Tomas coming to fetch me for our morning training. Eager as I was each day to grow stronger and learn inside the tower, I still had a hard time getting up in the morning. Sure enough, there was a knock on my one-room apartment door, and a familiar voice a few moments later.

"Hey, arse hat, if I'm up, you should be up. Let's move it, or we won't have time to grab a snack before training starts," Tomas said. Trying the knob and finding it unlocked, he entered.

Tomas had features common in the north, where snow clung to the ground year-round. He had bright blue eyes, a grin almost always on his face, and blonde hair tied into a small bun at the back of his head. His scruff was more persistent than my own, showing up no matter how often he shaved. And, as always, he already had a bag of some snack or another in his hands. Tomas was fit, though wiry; he was faster than I was when we sparred, but he didn't have the strength I could bring to bear.

"I'm up," I said, climbing out of bed and heading to the washbasin. I caught a glimpse of myself in the reflection of the water.

I was young-faced for a man of 25, but I didn't mind having to only shave one day in five. My brown, unruly hair stuck up in every direction, so I splashed it with a bit of water to tame the worst of it. I felt the strength in my arms and legs as I stretched, and my keen orange eyes, something I had gotten from my father, scanned the room, alert and ready for the day.

I set the chamber pot outside my door, then started getting dressed for the day.

"Still in your undergarments, eh?" Tomas asked, throwing a bit of something into his mouth and munching loudly.

"Give me five, and I'll be set," I said, pulling on my tunic, pants, boots, and lastly my father's red scarf. I wore it year-round to honor and remember him, but after today, I'd know what true potential it held, as I was almost certain it was a magical item.

Magical items were strange, though. Until you were 'Unlocked,' as they called it, you couldn't really use or benefit from them. It had something to do with the famed 'System' and how it worked. Whenever I tried to ask more about it, I always got the same dismissive answer: "Wait and see." But the waiting and seeing would be over soon. At midnight tonight, I'd be part of the ritual to unlock myself along with Tomas and Ryn, our other best friend.

"Ryn is going to kick you in the arse," Tomas said through the sound of him chewing. "You told her we'd meet her at the Starling Inn as the sun rose. That was at least twenty minutes ago, and I'm not taking the blame for this one; she already has it out for me because of that little mishap with the goblin."

"You mean when you hit it right into her and got her stabbed in the gut?" I asked, laughing only now that it had been a few months since. It was a sore topic for a while, as Ryn had nearly died because of the mistake Tomas had made.

"We had potions, she wasn't going to die," Tomas said, as if reading my mind.

"Yeah?" I asked, smiling. "Tell that to her. Maybe I'll bring it up as a way to get the heat off of me for being late." Pausing as I finished getting ready I said, "Let's go, I'm ready."

I grabbed my pack, which held my training gear and my nearly rusted-out sword. To say I was poor would be an understatement, but Tomas lived comfortably with his adoptive family, and Ryn worked hard as a town guard in the evenings, so I had friends who were reasonably well off.

Personally, I took the occasional shift at the docks on the west side of town when I really needed coin, which meant I worked about every two or three days. It was frustrating because I'd miss out on that day's training, leaving me quite a bit behind the other students in technique. Despite that, I hadn't been kicked out of the tower yet, so the day had finally come for me to be unlocked.

Of course, House Ravenlock was pretty lax with those they sponsored to go into the tower; it was more about trade and supporting local guilds and markets than anything. They'd adopted Tomas for one, which meant they had to be pretty relaxed about their rules, because well, Tomas was lax about everything, except for maybe being on time. That flaw fell to me alone out of our group of three.

There were two noble Houses in our town, Brackenford. One was much more militaristic than the other, basically claiming they alone kept the dungeon outside of town in check. When adventurers failed to purge it regularly, they'd go in and keep the numbers down, so the town was never at risk. They also used the tower; of course, it was technically open to all, but the two families kept a tight watch on it.

The Elder Spire loomed over the city at its center, like a sentinel constantly watching, ever-present and steadfast. I couldn't help but be drawn to the tower, despite being the oldest building in all of Brackenford, its construction and true purpose remained a mystery.

I lived in the Commons, as it was called, part of the outer ring of the city and the closest to the wall that stretched around the place. But I still liked to think of myself as a member of the Forge Quarter. It occupied the Southwest part of the town and was only a few streets away from where I stayed. The distinction mattered in a town that prized where you lived almost as much as where you were from.

"Should we hit up the Flowing Flask or the Amber Coin Tavern?" Tomas asked, finishing off his bag of treats and stuffing the remaining trash into his pockets.

"I kind of want to check out the new place, what was it called again?" I asked, trying to remember the silly name the tavern had been given.

"It was an odd name I've never heard before, Melon or Melish or something," Tomas said. "But I'm not sure about trying a new place. Might be best to stick with what we know works."

"Merlin's Pub," I said, raising a finger up and remembering the name at the same time.

"That sounds made up or like it's been used before. You sure you want to check it out?" Tomas asked.

"You're probably right," I said, shrugging it off. "Let's just hit up the Amber Coin Tavern, maybe we can look at the job boards while we are there."

"Oh," Tomas said suddenly as we neared the Starling Inn, where we were set to meet Ryn. "She looks pissed."

Sure enough, I looked up to see a sour-faced Ryn stomping her way over to us.

She was unique in this town; she came from the South about six years ago, around her 18th birthday, and we'd become fast friends since then, but she had a pretty intense temper when she wanted. Mostly, it was directed toward anyone who messed with Tomas or me, but now I could see it was directed toward us.

She had the skin and hair coloring of someone from the hot southern region of Vareth. Her black hair was shaved at the sides, with a small tuft of red at the front that hinted at Touched heritage somewhere in her bloodline. We joked that she must have a bit of Touched Fire Elemental in her ancestry, which would explain both her temper and that flash of red. She always disagreed, insisting that everyone in her family had the same tuft of hair and that it was simply part of who she was.

She had dark brown eyes and wore a tunic beneath a leather coat that doubled as armor when buttoned up. A belt at her waist held not one but two daggers, along with a sword. She even wore fingerless gloves, ready to draw and fight at any moment. Her nose was narrow at the bridge but widened significantly at the tip, and her eyebrows were almost always drawn together, whether in anger or concentration.

She spent her time either breaking up fights as a guard working the tavern circuit, starting fights herself on her off time, or sticking her nose in a book. No matter which she was doing, she wore the same concentrated-meets-constipated look on her face.

"You know how long I've waited for you two?" she said as we came within shouting distance.

Before I could answer, her eyes narrowed on me. I followed her gaze to see Tomas pointing at me with two fingers, jerking his head in my direction.

"Well, thanks, man," I said, chuckling despite the anger on Ryn's face. She was always angry about something or other. A little food and drink usually sorted that out for her.

"Uh, so, sorry about that, but we decided we should check out the

Amber Coin Tavern for some breakfast and maybe find a job we could take after tonight," I said, hoping the reminder that we were all set to leave on a journey together the next day might soften her up a bit.

"Ugh, why can't we just get some food here and get to training?" Ryn asked. We both made a face, but I was glad to have dodged most of her anger.

"Because old Morric has forgotten how to season his food since his wife passed," I said, and Tomas readily agreed, nodding his head vigorously.

"Yeah, their food stinks now. No flavor," he added, shaking his head to really drive the point home.

"I like it. Plus, he doesn't get many patrons anymore," Ryn said, showing she had a softer side despite her hard exterior.

"We can eat here tomorrow," I said. "I really want to check out the Adventurer's Guild board and see what jobs are available around here."

"They catch you looking before you've been unlocked, and they'll throw you out," Ryn said flatly.

"Oh, she's got a point," Tomas said, leaning hard on his walking stick, which doubled as his preferred weapon.

"Fine," I said. We'd wasted enough time as it was. "Let's eat bland food and drink sour ale."

"His ale is fine," Ryn said, slinging an arm over both of us and dragging us toward the entrance. "And don't think I've forgotten that you made me wait. You're paying today."

That hurt more than it should have. We all knew I was the poorest among us. I had enough coin to cover a meal or three, but not much else. All I carried were four scales and a single moon, saved for a rainy day. It was my entire fortune. A moon, a single silver coin, was worth a hundred copper scales, as they were commonly called.

Scales were thin copper coins that were just as likely to fall apart as stay together, so thin was the copper that the imprints of the noble house that minted them remained almost always indistinguishable. Moons were thin as well and had a hole in the middle, making them more like a ring than anything, but they were thick enough that you could still read the writing that went around it, usually just the name of the noble family that minted it on top.

Of course, all coins had different-sized holes, as was standard in most of Vareth, to make counting easier with rods. But I had once seen a coin from the south. It was like a scale but thicker and made of gold. It bore the face of some ruler from down south and words I couldn't understand, which was odd because, from what I had learned, most people on our continent spoke Varethian.

Even Ryn, when I'd told her about the coin, said it was odd and perhaps something they had gotten from the few trading boats that made it through the great sea separating us from our closest neighbors, the continent of

Sunreach. Of course, I knew about other continents, but the Tempest Veil and the Great Eastern Gyre made travel by boat, even for trade, nearly impossible. I had heard all this at the docks, where the river Veyne runs through the town.

All these thoughts ran through my head as we entered, and Mr. Althune, or Morric as most just called him, awaited us with an eagerness and energy that belied his old age.

"Welcome, welcome," he said. He had only one other person inside eating, an elderly woman whom I recognized as Mrs. Fenmere, Liora, I think her first name was, but she was also a widow, so I wondered immediately if we were interrupting time between them.

"Can you start us off with some coffee? I'll take mine black; he wants as much cream and sugar as you can spare," Ryn said, thumbing over to Tomas, who nodded eagerly. "And he wants just a splash of sugar and cream in his."

She was right, of course, but I frowned at her taking charge when I was going to be the one paying. My first order of business would have been to ask for a pitcher of water, which was much cheaper than three coffees.

"Fine," I said. "I mean, yes, that'll do fine."

"Sit anywhere you'd like, and I'll have those coffees up in a jiff," Old Morric said, turning and leaving for the back of the room in haste.

The Starling Inn was much what you'd expect from a two-story inn sandwiched between two large residential homes. The seating room had a dozen tables, only two of them occupied when we sat down. Sunlight streamed through the open window shutters, and lamplights glowed on the walls and at the tables. Despite all the trouble Ryn had given me about not making good time, it was still dim outside, the sun not yet fully cresting the horizon.

The room was decorated with various old weapons, tools, and even a few stuffed monster heads on the walls, all said to be trophies of Mr. and Mrs. Althune's conquests. It created an interesting vibe, as most of the decor was covered in a thick layer of dust and cobwebs. The prized weapon of Mr. Althune, a runed blue blade, remained polished and sat over the fireplace set into the south wall.

I'd asked him more than a few times if he wanted to sell the blade, but he'd always insisted that it would be buried with him when he died; it was the last blade he used before giving up adventuring and settling down with his wife.

"Here are your coffees. I hear congratulations are in store for the three of you, going to get Unlocked today, aren't you?" he asked, standing beside Tomas and leaning on his chair for support.

"We are," I said, taking charge before Ryn could. "We just haven't decided if we're leaving town to try for some weaker monsters around the dungeon ruins. I know the dungeon itself has higher-tier monsters, but maybe we could find something weaker."

"I'd suggest you go west if you can find a caravan heading that way. The monsters around here are pretty strong; you'd have to be very lucky to find anything weak enough to give you the essence you'll need to level up," Morric said, smiling widely, clearly enjoying the chance to pass on his knowledge to youngsters, I was sure.

"How about it, Morric?" I said, gesturing to his sword. "Ready to sell that to me?"

"You couldn't afford it, lad, even if I did sell it," Morric said, chuckling. "Did I tell you the time I got that sword? Myrren and I, along with our party, had just slain a lich that was giving one of the biggest cities trouble, and then, out of nowhere, a demon showed up—likely half-summoned by the lich. Lucky for us, it was malformed and only barely summoned, so we slayed it easily, and I got that sword as a drop. It stayed with me another five years, longer than any other blade, and I retired with it after we hit level 45."

"You're level 45?" I asked, surprised that he'd made it that high. "How long did it take you to reach that level?" I had an ulterior motive in asking. The book my father had given me before his death suggested a build that didn't earn a class until level 40, but it would be worth it if I could obtain the class of a Dragon Knight.

"Oh, we were pretty slow going, so it took us many years. Most can do it in half the time if they're willing to keep adventuring hardcore. I've even heard of a few who did it in just a few months, but those would have noble support and all, so it wouldn't be easy to replicate," Morric said, looking every bit his age as he leaned on the chair.

He was probably close to 80 years old now, but the years of adventuring had taken their toll on his body, and he looked a good ten years older than he was. I realized that in all the time I've known the man, all my life really, I'd never heard what his class had been. It was kind of a taboo question to ask someone, unless you were in their party, but I decided to ask anyway.

"Morric," I said. "What class did you and Myrren have?"

"Oh, nothing special. We took one of the first that were offered to us from our attribute spread. I was an Arcane Knight, and she was a Mystic Sentinel, both hardy classes worth every attribute we had sunk into the builds. You know how rare healers are, so as a Mystic Sentinel, Myrren could block damage before it occurred, keeping potion costs down. She did eventually get her hands on a staff of healing, allowing her to heal and block damage, but that's an entirely different story," Morric said, seemingly happy to talk about his good ole days.

"Arcane Knight, that is a Power and Arcana build, right? It takes only ten from each attribute, meaning you can get it at level 20," Ryn said as if reciting something she'd read.

We ordered quickly, and he nodded along. He was the cook as well, so when he didn't immediately leave, I knew we'd made a mistake coming here and striking up so much conversation. We were going to be late for sure.

"Have you youngsters decided what classes you are going for?" Morric asked, still leaning heavily on Tomas's chair.

"I'm going to be a Dervish," Tomas announced, and I snorted. He'd changed what he wanted to be on a daily basis; only yesterday, he was trying to convince me that Warden was the way to go, despite how long it would take to unlock the class. Not that I was one to talk, if I followed the path I had in mind, it would be level 40 before I even saw if my hard work paid off.

"I don't know, to be honest," Ryn said. "It depends on what attributes they decide to focus on, then I'll adjust accordingly."

Morric smiled, and then everyone looked at me. It was no secret what I wanted, as I'd told more than just my circle of friends, but it often got me laughed at, and so I hesitated only a moment or two before saying.

"I'm going to be a Dragon Knight."

CHAPTER 2
ELDER TOWER

Morric's chuckles annoyed me as he walked away, shaking his head. I could understand why. According to my father, there hadn't been a Dragon Knight on record for over a hundred years. To make matters worse, any records of how to become a Dragon Knight were either lost or deliberately kept secret by noble families, no doubt to maintain control over such a powerful class.

But I was raised on stories of dragons and Dragon Knights, how they were powerful enough to turn the tide of entire wars. I wanted that power, and I would get it one way or another. Sure, I had hoops to jump through, like my precious book saying that to become a Dragon Knight, I would have to slay a dragon.

Dragons hadn't been seen on the mainland for as long as the Dragon Knights had disappeared, according to the little research I had done and the lessons Ryn had repeated to me multiple times. There were about thirty known classes, each resulting from a different combination of the four main attributes: Power, Guard, Speed, and Arcana.

My book spoke of three additional classes that were once more common among more patient folk who truly wanted to change the world; Dragon Knight was among them.

I didn't care much for the others, Paragon and Epoch, despite them sounding cool. I wanted the class that was by far the most epic, as it involved me one day taming a dragon as a companion.

Dragon Knight.

"You know," Ryn said. "If you'd just keep that to yourself, you'd get laughed at a whole lot less. I mean, even if you do end up going the path of the Dragon Knight, assuming it's real and you don't waste years of your life on it, do you really need to tell everyone?"

"I know, I know," I said, drinking deeply from my coffee mug.

I didn't have to, but I couldn't help it. I was so enthralled by the idea of reaching that lofty goal that I couldn't do anything but tell anyone who cared to listen. It was foolish of me, sure, but I had my book to reassure me that all wasn't lost.

Besides, even if I wasted forty levels and did as the guide suggested, putting all attributes to ten, then that would mean I'd be one of the most balanced Adventurers around. Most people focused on one or two attributes, becoming either insanely strong, nearly impossible to injure, unbelievably fast, or masters of magic unrivaled by anyone else.

Saying it like that made me feel a bit down. I'd be decent at all attributes, but not exceptional at any of them. It was going to be alright, though, because each class had benefits and special abilities that would make up for it.

Morric arrived shortly after, carrying three plates of food, setting them down one by one.

"For the girl who doesn't know what she wants to be yet, here you are," he said, handing Ryn her plate. Then he acknowledged Tomas, mentioning the class he'd said, and then came over to me.

"And to our famed Dragon Knight, a plate of eggs, bacon, and an extra portion of potatoes," Morric said, chuckling again. "You might need my sword if you're going after a fairytale class like that, but I doubt you've got the Suns required to buy it. Speaking of which, that'll be three scales for the meal."

"That's more than it was last time," I said, complaining about the rising prices.

"It isn't, so pay up now, or I'll make you work it off," Morric said, holding out his hand.

I paid the man, handing him three of my four scales. Luckily, tipping wasn't customary in the central parts of Vareth; only the northern regions had that practice, and it was considered rude here.

We ate like people who hadn't eaten in days, knowing we were late and couldn't spare the time. The food was sparsely seasoned, so we barely tasted it, and then we stood and made for the door.

Before long, we were outside in the cool morning air. It was early in the year, but late enough that the snows had already melted everywhere except the northern lands. That meant monster migrations would begin soon, so there would be plenty of ways to get essence eventually.

But we still had one more day of training in the tower, and those goblins weren't going to kill themselves. We walked through the Forge Quarter, where smoke constantly filtered from the many shops and forges, stinking up the area and making us quicken our pace to escape it.

We made it to the main street and soon approached the Elder Tower, where various groups of youths practiced fighting alongside whichever house sponsored them. Our group was gone already, likely inside the tower after warm-ups and killing goblins.

"Well, shit," Ryn said, looking at me with judgment in her eyes. "They went in already, so we are going to have to hope they aren't too deep to reach, or we risk our lives because you can't wake up on time."

"I get it," I finally said. "I made us late, and now we might die. Let's just get in there and kill something already."

The tower had many doors, each one of the six we used put you into a different version of the tower, so you could face goblins, skeletons, imps, or any number of other monsters. We were scheduled for the goblin door today. Our last day inside was meant to take us all the way to the goblin mini-boss, where we would form groups and stage a raid-style fight, defeating him to prove we were ready for life as adventurers.

Of course, there was little risk when Velric, our mentor, led the group. But that all went out the window if you entered on your own, which we very much planned to do.

"How long ago did Velric's group enter?" I asked as we approached the door warden for the goblin door.

"Ten, almost fifteen minutes ago," he said. "I'd advise against going in until they return."

"Noted," I said. We stepped forward as one and pushed the six-foot-high door open. A rush of wind hit us, as always, and we stepped through the shimmering wall of light into the tower's first floor.

I felt my stomach drop for a moment, but it passed quickly as we focused on getting our armor on and leaving our packs by the interior door with the others. Velric brought his own, stocked with potions and even a rare healing wand. We always left ours behind because it was better to be ready to fight than to wrestle with a pack.

The twenty-pace circle around the door kept us safe from the goblins roaming the trees, so we didn't worry as we changed and pulled out our weapons. My armor was nothing more than hardened leather, cracked and worn in places from years of training. I had it mended as best I could, but it still didn't look like much.

My sword was chipped and a little rusty, but I had taken care of it, and it looked better than when I first got it. My shield was small, a buckler really, made of wood chipped and splintered along the edges. In a word, my gear was shoddy at best and trash at worst.

"I'm ready," I said, doing a quick check to make sure all the buckles were fastened on myself and the others.

Ryn had the best-looking gear of all of us, thanks to her steady job and income. Even Tomas, who was sponsored by his adoptive family, had armor that had seen better days. Still, we all knew our limitations and what we could expect from each other.

I played the role of the tank or front-line fighter, getting the attention of the monsters and drawing in their blows as my team flanked them. Tomas would come in hard with his staff, cracking skulls and ending goblin lives easily, while Ryn relied on her speed and either her short sword or her daggers to take them out while they weren't paying attention to her.

"Let's move," I said once they both indicated they were ready. We stepped forward, heading directly north toward the boss. Hopefully, they had cleared out most of the bigger groups for us, since goblins could swarm if not dealt with quickly.

The inside of the tower felt like its own little world. You could see the illusion of a sky on a ceiling some twenty paces above, but the trees seemed real enough, thick brush making it difficult at best and impossible at worst to follow anything but the path laid out for you.

We followed the tracks of a large party moving through the forest and soon came upon our first monster. The brush shook, and a little four-foot-tall green figure with a bulbous head and large ears leapt out. It wore scraps of cloth and wielded a sharpened stick. This was the weakest of all types of goblins you could encounter, and we didn't slow down as we engaged it with practiced ease.

The goblin stabbed forward with its stick. I raised my shield, catching the blow and deflecting it to the side before counterattacking with my sword. My strike cut a long groove across its cheek. It didn't cry out in pain; they never did inside the tower. Nor did they run like normal goblins were said to when they felt outmatched.

Instead, it reared back to stab at my midsection, but Tomas was there, smashing it down on the head and twirling his staff in a way that it took out the weak, sharpened stick before it could hit me. Ryn finished it off as it staggered, cutting her daggers across its neck.

No blood, as always, but it shimmered suddenly and burst into tiny pieces of light that faded a moment later. Also, unfortunately, tower monsters provided no loot at all; only dungeon monsters provided loot, and monsters that left a dungeon or were natural provided only what their corpses offered.

We continued on, facing off against two more weak goblins before we heard shouting ahead that indicated we'd caught up with the group. But as we neared, a goblin warrior appeared, wearing rusty chainmail and wielding a wicked-looking curved blade. This was meant to be fought by a team of six, so we were immediately at a disadvantage.

I caught the first strike of its blade as it snarled at us, but I wasn't expecting the kick to my knees that came from the slightly taller and stronger goblin. I fell backward, stumbling but keeping my footing after all.

Tomas was there, smashing his staff into the goblin's face, making it possible for me to recover. Ryn attacked from the side, but it was ready for her, and she had to dance back to avoid its blade. We poked at it, swords swinging and my shield doing its best to catch attacks, when finally Tomas managed to hit it in the head and stun it.

Ryn and I both lunged forward, blades held out before us, stabbing for the goblin's throat and gut. My blade pierced its chainmail and dug deep into its gut as she scored a critical hit on its throat, slicing it wide open. Again, no blood came, just the quick death of the goblin in a spray of light.

"About time you caught up," a voice called from further up the path. It was Velric Shadewyn, our mentor. I could just make out his face ahead, and we sprinted to join them, the sounds of battle already reaching us.

Sure enough, the goblin king, as he was known, stood six feet tall and just as wide, battling the rest of our class, all fifteen of them. Jareth, Sel, and Ashric, the group we normally partied up with, fought toward the back, waiting their chance to rotate in and fight.

"Well, go on. Join your party and get ready to rotate in when I call for it," Velric said, shooing us away with a hand.

Velric was an oddity in our small town. He was a Touched, specifically a Beastborn of the cat variety, with fur covering his entire body and cat ears atop his head, patterned with black-and-grey spots. He wore black leather armor with metal studs and carried a thin rapier at his side, never using a shield. His pack was set aside, but several potions hung from his belt, ready for use if needed. There, too, was the white-wood healing wand he kept for emergencies.

I could count on one hand how many Touched lived in our town that I knew of, and on two hands how many I had seen in my lifetime. They were rare, said to be shaped by the magic of the land—given different forms but still considered human, just touched by magic.

We rushed forward to join the waiting three, who gave us looks ranging from eye rolling to snickering to a touch of annoyance. Jareth wielded a thin sword like Velric's, and he was known to be fast and vicious in the damage he dealt. Meanwhile, Sel had a larger shield than mine and used a mace, very effective against the skeleton door but slightly less so against goblins. Ashric used a magical staff that shot forth pulsing blue light, preferring to stay back and use its charges rather than fight up close.

It was rare to almost unheard of for a magical item to work for someone not yet unlocked, but this staff was an artifact-level item from his House, House Ravenlock, to whom he was the second son. It required charging from someone with access to Mana, which he didn't have, so I knew, from experience and hard lessons learned, that his staff had four dozen charges before it went limp, and he was worthless in a fight.

He did carry a crossbow, but it was slow and cumbersome to reload. However, this was the team we had, and we'd grown to be fair enough friends with the lot. Ashric and Tomas were fast friends, having grown up together, but Jareth was a little distant, and Sel just thought of us as annoying, seeing as I missed so many days and inconvenienced the team on more occasions than not.

"Nice of you to join us," Sel said, her dark brown hair falling out of her helmet on the side. She had true armor, a mix of a cloth gambeson with hardened leather plates with metal studs over it. Her parents were well-off merchants and had amassed a good deal of wealth as adventurers back in the day.

"We aim to please," Tomas said. Somehow, he'd found a new bag of snacks and was eating some dried fruit or something similar while he waited for us to be called in.

"We can apologize later. Right now, we've gotta stay sharp," Ryn said, cutting off something Sel was about to say.

Meanwhile, Ashric was sneaking a few fruit chips from Tomas's bag despite Tomas's protests. Jareth stood to the side, as he did most days, fingering his blade and looking bored and disinterested.

"Switch!" Velric said, and suddenly our attention was back on the battle before us. The group to the left ran out, and we ran in to take their spot in the fight against the giant goblin king.

He lifted his massive cleaver and began to swing. The group on the right was calling shots and called for a block. I rushed forward with three other shields at my side, and we blocked the massive blow, each of us being thrown back by the sheer power of it.

"Attack!" came the call from someone on the right as we recovered and checked our shields for damage. Mine was nearly split in two, but it hadn't completely buckled, so I would be ready when shields were called.

I watched in awe as everyone unleashed attacks on the massive goblin. Jareth flashed his rapier out and stabbed and slashed with speed beyond reason for someone not yet unlocked. Ashric stood back and pelted it with bolts of light, blowing away small chunks of its flesh with each hit. It was a marvelous battle to behold, and I rushed forward to get a few strikes before the goblin king recovered and tried to strike again.

This raid fight was much easier than I thought it would be; it was more about having the right number of people than anything else. Or at least I thought I had it figured out, when it suddenly did something unexpected, throwing its cleaver down and stabbing it into the ground. It folded its arms as we attacked, and suddenly, goblin warriors, shamans, and stick goblins appeared, as well as a line of four archer goblin. We'd not faced archers before so we made ourselves ready for this change as best we could.

"Switch!" Velric called, and the right group switched out with the six that were resting. That would mean it was up to us to call the shots as we'd been in longer. Ryn was our shot caller, so she stepped forward and assessed the situation.

"Ranged, go for the archers! Shields, get ready to stop that charge, everyone else flank hard!" Ryn yelled, and we moved to follow her instructions.

One archer went down from a blast of magic, then an arrow from one of the other groups took another, but not before three arrows shot out and hit our group's backline. Luck was with us, though, as only one person on the other team was hit in the leg, non-lethal damage. The remaining archers went down before they could get another volley off, mostly because of some quick work by Ashric, casting his blasts faster than I'd seen him do before.

The charge of goblin warriors hit the wall just as the shamans began to cast their spells. We all knew from experience that they'd summon shields on themselves first, then begin to buff the other goblins, making them stronger and faster. Then, if they were allowed to live long enough, they'd cast a chain lightning attack on us that would hurt like hell.

Because of how slow it took them to do their spells, though, they weren't a priority, so instead we worked hard to bring down the dozen melee-fighter goblins, half stick-wielding and half warriors. I caught a blade and parried a follow-up attack as we stood with our shields ready, blocking their charge.

Our flanking attackers swarmed in. With our focus holding roughly six or seven goblins in place, the rest of the fighters were able to overwhelm the others, and they soon began to burst into sparkling lights .

I caught another blow, and my shield finally gave way, splitting in two. Sel shot me a look and rolled her eyes, but I stayed in the line, focusing on parrying attacks instead of striking. Where I could, I counterattacked, but I was seldom able to. Instead, I acted as a tank without a shield as best as I could, and it worked well enough that I held the line.

Sweat poured down my face as I gripped my sword with two hands and pushed it to the limits of its design. We were all running the risk of being too tired from how intense the combat was, but even so, we fought on.

Blow after blow came in from the warrior before me, and I slowly chipped away at his health until finally I scored a killing blow when I turned away his weapon and slammed my sword into his neck.

"Nice," I said, pushing through the line and slashing out at a stick-wielding goblin. It managed to get past my defenses in my rush of excitement, and I felt it stab into my stomach, just barely drawing blood.

I saw red, slashing for its neck and ending it a moment later.

The battle raged on for only a minute, but it felt like more. When they were finally cleared, a call for "Switch!" was issued, and we backed out to allow a fresh party to go in. It was a relief, because the constant fighting was starting to wear on me, and my breaths came in short, sharp bursts.

Half the party, myself included, took a knee as we recovered, but after a minutes, I was feeling much better. Years of fighting like this had drilled my body into getting used to short bursts of intense focus and work.

The call to switch us in never came, as the goblin boss exploded in a bright shower of light only a minute into the other group coming in to fight it.

"Hell yeah!" I cheered, along with everyone else, as we all shouted in celebration.

"That was your last challenge," Velric said. "You should be proud. Over the last five years, you have all grown strong enough to survive your Unlocking ceremony. It won't be easy, and I know you've been told very little about what to expect. Be ready, because nothing worth having is ever easy."

With that, we split up, had our injuries checked on, and healed if necessary. Mine was so slight that it didn't warrant using a charge from the healing wand or a healing potion, so we patched it up the old-fashioned way, and I dealt with the pain, slight as it was.

"We've got like twelve hours before the ritual, any plans?" Ashric asked, walking beside Tomas, Ryn, and me.

"I have work," Ryn said. "It's my last day, and they are throwing me a party."

"I'm free," Tomas said, shrugging.

"So am I, but I want to run by the library at some point. Ryn tells me they just got in some old books that I want to check for information about my future class," I said. I didn't say the name out loud, but everyone sort of chuckled or groaned at the mention of it anyway.

"I told you I already skimmed through them and didn't see anything to do with Dragon Knights. But there was a mention of a dragon class or perhaps a rumored class. It's the large, black-bound one with the gold bar down the spine. I forget the title, but you can't miss it," Ryn said, shrugging as we ventured casually through the tower and out into the courtyard beyond.

"Did you guys notice a door opened behind the goblin king after he was defeated?" Sel asked, looking to Jareth and Ashric more than my team.

"What?" Ashric asked. "Like it opened up access to the next floor or something?"

"Yeah, that's what it looked like," Sel said.

"Wonder what we'd face on a higher floor?" I asked, curious whether the goblin theme would remain.

"No idea," Sel said.

I knew precious little about Towers in general, but I did see a Climber once. They're adventurers who challenge towers exclusively, and they don't last long, or so the rumors around town said when one came to visit our tower. Something about getting only a quarter of the essence from monster kills in a tower and no loot except on the higher floors, and even that loot wasn't what you'd expect from a dungeon or a craftsman.

I had a lot to learn about adventuring and the world I was about to enter, but I wouldn't do it alone. I'd become a Dragon Knight with my friends at my side and a blade in my hands.

CHAPTER 3
TO THE LIBRARY

I made my way to the library, eager to learn what I could about any classes to do with dragons. The library in question was in the northern part of town in Scholar's Row. It was next to the second-largest building in the town walls, the Collegium Annex, a place where traveling adventurers who focused on Arcana could lecture or sell knowledge.

The weather was still cool and crisp, feeling great against my skin as I peeled off my armor and put on my normal clothes. Of course, I had a hole in my shirt now where I'd been stabbed, but the blood was under control, and my bandage held together after stripping away my armor.

I knew Mrs. Valtren wasn't going to be happy if she saw the blood as I entered the library, so I fished out a thin coat I had in my pack and put it on over my wound. Feeling as if I'd done my best, I ventured through the town and to the location in question.

People by the dozens went about their business; there were just as many adventurers as there were people who had retired and taken on more mundane jobs. The thing was, everyone was an adventurer at some point in their lives; it was just a matter of how long you stayed an adventurer.

For some, it was just a matter of weeks. Getting those first five to ten levels was easy, known as the ease in levels, as they came quickly and fast, getting you hooked on the feeling of growing in power. But after that, it gradually slowed until you approached level 50, when it became downright hard to level, or so I'd heard from those who had tried to go beyond.

All thoughts fled as I approached the library, and my excitement hit a crescendo. The library was small, considering the building beside it was some four stories tall. With a square design and a flat roof more commonly seen in the south, it stood out against the rest of the buildings. It was painted white with blue trim, and its door was the same deep blue.

The door swung open easily, and I was immediately overtaken by the smell and feel of so many books in one place. I wasn't Ryn, so I wasn't so obsessed with books that I had to spend all day, every day reading, but I had an appreciation for them.

"Welcome, young Grimholt, in search of dragons again, are you?" Mrs. Valtren asked, looking over her desk at me with several books stacked all around her.

"There was supposed to be a new shipment of some old books, Ryn told me," I said, looking about on the reading tables and the carts used to return books for anything matching the description she'd given.

"Oh, those books, I'm afraid all but one have been checked out already. They were donated by a wandering scholar, and the noble families took special note of them when I told them what they likely contained. We do have this one left," she said, raising up a book that matched the description Ryn had given. "Ryn told me you'd be interested in it, so I kept it aside, but they will realize and come for it soon, so you'd best get your reading done with haste."

"You are the best!" I said, wishing I could jump over the desk and hug her, but I knew she wouldn't be a fan of such touching. She placed the book at the end of her desk, and I carried it to a table, pulled out a chair, and sat down.

The book had no title, or rather, the title page had been ripped free, so there were only chapters with no titles, with information listed here and there, and little pen-written side notes. Such abuses of books would have Mrs. Valtren mad as a fox deprived of its meal.

Plunging headfirst into the book, I searched for any mention of a dragon class. I ended up finding notes on four classes considered rare, ones I'd never heard of before. First, there was the Blade Sage; you would be required to raise three attributes to the second threshold, which, knowing from past studies, meant 10. It would give you great control over the elements and a class ability called Elemental Dash.

Interesting, but not what I wanted. I moved to the next: War Monk. A martial brawler with endurance to match the gods. It had a class ability called Crushing Flurry and was famed for its ability to use blunt weapons effectively in almost any situation.

Then there was a super rare class, as it seemed to be focused around healing, which almost no classes were, as all healing was done by shielding, potions, or special items infused with healing magic. It was called Battle Priest, a defensive healer with a class ability called Divine Ward. So perhaps still a shielding type of healer after all.

The last one caught my eye, and my heart jumped a little. It wasn't Dragon Knight and didn't require the same as the class I had a book for, but it was called Dragon Vanguard, an elite anti-beast fighter that got a class ability called Drakebane Strike. And here it was, somewhere that actually mentioned Dragon Knights.

It said, roughly, that Dragon Vanguard is a precursor to the legendary class Dragon Knight, often filled with those who allied themselves with Dragon Knights, though few took the path of Dragon Knights anymore, the book said, because of the quest requirements being so deadly.

I kept reading, but it made no further mention of it and had no notes on it. But this proved that the class existed at least, and my book wasn't just an anomaly of text on the subject. No, it was something that could still be obtained, if only I could complete the quest it mentioned.

From reading my own book on the topic, I knew that the quest required me to slay a dragon, a feat that seemed impossible, but if I could manage it, there were talks in the book about me somehow getting a dragon's egg and raising a dragon myself. That of course meant I'd need to find a dragon somehow and then kill it, and then somehow find an egg so I could have my own dragon.

I'd all but memorized the small book I had on the topic, but besides giving the thresholds you had to reach and explaining the quest, the rest was stories of great riders and what they'd been able to accomplish. Because every Dragon Knight it spoke of was also a dragon rider. I could hardly wait to read out of the book again, even though I'd done so a million times before.

Leaving the library after committing the new classes to memory, I returned the book just as two men in House Deymorin livery arrived. I could guess what they were there for, but I slipped out before I could be questioned about the book. No one made a move to follow me, but I went straight home in the Commons, to change and meet up with my friends at the Amber Coin Tavern, where I was sure they'd be trying to catch a sneak peek at the Adventurer's Guild board.

As I was walking up to my room, I heard things being thrown about, and I quickened my pace, only to find two members of House Deymorin leaving my room.

"What in the hell are you doing?" I asked, blocking their path out of sheer annoyance and anger.

"Kaelric Grimholt?" one of them asked; he wore the black-and-gold colors of House Deymorin, with the serpent emblem on the front in gold.

"Who wants to know?" I asked, suddenly on the defensive. That was when I saw they had a certain small black leather book, the one my father had given me. "Give that back!" I lunged forward, but these were Unlocked individuals of who knew what level, and they easily stopped me. One of them extended a hand and struck me in the chest, throwing me back from an open palm attack.

I nearly fell down the stairs behind me, but I managed to catch myself.

"Take him and let's go," the guard on the left said.

I knew neither of them, for most of the guards and families of the guards lived out on the estate of House Deymorin, barely interacting with the town if they didn't have to. They prized themselves as the barrier of the town against the dungeon, but I suspected it was mostly talk. Adventurers kept the dungeon in check most of the time, so their services were barely needed, except during the monster migrations, which were to happen any week now.

One of the guards kept a firm grip on my arm, walking me through town like a prisoner, and catching the looks of many citizens who pointed and jeered at either the guards or me, I couldn't rightly tell. Either way, no one came to my rescue, and I didn't have the power to escape them myself.

We reached the city gate, and to my relief, Ryn was on gate duty for this side of the wall. She caught my eye and gave me a questioning look. I just shrugged and gestured to the two holding me. That was enough for her to go from passive looking to whistling and calling all the guards to attention, moving to block the two House Guards' path.

"State your business," Ryn said, her hand on her sword already. The other guards, three of them, were just as tense, putting their hands on their weapons.

You see, almost all the guards were 25 or younger and not Unlocked, so they had good reason to be worried about a confrontation with two Unlocked men. They wouldn't stand a chance, and I think Ryn knew that, but she wasn't one to just step aside.

"Step aside, now," ordered the first guard.

"Or we will remove you," said the other guard.

"You don't scare me, Tin," Ryn said, looking at the larger guard on the right. "You just barely Unlocked a season ago; you'll barely be any stronger than me."

"Want to bet on that?" Tin said, scowling under his black hood, his expression mostly hidden.

"I am more your match, I think," came a slimy reply from the other guard. "Try me, and I'll gut you like a fish."

"You willing to make all this trouble over old Kael here?" Ryn asked, relaxing her posture a little. "Just leave him here, and I'll pay whatever fines he owes you."

"He owes nothing; the head of our House requested him, and he will answer the summons, even if we must spill blood to get him there," said the slimy guard again.

"What seems to be the issue?" came a deep voice from behind them, and I saw now why Ryn relaxed. The captain of the town guard had arrived, and not all too soon. He was said to be level 75 and much more able to take on these thug guards.

Tin answered, the slimy-voiced guy suddenly unable to find his tongue.

"We are simply answering the summons and taking this boy to our house lord as requested; nothing afoul is happening," Tin explained. "Your guard refuses to let us pass."

"Do you want to go with these men?" Teyric Mornell, the Captain of the Guard, asked.

"It doesn't matter what he wants; he was found with House Deymorin property, and if we wished, we could have him charged. We don't want that, just that he comes with us to answer a few questions, that is all," answered the slimy guard.

"My question stands," Teyric said, walking to stand before us.

He was a massive figure, standing at 6'5" at least, and wearing gleaming silver armor with a massive blade on his back, and a helmet hanging from his belt. He had golden hair and blue eyes, looking very northern, except that I knew he was born and raised in this town, returning after giving up adventuring. Perhaps down the line, his heritage was northern, but he was a Brackenford through and through.

"I'll go with them," I said, surprising myself and Ryn in the process. My reasoning caught up with my mouth, and I understood why I needed to.

They knew about my book, so they might be able to tell me more about being a Dragon Knight. Also, if that truly was their book, then my father had stolen it, and I wanted to know more about that as well.

Ryn gave me a look, but I just gave her the most apologetic expression I could give her.

"Let it be known that we know you have him in your custody. If he isn't at the ceremony tonight, I will personally come for you two and find his whereabouts," Teyric said, his words heavy with threat and purpose. He wasn't someone to mess with, as his power rivaled or surpassed that of the House Lords.

"We understand and can assure you that after being questioned, he will be released. Should he be found guilty and put in our jail, word will be sent to you as well," Tin said, but he'd obviously made a mistake, because Teyric pulled his blade and took a step forward.

"You think to detain someone from their gods given right to be Unlocked? Not even a House has such authority. All who are able will be Unlocked," Teyric said, his voice fierce.

"He misspoke, of course, he will be released," said the slimy guard. "Detain us no longer, for time is fast approaching."

"Be gone," Teyric said, and they escorted me through and past a distraught-looking Ryn out onto the road toward House Deymorin's manor. It looked like she'd fight regardless of what Teyric had said, but I watched him put a hand on her shoulder, stopping her.

Then I turned my head, and we walked toward House Deymorin. The farther from Teyric we got, the rougher they were with me, pushing and grabbing at my arm with tight hands. I was not happy about this, but we might as well get it over with and then be done with it all. I knew for a fact they couldn't stop me from being Unlocked when my time came; no House had such authority, nor the kings or queens that ruled Vareth.

It took only a matter of ten minutes or so before we reached the outer gates, and another ten before reaching the house. The gates were grand, made of black metal, with many loops and hammered leaves decorating the exterior. Beside the gate, the wall around the complex was stone, standing as high as ten paces, as tall as our town's walls.

Each of the House manors had similar walls and defenses. It would be foolish to keep their estates unguarded when we get seasonal monster surges in our area. Even the farmers came into the city to sleep at night during the seasons, leaving their crops in the hands of whatever deity they worshiped.

The manor house was much what you'd expect, huge with many windows dotting the outside brickwork, and painted white with gold trim, making it awfully gawdy. We entered through a pair of massive black doors into a grand, open area with a staircase at the back and many paths leading to closed doors.

They marched me up the stairs and to the left, into a study of some kind, where a man in black and gold sat, tapping his chin with his finger. It was Lord Deymorin himself, not his eldest son or his third oldest, the one I dealt with on a daily basis, since we were in the same age group, but Mr. Head of the House himself.

"You may leave," Lord Deymorin said to the two guards, and they bowed and left.

I stared at the man; he was said to be one of the top five most powerful adventurers in the town, perhaps even the strongest. But I felt no fear, just apprehension about my book that they had laid out before him, and he was currently eyeing. He picked it up and began thumbing through it.

"It was a gift from my father," I said, which was true. I'd been given the scarf and the book the night of the fire, and my father had told me to watch over them. It was because of his gifts and my going out to celebrate with friends that I was away from the fire that took their lives.

"It wasn't a gift your father was meant to give out; he should have known better, or at least your mother should have," Lord Deymorin said, making a clicking noise with his tongue as he set it back down. "Shall we discuss the foolhardy notions of you becoming a Dragon Knight then?"

"What's to discuss?" I asked. "It is the path I've chosen, and I will reach it someday."

"Perhaps I can dissuade you," he said. "I'm willing to sponsor your first ten months of adventuring, if you promise to choose any class other than Dragon Knight. That would mean a weekly stipend, gear you can rely on, and a party that will help you rise in the ranks quickly. However, you must never mention or speak of Dragon Knights again."

No is what I wanted to say right away, but his offer warranted some thought, so I gave it some. To be sponsored would be a great boon, meaning

I'd get basically the top-notch gear and help with the toughest monsters that gave the most essence. It would guarantee that I hit level 20 or higher within weeks of Unlocking.

All I had to do was give up my one true goal, the one thing I promised both the heavens above and the ground below, that I'd do so not just for myself, but for the memory of my father and mother. I would be the greatest there was to make them proud, and that meant being a Dragon Knight.

"I'm sorry, but I can't. I will be a Dragon Knight someday," I said, meeting his eyes with as much fire as possible, while he stared lazily back at me.

"Adventuring is a dangerous job, one that almost all citizens take up for at least a while, but where will you be if an accident were to befall you and your party? You wouldn't want to risk the lives of your friends over some foolhardy dream, would you?" he asked, lifting one eyebrow in question.

"I accept all the dangers that come with being an adventurer, even the threats you openly lay at my feet," I said with a bit of a snarl in my voice that I wasn't expecting. Sure, he was threatening me, which made me angry, but this guy was also one of the most powerful people in the town, both economically and physically.

"Very well," he said. "I've got my book returned, and you are on the path that you are. Should you survive long enough to obtain it, return to me, and I will have a sponsorship for you and your team, among many other gifts. A part of me is tempted to sponsor you now, but should any other Houses hear of your ambitions, you'll be in more danger than you know, so be careful and good luck at tonight's ceremony. You may leave."

My head spun from is sudden tonal change and what almost seemed like his potential support of me. I'd have to ponder of that later, but for now I stood immediately and began to walk away, but I had to try. Turning, I went for the book, but he was faster, scooping it up and tsking his tongue.

"Try that again, and I'll throw you in my jail until it's time for your unlocking; it won't be pleasant either," he said, and I withdrew my hand.

"Fine, but I will become a Dragon Knight, and when I do, nothing will stand in my way any longer," I said, standing firm before Lord Deymorin.

I turned and was greeted by two guards waiting for me.

"Take him back to town," Lord Deymorin called out to them, and they nodded, taking me firmly in their grasp once more.

I wiggled and wormed the entire way back to town, eager to find my friends and be done with this little interruption.

CHAPTER 4
AMBER COIN TAVERN

I made a beeline for the Amber Coin Tavern, known to most simply as the Adventurer's Guild. It was one of only two locations in town officially sponsored by the larger guild.

It was a hub of activity for the area, but it allowed non-unlocked to come and dine in as well, which is where my friends would be now, trying to get a peek at the adventurer's job board. The entire idea of looking before we could actually do anything was silly, since most of the jobs in our area would be out of our level range, but I was eager to check it out as well.

I moved with haste to my apartment first, making sure my door was locked and secure. It wasn't, and the lock was destroyed along with the hinge, so the door kind of just hung there. Luckily, all I had of worth to be stolen was either on my person, namely my red scarf, or my book, which had already been stolen. With that in mind, I left my apartment and made my way to the Amber Coin Tavern.

It was located in the Northwest part of town, in Guildrow, where other guild halls were also located. The building stood two stories high with several windows that glowed an amber color from the light within. Part of why they named it such, at least the word on the street, was because its windows had an amber tint to them, unlike any others around town.

The bottom floor was cobblestone, including the doorframe from where a single wooden door stood, thick and heavy, but it always opened very smoothly. A line of people came in and out pretty regularly, so I waited my turn and got inside when I could.

As I stepped through the heavy oak door, I was hit by a wall of noise and warmth. The main hall was broad and open with thick timbers overhead, darkened by years of smoke from the massive stone hearth roaring beside the southern wall. Lanterns hung from hooks cast a golden glow across the hall, illuminating scuffed, marred floors.

At the center of the room were long communal tables, equally scarred by hundreds of blades and tankards. Adventurers ate side by side here, no qualms given to what level or gear they might have, just coming together to eat a meal. Some groups were boisterous, laughing heartily, while others were quiet and reserved.

A few round tables, closer to the job board, were occupied by random patrons, and that is where I found my friends, all peeking at the board while sipping from their drinks. Tomas, Jareth, Sel, and Ashric looked a sight to be seen, leaning and squinting at the board. I decided to wow them and walked right up to the board, quickly looking for anything in the level 10 or under bracket.

Surprisingly, I found two right off: one called for a group to take on some mutated, large rats growing in the sewers, and another said that south of town, some weaker goblins had moved in; neither paid much coin, which was why they were still on the board. Barely five moons each, which wasn't even enough for each member to get a silver for themselves.

"If I recall," came a burly voice from behind me. "You ain't to be Unlocked until tonight. Keep to the rules, boys, or you may get blacklisted from the Adventurer's Guild, and that, my friend, is a life of hardship."

I turned to see old Rurik Dane, who looked like a broader, older version of Tomas. Like most northerners, he had long blond hair and blue eyes, and at times it felt hard to tell them apart.

"Sorry, Rurik," I said, averting my eyes from the board and heading over to the table.

He chuckled and went about his business, checking the board for anything around his level. He'd been in town for at least a year now, and he'd need to move on to stronger areas if he wanted to progress, but it wasn't my place to critique him.

"Well?" Tomas said, looking at me with expectation. I decided to keep him on the hook.

"Not sure what I saw or didn't see, but I sure am thirsty," I said, and Tomas groaned, lifting a hand and summoning a serving girl.

"Another round for us all, and one for him as well," he said, pointing at me. "Oh, and give me another plate of those crunchy salty things you brought us earlier, and a bag of Spiced Chickpeas while you're at it."

I chuckled and decided it was time to reveal my secret.

"You won't guess what happened to me before I came here," I said, keeping them on the hook for even longer as I tried to explain my kidnapping.

"What'd you see on the board?" Sel asked, obviously uninterested in my other story. She sneered at me, but I could tell it wasn't as serious as her normal disdain for us, more a mocking blow among friends.

"I'll get to that, I will," I said. "But first, I need to tell you. I was taken by Lord Deymorin, and he threatened me, sort of. He was all sorts of bent out of shape to hear I wanted to be a Dragon Knight. He even tossed my room and stole my father's book. I'll get it back someday, but the joke is on him; I memorized that book years ago."

"He did what?" Ashric asked, as Tomas looked at me with wide eyes, all mention of the job board forgotten.

"Yeah, and he also implied that I might have an accident after becoming an adventurer. Then he went all sideways and said if I did manage to become a Dragon Knight, that I should come to him and he'd sponsor me. It had my head all sorts of twisted if I'm being honest."

"I need to tell my father; he might want to have words with you as well," Ashric said, standing suddenly.

"Don't you want to hear about the job board?" I asked, and he looked conflicted.

"If you found us a job, then good, but I need to get this news to my father now," Ashric said, taking it far more seriously than I thought he might.

"I want to hear," Tomas said. "I'll meet up with you back at home, alright, Ashri? Go tell Father, and I'll bring Kaelric by after we finish up here, just in case he wants to talk to him."

"Deal," Ashric said, turning and leaving the Amber Coin Tavern.

"So, about that job board?" Tomas asked. Turning his attention back to me.

"What if I don't want to meet with Lord Ravenlock?" I asked, giving my friend a look that said, "Think shit through before you speak."

"Why wouldn't you?" Tomas asked. "He's a really nice guy. I bet the fact that Deymorin is interested in you might even make him want to sponsor you, too. Which would be nice because Ashric and I have already turned down his sponsorship, well, any further help we've refused, but it might be nice for you to get a little starting help. Your gear isn't the greatest, and your last shield just broke."

"I don't need a sponsorship," I said. I'd gotten by all by myself for the last nine years; I didn't need help now. Sure, I was being a little prideful, but it was my right to be so, having earned it by my years of hard work and sweat to get where I was today.

"The job board?" Jareth asked, his voice carrying its usual boredom, though deeper than most of ours.

"Right," I said. "Thanks, Jareth. There is bad news and good news."

"Give us the good news," Tomas said, as his food and our drinks arrived.

I took a long pull on my ale and wet my lips. "Good news is there are two jobs we might be able to take care of that others won't want to do."

"Bad news?" Sel asked.

"They each only pay a few moons, so until we do both, it won't be an even split," I said.

"Only a few moons? That seems pretty low," Tomas said, but he was used to spending a moon a week on drinks and snacks alone. I'd scrimped and saved for the single moon I had.

"It is," Sel said. "Probably not worth doing."

"Which is why we will do them both," I said. "It'll give us a head-up on others, getting kills right off the bat. Plus, if you aren't interested, I'm sure Ryn, Tomas, and I could hammer it out ourselves."

"Then do it, I'm not participating in such a shit job," Sel said, and Jareth nodded his assent.

"In that case, the moons will be more than enough pay," I said, but I could see Tomas wasn't super convinced. "We gotta start somewhere."

"I know," Tomas said, munching on his food. "Fine, I'm down for whatever."

Now I just needed to get Ryn on board, which should be easy enough, since she earned a moon a week at her job. Getting potentially two moons for two easy jobs would be like a prize worthy of celebrating.

"Are we sticking together as a group?" I asked, looking mostly at Sel. "I mean, I know you don't want to do these smaller jobs, but we need to decide where we are going soon if we want to get the levels coming in."

"I don't know," Sel said, speaking honestly and without malice for once. "We work well enough together, and I guess you'll be pretty focused now that you don't have to work on anything but being an adventurer, but you three haven't been the most reliable over the last few years."

"We might have to work still," I said, shrugging. "We need to get enough moons together to get a place in a caravan if we want to make it to another town or city with monsters closer to our levels, but I get your point. If there is any way to get the coin as an adventurer, then that is what we will do, right, Tomas?"

"Right," Tomas said with a mouth full of food. It was a wonder how he stayed so fit, given how much he ate, but he looked almost as ripped as me with my shirt off, which was saying something, because I didn't eat much most days, so I stayed pretty lean, yet surprisingly bulky from our constant training and fighting.

There were twenty of us coming of age this year, meaning we'd have to compete for work and kills, but that didn't mean they were likely to take the shit jobs we would, so I didn't worry too much. If Sel didn't want to do the work for so little, it was laughable to think that any of the others would.

"You losers hear to peek at the board, are you?" came a voice I hated to hear. It was Craven Deymorin, third son of the Lord Deymorin, and a constant pain in my ass.

"That's right, and guess what?" I asked him, answering before he could say anything. "All the jobs up there say no asshats, so you better try looking elsewhere."

Tomas snorted and grinned over at the black-haired man. I looked over at him and took in his appearance. He wore black, hardened leather armor with gold-colored metal squares all over it for extra protection. He had a large nose, like all Deymorin's, and small, beady, dark eyes, also a typical trait of his family. His eyes were slightly too close together, and it gave him an odd look.

He showed no signs of caring what I'd said, but smirked and leaned in a little.

"Father says you are on his shit list, so you better watch out, because that means you are fair game now," Craven whispered.

"I'll manage, thanks," I said, shaking my head at his display of bravado.

"I won't be coming back here for a while," Craven said. "You see, my father has several jobs lined up for my party, enough that we will reach level 20 before you halfwits manage to figure a way out of town."

"How about you go brag to someone who gives a shit, because we don't," Sel said, directing her scorn toward someone other than me for once.

"Oh, I will, I just needed to come here and see which of my competitors were lame enough to try to get a peek at the board before Unlocking. Better watch out who you ally yourself with, Sel. Some among you aren't going to last long," Craven said, turning on his heels and leaving.

Sel started to stand, but Jareth put a hand on her arm and shook his head 'no'. For a man of few words, he knew when to act; that much was true. With the table all unsettled now, I was surprised to see Sel smile and nod to Jareth.

"We are leaving for now. See you later tonight," Sel said, then they both got up and left Tomas and me alone.

"Let me finish, and we can swing by the manor before we head to the tower for the ceremony," Tomas said, licking his fingers as he spoke, making a smacking noise between every few words.

I found myself waiting outside Lord Ravenlock's study while Tomas and Ashric were inside speaking to the man. Whatever they were talking about, I could almost make out the words, as some of them shouted, and then it quieted before the door finally swung open.

"Come on in," Tomas said, gesturing for me to enter.

"Welcome, Mr. Grimholt," Lord Ravenlock said, gesturing for me to sit in one of three chairs opposite his desk.

He had hawk-like features, with a peaked nose, narrowed eyes, and a sharp chin, features his son inherited but not as harshly as his own. He had green eyes that held an intelligence that was hard to deny.

"Are you aware of why you are here?" he asked, and I nodded.

Then, thinking better of it, I spoke, "I am."

"And if I'd known of your ambitions before today, I'd have called you in to warn you against sharing such dreams aloud in such times as these," he said.

"I will be a Dragon Knight someday," I said, and he nodded, pinching the bridge of his hooked nose.

"I daresay that you will. Your friends speak of your determination and circumstances. They want me to sponsor you, but I feel as if such an offer would be wasted on someone who does not want it. Instead, allow me to give you a boon and a promise. If you are to become a Dragon Knight, you will be putting yourself in the middle of the qualms of kings and queens. Should you accomplish such a feat, come see me, and I will help direct you forward," he said, looking straight into my soul as he spoke.

"I understand, but why are so many people getting upset that I want to be a Dragon Knight? I've said as much for years," I said.

"And had I heard you even years ago, I'd make you this same offer. House Deymorin might try a more hands-on approach at stopping you or aiding you, but I can't put my House in that position. I would offer this word of advice, though. Keep it to yourself; our Houses may be more understanding than you realize, as you are one of us. But outside of Brackenford, you will find a blade in your back sooner than you can imagine should you share your ambitions."

"I understand," I said, but in truth I didn't. Why did so many people fear the Dragon Knight class and what it could do? I'd heard only great stories and tales of the power they could wield. Would it truly make me so powerful as to make kings and queens quake?

"I doubt you do, but you will if you persist in telling everyone who will listen about your plans. You are an adult now, begin to think and act like one," he said, shifting in his chair and looking to his son. "I would also caution you, son, from being around someone with such ambitions."

"Yes, Father," Ashric said, bowing his head down to his father.

"Very well, I've said what I've said. Give the boy some gear from our armory and a week's stipend, then be gone. This is all I can do for you, but it is better than you'll get from most. And be wary of accepting promises and gifts from others. Mine have no strings attached, but almost all others will," Lord Ravenlock said, gesturing with his hand that we should leave.

We did so, and I followed Ashric out.

"I don't need the gear," I said, and Tomas huffed out some air.

"The hells you don't," he said. "If we are going to adventure with you, then at least accept some baseline gear. It won't even be enchanted in any way, just some basic stuff to get you started."

I thought about my gear and how bad shape it was in. With my shield gone, I couldn't even properly tank a fight. It didn't take much more convincing before I relented.

"Fine, but that's it. After this, I don't need anyone's help," I said, trying to remain defiant despite the situation.

The House Ravenlock guards took us down the stairs and down another hidden flight of stairs until we reached an armory of sorts, with all manner of swords, shields, and armor laid out on tables and on mannequins.

Ashric went over to a set of leather armor with metal studs on it and pulled it off.

"Try it on and see if it fits. We can have it adjusted if not, but it has a little bit of give or take either way built into it," he said, handing over the chest plate.

I tried it all on, and with a few adjustments to let out the chest and legs, it fit like a charm. I admired my reflection in the mirror, my messy hair sticking up in all directions, no matter how much I washed and tried to tame it down.

The armor looked amazing. It needed a bit of breaking in, but I could move in it without too much trouble. It was stained a dark brown, with silver metallic squares woven through it for added defense. Once I was finished testing it, I took it off and added it to my pack. The strap nearly tore as I did, and Ashric quickly fetched a massive backpack with a bedroll and everything else already attached. It was already half full, and I gave him an odd look before accepting it anyway.

"Every adventurer needs a sturdy backpack," he said, and I accepted it.

I transferred all my goods, leaving my broken shield, sword, and shit armor on the ground as I was going to get new ones of each of those. Next, we picked out a sword. I got a plain arming sword about the length of my forearm from the tips of my elbow to the tip of my fingers. It was solid steel and would do well in a fight, polished and oiled as it was.

The final addition to my gear after sheathing my sword on the side of my backpack was a shield. I picked out a round shield, bigger than what I was used to, but big enough to actually offer some decent protection. It covered my entire midsection without being too bulky or heavy.

It had metal banding around the outside, a small metal dome in the middle, and metal rivets along the edge. Meanwhile, the inside was layered in sturdy leather, soft to the touch where my arm hit, but otherwise able to take a beating.

The shield was attached to the back of my bag, hanging from the bottom half, and would be easy to remove when needed. In all, it felt good to be properly outfitted for my life as an adventurer, even though I knew none of it would be enchanted gear; it was far better than what I had currently.

What came next had me tasting bile, bubbling up from my throat. I wanted to deny it, but at the same time, I shouldn't deny a gift given without strings. It was a money pouch made of thick, dark brown leather, sturdy enough that it would not be easily cut by thieves. Inside were ten moons and dozens of scales, more wealth than I had ever carried on me at once.

"I really shouldn't," I said, offering it back after taking it from Ashric.

"You will keep it and use it to help the party. Think of it as our first party reward," Tomas said, stepping between me and the offer to return it.

"Fine, but it is party funds, not mine. Got it?" I said, pointing an accusing finger at them both.

A clock toned somewhere distant, and Ashric pulled out a round, golden pocket watch, the kind only the rich had, and checked the time.

"We've got an hour before showtime, we ought to get moving," he said, and I nodded.

"Let's do it," I said, remembering that we were meant to wear our armor during the ceremony, so I started to change as they ran off to do the same in their rooms.

Before too long, the three of us were well-armored and well-armed as we left the manor house, ready to accept our destinies and be Unlocked. For the first time in our lives, we'd learn what true power felt like.

CHAPTER 5
UNLOCKED

The ceremony was to take place at the Elder Tower, through the infamous seventh door. It was the one door that we had never entered, and for good reason, as to do so was said to be a death sentence. But now, when the moons above aligned and their brightness rivaled that of the sun at midnight, we'd enter and be changed forever.

Tomorrow would be the first day of a week-long festival that would follow as a celebration and was also a yearly event in which parades and all manner of fun would be had. As new recruits being Unlocked, we'd walk in the parade and allow everyone to get a good look at us, as was customary. But I wasn't worried about any of that yet; my mind was singularly focused on what would happen to us when we went into that seventh door in the tower.

We approached the tower in silence, each of us in our own heads as we met up with the rest of our party, also silent as we neared the tower. Family, friends, and well, anyone who supported you could be found ringed outside the main area of the tower, all waiting for us to take a step they'd all taken before.

I saw our mentor, Velric, and the rest of the potentials, so we joined them in quiet ceremony.

"I'll make it simple, follow me now and keep quiet. Remember that what you see inside isn't to be spoken of to anyone, no matter if they know the same as you, it just isn't, alright?" he asked, and we all nodded, following him as he headed for the famed seventh door.

It was the simplest of the seven, opening easily as he pushed, and a dim blue light pulsed from somewhere within. I was near the front of the line as we entered and was surprised to find stairs leading down. The blue light lit up the walls in harmony with a faint pulsing sound, like a humming.

The walls were covered in ancient depictions of people and monsters, fighting and dying. Among them were Dragons, and atop some dragons were people, no doubt Dragon Knights. But as I searched the depictions, I saw almost every class I knew of, and many I didn't, being depicted using their signature class abilities. I knew maybe half of the known ones, but still, I just knew that this was what they were meant to be, and there were hundreds, not dozens, as we thought.

Still, I felt something in my chest growing heavier as we got lower, and almost all instincts I had told me to turn and run. But I walked along with the others, with my own fears quieted and burning in my chest. I would be a Dragon Knight, I told myself. I wouldn't let fear control me.

Swallowing hard, I pushed the fear down until only excitement lingered. We finally reached the bottom of the spiraling staircase, and what was at the bottom took my breath away. A pillar of stone with words that I'd never seen anywhere before, pulsing blue light that seemed to penetrate the very stone all around us, making it glow softly.

"This is the Everstone," Velric said, gesturing to the stone. "Each of you will take turns touching it and allowing its light to unlock your true potential. Then you will leave, keeping whatever you hear or experience to yourself. The truths or lack thereof are meant for you and you alone."

He gestured, and the first in the line stepped forward, touching the stone. Blue light surged as they did so, and he was lifted off his feet for just a moment before falling back down and catching himself. His eyes glowed blue as he turned to look at us, but his face wore an eerie smile for only a moment before changing back to normal.

One after another, each of us did this, each one with an odd smile of elation on their face afterward. But as my turn neared, I began to wonder what was truly happening and if I wanted to be a part of it. But it was too late, it was my turn, and I was walking forward with my hand out.

I touched the stone, and suddenly I felt my body go rigid, and I was someplace different. I stood on an island somewhere, and in the distance, I could hear the roar of a creature so fierce, so powerful that I couldn't help but be afraid.

"That is the dragon you seek," came a voice, ethereal and hollow at the same time. "Come here and put an end to his suffering, then and only then will you become what you seek."

Suddenly, I was being drawn back to my body. I saw, as I left, that this island was just off the coast of Vareth, and I saw a ship with red sails docked at the island. I would find this ship with red sails, defeat this fierce dragon, and become a Dragon Knight.

Blinking rapidly, I shook my head as I felt myself return to my body. Immediately, I was ushered up and out of the secret chamber, but I couldn't help but notice the difference in my vision. A small blinking icon appeared in my field of view, and when I focused on it, careful not to fall on the steps, a window appeared with information about me.

Name: Kaelric Grimholt
Level: 0
Essence: 6,320/100 Until Next Level
Attributes:
    Power: 0
    Guard: 0
    Speed: 10(Base 0)
    Arcana: 0
Equipped Abilities:
    Slot 1: Empty
    Slot 2: Empty
Slot 3: Empty
    Slot 4: Empty
Class: Empty
Class Passive: Empty
Class Slot Ability: Empty

Then a prompt appeared, flashing from the right corner of my information.

Would you like to Level up x5? Yes/No

"Yes," I said, my voice breaking the silence of the thrumming. Instantly, I knew I had five attribute points to assign, and I was both confused and excited. How had I gotten essence before I was even unlocked? Was everyone going to start at level 5? I hadn't read that anywhere, but the whole of Unlocking wasn't something many, if any, would write about or share.

I reached the top of the steps, dismissing all screens with a thought, and joined the crowd to wait for my friends to come out, as I had been the first among them. A cheer rose from the crowd as I stepped out, and I joined the others waiting in line for our mentor to return and guide us.

While I waited, I thought I'd need to decide what to do next, and why had my attributes said I had a speed of ten but a base of zero? The only item I had that I remotely thought might be magical was the scarf from my father, a bit ragged from age, but it held up pretty well, all things considered.

He'd used it his whole life, he'd said, and was passing it to me, which at the time was confusing because I was only sixteen. But that brought up another thought: maybe he knew death was close at hand? Surely, he couldn't have known there would be a fire, or that he'd be sleeping when it hit. Or perhaps he did...

I couldn't think about that right now, so I pushed those thoughts aside to go over what I'd already talked to Ryn and Tomas about. I was going to take my first five attribute points into Guard, then Power, so I'd have access to a guard ability and a power ability. We'd talked about maybe going speed second, but with it at 10 now, even with a base of 0, that meant I'd be faster than everyone at my level, so no need there.

Trying as best I could to remember the abilities you gained access to at five attribute points per attribute was easier than I thought, as I'd basically memorized the first three for each, years ago.

For Power, they were Heavy Strike, Iron Grip, and Shove. Heavy Strike increased the damage of the next attack by fifty percent, whereas Iron Grip made it impossible to be disarmed for a dozen seconds. Lastly, Shove was a supernatural way to push someone back, using no weapons or hands.

I knew which of the three I wanted. Shove was just too overpowered in too many situations not to choose. Plus, there were better attack-improving abilities down the line, or so it was said.

When considering the Guard abilities, they were as follows: Iron Skin, Brace, and Block.

Iron Skin did what it sounded like: it turned your skin into the toughness of iron and was considered the best of the three available options for almost anyone considering tanking. Not only would I turn away strikes on your skin, but it would also give you increased resistance to puncture attacks, like needles or darts that would be used to poison you.

Brace made you resistant to knockbacks, stuns, and staggers, pretty straightforward, and could be useful in the right situation. Then there was Block, allowing you to stop an attack similar to Shove, with your mind or magic or whatever, stopping a blow every few seconds without having to block it physically. It can also be used up to ten feet away from you, so it's super useful for those going for a block/barrier build.

I even knew the Speed and Arcana ones, so I went over them as well, despite knowing I wouldn't pick one until after level 10 or so. My plan was to reach 5 in each to unlock an ability for each, then bring them to 10 so I could qualify for the Dragon Knight class by level 40.

Speed's options for the first five attributes were Quickstep, Fleet Foot, and Fast Hands. Quickstep let you supernaturally dash in any direction without regard for the momentum you'd carried from your previous move. Very popular and almost always taken by those wanting an edge.

Fleet Foot increased your movement speed by a flat fifteen percent, meaning you could get around much faster, but it didn't affect your reflexes or attack speed, except that your arm moves fifteen percent faster, so it hits a bit harder.

Next was Fast Hands, giving you a fifteen percent boost to attack speed and reaction time, a choice often taken by Tanking classes for the flat edge it gives you over similarly strong, fast opponents.

Finally, there were the first three Arcana that you unlocked when you hit five in that attribute, which were Mana Bolt, Spark, and Magic Ward. Mana Bolt sent out a small magical projectile that grew more powerful the higher your Arcana and the time spent channeling the spell before releasing it.

Spark was what it sounded like; you could hit someone or something with a spark of lightning that could start fires in a pinch or hit from short range with a chance to stun an enemy. Whereas Magic Ward was a buffing ability that you could place on someone or something for an hour, making it reduce the magical and elemental damage they took by fifteen percent.

Those who prioritized tanking damage often took Magic Ward, as only those not looking to deal damage ignored Mana Bolt or Spark. I had no plans on taking Magic Ward, though, as I thought the idea of Spark was far too enticing. But that would be for another time, as I had to prioritize my other attributes first.

My thoughts were interrupted as the last of the newly Unlocked appeared, and our mentor cleared his throat to speak.

"You are now one of us, and I am no longer your mentor. Go out and do good for the world," he said, bowing as the crowd cheered.

We'd done it! We were free to finally live our lives as adventurers! I was going to be a Dragon Knight, and tonight would be me taking my first steps toward that. I found my friends and told Ryn of our plan to take out some rats and goblins. She nodded, still obviously stunned by whatever had happened down below the Elder Tower.

"Let's do this," I said, grinning as my two closest friends nodded their agreement.

"So, super odd," I said as we walked away and headed for the Amber Coin Tavern. We knew it would be open this late, since adventurers operated at all hours of the night. We wanted to try at the sewer rats while our energy and excitement were at an all-time high.

"You're level 5, too?" Ryn said. "It was surprising to me as well, but I read a few passages that hinted at such advancement, and I have a theory."

"It was probably the tower," Tomas said, munching his snack as we walked, and Ryn made an exaggerated sigh.

"Of course it was the tower," Ryn said. "We've been inside almost every day absorbing latent essence from the kills, even though we weren't Unlocked yet, a small portion of that essence clung to us."

"Should we be talking about this?" I asked, suddenly nervous we'd stumbled upon something taboo that wasn't talked about.

"As long as we don't try to pass it around or write it down, we ought to be alright," Ryn answered, throwing a hand around both of us and pulling us in close. "So, which attribute are you each raising first, and which skill are you choosing? We need to plan this out if we are going to do it right."

"First, I need to tell you guys about the four classes I discovered at the library, just in case you wanted to go for one of them," I said, then launched into the four: Blade Sage, War Monk, Battle Priest, and Dragon Vanguard. I explained that each required 10 in various attributes, and that three had to be raised before the class would present itself.

"I know, I looked over the book as well," Ryn said, smiling and yet rolling her eyes at me. "I'm thinking of taking the Blade Sage path. It would be hard to wait so long for a class, but it would give me a goal to work toward. Plus, Power, Speed, and Arcana would be a versatile mix."

"I'm going for War Monk," Tomas announced. "Unless, of course, something better comes my way before then. But War Monk sounds really cool and right up my alley."

Ryn and I both rolled our eyes this time. Tomas always saw the newest and shiniest thing, latching onto it, so it was no surprise he'd given up his last obsession with a class to pick one of the harder and rarer paths with us.

"Are you going for Dragon Vanguard, just in case Dragon Knight ends up not working? It couldn't hurt to make sure you raise Power, Guard, and Arcana up first, then worry about speed if you want to chase the Dragon Knight class," Ryn said, biting her lip as she said it. She knew I was committed to the Dragon Knight class, and even the cool-sounding Dragon Vanguard class wouldn't do it for me.

"I was already planning on doing Speed last, so I guess I could hold off adding any to it until I'm level 30," I said, relenting a little for the sake of my friends. "But let me tell you why I'm okay with waiting on my Speed."

"Alright," Ryn said, smirking. "What is it?"

I leaned in close and whispered to them, because letting anyone know about this could get us all killed for the item, and I didn't want to be watching over my back.

"My father's scarf gives plus ten to the Speed attribute," I whispered, and Ryn looked at me as if I'd hit my head.

"Attribute-raising gear is more commonly dropped from dungeons and such, but a plus ten to anything without a prior attribute requirement is huge, like artifact-level gear huge," she said as if that disproved what I'd seen with my own eyes. "Are you sure you are seeing it right?"

"I am," I said. "But let's not talk about it, I don't want it to be stolen. It's literally the last thing I have that ties me to my family."

"Alright," Ryn said, drawing out the word. "Let's get back on topic. I'm thinking of raising my Speed first, as I think it'll give me an edge, and then I can pick up Quickstep. What are you thinking, Tomas?"

"Uh, hmm, so I was actually thinking it might be a good idea to grab Heavy Strike, with 5 into my Power attribute," Tomas said, throwing more snacks into his mouth as we walked.

"You aren't considering Shove? I hear most people take it as it's pretty powerful and big on utility," I said, reiterating the same logic that had convinced me.

"Yeah, but I'm sure we'll have enough people taking it, but very few will take Heavy Strike, so I'll have an advantage, as I'll be able to deal more damage with a surge of power," Tomas said, shrugging. "I mean, technically, I already assigned my points and picked it, so I can't really go back now."

"Tomas!" Ryn said, practically hissing his name at him. "We were meant to discuss and plan accordingly."

"We've been planning this for years, we all knew you would go Speed, and Kaelric would go Guard, although I don't know which he said he'd pick. Did you ever decide?" Tomas asked.

"I'm leaning toward Iron Skin, but Block has so much potential if I can master it," I said, and they both nodded along, agreeing with my assessment.

"I'd say go Iron Skin if you want to fill the tank role and be more durable. Choose Block if you want to be a hybrid damage reducer and tank, or say screw it to both of them and take Bracer. I heard that at higher Guard, it makes you unstoppable; nothing can stun you or stop you when you move forward. It isn't without merit," Ryn said, not helping the situation at all.

"I'm going to stick to my gut feeling and take Iron Skin. If I do end up having to face a dragon," I said, lowering my voice when mentioning a dragon. "Then I will want to be able to take the heat, and higher Guard attributes are said to increase your ability to block and resist all manner of elemental and types of damage. Or at least you've told me as much, right Ryn?"

"That's right, it is pretty standard for almost all main tanks for that very reason. It is also the most passive and easiest ability to take, making it helpful in all manner of situations," Ryn said as we neared Amber Coin Tavern.

"Let's lock it in then," I said, and we stopped. Mentally pulling up my menu, I locked in my first five attributes.

Before I even got my pick of abilities, I felt myself grow more sturdy, my muscles bulged a little, and I knew I was much more durable than I'd just been a few seconds ago. Five attributes, according to Ryn, represented literally doubling your normal limits in that attribute.

Which meant that at five, you were twice as capable; at 10, you were twice as capable as you were at five, indicating it had a scaling effect. My Speed was four times as fast as it had been before, and that also affected my perception, I think, because when I focused, I could almost slow down time a little.

It would be interesting to see how much that threw me off in combat. Being faster by a measure of four would obviously be a problem, but I also felt my body had adjusted to it; my muscles were more limber and bounced back with greater elasticity than ever before.

I saw a blinking shield icon in the corner of my vision and focused on it, bringing it up. It gave me three options, as I'd thought, and listed each of them.

Iron Skin, Brace, Block.

When I focused on one, I got more information, but I already knew all that, so I did a quick check to be sure it was the same as I'd thought. It was, and then I locked in my choice.

You have selected Iron Skin. Are you sure you wish to lock in this Ability and assign it to your first Ability Slot? Yes/No

Mentally, I selected 'Yes,' and I felt knowledge of the technique fill my mind, my skin hardened, and I knew it would take a good effort to cut or scratch me now. It was also the lowest and weakest form of Iron Skin, but it would grow more effective the longer I had it and the higher my Guard became.

All this I knew instinctively, and oddly enough, I also realized I could turn it off if I removed it from the Ability Slot. Not sure why I'd do that, but perhaps greater level abilities were better than even Iron Skin. I'd only read of the first tier, as the rest were kept mostly secret. Sure, you heard rumors about abilities and such, but rarely could you trust such things.

"I did it," I said, and Ryn gave me a thumbs up.

"I now have Quickstep," she said, then suddenly she blurred and appeared five feet away at an odd angle. "And I'm awesome."

"Well, damn," I said, sort of regretting I didn't choose something cool for my first pick, but knowing that planning for the future was the best bet, I stood behind my choice. "Let's get in and grab those job postings and register with the guild; we've got work to do."

With that, we entered the Amber Coin Tavern for the first time as adventurers, ready to take on the world.

CHAPTER 6
SEWER RATS

Walking right up to the board, I was overcome by the scents and smells of the place. It smelled like opportunity, and we weren't going to miss out. There was great adventure in store for us; we just had to take what jobs we could and begin to make a name for ourselves. Sure, these wouldn't be the most glorious first few jobs, but they'd give us essence, and we needed it to level up.

According to everything Ryn had told us, the first ten levels were easy enough to gain; they just required a small amount of essence compared to later levels. And I knew we couldn't enter a dungeon or risk leaving our hometown until we were at least level 10. Monsters outside these walls would just be too strong; even so, we needed to start saving to join a caravan to an area with lower-level monsters. So much to do, so little time!

I grabbed the two job postings and took them over to the registration desk, an oak desk in the eastern corner of the tavern where a mousy girl with a small nose and big eyes awaited us.

"New adventurers, I take it?" she asked, and we nodded.

"Yeah," I said. "How'd you know?"

"Because you removed the job posting from the board, that's a big 'no-no.' Go put them back, and I'll give you a copy. The job board operates on a first-come, first-served basis, but I can tell you which have already been applied for or accepted, so you don't waste your time. These two jobs remain untaken, so I'll get you assigned to them if you return the jobs to the board," she said, all business.

"I will right away," I said, spinning and returning them to the board. A few older and drunk adventurers, still up for whatever reason, laughed at me as I did so, and I just ignored them. "Okay, all done."

"Good, my name is Serif, and I'll be your point of contact on this job and any others you pick up around town from our guild hall. I'll also need you to fill out these forms and formally register with the Adventurer's Guild. You'll get a guild coin that can be shown at any location to give you a day's rest and food free of charge once per week. So, if you fall on hard times, remember, the guild is always there for you. It'll be one moon each for registration."

I cringed at hearing that, but we were about to make some moons, so I took out my only moon, the silver coin glistening in the light of the fireplace, and placed it on the desk, along with two others from Ryn and Tomas. I'd been saving for this exact reason, but it still hurt to lose all my wealth. I literally had a single scale left, and it wasn't even a good one; it was half falling apart, and I doubted most would take it for its value. Sure, I had the ten silvers from Ashric's father, but I wasn't about to use those for anything but group supplies.

We filled out the forms, which asked for our current level, names, any chosen abilities, and whether we knew which classes we'd be taking. A mutual agreement was passed between us then, and we all left ours blank. If we were going to chase rare classes, it wouldn't do any good to let everyone know about them. Returning the forms a few minutes later, we were given guild coins.

They had the Adventurer's Guild emblem on it: a sword, a staff, and a dagger crossing on a shield. The coin itself was lighter than I'd expect from the iron color, but I pocketed it, and we turned to leave after getting our copy of the job posting. I looked closely at the rat one first.

Job: Sewer Rats of Unusual Size
Rank: *[Common]*
Location: *Brackenford Sewers (East Drainage)*
Details: *Reports of oversized rats, twisted by some unknown taint, have been sighted in the sewers beneath the city. They've been gnawing through grain stores, biting workers, and spreading disease. The city guard refuses to descend into the tunnels, leaving this matter to adventurers.*

Objective: *Clear out the infestation and return with proof of at least five slain mutated rats.*

Reward: *5 Moons (split among party)*

Notes: *Guild rumors whisper the rats may be feeding on something magical discarded below.*

Next, I pulled open the goblin one and took a look at it as well.

Job: Goblin Encroachment
Rank: *[Common]*
Location: *South Farmlands, near the Old Mill Road*
Details: *A small band of weak goblins has been spotted making camp*

among the abandoned sheds near the southern fields. Farmers complain of stolen chickens and nightly raids. The goblins are unorganized but dangerous in numbers.

*   **Objective:** Drive off or slay the goblins (estimated group: 6–10). Bring back their ears as proof.*

*   **Reward:** 5 Moons (split among party)*

*   **Notes:** These goblins seem weaker than the cave-born kind. Locals suspect they've been forced out of deeper territory.*

That would net us 10 silver moons or three each and one for the party if we completed both of these jobs today. It would be wise to wait until daytime to hunt the goblins, as scarier things awaited us out in the dark than goblins, but in the sewers, it didn't really matter, as light wouldn't really reach there.

I showed the listings to the group, and Ryn spoke up first.

"We will need to grab a lamp and a few other supplies," Ryn said. "Like maybe a cure-all for poisons. I'm alright paying for it all, but I want to be repaid out of the moons we'll earn. It shouldn't cost more than a moon to get all the supplies I'm thinking of, and we can use most of them again, so that's good. Also, I was going to suggest we get Kael some better armor, but seeing as Tomas took care of that, we should be good to take on those rats now."

"I have some silver moons that will pay for that," I said, tossing her the coin purse I'd gotten.

"Do you think that we will find the reason behind why the rats are becoming mutated?" Tomas asked, snacking as we went. "I mean, if it's a magical item or something, maybe it'll be worth something."

"Our job is to kill at least five rats," Ryn said. "We stick to the bare minimum for now and get our reward."

"Technically, it says clear out the infestation, but we should do our best to solve the mystery of why as well," I said, and Ryn rolled her eyes at me. She did that a lot, a holdover from when we were younger, but Tomas and I found it amusing, so I think that's why she kept doing it.

"Let's see what we face and then decide," Ryn said, as we headed to one of the few shops that would be open this late. It catered to adventurers, as they could come at any time of night.

It was called Gallywot's Emporium, and it was the strangest building, with white and black brick, each painted the opposite color, creating a pattern that disturbed the eye if you stared too long. He had his sign hanging out front, made of wood and painted white with black lettering. When we entered, we got a hearty greeting from Mr. Gallywot himself.

"Hello, adventurers! What can I assist you with this fine evening?" he called out from the back of the store, waddling our way.

The inside of the room smelled of mold, and the air was damp, but I saw no signs of mildew, and the goods were spread out on tables and shelves all around. They had all manner of items, including magical items in glass cases lining the walls. I watched the plump Gallywot waddle over to us and took a good look at him. I hadn't been inside here for years, but he looked exactly the same as before.

Red-faced and plump, with beady brown eyes, taller than most, but just as wide. He wore a black-and-white suit that seemed to be bursting at the seams, and he had the most worn-out brown dress shoes that I'd ever seen, the exact same condition as they'd been when I'd last visited. He was an enigma for sure, and not one that I cared to figure out.

Ryn told him what we needed, and he took us around the store trying to upsell us on every purchase. We wanted a lamp, but he tried to sell us one with an Everglow enchantment, which meant it didn't require any oil, but it cost four times as much. We wanted a basic poison cure; he wanted to sell us a variety of potions in a case that would heal you, another that would increase your attributes, and even one that would give you luck for a short period of time.

We refused him on every turn, except to purchase a case of six small potion vials, costing a single moon by themselves. We would need an emergency healing potion just in case, and Gallywot was generous, throwing in three leather belt attachments that could be used to hold up to three potions each.

Slotting the two potions onto our belts, we paid for the rest of the supplies we needed and left. It cost two moons total, which meant we'd have only 8 left. We'd figure it out, but for now, we were ready to go check out the Eastern Sewer entrance.

We made it there with only encountering one guard, who nodded to Ryn and let us pass despite the late hour. We could have shown our coins, which meant we were on the business of the Adventurer's Guild, but there was no need when you had a former guard on your side.

The sewer grate was heavy, and we ended up having to rely on Tomas, now stronger than ever thanks to his five points in Power, to lift it free. The metal groaned as he struggled against it, but it was no match for him and his staff; it came free, and he set it aside so we could exit without worry.

We lit the lantern; we had extra oil ready to go, and Ryn was manning it all and taking a position near the front while I slipped my shield off and readied my sword. I wish I had some special skill to help me fight; instead, my skin was as hard as iron, so I'd be the whipping boy up in front. That was what I wanted, so I couldn't complain too much, but it felt a little anti-climactic.

The darkness of the ten-foot-high tunnels escaped slowly before us as the light shone. It withered away like it didn't want to be exposed to the light, and so when we first saw a rat, I almost mistook its tail for the odd way the light was receding.

"Rat!" I called, as it turned and entered the light.

It was roughly the size of a large dog, standing three feet high and over six feet long, with a tail as thick as my forearm. It snarled and retreated from the light, staying half in the dark and half in the light.

It had beady red eyes and gray fur that split all around, showing red, bloody flesh, as if it had been slashed down the length of its body. It had two massive front teeth and a bunch of razor-sharp teeth up and down its open maw as it screeched at us.

When it lunged, it almost seemed as if it were in slow motion. I moved to intercept it with my shield and found myself waiting for the impact. When it did finally hit, it rocked me backward, and I stabbed out with my sword.

My blade hit flesh but barely got past the fur, drawing very little blood. Tomas appeared next, his staff coming down on its head from the side. The end of it lit up with a red crackling light, and the blow shattered the rat's skull, dropping it stunned to the ground.

"Hurry," I said. "Finish it off while it's stunned."

I stabbed over and over again into its back, and Ryn appeared, stabbing her daggers into its neck until the body stopped twitching and fell still.

"That wasn't even that hard," I said, checking my status screen to see how much essence I'd gotten from the kill. "Well, that wasn't very lucrative. I only got 100 essence from killing it."

"Same," Ryn said. "Rats are pretty lowbie monsters, if they are considered monsters at all. By my calculations, we will need to kill another ten to twenty more before we level. If you guys have the same essence as me, that is."

I did some mental math, and mine was about the same; roughly ten rats ought to do it. I didn't know if we'd find that many rats down here, but I was all for getting more than five now.

"Should we check for a monster core?" Ryn asked, looking down at the rat with more than a little apprehension.

"Will it have one?" Tomas asked. His snack bag was empty, and he was using it to guard his nose against the pungent smell of the sewers. Luckily, the side we'd fought on was pretty dry, a narrow groove down the middle of the six-foot-wide space that contained sewage and water flowing down and out to wherever sewage went.

"It should, right?" I asked, looking to Ryn, the only one among us that studied this stuff enough to really know.

"It gave us essence, so it has a core," Ryn said. "But it's normally attached to the back of the head, so Tomas might have crushed it."

"Let's dig in then," I said, swallowing hard as I tried to imagine what would be required. We ended up drawing straws from threads Tomas produced, and I got the shortest one, so Ryn passed over one of her daggers, and I went to town. First we cut off its tail as proof of the kill, putting the large thing into Tomas's pack, then I dug into its head, being careful enough not to destroy the core if it was intact.

All we found was chunks of it, which we collected because Ryn said they were normally turned to dust after essence was used, so it didn't matter as much, just harder to sell as pieces. We managed to get four marble-sized pieces before I was so covered in blood and gore that I almost used the nasty wastewater to clean myself, but I had better sense than that.

Instead, I used my canteen to wash as much as I could off me, then I returned the dagger to Ryn before we ventured deeper into the tunnels. Every few hundred feet were iron grates; they were all open, but it appeared as if you could slam them down and they'd stay in place. The oddity of it, why were grates like this needed inside the actual sewer? It was a mystery that not even Ryn had the answer to.

The sewer had been created in the time of the tower, they said, with the old magics and constructions of the time. We knew precious little about it, other than it worked and we used it. Sure, there was maintenance to be done, and from what Ryn said, they knew enough to do that, but not much else.

It twisted and turned, but we encountered another rat almost immediately, this one smaller than the first, but I readied my shield all the same. When it came, I had to angle my shield down as it scratched and bit at me. It managed to get to the side before Tomas could bash it, and teeth sunk into my arm, or at least they should have, instead it felt like someone was firmly pressing on my arm.

Tomas struck a blow to its spine, forcing it back but not stunning it. I checked my arm in between the armor, and it was fine, my Iron Skin worked after all! That made me a little more brave, I rushed in and slammed it in the head with my shield and took another bite as I slashed down at it, scoring a cut down its back.

It came back with a tail swipe at Tomas, catching him off guard, and he slipped into the muck in the middle of the tunnel, cursing as he fell. Ryn appeared suddenly behind the rat and slammed her dagger into its back. It let out a screech, then fell silent as we got our second kill as Adventurers!

I felt pretty invincible with my Iron Skin ability, so I couldn't stop smiling as I looked over the group. Tomas must have thought I was smiling at his bad luck, because he narrowed his eyes at me.

"I'll dunk you in this shit if you'd like, we can all stink up to high heaven," Tomas said, unusually irritated. He took a deep breath and calmed within seconds. "I drew the shit straw this time, so I might as well dig into the rat and find its core."

With that, Tomas borrowed a dagger from Ryn and began to cut into the rat, one slice at a time, making headway much faster than I did and finding a fully intact, but small core. He held it up for us all to see, and I marveled at its geometric look.

It was a semi-flat oval-like thing with flat small sections meeting up. I didn't know the name for the shape, but it was odd to say the least. Covered in blood as it was, I couldn't tell what color it was meant to be until Tomas cleaned it off with his canteen of water.

The thing was crystal clear under the blood, with a tiny light glowing inside.

We continued on carefully and slowly, finding another two rats and killing them in short order. We made sure to collect the tails as we hunted for our fifth and final rat to meet the minimum requirements of the job. I could tell already though, that Ryn was in it for the long haul now that we knew we could farm these bastards for essence.

"Does it feel like it's getting less stinky the deeper we get?" Tomas asked, plugging and unplugging his nose as if testing the air.

I hadn't really noticed it, but he was right, the sewage didn't seem so harsh this deep in, and I wasn't sure why that was.

"We must be getting close to the cleansing system, although if we are as close as I think we are, it shouldn't smell at all. I think we might have stumbled on what is happening," Ryn said as we turned a sharp corner, and before us lay a bright blue light illuminating a horde of giant rats.

We quickly backtracked and peeked around the bend, taking a count before I snuck back several feet, holding my breath as if that might keep them from detecting us.

"There are twelve of those things all huddled together around that blue light," I whispered. "How are we supposed to take care of twelve of those things at once?"

"I don't know," Ryn said, scratching at her chin. "Let's see what we can come up with."

"We could leave and come back with more people, the quest board only called for five tails after all, and we have four, so we find one more roaming around and then call it good, allow them to make another posting for this more difficult problem," Tomas suggested.

I sighed. We were in over our heads, but surely we could come up with a solution. A way to draw them out one at a time. I strained my brain, but I was missing some facts, so I asked Ryn about the glowing device in the middle of the swarm of rats.

"What is the deal with that device? Is it broken? It obviously shouldn't be mutating rats, right?" I asked, trying to get my facts straight.

"That's beyond even my knowledge. I'm sure if we can clear the rats out, they will send someone to fix it," Ryn said, as we sat and pondered the best way to do this.

"I've got a crazy idea," I said. "What if we use those metal gates to funnel them down, so we can kill one or two at a time. I can run out and get their attention, since I'm the fastest and most durable right now. Then you guys get ready at the nearest gate and close it on them. Tomas will hold it closed, and we will deal with the rats, one at a time."

"And if more than a few get through?" Ryn asked, but I shrugged.

"The opening for the gate is only a few feet wide at best, so only a couple could get through at a time. We just have to trust that Tomas is strong enough to hold them back for a while," I said. "Can you do it, Tomas?"

"Sure, why not? I don't see any other way," Tomas said. "I think I'm up for it."

"It's a bad plan," Ryn repeated, but she offered up no alternative, so we continued forward with my plan.

We had one bow between us, and I put Ryn on it, telling her to shoot as many arrows as possible into the mix while I stood ready to grab their attention, and when they reached the halfway point to us, she would run, with me only running right at the end to make sure I had their attention. Meanwhile, Tomas would be at the sewer gates closest to us waiting to slam it closed.

The plan started off nicely, with both of us in position and our hearts pounding with the expectation of action to come. I bit my lip as I readied myself with sword and shield, a tad nervous, but I knew life as an adventurer would include some risks. This was just one of the many I'd be taking with my life.

An arrow whistled through the air, and I began shouting at the rats. Immediately they turned as one and began to charge. Another arrow flew past me, striking the lead rat and slowing it as it took the arrow right into the eye.

"Run!" I yelled to Ryn, but she was already on the way after firing a final arrow into the horde.

I waited a second longer, they were faster than they looked, before turning and sprinting away. I caught up with Ryn almost immediately, and I had to slow myself. This scarf was amazing. I could run at a dead sprint and feel completely in control despite moving four times faster than I ever could have managed before.

Stopping again, I checked to make sure they were following me, most were, but we'd obviously lost a few. But there was no helping that now, so I turned and jogged at what felt like a slow pace, but it was well beyond what the rats could muster.

As I got through the gate, I saw Tomas standing ready as Ryn entered. I jumped through, and we waited the few seconds it took for the rats to catch up. Panting and out of breath, Ryn spoke.

"When did you get so damn fast?" she said, half laughing as she spoke.

I tugged on my scarf and laughed with her as the rats reached us.

Two squeezed through just as Tomas slammed it shut, blocking the rest. He didn't even have to struggle much as the door latched into place, and the rats were too dumb to figure out a door latch. We descended on the two rats with vicious fury, slicing, stabbing, and bashing away at them as they tried to rip us up with their teeth.

I took the brunt of the damage, their teeth leaving shallow bruises but not getting through my flesh at all. We ended the first set with relative ease and realized the rats were dumb enough that we might get a few more kills as they threw themselves against the gate.

I stabbed through the bars and scored another two kills before they got wise and backed off a little.

"I'll open the gate and outrun them, go to the next one and be ready," I said. This continued for three more gates until the last one, with three left, didn't want to work for us.

"It won't shut," Tomas yelled as I neared with three rats on my tail.

"Then we fight, be ready!" I shouted ahead of me. I was getting tired too, but we had to fight on into the night; we had to finish this job.

I jumped through the gate, and Tomas was ready, bashing in the head of the lead one with his Heavy Strike just as Ryn slashed out with her daggers around its thick neck. It died nearly instantly, forcing the other two to climb over it, which they did in quick succession.

That left us with just two, but the biggest and slowest two of the bunch. When the one on the left came in, I caught it on my shield and slashed out with my blade. The other rat barreled right into me as well, knocking me back. I tripped and fell on my ass as two hungry rats went for my throat.

But my team was with me, and they had other plans for these rats. Tomas activated his ability, stunning one, just as Ryn appeared behind another, stabbing deeply into it but not killing it. She called out to me as the wounded one dug its teeth into my neck, drawing blood for the first time since this fight down under had started.

I felt pain, raw and somewhat withdrawn, in my neck, but I wasn't going down so easily. Kicking off with my feet, I managed to get my shield back under me and I blocked my neck, then shoved it to the side with all my strength. It rolled off, screeching all the while, as Tomas took it in the head with his ability. It didn't hit as hard as the prior ones, and I knew I was seeing the fall off of using an ability too close to another use, meaning it wouldn't be as effective as it would if you rested.

But effective or not, the rats fell to repeated blows and attacks by Ryn, Tomas, and eventually, as I got to my feet, myself. It was a bloody affair, not just for the rats but for us as well. But we'd done it, killing a total of 14 rats, all said and done.

We went back to the crystal to check it out, but when we got close, our skin began to warm, and we backed off, not trusting whatever was at work ahead. We'd report it in and let someone else take care of it. Oddly enough, no more rats were around the area, so our kill count ended at 14, meaning we gathered around 1,400 experience, enough to reach level 6 on our first night of adventuring. I know they say the first 10 levels are easy, but this felt amazing.

I leveled up to 6 and felt myself fill with elation; whether it was the process of leveling or just the joy of progression, I couldn't say. I turned to my friends, our bags filled with giant rat tails, and we shared a potion that healed our minor wounds.

"What attribute should I focus on next? I was actually thinking it might be nice to put five into Arcana to give me an edge with Spark, no one expects a tank to be able to cast any quick and dirty magic," I said, imagining the surprise on my attackers' faces as I cast Spark, stunning them right before I struck.

"Sounds good to me," Ryn said. "I think I'll go Power next, give me an ability I can use like Heavy Strike or Shove, probably Shove as it has the most utility."

"And what about you, Tomas?" I asked. "What path you taking next?"

"Arcana sounds cool, maybe I'll do that too," Tomas said, and I facepalmed.

"If you are going after the War Monk class, you need to focus on Power, Guard, and Speed, remember?" I asked, and he seemed surprised.

"Oh, right, right," he said. "Then I'll go Speed next."

With that figured out, we exited the sewers to find a few guards posted at the exit we'd left open and a sour expression on their faces.

"Aye, boys," Ryn said as we climbed out. "Just doing some Adventurer's Guild business, we can close it up now."

"Right," one of them said, recognizing Ryn. "We thought someone was up to something when we noticed the grate, but we trust you, Ryn. Go along then."

We shut the grate and headed back to the Adventurer's Hall, the Amber Coin Tavern, to turn our rat tails in and get some sleep. It was mid-morning already, but we decided to catch a few hours before setting out, that and a long bath, a very long bath.

CHAPTER 7
PREPARATION

"We will throw in an extra two moons for going above and beyond," Serif said, seeing the large collection of sewer rat tails. "Now, tell me again what you found down there, some sort of malfunctioning cleaning crystal?"

"Yeah," Ryn said, taking point. She described it as best she could, better than I would have, and Serif made a report, saying she'd get someone on it from the city.

With that, we left the guild hall and split off to deal with our bathing and sleeping, with promises to meet up in four hours, while we still had plenty of daylight. The festival started this evening, so we'd be busy later in the night, but until then, we had goblins to kill.

I was distracted as I walked to the nearest bathhouse, ready to wash away my troubles and spend a little of the two moons I'd earned. More coin than I'd ever had before, wearing gear more expensive than I'd ever worn before, I felt pretty nice all things considered.

While daydreaming and enjoying my day, I nearly walked right into Craven Deymorin and his group of thugs. Oh, what a day, I thought, ruined by the likes of Craven.

"Watch where you're going, Commons boy," Craven said, and I made it a point to stop and look him right in the eye.

"I'd watch what you say to me," I said, grinning at him.

"Oh yeah, why is that?" Craven asked, smirking at his friends.

"Because I'd hate to beat your ass in front of your friends, but I'll do it," I said.

Craven, quick to anger as he was, put a hand on his massive two-handed sword as if he were about to draw it. But one of his lackeys, a girl with brown hair and green eyes, put a hand on his shoulder. I didn't know her name as she hadn't been one of the newer adventurers unlocked last night.

Craven visibly calmed, and then the girl spoke, her voice much more mature than her age portrayed.

"Be careful, young adventurer, even easy jobs like goblin hunting can be dangerous, I'd hate to have you die before you could become the next great Dragon Knight," she said, and all of them chuckled at me.

"I'll be fine," I said, not letting them get to me as they moved off and away without saying another word.

There was a threat in their words, but I couldn't do anything about that now. I'd tell Ryn and Tomas, make sure they knew what they were getting into, but I knew my friends all too well. They'd risk life and limb for me every time without fail. And I loved them for it.

People like Craven and his father's goons would always be there, threatening or trying to discourage. It was up to people like me to stand up and do good anyway. Beyond doubt and fear is where we must live.

So I took my time getting to the bathhouse, trying to think of ways I could ensure our safety for the upcoming goblin hunt. They obviously knew we were on the case, but what else did they know? Perhaps a danger that the posting hadn't eluded to or known about? It was worth considering, but not worth stopping our hunt for. That much I was confident about.

The bathhouse I chose was one close to the Commons, but far enough away that it cost ten scales to use, instead of the two I normally spent. But that meant I had access to all the good oils and heated tubs. It was early in the morning, and the men's baths were half full, but not so full that I would seek a bath elsewhere.

The building was made of stone and had heating provided by some enchantment or item that other, less fancy bathhouses wouldn't have. So there was no lingering smoke smell, like from the Commons bathhouses, from the wood that burned to heat the baths. Instead, it smelt of aged wood and flowers.

The flowery scents mostly came from the women's side of the bathhouse, where they prioritized the scents of pretty things over more manly smells. I oiled my body all over, giving special attention to my neck where I had small scars from the bite I'd taken.

There were ointments that could lessen the scarring caused by the quick and dirty potion healing, but it was so slight that I didn't need any right now nor did I think I could afford it. Ointments like that cost several moons each, a pittance for a full-time adventurer that had access to the wealth of dungeons, but much more than I could muster up at the moment.

Hot water washed over me as I plunged my head under the surface and soaked myself thoroughly. It felt so good. I was happy that almost no one made conversation while in the baths. Even so, I kept an eye on the door and occasionally looked at all present, always watchful for threats after two members of House Deymorin alluded to my possible harm or death.

I needed to get out of this town and see the wide world, explore and discover the wonders of dungeons and other places. My father and mother had never liked the idea of travel, but you'd never know it from the stories they told of grand adventures, and, of course, my father was obsessed with dragons, even going so far as to claim he'd seen one once as a boy.

I could never get him to tell me more than that little detail on the matter, and only when he'd drunk one too many ales. He kept secrets, like where he'd gotten such an amazing scarf, or where they came from before coming here in their late twenties. I was a product of them settling down, but everyone had tales of adventuring, yet my parents never attributed the stories they told to themselves, always to someone else.

Whether they had planned to tell me when I was older, I could not know, but I missed them dearly when I let myself dwell on it. Their bodies had been so badly burnt from the fires that, if they hadn't been lying together in their room where they were found, you wouldn't be able to even tell it was them.

That fire took the lives of many mothers, fathers, and children. A scar on the town's history and one that no one liked to speak of. Nearly a fourth of the town was burnt down at the time, and only now, some ten years later, are we fully recovering from the loss of life and buildings. No more charred remains, except in a small section of the Commons, remained, where the fire was said to have started.

Of course, not everyone agreed on how the fire started. Some say a house caught fire from a rogue lamp falling, while others claim to have seen hooded figures fleeing the burning house, as if it were sabotage or something. I didn't know what to believe, and I'd tried to work out what truly happened over the years, but I was no closer to knowing than I had been the day it happened.

I finished my bath as I let my mind wander to one of the stories of dragons my father had told me. One about an old, wise dragon who had somehow avoided the curse of the mind sickness. My father explained that as dragons grew older, they inherited memories from other dragons of the same type, which inevitably merged with the first elemental wild dragons, driving them mad as well.

But this story was about one such dragon that avoided that fate by sharing its madness with its rider, a Dragon Knight. By doing so, they were able to fight the urges and become a force for good across the continent. I remembered the details well: the dragon had been a great red dragon, and his rider wore armor made from his own scales.

How they'd travel the continent and beyond, settling wars and rumors of wars by their very presence. It was no wonder people didn't want me to become a Dragon Knight; the stories made them seem unstoppable and more powerful than anyone ought to be. But I wanted that power, not for the sake of power, but for the opportunities it would give me for good.

No longer would I be the outcast orphan boy barely making it through life; I'd be the great Dragon Knight who ended wars and conflicts. A Knight that others could look up to, and with my dragon, I'd bring peace to the lands as they had once been. So many dreams and aspirations filled my head, but it would take time and a lot of hard work, so I had to be ready for that.

If my calculations were right and they were based on me speaking to so many adventurers, then it would take me at the very least years to reach level 40 and unlock my class. And when I did finally accomplish that, I'd need to do the hardest part yet, find and kill a mad dragon.

It was a shame to have to kill a dragon, but it almost always fell to Dragon Knights to kill the older dragons as they became global threats when their minds were lost. I didn't know if someday I'd have to kill my own dragon, but that was a bridge I'd cross if I ever reached it.

Finishing my bath, I got up, found a towel, dried myself, and returned to my armor. I'd paid an extra ten scales to have it cleaned while I bathed, but they weren't finished yet, so I waited with my towel on as they made the final adjustments to my armor, getting all the blood and stink off it.

"Thank you," I said, as the young dark-haired girl returned it to me. She bowed, and I returned the gesture before returning to the locker room and dressing in my clothing and armor.

How they managed to dry them so fast with those odd rocks of theirs, I didn't know, but I did know that this place was fancy, and if any bath house could do it, it would be this one. I checked the name again as I left, in appreciation of their quick service. The sign out front called the place, 'The Dripping Goose'. An odd name for sure, but I moved off toward the Commons and to my one-bedroom apartment.

My landlord saw me coming. He lived on the first floor with his family, and he did not look happy.

"You will pay 25 scales for the work I did to fix your door," he shouted to me. I reached into my coin purse and paid him 75, which covered the repairs and another two weeks' rent. "Oh," he said, probably surprised I could pay him. "Thank you. You're a big adventurer now, aren't you, boy? Maybe I should charge you normal rates now?"

"Charge what you must, I'm not sure how long I'll be in town, but I do need a place to stay while I'm here," I said, though I was already thinking about moving into a nicer place for the meantime and to have a place that people didn't know where I stayed.

"No, you're a good boy, I'll keep the discount for you," Mr. Moroto said, bowing to me as he left back into his bottom apartment.

"Thanks," I said, walking up the stairs and to my room on the left.

My key worked, and the door swung open, the lock and hatch having been fixed from before. Mr. Moroto was an abrasive guy most of the time to me, but having just been paid, he was nicer than I'd ever seen him, despite having to fix my broken door.

My room was no more than ten paces long and just over half that wide, but it fit all I needed: a bed, a trunk with a lock that had been broken along with a large portion of the trunk, and my belongings thrown about the room.

I changed out of my armor and lay on my bed in my newly laundered clothing. I'd need to drop off my clothes at a bathhouse for cleaning, as I was on my last outfit now, but I'd use the old place that did it for a scale a stone's worth of weight. The stone in question, being about the size of my fists put together.

Slipping off to sleep was easy after I latched the door shut and wedged my shield under the door handle. It was the banging on my door after what felt like only a minute or two of sleeping that was annoying.

"Come on, it's been nearly three hours, we need to get a move on," Ryn was saying from outside the door.

It couldn't possibly have been that long, I thought, as I groggily got up and unlocked my door, letting her in, Tomas following after with a bag of dried fruit covered in a light dusting of sugar. The brown sack he held scattered sugar across my floor as he reached inside to grab more.

"I'm up," I said, finally sitting back down and looking for my armor on the ground where I'd set it.

Pulling piece by piece on, Ryn watched me, looking around my room and shaking her head. "You uh, need to clean up, you can't be this messy all the time," she said, having only really seen my room in this state in the few times she'd visited.

"I have a reason this time, my room was tossed by some Deymorin thugs, hardly my fault," I said, though if I was being truthful, it wasn't that clean before; it was organized, chaotic or not, so I could find stuff. As it was, I couldn't tell you where anything was anymore.

"We wanted to get a bite to eat and grab another meal to go so we don't have to come back into town until dark," Ryn said, hurrying me along.

"That'll make us late for the start of the festival," Tomas said, as if just now realizing it. "I'd hate to miss all that yummy food."

"They'll still have plenty of pies and cakes waiting for you, don't you worry,1 bud," I said, chuckling at his voracious appetite. "We sure we can't convince Ashric and his crew to join us?"

"Nah, Lord Ravenlock sent them on an errand with some of his men and they'll be getting a ton of essence off of it, we could have gone with them, Ashric said, but I figured we wanted to do it our own way," Tomas explained, sitting on the bed next to me while I stood and struggled into the rest of the armor. It was harder than it looked, and Ryn had to help me get the last few pieces on before we were set to go.

"Wonder what it was," I said as an afterthought, putting my pack on and heading for the door.

"A den of harpies is what Ashric said, but he wasn't one hundred percent sure," Tomas said, and I nodded my head.

"Harpies around here are likely closer to level 25, so they'd get a decent amount of essence if they could manage to stay safe while the harpies are killed. I doubt they'll be much help, it's straight up boosting at that point," Ryn said, scoffing.

Boosting wasn't uncommon, but it was highly frowned upon by almost all adventurers. It basically meant having a higher-level person kill something that wasn't too strong for them, but also not too high for you, as after about 20 levels, either way, you stopped getting essence from it. Nobles, of course, would do shit like that and no one bats an eye, but if a commoner was caught doing it, the Adventurer's Guild would fine them and threaten banning them.

"They better be careful that not everyone finds out about that," I said, and Ryn nodded in agreement.

"Right," she said. "Risky if you ask me, especially if they told Tomas. He keeps a secret about as well as he keeps snacks around for longer than a day."

"Hey," Tomas said, his face screwing up in a frown and looking mighty offended. Then he laughed and said, "Well, you got me. But I'll keep this one under wraps, I don't want Ashric to get into trouble. So, uh, pretend I didn't tell you any of that."

"Deal," I said, respecting his trying to keep the secret, despite knowing it wouldn't last long. He had loose lips and often spoke before thinking.

We ventured off into the early afternoon to get some food. We'd gotten our free ration from the Amber Coin Tavern, but we had another place in mind for our lunch. There were rows and rows of booths set up in the festival space in the center of town, and almost all of the temporary food areas were open already.

We split up, each of us going to the area and kind of food we preferred. So Tomas went for sweet stuff, Ryn for savory, and me for a place that not many went to, a visiting merchant from down south that made these wonderful things called burritos. Mine had a mix of chicken, spiced to perfection, beans, rice, tomato, lettuce, and other things I couldn't identify.

In a word, though, it was perfection. I paid the ridiculous 10 scales for it and was so happy I could afford it this year around. I'd only eaten it twice, once when Tomas paid for it and didn't like it, and another when I'd saved specifically for it. But this year I'd eat my fill of them and be all the happier for it.

"Thank you," I told the man, a Mr. Horitos. "I'll be back for some later, so don't sell out."

"A deal for you, young sir, come back and I'll knock off a scale just for you," he said, tipping his large hat in my direction.

With all our food gathered, we came together and feasted like kings. Tomas, of course, bought more than he could handle, and we ended up sharing in his leftovers as a dessert. While Ryn ate her small portion and called it good.

"You guys have to try this burrito," I said, not offering mine up but gesturing to the cart.

"I did, remember?" Tomas said. "Too spicy for me."

"If I'm expected to eat the entire thing, I'm not sure I could, but perhaps a bite will tell me if it's worth it?" Ryn said, gesturing to my burrito, half finished.

"Fine," I said, offering it to her and allowing her to take a bite.

She did so, and her face screwed up in all sorts of different emotions before settling on one of satisfaction.

"That's not bad," she said. "Maybe we can go halves on one some other time."

"It'll have to be tonight or tomorrow, he always sells out," I explained.

"Oh, I bet, even the aftertaste is tasty," Ryn said, her expression growing light.

"Let me try another bite," Tomas said, likely intrigued by Ryn's acceptance of it.

I sighed and relented.

"Oh wow, that isn't as spicy as I remembered. Maybe I shouldn't have used so much of that red sauce on it last time," Tomas said, then he went for a second bite, and I had to wrestle my burrito from his hands.

"That's enough, get your own," I said, munching on my burrito and taking a tad bit too big a bite. It took a second, but I managed to get it all down. Then I conquered the rest of the burrito.

What followed was too many sweets from Tomas's leftovers and random talking about various subjects. It was fun, but then we got serious and tried to figure out how we'd take on the goblins.

"Goblins are known to group up for strength in numbers," Ryn said. "So we will need to figure out a way to separate and destroy them. Any ideas?"

"What if we try to lure some away with something shiny? I hear goblins have gold lust as bad as stories claim dragons have it, so maybe we can use that to our advantage?" I asked, thinking hard about how else we'd be able to defeat the goblins if they outnumbered us.

"I think how we killed the rats might apply; we get them to follow us into a narrow gorge or something, then just kill them off one by one," Tomas suggested.

"What if we used a controlled fire to surround and scare them into a confined space, and we fire arrows in and kill them all. We'd need to pick up two new bows and some arrows, but that shouldn't be much more than a moon," Ryn said, her suggestion the most promising of the three.

"Or," I said, smiling. "We do a combination of all three."

With a tentative plan put together, we ventured off to grab a few bows and a bundle or three of arrows. If our plan worked, we'd need to be fast at putting out the fire as well, so we spent two silver for a trinket that was made for just that, putting out fires by some odd magical means. They'd grown in popularity after the fire, but having been overproduced the price of them had hit rock bottom.

With all our supplies together and a plan put forth, we ventured toward the gates and into the wilds.

CHAPTER 8
GOBLINS

Ryn got us waived through the gate without so much as a question about what three weaker adventurers might be off doing in the middle of the day in an area known for its stronger monsters, like gnolls, hobgoblins, bugbears, and the like. Adventurers kept the first few miles around the town cleared, sometimes even deeper, and it was in these first few miles that the goblins had gathered.

They were seen as so weak that only children would have trouble with them, but they could be a nuisance if allowed to gather together like they were now. So a posting that no one cared to deal with had been posted, and now it was up to us to find and destroy them.

The forest around the town, at least for a mile coming up to all sides of the walls, was cleared of almost all trees, so we ventured through open country together toward the thicker trees in hope of finding the goblins. To our surprise, we ran into a pack of three goblins almost immediately after entering the thick trees.

One had a bow, one a staff, and the other a rusty sword, so already better equipped than the job notice made them out to be.

Rushing in, I slashed out with my sword after hitting the bowmen back on his ass. My blade cut into the staff-wielding goblin just as it began to chant, breaking its concentration. Tomas hit the warrior in the chest with his Heavy Strike attack, and it went flying backward into a tree, crunching hard and falling into a pile, still as ever and obviously dead.

I was momentarily distracted; we'd killed hundreds if not thousands of goblins over the last five years of training, but this was the first time I'd heard them scream out in pain and bleed. But I didn't let it bother me, instead I pushed it down and stabbed the fallen bowmen as he tried to climb to his feet, relying on Ryn to take out the caster.

Which she did, stabbing her daggers right into its neck, and ending any possible casting from happening.

"That was easy," I said, panting only a little. "That was even easier than the tower goblins."

"A lot more messy, though," Ryn said, wiping her dagger free of blood on the dead goblin. "Check out the essence we get for each one, though, that's pretty awesome."

We'd gotten one hundred and seventy-five essence per kill, it appeared.

"Who is getting their cores, because I am not going first again," I said, then Ryn shrugged and made a point of counting them.

"One for each of us, let's go for it, loot and keep whichever one you killed, I suppose," she said, cutting into the shaman.

"That means you'll get the biggest core right, because ones that can use magic have bigger cores from what you've told us," I said, kneeling down and digging into the spine of the one before me with my newly purchased dagger, it was a small thing and would mostly be used for getting cores, not combat, but I had a sheath for it on my belt regardless.

"So you do listen," Ryn said in mock surprise. "Well I guess you do learn."

She made no move to stop what she was doing, though, finding her core around the same time I found mine. It wasn't that much bigger, but it was noticeable. I made a show of inspecting mine and washing it clean.

Tomas came over with his and said, "It's like they always say. Size doesn't matter, it's how you use it!"

"Who says that?" Ryn asked, snickering.

"You mean, it's not true?" Tomas asked, making a show of being shocked. "She lied to me then!"

"Okay, knock it off, we've got goblins to kill, remember," I said, cleaning my dagger and sword off before stacking up the bodies. "Oh, don't forget to get some ears as proof of kills. Does that mean we need both or...?"

"Just the left ear is common practice, as long as we have all the same, they'll count them. If we bring half left and half right, we will only get half credit for each singular ear," Ryn said. She always knew way more about this than we did.

"Okay, left ears it is," I said, pulling out my dagger and cutting the ear off. It wasn't as easy or clean as you'd think, as I cut a part of its fleshy head skin off as well. But I knew the more I did it, the better I'd get.

Cleaning my blade once more, I sheathed it and led the party forward. We would head in the direction they'd been coming from, going deeper and more to the west. It would be a test of bravery, though, as the deeper we went, the bigger chance we had of encountering stronger monsters.

As I walked, it felt like the forest pressed in around me, my feet sinking into the soft ground all around me. Every crunch of a twig and leaf had me on edge, as if each sound I made might invite one of the monsters stronger than us to attack us. No shapes lurked in the shadows around us, no glint of eyes staring at us, yet still I wondered what could be.

The air was thick with the scent of tree leaves, the kind I'd smelled all my life growing up in a town filled with them. Pine needles had a very unique scent, and I actually found it rather calming. There was a mix of other trees, with broad leaves and whatnot, but mostly just pines. A raven croaked overhead, the sound split the silence that reigned over the forest.

It was so strange being out here in the forest. Sure, we'd ventured out as kids, Tomas and I, but the reality of the dangers became real around the time Ryn showed up in town, so this was the first time I'd been out with all three of us. The few miles were said to be safe around town, but you never knew when a monster might roam closer to the walls.

That was the case with little Jonny, back all those years before. It was said to have been a hobgoblin, a larger goblin with more brute strength and cunning than normal goblins. It snatched him up while he played only a mile or so away from the main eastern gate. The other kids escaped, but it snacked on Jonny, leaving only scraps behind by the time the guards and adventurers could be mustered.

As we ventured through the woods, I tried my best to push all the horror stories away and remember that I was now an adventurer and no longer did I need to fear the monsters or the stories I'd heard about them. I'd be stupid not to be wary of them, though, so I found myself someplace between scared and brave, but not quite either.

So when we heard snickering up ahead, I was ready to attack whatever it might be, except perhaps what we found: four teenage boys with sharp sticks poking at a goblin corpse.

"What on Avaris are you doing out here?" Ryn admonished them.

"Oh shit," a dark-haired youth said, dropping his stick and trying to look innocent.

"We were goblin hunting," another said with lighter hair but a bigger thicker build.

"You'd best get back, we are hunting the remaining goblins, and you guys are getting closer to their camp. You might be able to kill one goblin, but how do you feel against twenty?" I asked, clearing my voice and speaking with as much authority as I could.

"Fuck all if we care, we can take them," another said, just as a whistle filled the air, and he took an arrow to the gut. "Shit." He managed to say as he fell to his knees.

"Protect them and find the archer!" I commanded, moving in front of where the arrow had come, catching another on my shield. "Right there, I see at least two of them!"

I rushed forward with Tomas as Ryn helped the injured boy. Tomas dodged an arrow, then smacked another out of the air with his stick, before we reached the space where the goblins lay in wait.

The first one went down by Tomas's Heavy Strike, and I bashed apart the bow of another, following up with a stab to its arm. It shrieked, speaking in that gibberish language goblins used, before turning to run. I was much faster, however, and overtook it with a blade to its spine.

Grabbing the corpses, we brought them back to the clearing as the boy sipped on a potion. I'd faintly heard his screams echo through the woods as she removed the arrow, but being in combat had narrowed my focus enough that I hadn't really even thought about it.

"It'll hurt, but you can make it back to the town now, hurry and avoid the deeper woods," Ryn said to them as the other stood and made ready to leave.

They nodded, no longer thinking this adventure was cool or fun after their buddy took one to the gut. We gathered the three, took their left ears, destroyed their right ones, so no one could claim it by finding and taking the right ones.

With the young adults taken care of, we ventured deeper until finally we found a camp. We stayed on the outskirts of it, but there had to be at least three, maybe four dozen goblins here. As we waited, we saw a group of three leaving, and we stalked them waiting to ambush them when they got far enough away.

Our ambush was quick and effective. Killing all three in a matter of seconds instead of a minute or longer. At one hundred and seventy-five a pop, this was going to fast-track us to higher levels. At least until level 10.

"Let's do this for a while," I suggested. "We can keep waiting for them to venture out alone and take them on three at a time."

"That's smart, plus I'm not confident fire is the answer anymore. You see how dry these woods are. I don't know if we'd be able to stop it if it got out of control."

"They are so weak, we might be fine to just rush them," Tomas said, snacking on something out of a bag he'd picked up in town.

"I'd like to bring down their numbers first, because an arrow hurts no matter how weak, the monster is strong enough to fire arrows that pierce flesh," Ryn said, thumbing behind as if mentioning the youths who'd gotten the arrow to the gut.

"Not my skin, maybe I could go in and take them on," I said jokingly, but Tomas seemed to consider it and nodded.

"You probably could, until the magic started, then you'd be in trouble," Tomas said.

With that decided, we ventured back to the camp just in time for three more to leave. We followed after them, but not before noticing something. The three that had left had come from a cave in the camp, where something else could be hiding. We continued to kill them in threes for the next six hours, with nighttime ready to fall at any hour, we decided it was time for more drastic measures.

We'd already gained two levels from killing over 30 goblins in the slow manner of waiting for them to come out, and that left the camp with only about a dozen goblins, and they no longer looked to be sending out more groups. As we watched, we heard a grunt and a call for something. Five goblins went into the cave, and only three came out, leaving ten goblins to deal with. Except, the three left, and we decided to hunt them as we had the others.

That left seven to deal with, and we marveled at how this job or quest had just worked itself out. Making our way back to the camp, five goblins had left, leaving only two, so we walked right in with my shield in front of me.

The remaining two were warriors, so they came in with swords, screaming something toward the cave but rushing us. I caught the first sword, more confident than I'd ever been from a day filled with killing goblins. I slashed out, taking one right in the neck and ending it. Tomas and Ryn dispatched the last one just as a roar split the air and something stepped free of the cave's shadows.

I didn't know what I was looking at, but Ryn did and informed us almost immediately.

"It's a hobgoblin! We need to run!" Ryn shouted, but I had other plans.

"We are already level 8, it can't be more than double that, together we can take it!" I yelled back as the eight-foot-tall monster with a massive club lumbered over toward us, moving slowly. This monster would have all its attributes put into a mixture of Guard and Power, so we needed to be wary of its strength most of all.

"Dodge!" I yelled as the club came down for me. I caught a little of it on my shield, but mostly I got the hell out of the way.

"Tomas moved in, slamming his staff against the back of the hobgoblin's leg and dropping it to a knee as Ryn rushed forward and stabbed it in the left eye.

We were doing it! We were doing it!

I rushed forward and watched as Ryn dodged an attack with her Quick-step and Tomas hit it again, this time on the head, with a Heavy Strike. It swayed as I got to its back leg and sliced with all my might. My sword cut deep, and I realized in that moment that we'd gotten lucky; this monster must have put all its attributes into strength and not in guard.

Then suddenly it rolled, and Tomas was knocked back. It got to its feet and roared defiantly into the air. With a wave of its hand, we all went flying back from the force of the attack or perhaps an ability it had. I knocked my head hard onto a tree, but my vision focused only a moment later, and I saw Ryn about to be rushed by a blow from its club.

I moved as fast as the wind, my scarf boosting my speed beyond what I could achieve before, and I positioned myself in the middle of the attack with my shield raised. It hit and shattered my sturdy shield in a single blow, hammering me down into the ground. My knees ached, my arm was clearly broken, and my sword had been knocked aside.

Luckily for me, it wasn't over, because Tomas was back on his feet and came at the hobgoblin from the side. His staff crackled with red energy as he struck down with great power. It smashed and shattered on the head of the hobgoblin. But it had done the trick, perhaps not killing it but stunning it for sure.

I grabbed hold of my sword, Ryn was on her feet as well, and we rushed the fallen hobgoblin, ready to kill it for good. Our strikes found home, my sword going deep into its good eye, and Ryn's daggers slitting the throat. Then I watched as Ryn took its head off completely, ending the threat and releasing the essence into the air.

"That hurt," I said, looking at the pieces of my shield. "I'm pretty sure the bones in my arm are shattered as well."

"Let's get its core and get home, we are far too close to the deep woods for my liking," Ryn said, wrapping the entire head and putting it in her pack.

We found the core just below where she took the head, a medium core worth its weight in moons and even perhaps a few suns, or golden coins.

I took a potion, but it would take another to heal the bones completely. But to do that, I'd have to wait a while before using another potion.

"Two levels and all these cores," Tomas said, walking happily despite losing his staff. "Even after replacing our equipment, we will have more moons than even I've ever had before. We will be able to afford to have some festival fun and get a gig on a caravan, making our way to a town with a lower-level dungeon and monsters we can kill without nearly dying."

"I'm just glad my shield held long enough to keep more than my arm from breaking apart," I said, my arm lay in a makeshift sling where it would stay for another two hours until I could safely take another potion and hope it healed the bones enough.

"Thank you," Ryn said. "I'd have been flattened if not for you. That push attack he had was oddly similar to Shove, and I wasn't expecting a monster to have that ability."

"Yeah, that was odd, wasn't it? I wonder, do monsters have access to the same attributes and abilities as us?" I asked, directing my question to the all-knowing Ryn.

"I don't know," she said, surprising me. "Honestly, I've done precious little monster research, but I'll be hitting the books tomorrow to find out."

We'd killed a total of 38 goblins and 1 hobgoblin in a single day. It had to be a record of some kind, and I was very much expecting extra compensation for what we'd collected. The job posting had alluded to roughly 12 goblins total, and we'd killed three times that many.

We'd also missed out on just as much essence, seeing as the cave was literally filled with goblin corpses. Ryn theorized, as we left, that the hobgoblin had been trying to power level himself by killing the weaker goblins off a few at a time. It was an interesting theory, but I just wanted to turn in our quest rewards and see what we'd be given in return.

"You encountered a hobgoblin within the safe zone of the woods. We will dispense a group out to kill it at once," Serif said, her eyes wide with surprise. "It is a wonder you are still alive to tell the tale. Probably a slow monster, they always tend to go Guard or Power."

"You misunderstand me," Ryn said, lifting the head and putting it on the desk. "We took care of it, as well as 38 goblins."

We took turns emptying out ears onto the table.

"Thirty-eight!?" Serif said. "That's a small army. And they were all within the safe zone?"

"Yes," I said, putting my final two ears on the table. "It would have been more, but half their numbers had been killed by the hobgoblin."

"That's odd behavior. I'll make sure it is reported and teams are sent to scour and cleanse the safe zone to ensure it is safe once more," Serif said. "This calls for another job done well beyond the posting. I will give you a sun for your efforts and our apologies for sending you off on a mission that might have ended you."

"Whoa, are you serious?" I asked, accepting the coin as she offered it. That represented 100 moons, more wealth than any of us could have hoped to gather in such a short time.

"Hobgoblins are worth about half that, and you brought the head, so we can't doubt you did it. That, plus the danger and sheer amount of goblins you've taken care of, a sun is the best we can do though," Serif said, taking the head and walking to the back with it.

I shared a look with both Ryn and Tomas, then we all hooted and hollered in sudden surprise.

"Yes!" I said. "Let's get this broken up and split up, then we can set aside a quarter for supplies and caravan costs. We are set, and nearly level 10 at that!"

"I'm almost level 9, not 10," Ryn said, looking at me oddly. "Are you getting more essence than me?"

"No," I said, chuckling. "I was just getting ahead of myself. I'm at the same level as you."

We all shared a laugh, and when Serif returned, she was able to split the sun into a hundred moons for us, so we could split it amongst ourselves. By the end, I had a crazy 34 moons and a few dozen scales.

My coin purse was never so fat as it was today. We agreed, since we'd kind of gotten a landfall, that we'd use our personal coin to replace broken items. So I made a note that I needed to find a place to buy a shield, maybe a magical one even, since I had so much coin in my purse.

It was time to go enjoy the festival, but first I ran my coin back to my room and lifted a baseboard to hide the majority of my coins from any intruders. I could have just gotten a better place, but that took time, and this worked just as well.

Before I knew it, I was meeting up with my friends, including Jareth, Sel, and Ashric, to have some fun at the festival. They had all made it to level 10, but we had a better story to tell than they did, so it all worked out. We'd reach ten within the next day or so, and then we'd be on the slow grind forward like everyone else.

It was a marvelous start to a marvelous night. And I took every moment to enjoy the time we had together, because here soon we'd probably go our separate ways, at least Jareth, Sel, and Arshic, but not my closest friends. We shared a similar goal to become powerful adventurers, and we wouldn't let anything stand in our way.

CHAPTER 9
FESTIVAL

The first day of the festival was little more than vendors selling food and merchants pushing cool lanterns and the like that would be lit on the day of remembrance, the second day of the festival.

Also on the second day, there would be time for all the competitions, from eating to racing to a tournament that only non-unlocked players could enter. Which was a shame, because I loved that sword tournament, and now I'd need to register as a level eight Adventurer. Which would put me in the level 5 to 10 bracket of fighters.

But tonight was all about eating and having fun, maybe even buying a few trinkets and bits and bobs from some of the merchants. Walking with all six of us together, we decided to check out the merchants first, then head over and get some food just in time for one of the nightly plays to reenact some great deed or heroism.

"So level 10 already?" I asked the other three. "How's that feel?"

"A bit shitty," Jareth said, surprising us with his words. He was always so reserved and rarely spoke.

"It just feels like we didn't earn it," Sel said, her eyes downcast. "I'm not sure we should even talk about it, because it was borderline boosting if you ask me."

"Nonsense," Ashric said. "We went out to see more powerful adventurers at work, and got ambushed. How could we have known all those goblins and hobgoblins would be watching the road? Plus, we got a number of goblin kills, so it wasn't like we did nothing."

"Yeah," Tomas said, eating from a plate of sweet pies that he'd had us stop for him to get before going to the merchants. "You fought and happened to get a few extra essence from the stronger monsters. It isn't all too uncommon. But to hit level 10 in a night, that must have been exhilarating."

"I hear Craven and his five made level 10 as well," I said, shaking my head. "A shame we didn't make it all the way to 10 as well, we are super close though."

"Tell me again how you three managed to kill one of those crazy hobgoblins by yourselves?" Sel said, seeming skeptical.

"It wasn't without injury," I said, showing my arm. It was sore but the bones had knitted back together with my second potion. There would be a period before it healed completely, but unless I got a rare regeneration ring or something, I'd just have to deal with the soreness. We'd all need regeneration rings eventually; they were rare but an integral part of being an adventurer.

"We killed something like 40 goblins right, three at a time for hours and hours, and finally this giant of a goblin came out," Tomas said, going into another retelling of our tale. He made it sound much more exciting and longer than it had actually been, but we all ate it up, Sel included. Finally, we reached the merchant quarter of the square and decided to split up to look at everything and meet up in an hour or so.

I moved to the first booth, Ryn stayed at my side, and this one had all manner of magical trinkets said to be for adventurers specifically, which wasn't uncommon, as most folk were adventurers before they were anything else.

The first item that caught my eye was an Emberlight Lantern, similar to what Gallywot had tried to sell us, but for twice the price at 20 silver moons. This one was smaller than the other, allowing it to be held easily in the palm of my hand if I wanted, but lamps were easier to hold when they had a handle and were a tad bigger, so I went to the next item that caught my eye and read the inscription next to it.

A Featherfall Token, a coin that, if held in your hand and squeezed while falling, would allow you to fall slowly once per day. At fifteen silver moons, it was tempting, but just because I had more wealth than before didn't mean I wanted to spend it all. For that very reason, I'd only brought ten silver moons with me to the festival.

Then I saw several sunburst-shaped pins. When pinned, the "Everdry cloak pin" would do as its name suggested, keeping your clothes dry even in the wettest of conditions. A common magical item that I'd seen many a traveler wear. I picked it up and looked at the price. At only 4 silver moons, it was a bargain, and I set it down, seriously considering it.

There were a few other items: a pair of pebbles that could share a whisper from a mile away, a wrap that let you blend in with your surroundings, a pocket-warming stone that kept your body temperature even in cold climates, and several others.

I looked at Ryn, who was clutching a pair of brass spectacles, and down at the placard to see what they were called and how much they cost.

Identifying Glasses: fifty silver moons. Brass-rimmed spectacles with faint rune-etchings all around them. They were said to allow the wearer to appraise items or creatures within a few levels of themselves. Overuse will cause a mild headache, until finally it will stop working until you've taken a short rest.

"Those are pretty pricey," I said, but I couldn't deny they'd be useful to have around.

"I have nearly enough, but I'd need to cut into our group fund for the rest," Ryn said. She'd been charged with holding the group coin, so she could buy it if she wanted and felt it was a good item for us to have as a group, but Tomas would want a say in it as well.

"What if we all throw in ten silver moons, and the party fund puts in twenty, that way it's even?" I asked, we'd need an item like this eventually, and paying someone for scrolls would get pricy after a while. According to Ry,n most scrolls cost about 1 silver moon, or greater if they needed to identify higher-level items.

"That could work," Ryn said, seeming surprised at my offer. "Let's find Tomas and see if he agrees."

He did, of course, and soon the three of us were back and purchasing one of the most expensive items on the table. We, or I should say Ryn, haggled him down to 45 Silver moons before we finalized the purchase. I told Ryn I'd pay her back as I'd only brought so much, and she was fine with it.

"Try to identify my scarf now," I said, excited to learn of its properties officially.

"I'm trying, but I keep getting either your armor or yourself. The scarf isn't registering. Take it off and let me hold it, maybe?" Ryn asked, and I took it off, feeling my Perception fall a fair bit as I did so. I felt sluggish, and everyone moved differently than before, in ways I couldn't as easily predict.

"Hurry up, it feels weird not having it on," I said. I'd been so tired when I'd bathed that I hadn't really noticed much of a difference.

"Nope, still won't work. Not even telling me a little bit about it. Maybe it's a rare item, and that puts it outside our level range of identifying," Ryn said, handing it back, and I put it on immediately, returning everything to the state it was before.

Because of this, I felt someone approaching from the side, and I turned to see none other than Craven with his five teammates, all wearing armor and carrying weapons, as if they'd come back from a hunt, yet not a one of them was dirty or bloody, so it wasn't clear what they'd hunted.

"Let me guess, you lot didn't make it to level 10, but you did manage to stay alive from that goblin raid. Was it harder than you expected?" Craven asked, chuckling to his friends.

"You dick," Ryn said. "You knew somehow that a hobgoblin had joined forces with those goblins, didn't you! You know I could get you fined for not reporting that to the Adventurer's Guild!"

"Easy now, maybe we just learned recently about it, not nearly fast enough to report it and get you informed. Either way, try if you want, no fine will keep the joy off my face of knowing you guys barely made it out alive," Craven said.

"Why do you act like this?" I asked, so fed up with his stupid childish antics.

"Because common trash like you shouldn't even be allowed to be Unlocked. Go give up on the life and become a tavern owner or something, serve people like you are meant to," Craven said, sneering the words at me.

"Let's go, Ryn. This guy just likes getting off on others' pains. We don't need to fuel the fire," I said, keeping my calm as Ryn clenched her fists and readied to punch Craven in the face.

I had to turn back and take her by the arm. She was fuming visibly, and it was a good thing Craven didn't say anything else, because level 10 or not, a level 8 Ryn was about ready to kick his ass.

We found another table with goodies, but the will to buy anything had passed. I kept hold of my coin, and we stayed in silence until Ryn finally spoke.

"We could have taken them, injured arm or not; they didn't earn their levels," Ryn said. "I hate that they treat you like scum just because you happen to live in the Commons. They are just jealous because they know how great you and Tomas are."

"Yeah," I said, agreeing. "Jealously has an odd way of showing up on Craven's ugly mug. But once we leave this town, we won't have to deal with him, and I'll be all the happier for it."

"There will always be Cravens, no matter where we go, and since we've decided to play the long game and pick classes that take a while, all those classed idiots who took the easy road will be laughing at us up until we prove them wrong," Ryn said and I nodded, figuring it might be that way, but it would be worth it in the end.

"And when we stand at the top of the adventuring world with classes that no one can match, they'll know they should have waited as well," I said, speaking proudly as I imagined it being so.

"Hey, there is Analese," Ryn said, nudging me with her shoulder. "I bet she didn't allow her party to be boosted, we should go talk to her and see if she still wants to kiss your face."

"That was a one-night kind of deal, and it was a freaking year ago. When are you going to let me live it down?" I asked, then, smirking, I added. "Maybe you want a go at her, and you figure I can break the ice?"

"Hah!" Ryn said, elbowing me hard in the ribs before waving down

Analese, a party leader from the third group of Unlocked. Her group was the most humble of types, and I knew they'd be working hard to find ways to level.

"You guys make it to level 10, too?" she asked, giving us a side-eye look that explained to me perfectly that she hadn't, but she'd heard of the others who had.

"Nah, we ain't no boosters," Ryn said. "We did make it to level 8, though."

"Really?" Analese asked. "We got to level 7 by clearing out some skeletons that kept rising up in the graveyard last night. It was a job posted and picked up immediately by yours truly. Then we hunted a pack of weak kobolds who'd thrown their lot with a pair of cultists. Must have been level 10, but still, their magic was weak as they'd allowed themselves to be drained to try and summon up a greater demon. Luckily, it didn't work; instead, it summoned a random guy who spoke our language, but oddly. He kept claiming he was in the middle of reading about some guy named Carl and his cat, that he should be here, blah blah. We took him to the Adventurer's Guild and got a bonus for it."

"Oh, you found someone who's been Isekai'd from another world?" Ryn said. "I hear summonings and other methods bring them here, but he's likely going to have a rough go at it. From what I hear, they arrive already Unlocked, but they start at level 1. To make up for that, they also seem to gain essence faster than most and get extra attributes and abilities. It's a whole thing, but they are so rare, I can't believe you found one!"

"What are you saying? That people from other worlds are being brought here and have the potential of being way stronger than us?" I asked, truly dumbfounded. "That seems a bit unfair."

"Right?" Ryn agreed. "Anyway almost all of them die heroic stupid deaths early on, with only one in a thousand of these super rare beings making it anywhere."

We chatted for a bit longer on the subject before Analese put her hand on my arm and caught my eye. I gave her a look, and she backed off, but it was too late, Ryn caught the interaction and grinned.

"I've got to go check a thing, over someplace else," she said, then sauntered off by herself.

"Sorry," Analese said. "I thought she knew."

I took Analese by the hand, and we slipped into a darkened alley, where we shared a deep, long kiss. When we released we were both out of breath and giggling. I tried to keep it a secret, but Analese, or Ana as I called her most days, we'd been an item since that one night we'd spent together. We both knew our lives would change when we got Unlocked, so we always said it wasn't serious, but I cared for her and she for me.

She had long brown hair tied in a braid, with green eyes. She had a narrow face with a thin nose and sharp eyes, but in a beautiful way. Her body was firm from years of training, but her womanly curves weren't there without notice. I brushed my hand down her side and followed the curve of her hips as I took in a breath of her.

"I love it when you do that," she said, giggling at me.

"What?" I asked, finishing my deep breath and letting my eyes wash over every inch of her once more.

"The way you breathe me in and then just look at me as if I'm the most beautiful thing you've ever seen, it's intoxicating," she said.

"We shouldn't be doing this," I said, as my brain and mouth took action while my other parts refused.

"We have another week or two at least before we all go our separate ways. Besides, I'll be on the first caravan out of here, and I suspect you will be too, so really, why should we stop?" she asked, biting her lip and her green eyes melting away any resistance I had to her.

"Fine, but promise me you won't get jealous when I take other partners, years down the line," I said, adding the last part as a sort of soft-hitting barrier between my words.

"Years, eh? What if I take a new bed partner the first night away from you? Will you be mad?" she asked, teasingly.

"No," I said a bit too quickly. "I uhh, I understand that we aren't officially anything, so should you seek comfort somewhere else, then so be it."

"What about after we accomplish all we want from a life of adventuring? Will you return here and make me your bride?" Ana asked, catching me off guard. We'd never spoken of what we'd do if or when we hung up the adventuring hat.

"I don't think I will ever hang it up for good," I said. "I'm going to be a Dragon Knight, and I doubt there will ever be a time when I can slow things down."

"Then visit me at least. I won't be in this life forever, and I will return here. Fly to me on your mighty dragon and give me a night to remember every few years," Ana said, and she spoke without jest in her voice, which caught me even more off guard.

"I will," I found myself promising. Despite it all, I felt a hunger for her when she was away, and I knew that despite not ever saying it, I'd fallen hard for her. But I also knew that with time, that would fade, and as I grew more and more into the life of an adventurer, I'd likely find love in the arms of others. But I still promised her I would return from time to time.

We made out for the next several minutes before promising to meet at her place tonight. I watched her go from the shadows and back into the light, and I admired her all the way until I lost sight of her. From there, I met up with my friends, and we ate, hung out, and talked about all kinds of random things. It was a night to remember, a night to look back on when the darker nights of the future loomed over us.

Today I was all I wanted to be: an adventurer, a friend, a lover, and a future Dragon Knight. Only time would tell if my dreams would come true, but it would take my own death to stop me from reaching my goals. A promise I made to the world around me with my every waking breath.

CHAPTER 10
COMPETITION

Ana and I had a wonderful night, and I didn't make it back to my own place until early the next morning. My life was truly coming together, and I couldn't imagine what could go wrong.

To start things off, I got my extra silver moons to pay Ryn, then I changed my clothes, stored my armor, and went to the bathhouses with my bag of laundry. I splurged a little, going to one where my clothing wouldn't disappear a few articles at a time. With that taken care of while I washed myself, I headed back to my apartment to return my clothes.

"You haven't left for a better place yet?" Mr. Moroto asked, catching me with a handful of laundry as I headed for the stairs.

I walked up to my room, used my key, and slid my clothes inside, nice and folded. Before coming out to talk with him.

"Not yet," I said. "I'm fond of the time I've spent here."

"No reason to be fond, move on and live life," Mr. Moroto said through puffs of his pipe. It smelled of Granger Weed, a popular weed that helped relax the mind and muscles after a tense day at work. I never touched the stuff unless offered for free, as it was occasionally pricey depending on how much was collected outside the walls.

"I know," I said, and he passed the pipe to me, so I took a puff and passed it back. "I did pay for a few weeks, though. It's best to be frugal and not waste any coin."

"Might waste coin by keeping it here, security ain't great these days. Couldn't even stop the House Guards from tossing your place," he said, chuckling. "Not that I tried much after they showed their blades."

"Can I ask you a personal question?" I asked, taking a long look at Mr. Moroto and trying to guess what class he had picked before retiring.

"Can't see why not," Mr. Moroto said, his facial features scrunching up as he examined me.

"What class did you pick when you were an adventurer?" I asked, and he chuckled.

"You would not believe me if I told you the truth of the matter. I am from another land, it is a bit different where I am from," Mr. Moroto said, shrugging. Perhaps it was the Granger Weed, or just him being more friendly to me, but he was opening up about something I'd never heard of.

"Can you tell me more? What continent are you from?" I asked.

I knew, as most did, that there were three continents on the world of Avaris, but the coming and going between them is so few and far between that reliable trade routes have never been set up. Instead, we get random ships that'll make it through and they'll sell their goods then go off, never to be seen again. I only knew this because of Ryn and her fascination with other continents, but ships and sailing the open waters were one of the most dangerous things a person could do.

"I'm from the continent of Sunreach, as we call it, I forget if you call it different here, so little talk of my homeland that it's easy to forget. I came here as a young man, seeking glory and new techniques in a foreign land. Instead, all I learned was that your magic is very different than the magic of my lands. And with time, my techniques and abilities began to fade, leaving me with only a fraction of the power I once held. Maybe I'd sneak into your tower and unlock myself. I had thought about it for many years, but I have a family now. I've settled into the life of an apartment owner. It pays enough to keep my family fed and clothed."

"What of your son, Ashiro? He will reach 25 years old next year, will he not? I know he's been training in the tower for the last five years under Aelric of House Deymorin, right?" I asked, curious if he tried to teach his son his old magics from Sunreach or just accepted that he would be Unlocked as all others I'd ever heard of.

This news was a little more than startling for me, but I took it in stride, mostly with the help of the Granger flora easing my mind. Its dried leaves were nothing if not mind-opening and allowing you to accept even the impossible.

"He will walk the path of a Vareth adventurer. Maybe someday when he is powerful enough, we will attempt the crossing back to my lands, where I can teach him what true power looks like, unbridled and drawn from the very land around him. We called ourselves Cultivators in my land. Here, we are nothing but weak citizens compared to the power each person is able to wield. But that doesn't mean I am without a trick or two myself," Mr. Moroto said, his eyes went hard, and he unfurled his hand, a flash of smoke and a little fire appeared.

Where had that come from, I wondered as I watched the ash fall slowly to the ground. Was that just some trick of powders, or had he actually done some of his cultivation magic?

"Can you teach it to me?" I asked, wondering if I could learn of this foreign magic to give me an edge.

"What you saw was the extent of my powers here, minus several body modifications I underwent as a young master that leave me stronger and faster than you, at least, but not by much. Your attribute system, as much as I've been able to learn about it, seems superior in the getting of the power, if not the extent of power it grants. But I tire of conversation. Keep my secret, and I will do my best to guard your sanctum and that which you keep within it with my life. I feel shamed at letting those guards take your beloved book, but they threatened to drop my son from training and sponsorship, and I couldn't have that," he said, rubbing at the balding spot atop his head.

"Thank you for sharing," I said, unsure what else to say. "And tell Ashiro I wish him the best. If he were just a little older he'd might have been on my team or at least in my same group. It's a shame, he seems like an honorable man, I'd have liked to work with him."

"You honor me by saying as much," Mr. Moroto said, bowing his head.

I took it as what it was, an invitation to leave, so I returned a bow and went on my way. This cultivation magic he spoke of sounded interesting, but I had a mission in life already, a grand quest that I needed to follow; there was no point in getting distracted along the way with the next new shiny thing to appear.

I roamed the Commons a little, something I rarely did, as the mud-filled streets were just as likely to welcome me in as they were to try to rob me for whatever coin I had in my purse. But most thugs were not Unlocked yet, so I'd have an advantage if anyone tried anything. On that note, I did as most adventurers did, I had my sword at my waist. Despite not having my shield and armor, it would do plenty to signal to those around I wasn't an easy target.

My hunch was right, and when I saw a group of younger thugs, they left me alone as I walked confidently from shop to shop. Most were closed for the festival, going off to sell their wares at the place everyone would be. Common or not, if their food was good enough, they could make a killing.

However, my favorite bread shop remained open and hardworking. Mrs. Elise toiled away making low-cost rolls and sweet rolls that I enjoyed. She also had more expensive donuts, specialty types of sweet rolls that really packed in the sugars, but I hadn't really been able to buy one up until now. I decided to get a half dozen for my friends, as well as a sweet roll, the cheap kind, for a snack, as it was somewhat of a comfort food for me.

"Welcome in, young Grimholt, a sweet roll for you this morning?" she asked, then launched right into another string of words before I could answer. "Here you are. I haven't seen you here in a few days, that is odd for sure. I was about to call on the guards to check on you, lucky you came when you did."

"I'll take six of your donuts," I said, gesturing to the variety of colors and sweet circular rolls she had on display.

"Oh, those are ten scales a piece, let me just get you another sweet roll, eh?" she asked, but I shook my head.

"I'll have the donuts," I said, pulling out a single silver moon and handing it over. She'd give me change, but I wanted to show her I wasn't as poor as I'd once been.

"Oh dear, you must have been Unlocked. Time just flies, I remember when your pa would bring you by for sweet rolls every other day. Now look atcha, all grown up. I'll fulfil your order right away me-lord. Just enjoy that sweet roll and don't forget where you've come from, now won'tcha?" she asked in the odd way of speaking she had. I wasn't sure what part of Vareth she was from, but wherever it was, it gave her an odd accent that I couldn't really pin down.

I watched her work; she moved with the speed of someone with an attribute spread akin to the scarf that I wore, her rotund form weaving here and there with grace and agility. While she worked, I decided to have her add another dozen sweet rolls, just in case I needed something to eat later.

Before long, she'd gathered the donuts and sweet rolls, given me my change, and sent me on my way as a small line formed behind me for her sweet rolls. It didn't surprise me. At only a scale, they were the best food you could hope to find in the morning. And since she didn't attend the festival, she got all the common folk coming in to fill their bellies before heading to the more expensive festival locations.

Today was the day of competitions, from food to arms to footraces; it was all open to the Non-Unlocked, with only a few games open to newly Unlocked who wished to participate. I was going to do the foot race and the sword competition, but those at level 10 would have an advantage over me, since abilities would be allowed if you'd Unlocked them.

I made it out of the Commons and into the Forge Quarter, heading for the area around the tower and the surrounding square where all the activities would be held. Thousands gathered here and there, collecting wares and foodstuffs for close to double the price you'd find them elsewhere, in most cases.

Magical items seemed to be the exception, as I found more I might want to buy before I found Ryn and the group. I examined a compass that didn't point north, but rather to the largest settlement. Which sounded intriguing; however, I was warned that it could sometimes mean monster settlements, like goblins and the like.

There was also a pocketwatch, a rare item without being magical, that told you the time and a smaller timing device that could tell you approximately how long until you leveled, if it were going to be within the next twenty-four hours at least. A handy little device, I guessed, but for fifteen silver moons, I couldn't talk myself into buying it. First, I needed to pay Ryn, then find a reasonably priced item to spend my silver on.

Brackenford was out in force today. Tomorrow was the parade, when people would line the streets, and we'd march all through town, but today was the most exciting day with all the competitions and events.

I found my group at the registration tables, already in line, and snuck in with them without anyone noticing or saying anything harsh to us. It helped that it was so busy and already five waited in line, so what was one more?

"Always late," Ryn said, shaking her head.

"Here," I said, passing her the coin, then showing the donuts. "I brought breakfast!"

"Oh, lovely!" Ryn said, pulling out a donut as the others turned and did the same, with muttered thank yous and such.

I took the final one and enjoyed every bite. They were light and airy, with a balanced sweetness that left me salivating for more. Now we needed to find some hot coffee to fully awaken my soul before the competitions began.

"So, anyone else doing the foot race or the sword tourney?" I asked, and Jareth raised his hand but said nothing, so whether he was doing one or the other, or perhaps both, I didn't know.

Sel sort of huffed after finishing her donut. "I wish they'd allow maces in the tourney, I don't get the obsession with swords."

"I think they are doing an open format this year. You should be able to use whatever weapon you want," Ryn said, always on the up and up on information about the town and its happenings.

"I heard that too," Ashric said. "I think I'm going to stick to watching this year. My full dive into my Arcana attribute has yielded me two cool abilities, but neither can help me in a foot race or combat with a weapon."

"You went full Arcana already?" I asked, surprised. "What class are you going for?"

"I'm a simple man," Ashric said, shrugging. "So I'm going for a relatively simple but powerful class, Archmage. If my studies are correct, it'll raise my spell damage by a massive amount and give me a pretty unique and powerful spell. Not many walk the one-attribute paths, but they have merit. I'll be able to choose my class at level 15 if I stay the course."

"Yeah, but you'll be weaker physically than all other classes. I hope you trust your tanks to keep you safe," I said, nudging Sel and getting a glare for my trouble.

"I'll be doing the eating competition. This will be the first year I'll be participating as an Unlocked, but of course you all know I'm a five year in a row champion of the food competition, so this won't be any different," Tomas said, snacking on some salty fried potato skins as he boasted how he'd be eating even more this same day. He'd already eaten his donut and two of my sweet rolls, but I didn't doubt he could eat even more.

"You have a bottomless pit for a stomach. I swear it has to be some kind of magic. Did you swallow a bag of holding?" Ashric teased him, and I perked up at the mention of a dimensional item.

They were so rare as to be considered myths. They came in all forms, from bags to rings to cubes, and spheres. They popped up in stories with high-level adventurers, when the bards sang of their exploits, there was almost always at least a mention of the item.

But to get one would cost hundreds of platinum crowns, and no one had that kind of money to spend on an item such as that, not even the two great Houses of Brackenford could pull off that kind of purchase without breaking the bank. Or at least I assumed as much; I didn't know their finances.

"And you?" I asked Ryn. "Are you competing?"

"I am, in both the foot race and the weapons tourney," she said, smirking at me when I mocked surprise. She always competed with me, and she almost always won, but this time it would be different. I had the speed of my scarf, the guard reinforcing my body, and a few points in Arcana to strengthen my mind, maybe?

We finally reached the front after another half hour of chatting and waiting, and we started our registrations. Jareth did both the foot race and the weapons tourney, along with Ryn, Sel, and me. Tomas, of course, did the foot competition and nothing else, but there were four going on today, and he tried to register for each of them, even the Non-Unlocked one. They told him max he could do was two, so he did a fruit pie eating contest and a meat pie eating contest. They were roughly four hours apart as well, so he'd have time to recover.

"Foot race starts soon, should we head over?" I asked, and everyone nodded, as we left as one group toward the footrace area.

Once we arrived, we gave our tickets to an event coordinator who set us up with an overhead apron of sorts with numbers on it. I was number 31, Ryn, 65, and lastly, Jareth got number 2. Seemed a bit random, but I didn't worry about that. Instead I focused on my competition as the race line was set and the course explained. It was more than just a test of speed; it was also a test of endurance.

The first leg was just a two-hundred-pace section, where the winner would be selected from the fastest, but they were also expected to continue the race around town, following yellow markers and cleared streets. We'd weave through the River Quarter, into the Guildrow and then back to the center of town where we started. They said it would take about half an hour to complete the longer race, so we were told to pace ourselves.

I'd done this before, but never this long, and never with a sprint at the start. If nothing else, I told myself I'd win the first leg of the race, and if I failed at that, then I'd have to take the longer race as my own.

We lined up and waited for the clank of the mallet on the metal disc, as was normal to start the race or any event, really. With a sudden, clank, we were off. I ran with all my power and speed, instantly moving ahead of all the other competitors but one, a dark-haired man who I didn't recognize. He had to be level ten or below, so he must have gone all into Speed to match the ten I had personally.

Even so, I barely managed to stay ahead of him, and Ryn was hot on our heels, moving with speed beyond what her five in that attribute ought to give her. Though, I knew she was naturally really fast, so that helped a fair bit as well, since the attributes increased what you already had, improving on the baseline that you personally could achieve.

Then, just as we reached the line for the end of the sprint, Ryn zipped ahead, using her ability, just as the other man did. But Ryn somehow got further and made it past the line first, winning the first leg of the race. However, she ran with such speed that she instantly slowed after going through the line.

I slowed as well, but not nearly as much as she did. Despite how out of breath I was, I needed to catch the dark-haired man who was now some ten paces ahead of me and running strong still. The Speed attribute was meant to give you speed in all things, but it didn't provide endurance. It was commonly accepted that Guard did that, so I had an advantage as I had five in my Guard and ten in my Speed thanks to the scarf.

Sure enough, I began to pull closer to him and after only two minutes I was ahead, following the markings on the road and keeping a powerfully fast pace. I'd be able to maintain it for another minute, maybe more, before I'd need to slow, but already I noticed with a quick check that the dark-haired guy and all the others had slowed to a more reasonable pace.

I slowed as well, but kept my distance from the pack, so I could increase my speed if needed. I had to win this long-form race now, since Ryn had stolen the sprint from me. My breathing flagged, and I slowed more, the distance between me and the others closing. I'd pushed too hard too fast, and now I was paying for it.

Then, as I turned the bend, to the final leg of the race, right along with the others at my heels. I heard someone cry out in the crowd.

"Run, Kael, run!" I turned my head to see who it could be, but in doing so I saw the dark-haired man sprinting at a full run to catch me and overtake me. Something inside of me jolted me back to full consciousness, and I sprinted out of there like the wind itself.

I could feel him at my heels as he ran to overtake me, but all worry and exhaustion had fled me as I ran, my heart booming in my chest. My steps became erratic and misplaced as I neared the finish line, but with one final push of exertion, I made it over the line before the dark-haired man.

Then the stars came as I dropped to a knee and struggled to pull in enough breath. I'd trained hard my entire life, especially for the last five years, but I was so spent that I couldn't imagine being more tired now than I'd ever been. For five minutes, I struggled to breathe until I finally got a sense of my surroundings and realized people were cheering for me.

Ryn and I were both awarded a prize bounty of ten silver moons each and a brass amulet that marked our victory in the race. This was much more than the single silver moon you got as a Non-Unlocked, so I gratefully took it and held the medal high to the praise of all the crowd.

The dark-haired man came up to me. He was older than me, but not by much, so why had he remained level 10? I wondered quietly as he approached.

"Good race," he said, holding out a hand. "I didn't think you'd be able to beat me, but you have some pretty intense attributes for someone under level ten."

"Aren't we all level ten or under?" I joked, thinking myself clever.

"Oh, no," he said in return. "They opened it up to level 15 and lower this year. I'm level 15, and how you beat me at level 10, I won't ever know."

"I'm level 8, actually," I said, and the man face-palmed.

"I'm going to go drown myself in some ale now, thanks for the good race," he said, turning and leaving without ever even giving his name. His number was zero, oddly enough, so I just called him Zero in my head.

Hopefully, Zero wouldn't drink too much after so much exercise. That might be bad for the muscles' recovery. Speaking of recovery, I thought to myself, I saw Ryn sneak a potion when I wasn't looking right at her, so I pulled out one as well and drank it. The weapons tourney was only an hour away, so it would help me recover in time.

Jareth found us and cursed at us, saying, "Damn, you guys are fast." Then he went back into his quiet reflection, which he always seemed to be in the middle of.

CHAPTER 11
SWORDS AND PIES

"If we hurry, we can catch the first pie eating contest before the first weapons tourney matches begin," Ryn said, grabbing my hand and pulling me along. Jareth followed after us without needing handholding.

We twisted and turned through the crowd, slowly making our way to the area designated for the pie eating contest. Several hundred chairs had been set up in front of a stage, and we found seats in front next to Sel and Ashric, who were kind enough to save us three seats.

"Ready to see Tomas eat more than any human ought to be able to eat?" Ashric said, chuckling as we sat down.

"He's got this," I said, then they started announcing the names of the competitors. When they got to Tomas, we all stood and cheered as loud as the rest of the crowd combined, supporting our friend in his friendly competition.

"They've got Gruk participating this year," Ashric said. "That might be a problem."

I looked at who he meant and saw immediately who this Gruk person was. A Beastborn of a hog variety, with tusks and a snout, looking almost like a monster, but he had the signs that marked him as beastborn and not some goblin variant. He had coarse red hair, green eyes, and a massive, bulky build. But worst of all, he had a massive mouth and a gut to match; this man was made to eat.

Suddenly, I felt like Tomas had himself a challenge. This competition was the one with the sweet pies made with some kind of white, fleshy fruit, maybe moonapple or the more common sunpear around here. Either way, it would be sweet and tasty, enough so that I wanted to sneak a pie myself.

Each pie was about the size of my open palm, and each competitor had roughly twenty-five on a plate in front of them, with two more plates waiting in the wings should the time not run out fast enough. They also had large cups filled with water and pitchers nearby.

The announcer readied the gong and yelled that the match was about to begin. Tomas looked hungrily down at the pies, licking his lips as he readied himself. Meanwhile, Gruk was dripping saliva from his massive mouth and tusks.

The gong sounded, and the competitors began eating. Tomas took a quick lead, grabbing two pies and stuffing them in, then grabbing two more to stuff in seconds later. However, Gruk took his time, lifted four in a single massive hand, and stuffed them into his mouth. He munched down and ate just as fast as Tomas.

None of the others were going as fast, but Tomas and Gruk were hammering them down faster than seemed possible. They were neck and neck, with only Gruk seemingly behind because for every three pies he got into his mouth, a pie's worth of extra fell down all around him and made a mess of the table.

Tomas did not miss a single bite as the timer counted down.

With only half the time gone, neither side seemed to be slowing down, and Gruk took a late lead, moving to his next plate while Tomas still had two remaining on his first. Back and forth they fought, eating up pies at an alarming rate. Finally, the gong was rung again, and the competition was over.

It was clear that Gruk had the least on his second plate, but the judges were speaking to each other, walking to each competitor, and pointing at the leftovers that Gruk had amassed all around himself.

They started picking up the remaining pieces and adding them to his plate, adding at least six pies' worth of material. Then they counted, and finally the announcement came.

"Gruk has eaten the most pies; however, he also left the most waste. We've determined that based on the weight of the waste, the true winner of this competition is Tomas Reed!"

Gruk roared, a mighty roar, and nearly flipped the table as he stood, but Tomas just sat there for a second, slowly finishing another pie in front of himself before burping loudly and raising his hands in the air. The crowd ate it up, cheering his victory and watching him as he took four pies to go before leaving the table.

We found Tomas, and I clasped a hand around him.

"You beat that hog at his own game," I said. "That stomach of yours is truly remarkable."

"I know," Tomas said, biting slowly into another pie and handing one over to me. "Want to try one? They're great!"

I ate one, and sure enough, they were amazing. It almost seemed like a waste to have so many made and left there. So I snuck, with Tomas at my side, back to the table and we snuck an entire plate, passing them out liberally to anyone who looked our way.

"We've got to hurry," I said, reaching our team. "We don't want to be late for the weapons tourney, who knows who is set to go first?"

"My coin is on Ryn and Kaelric going at it in round one," Sel said, chuckling and being a little more light-hearted than I'd seen her before. She must really be excited for the upcoming fights.

The rules of the tourney were simple: you wore the armor provided by the tourney so everyone was on equal footing. I hoped I'd still be able to use my scarf, but I knew all other armor would be stripped from me. The rules also stipulated that you provide your own weapon and are given a shield if you wish to use one. Then you fight for five minutes or until someone yields or is too injured to continue fighting.

If the fights are opened up to level 15's, which a quick check with Ryn told me was the case, then we'd have our work cut out for us in the upcoming battles. I didn't have any ambitions of coming in first once I found that out, but I sure as hells would try my best. If I could at least beat Ryn, I'd consider it a victory.

The morning dew was still in full effect, making the air feel wet and the day's adventure feel fresh. We moved as one to the area and found the listings of the first matchups. I was going up against someone I didn't know, simply put down as 'Dawnson'. Likely a level 15 person who was getting ready for a quick victory over a level 8 like me. But I had an edge, a ten-levels-worth edge with my Speed attribute scarf.

Although he could have an edge, too. At level 15, he'll have gone into dungeons and gotten dungeon loot by now. If that didn't include an accessory that he could wear, then we might be on even footing if the odds were on my side. If it were not in my favor, then I'd be looking at a crushing defeat. I'd hate to be out in the first round, since it was double elimination. Even if I lost one, I could still have a chance of fighting my way back to the top.

My match was one of the first, so I hurried over to the staging area and got ready. The armor they provided was light but sturdy, with special enchantments that could resize up to a certain extent. So when I slipped on the armor, it tightened around me, and soon I was wearing a full suit of hardened leather. I went over to the shields and began inspecting the different kinds.

They had the smaller buckler I was used to using from years of training on the only shield I could really afford. But they also had the round, bigger shield I'd gotten from House Ravenlock, which I'd had a fair bit of practice using recently. Then they had larger shields that protected your entire body, but they looked cumbersome and unlike what I was used to.

I picked the kind Ravenlock had gifted me, a circular shield with enough space to guard my upper torso and light enough not to inhibit me too much. As I finished getting ready, I felt someone behind me and turned to see a man standing by the armor racks, examining the armor. He turned to regard me, hard dark eyes boring into me.

"You must be Kaelric," he said in a knowing tone.

"That's me, are you Dawnson?" I asked, curious if this was my opponent.

"I am," he said, his light hair the color of the newly risen sun and his skin pale, as if he hadn't seen much sun. But his eyes were what I fixated on, brown yet so dark they could be black, and the whites of his eyes looked a tad yellow, with red veins visible.

"Good luck on the upcoming match," I said, holding out a hand. He took it, and I immediately knew he'd put many points into his Power Attribute, because he nearly squeezed the life out of my hand without so much as a grimace on his face from the effort.

"Same to you. Have you ever fought a classed person before?" he asked, smirking at me now that he'd released my hand.

Classed? I thought. Did that mean he'd taken one of the first four options? They could be popular, but they required total focus on a single attribute, leaving you weak in others until after you'd claimed your class. If he'd gone the Power route, he'd be a Titan, someone able to deal massive amounts of damage and have the class skill Colossus Strike along with three others from the Power tree of attributes.

"You are a Titan, then?" I asked, and he nodded. "Well, I'll do my best. Don't think I'll be an easy target."

"I'll crush you, the same as I will anyone in this tourney. I just wish I had someone stronger as my first opponent. I hear you aren't even level 15 yet. A shame, really, but I'll make the victory quick and painful," he said, a hint of a sneer in his voice as he finished.

But I caught myself smiling as well as I thought about my own attribute layout. With five in Guard and Iron Skin in full effect, I'd be able to take more punishment than others he might face; besides that, I had a ten in Speed because of my scarf, which meant I'd be hard to hit for him with no increase to his speed at all. Power, of course, made you stronger, which could lend some speed, but the Speed Attribute was by far the best way to increase your snap, quick movements, and overall speed.

"We'll see," I finally said, clearing my thoughts and readying myself by cracking my neck to each side.

"Don't think I don't know which attributes you spent points into," he said, apparently not yet done with the conversation. "I saw how fast you were. You are an all out Speed attribute spread, or I'd eat my own boot. Don't think you'll be able to dance around me the entire time. You'll run out of endurance before I will. Power gives me incredible endurance when it comes to my muscles. So watch yourself."

"I will endeavor to give you a proper match," I said, unable to keep myself from smiling.

"It's about time, move aside so I can get ready," he said. Stepping forward, he pulled on his armor, a larger suit than my own, with nearly twice my girth around the shoulders and bulging muscles.

At first glance, between the two of us, it seemed an easy guess who might win, but I wasn't such a pushover, and I'd give him the fight of his life before I gave up. I would keep it going for five minutes, get all the strikes I could, and hope to win by points rather than knockout. My speed would allow me to do that, and my Iron Skin would help me weather his impressive blows.

With my confidence building, I made my way to the opening on my side of the arena. The fighting area was a pit with soft layers of dirt on the ground, but no mud. There was a wooden fence, three planks rising to waist height, meant to mark the area more than anything else and low enough to allow everyone to see.

It was an area roughly thirty paces from one side to the other, square in shape. An announcer spoke my name as I took my position and then Dawnson's name as he came into his area. He had no shield, so that was good, but he was using a massive hammer that stood as tall as he did. A weapon like that would give him reach and keep me at bay more than I'd like to admit. I would have to be careful to attack only after he did, in the few seconds it would take him to reset himself from smashing down with such a large weapon.

However, he held it on his shoulder with a single hand, and suddenly I wondered, with an attribute of 15 in Power, whether it would be hard for him to reset after all. But now wasn't the time to work out that bit of information. I'd learn soon enough as it was, so I stepped into the ring, drew my sword, and put my shield into position. My plan was to keep moving and not allow him to get any direct hits.

"The fight between Kaelric and Dawnson has begun!" yelled the announcer, and I heard the gong sound, signaling that the timer had started.

Dawnson moved with incredible speed, given his attributes in Power. But I was at least half as quick, and I moved out of the way as his hammer glowed red and came slamming down. Just as I moved out of the way enough, a force pushed me back into place, and I raised my shield, catching the glancing blow. My body was rocked by the blow, but I held on well enough to twirl out of the way of his upswing, which came just as fast as the downswing.

He had Shove, the super useful five attribute ability, so he had some tactics after all, not just brute strength. This would be difficult if he could adjust me right before his strike, so I had to make sure I dodged even wider than I expected.

I swung in as I dodged a normal strike by him, scoring two quick strikes to his arm and side, the armor absorbing the blows easily. Then he came back with his hammer glowing red and sparking as he activated a Power skill. I dodged backward, but again the force pushed me back, but I planned on this and rolled forward into his blow.

I managed to get under the blow, and I struck hard at his shin with my shield before getting all the way back to my feet behind him. Turning quick I struck out once, twice, and a third time in quick succession. That was the moment that I caught the end of his hammer in my gut. I should have gone for that last strike; it left me too close and open to an attack.

I caught my breath just in time to get my shield above me as he struck down at me. It wasn't going to be a glancing blow, and I grit my teeth to brace against the powerful strike. The blow cracked the shield, I felt it begin to give, and my bones rattled from the force of the attack. But I was still alive and hadn't broken any bones, so I was still in this!

I backstepped and shook myself out, much to Dawnson's surprise.

"You should be knocked out cold, shield or no," Dawnson said, shouting across the field.

"I'm a bit sturdier than you give me credit," I said, willing to trade words over blows if he wanted to waste time.

"You're forcing me to use my ultimate ability, I didn't want to, but brace yourself, you'll probably survive," he shouted as a new color appeared around his weapon. A golden aura with matching crackling energy as he rushed forward with impossible speed, hammer raised above his head.

The massive head would collide right with me, so I raised my shield and pretended like I'd take the blow head-on. I heard cries of surprise from the crowd, and I waited until I felt the wind of the attack on my shield before pivoting to the side, only allowing a glancing blow to hit the shield as my body moved all the way out of the way.

Regardless of what I'd planned, the force of the attack threw me backward and off my feet. My back hit the fence hard, but I scrambled to my feet as I saw Dawnson moving again, having left a crater in the dirt arena floor. But his hammer wasn't glowing anymore, and he was so slow as to be laughable now.

I got into position, realized my shield was split entirely in two, so I threw it aside and focused on attack and dodging. That meant, of course, that I shouldn't let even a single blow through because it would break my bones instead of my shield.

He came in slowly but powerfully, and I dodged to the left. Slashing at his chest as I passed him by, then as he attempted to catch me with his backswing, I cut under him and got an attack on his legs. A few more hits to his legs, and maybe I'd manage to slow him down.

He was slowing, and I wasn't, so I felt like I had this fight well in hand, having survived the worst of it. Then he shoved me with his Power ability as

I danced around him. His hammer ignited in a red color haze of crackling lightning and hit me square in the chest. Blood spewed forth from my mouth, and my vision danced from complete darkness to blurry realization that I'd gotten a bit too cocky and taken a bad hit.

But like a lever being pulled, my mind snapped back together, and I rolled, painful as it was, out of the way of a follow-up blow. This allowed me to assess the damage: a broken rib or two, and a really hard time breathing. So much so, in fac,t that I wasn't sure how much I had in me. Luckily for me, the gong went off, signifying that the match was over.

I stood as tall as I could, trying not to show how much it hurt, but it was difficult.

"How are you still alive?" Dawnson asked. "A direct hit like that, and you should be bleeding out from internal injuries. Unless you have Iron Skin ,don't you, that would explain a lot. But how are you so fast?"

Dawnson had come over with his questions, but I was doing all I could to stay standing, so I limped over to the edge of the fence and followed it to my exit without answering him. Ryn met me at the opening, her face furious in rage, but immediately before even speaking, she shoved a potion down my throat.

"I can't believe they raised it to level 15 and now we have classed people fighting in the beginner brackets. This is beyond ridiculous," she said, each word spoken with slightly less rage as she vented her frustrations.

The potion worked like magic, healing my ability to breathe first, probably a collapsed lung, and then knitting together the fractured ribs. Whatever potion she'd given me, it was better quality than the ones I'd used before, and I was grateful to her for helping me.

"Thank you," I said when I could finally speak, spitting blood from my mouth and realizing I had bitten my tongue badly as well, but the potion was hard at work healing that wound, too.

"Let's get you out of that armor and me into a suit. I'm up after this next fight. Oh, and try to watch the fight as well, Sel is fighting now," Ryn said, and I turned my head to see her facing off against an Aether-Touched of all people.

Aether-Touched were easy to identify, and we had only a couple in town, working mainly as enchanters because they were prized for their ability to see magic in a way others couldn't, which meant they made far fewer mistakes than we normal people. The Aether-Touched she fought against had long silver hair that shimmered, as with all Aether-Touched.

Otherwise, they looked rather normal, except that instead of the blue veins most people had, they had crystal-white veins beneath thin, pale skin. Their eyes always seemed to glow, no matter what color. For instance, this particular Aethor-Touched had blue eyes, but they glowed enough to cast a blue hue around her pale, semi-sunken eyes.

I'd never heard of one being a fighter, but here she was, wielding a long sword, spear-like weapon, twirling it around and striking out against Sel before she could close the gap to get any attacks herself. It was fascinating to watch, and a bit mesmerizing as the spear left an afterglow as she twirled it, obviously enchanted with speed or something similar.

I wished Sel luck under my breath as I turned and stripped out of my armor. Dawnson was there, and it looked like he wanted to say something again, but he fell short when Ryn sent a glare in his direction. The fights would be announced, with winners and losers, after the first round finished, which meant at least five more fights.

Once I'd gotten out of my armor, the fight between Sel and the Aether-Touched was already over, with Sel yielding for some reason. I jogged with Ryn over to meet Sel and see what had happened.

"Why the yield?" I asked. The fight was only about three minutes in so far.

"Because the spear-wielding bitch started cutting through my armor, any deeper and I'd be bleeding to death. And by the look on her face, she was ready to start cutting deeper. It's fine, I'm not out yet, I just hope someone else gets her and knocks her out during the single elimination rounds," Sel said, obviously heated by the fight and wanting nothing more than to smash her mace into someone's face.

"I'm up then," Ryn said. She'd put on the armor, drawn her sword, and grabbed a shield, something I rarely saw her use. Her opponent was none other than Craven Deymorin, I realized as the announcer gave the call.

Craven wielded a massive two-handed sword, no shield, and his armor was the same we were all forced to wear, but he had a cloak and a shimmering necklace that would be enchanted, I was sure. House Deymorin would parade alongside House Ravenlock and the newly Unlocked in the Parade tomorrow, where they'd display their most powerful relics for us peasants to see.

But it appeared we were getting an early show, since I recognized the cloak and necklace from last year, though I couldn't say what they did, as it wasn't common knowledge. Instead, I just turned to Ryn and smiled at her.

"Kick his ass, relics and all," I said, and she nodded.

"You bet your ass I will," she said, and she entered the ring as her name was called, ready to do her best to cave in Craven's face.

CHAPTER 12
TOURNEY CONTINUES

Ryn went in swinging, her sword scoring several hits on Craven before he could even think to respond with his massive sword. When he did, activating an attack of some kind, she used Quickstep and shot off to the side. It was with such speed and precision that she delivered two more blows before he could react.

The fight went on for the full five minutes, but anyone watching would agree that Ryn won, with her quick and many strikes. Craven got a few hits here and there, but almost all were glancing blows, and only one hit home without resistance, smashing into her shoulder and throwing her back. But she recovered quickly, changing from sword and shield to sword and dagger. She caught his neck blow and stabbed him multiple times in the gut before breaking away.

"You did it!" I called out to her as she neared the exit. Then I saw Craven coming up behind her, blade raised to strike. "Watch out!" I yelled, but it was too late. The sword strike hit her in the spine, and she crumpled to the ground as guards rushed forward to defend her, but I was over the gate and sword out before anyone else could respond.

I hit him three times with all the force I could muster, then kicked his feet out from under him, and reared the blade back, ready to stab him in the neck. That was when the guards got there, pulling me off and forcing me back.

Ryn was all right; she took a potion, but the underhanded strike had rattled her that much was clear to see. She was red-faced and wouldn't look anyone in the eye.

"It's alright, he's disqualified, you won for sure now," I said, patting her lightly on the back. "Besides, we all knew he was a piece of shit; now everyone can see what we already knew."

"I should have seen it coming," Ryn said, shaking her head and finally meeting my eyes. She was angry, very angry, and I would have to watch her to make sure she didn't do anything stupid.

"Let the judges handle it, Ryn. We don't need more trouble, and his embarrassment will have to be enough," I said, and Ryn just smiled and looked over to where he stood, his House men already dismissed the guards and paid any fine that would be incurred from the unsportsmanlike conduct.

"We'll see," she said, never moving her eyes off him as she began to pull off the armor.

"You all right?" Tomas asked, finally making it back from wherever he had been. "I heard what happened, Kaelric got messed up by a classed guy, and then that blockhead Craven sucker punched you. I can't leave you guys alone for a second without you getting in trouble."

"I guess not," I said, my hand going to my ribs, which were sore but definitely not broken any longer. "Two more fights, then the results will come out. Let's go grab some food and circle back."

So we did just that, moving through the crowd to the nearby food vendors, finding one that sold ham on the bone, and digging into it with a hunger that only those who worked themselves to the edge could feel. Even Tomas got something to eat, a snack food of dried fruits in a bag, before we made it back in time for the scores to be announced.

Mine came first, and my heart sank as I heard the announcement. I'd lost 59 to 61 points-wise, Ryn won her match-up by points and forfeit, and Sel lost hers by forfeit. I had a single elimination round coming up next against a man I didn't know who had also lost. Only one of us could move forward and have a chance to win.

I was a bit sour to hear I'd lost by so few points; if I hadn't taken that hit at the end, it would have meant I'd won, I was sure of it. But if I wanted a chance to fight Ryn, I had to survive this next fight and win outright. I hadn't watched my opponent fight; he was one of the last ones to do so, but I had a feeling I could take him.

Time passed, and I got ready as our ticket was called, with Ryn and Tomas by my side, cheering me on. I entered the field of battle and brandished my sword and new shield. I'd make quick work of this fight and be ready for the next. My opponent's name was Hinkle, and I swear I'd seen him around town before, but I didn't know him well enough to know what to expect. I was sure I'd seen him the year before, when he was Unlocked.

So if he wasn't level 15 already, then what was he doing with his life moving so slowly up the levels? In a year's time, I had ambitions to be twice that level. But who could say where time would take us or how fast progress would come after we got into dungeons?

He had short hair, brown like what was common around here, dull yellow eyes that were almost golden, and a stocky build. Likely another

Power attribute person looking to get a quick victory by using sheer force. But with how he moved, I would guess he had points in Guard and perhaps even Speed.

Sure enough, as he came closer, he zipped past my guard using Quick-step and struck at my back. I turned and caught his blade just in time on my shield and stabbed him on the side. Then I kicked hard at his knee, staggering him back. Before the fight could even really get going, I saw an opening as he struck forward.

I took the hit to the shoulder and slammed my shield edge-first into his nose, spraying blood and crunching hard against the cartilage. He fell backward in pain, but I wasn't ready to relent. I fell atop him, shield first, and pummeled his face with the pommel of my blade until he called for the fight to stop.

Face a bloody mess and looking more than a little pissed off, Hinkle spit blood and spoke as I helped him up. "Damn man, you are vicious, you barely let me get started."

"I had to win, and I saw an opening," I said in response. Not one to say sorry for no reason, I patted him on the back as he walked past, his sword and shield hanging limp in his arms.

"Great job!" Tomas said. "That is more what I expected from you, not hearing you get your ass kicked."

"I didn't lose that badly last time; it was a close fight, and he had like seven levels and a class on me," I said, shaking my head.

"Don't listen to him," Ryn said. "Tomas was too busy stuffing his face to even watch us."

"I wasn't! Well, in a way I guess I was, but that's neither here nor there," Tomas said, chuckling as he threw some more food into his mouth.

"When is your next food competition?" I asked, remembering that he had one more this evening, but I was clearly losing track of time.

"It doesn't start until the tourney ends; something about wanting to have enough people in the crowd, so later this evening," Tomas said, elbowing me and adding, "I bet I win. Too bad you can't win something, too."

"Watch me," I said, more determined than ever to win the entire weapons tourney.

It wouldn't be enough to just beat Ryn now. I wanted to take the top spot, and if I got another chance against the classed guy, I knew I could beat him now. Level 15 or not, class or not, I'd be victorious.

With my first single elimination fight taken care of, I had one more to beat before I'd be back in the running to actually win this thing. I had to wait for the next two fights, though, as the other losers would fight for a chance to win as well. Sel would have a fight on her hands next, then two others I hadn't paid much attention to.

Despite having lost by forfeit, she was still given a chance to move forward if she wanted, but I could tell her heart wasn't in it as soon as her fight started. The fire that burned in her seemed to be only going at half power, but despite this, her opponent was weak enough that it was also clear that she was probably still going to win.

Sure enough, about four minutes into the five-minute fight, she scored a blow against the side of the guy's head with her mace and laid him out flat, knocking him out cold. That meant she'd be going on, along with two others, to the next round of single elimination.

After that, we'd have the next round of fights with the winners, where they'd all go through a single elimination round as well to bring the numbers down, then the final bouts to determine the final four in the tournament. It was all very exciting, and I watched with a certain amount of glee as the two fighters, a spear wielder and a long sword and dagger user, fought it out for a spot in the next round.

It was crazy to me how many were choosing weapons with superior reach after they'd opened the tourney up to weapons other than just swords, but I guessed it was probably the smart play; I was just too fond of using a sword to use any other weapon. It was a matter of style and familiarity, but mostly, I'd trained with only a sword for so long that using another weapon would be putting myself at a disadvantage.

With the final fight being decided, the spear-wielder forced a forfeit from the swordsman in a display of speed that made me quite sure he had a ten in speed similar to mine. The final single elimination was a change from what I expected. After a sword intermission, I was told that all four remaining fighters would participate in an all-versus-all fight, deciding the winner who would get a spot back in the tourney.

I suddenly wondered whether this format would continue into the higher-level fights, but I didn't ask anyone, as I had to get into armor and be ready for the upcoming fight. Sel was there with me, and I looked over to her. She looked defeated already, not something I was used to seeing on her face.

"We've got one more chance, don't give up just yet," I said, trying to cheer her up.

"You didn't fight that spear-wielding girl. I have no chance of beating her or anyone that could beat her, so I'm just wasting my time with this," she said, and I could tell she was a breath away from quitting altogether.

"Then think of it like this, you can help me out by teaming up with me to take down the other two. I might still have a chance against that spear girl, whatever her name was, and that way I could get a little revenge for you. How's that sound?" I asked, eager to not only cheer up someone I'd been friends with for the past five years, despite her animosity toward me on almost every occasion, but also to secure an ally in the upcoming fight to give me an edge.

"You think you can beat her?" she asked, a light in her eyes as she considered it. "You are fast, much faster than you have any right to be at your level. Maybe you could get lucky." I could see the cogs going around in her head as she considered it. "Fine," she finally said. "I'll be your ally and help you back into the tourney, but don't think I'll give you an easy victory after we take down the other two. I want to know you can truly deliver, so you'll be fighting me at my best."

A change washed over her as she spoke, and I knew I'd have my work cut out for me against her now. With that settled, we shook on it before taking up our shields and heading to the fighting arena.

They announced the fighters and the format, and soon all four of us were inside getting ready to fight. The two on the other side of us saw us together and made a snap decision to also team up, going arm to arm as they moved forward. I smiled, knowing it wouldn't help them in the least. Sel and I were good at fighting together; both of us practiced tanks, ready to take whatever damage they might throw at us and deliver it right back.

The spear-wielder poked at a distance, as the other swordsman tried to flank me on the right side. I trusted Sel to catch the next blow from the spearman, and I lunged forward, shield out, and scored a cut on the swordsman before he could react. It was his fault for leaving himself so open, given that I had an effective Speed attribute of 10.

His weapon glowed a harsh red, lightning crackling around it as he lunged back at me, using his Power attribute ability; no doubt Heavy Strike was being employed by him, so I didn't have to worry about Shove, which was a nice change of pace. However, as I dodged, I left my shield a bit lower when I didn't catch the next attack, leaving me open to another type of attack.

The swordsman held out his sword arm and suddenly blue lightning arced down his blade and struck me in the chest, spinning me hard as I felt what Spark could do in close quarters. My muscles twitched, but remained under my control, and I felt a ringing in my ears as I took up a stance, catching his next blow.

The swordsman then showed his final Attribute-gained ability by Quickstepping in front and then to the side of me, getting a lucky strike on my exposed left side. This was not going as well as I'd hoped, and surely he was ahead in points right now, so I'd need to try something new.

As he took a step back, I rushed him, my speed a match for his own, and I slammed my shield hard into his face, nearly knocking his weapon free of his hand as I did so. But I didn't stop there, no, I took a strike to my side in exchange for a powerful sword strike to his head. His helmet, being the same as all the ones we wore, a cap more than a full-faced helm, did enough to stop the blade and keep him alive.

However, the strike hit him hard enough that his eyes rolled to the back of his head, and he slumped forward into my arms. I caught him and dragged him to the side so the attendants could see to him, before turning to see that Sel had just taken care of the spear-wielder, breaking their weapon in two and delivering a knockout blow to their head with her powerful mace.

Considering she was only level 10, and her opponent was likely level 15, this was a pretty powerful win for her, but I'd done more with less, I reminded myself as I faced off against her. She had the glint back in her eye, and I knew this wouldn't be an easy fight.

I rushed forward, ready to employ my speed to its full advantage, but she hid behind her shield, not giving me an opportunity to get a strike in other than on her shield. When I finally stopped to back off and reconsider my strategy, she opened herself up and swung with her mace.

It battered my shield with immense force, and I knew in that moment she'd taken five points into Guard and five into Power. The fact was confirmed when her mace glowed a vicious red, and she struck my shield again, but this time with over twice the power of the last attack.

I reeled backward, my shield battered to the side in an attempt to catch her blow, then an idea hit me, and I let myself stumble to see if she'd take advantage of my folly. She did, of course, and I pivoted quickly to my sturdy backfoot, slipping to the side and cutting her hard on the rib cage. She grunted in pain, but took the attack with ease otherwise.

As I was in position for it, I took another attack on her back, before she could fully turn and face me. More points for me, I thought as I realized the fight was easily more than halfway over. I'd need as many points against her as possible, but I didn't really want to knock her out, simply show her I had what it took.

With that, I kicked at her shield, just as she braced herself. The speed of my kick brought extra power as I focused on the edge, forcing her shield to the side and gaining an additional point or two with a thrust into her gut. However, she batted at my arm with her mace, getting a glancing blow that hurt more than it should have, in my opinion.

Gritting my teeth, I wished I were level 10 so I could zap her with Spark, but instead I feigned an attack and scored another blow with my superior agility. Speed was truly an overpowered attribute, I decided, as I leveraged it to close the gap in her skill as a tank and my skill as a damage dealer.

The gong went off even sooner than I expected, both of us sweating and breathing hard, but I was clearly the winner; I'd scored more blows on her than she had on me by twice the amount. Now it was just a matter of waiting and seeing what would happen next.

"Good match, but I'm not convinced you have the power to take on the woman who beat me. She was so far beyond me that I felt like the first week of our training, where every fight was one that almost ended our lives in that tower. Best hope you've got a bit of luck on your side," Sel said, then punching me in the arm, she added. "Also, you should try not to be late anymore, fix that little quirk, and you aren't a half-bad guy."

She smiled at me in a way that stirred something inside of me. I had never felt that way about Sel before, but seeing her smile like that and being playful made me reconsider my feelings. However, I was with Analese, at least until I left this town to explore greater opportunities. Both Analese and I understood that we wouldn't be together forever; my ambition was to become a Dragon Knight, while she wanted to reach level 30 and settle down. Time would reveal where our lives would lead, but the last thing I needed was more distractions.

Luckily for me, Sel's dour expression returned not too long after when we joined our friends. Tomas teased her about losing to me, and I stayed out of it as Tomas tried and failed to dodge a punch to his gut. He spat out some of his food and put distance between himself and Sel before eating more of his dried fruit snacks.

"Alright," I said, holding up my hands. "Let's behave and go watch Ryn as she kicks someone's ass."

"Yeah," Ryn said, grinning. "I need to get ready, they are announcing the winner soon, then I'm the first one up against some guy with a mace. I got to watch his fight, and I think I know how to beat him."

"He barely won his first fight," Sel said. "You'll clobber him in no time."

"Watch out for his Shield Bash," Jareth said, surprising us by talking as he remained silent basically this entire time so far.

"What do you mean?" Ryn asked. "I noticed he had Speed and probably Guard. Do you think his Guard is high enough to give him an additional move that I didn't see during the fight?"

"He used it right at the end, finishing off his opponent when it looked like he'd lose. He was holding back the entire time. Be careful," Jareth said, and Ryn nodded, taking in everything he had to say.

With that out of the way, I followed Ryn over to the armor area and watched as she suited up. The announcements went out during that time, and I won my fight against Sel by an impressive twenty points. I glanced over to her then, and she just nodded her head to me, saying nothing.

"Well, that is a relief," I said, as Ryn finished putting her armor on.

"You thought you might not have won?" Ryn asked, cracking her neck to the side and picking up a shield. "It was pretty clear you were the winner."

"I know, but the scores betrayed me once; I figured it could happen again," I said, trying my best to hide my nervous energy. I was nervous for Ryn, not really myself, but I didn't want it to show, so she'd keep an even head.

She didn't seem to notice and walked up to me, pulling me into a hug before going toward the fighting arena, easily jumping over the low gate and entering as her name was called out. Then they called the second guy, but I was too focused on Ryn to care about the guy's name. Instead, I sent my thoughts to her, hoping she would have enough to conquer her foe so I'd have a crack at her later.

The fight started off pretty tame, with them trading blows here and there, but nothing crazy. It wasn't until Ryn used her Quickstep to get around his defenses and land a headshot that things started to get interesting.

Suddenly, her opponent was moving much quicker, anticipating her blows and even getting more hits in than she was getting with her superior speed. It was hard to watch because it looked like she'd lose for sure now, but after only a minute of this, he began to slow again, whatever adrenaline he had coursing through him fading as the fight wore on.

But Ryn never slowed, and she started getting hit after hit on him, until finally he showed his hand, slamming out with his shield right for her head. But she was too fast for him, even with his special skill being activated. She brought her own shield up, and in a clang of metal and wood, she took the blow right on.

It sent them both staggering back, but Ryn was the first to recover and go in for another attack. Her blow hit high on his helmet, and I saw his eyes roll to the back of his head.

The fight was won, Ryn had done it!

CHAPTER 13
TOURNEY RESULTS

"You are amazing!" I said to Ryn as she came out of her bout, the single-elimination round over, her opponent knocked out cold.

"He underestimated me, and I got a victory because of it," she said casually.

"Either way, I don't think anyone will be underestimating you now. That was amazing," I said, turning to Tomas as he approached with Ashric in tow.

"Way to end it with style," Tomas said, munching on his treats.

"Yeah, that was pretty impressive," Ashric said, smiling at Tomas as if they were sharing in a secret joke.

I ignored them and listened to the announcements. The spear-wielding girl who had beaten Sel—her name was Fen—was going up against another winner, but not Dawnson. I moved to the edge and decided to watch her fight, to see if she was truly the deadly opponent that Sel believed her to be.

I noticed she had three rings on her fingers, two on the left and one on the right, with an amulet that appeared to be magical, as well as her magical spear that gleamed with light as she swirled it around herself in dance-like movements. She was quick, that much was easy to see, but she also appeared sturdy, the way she took hits on her weapon and bore the brunt of the force without moving a foot.

And she struck out with the strength of someone much more powerful than a level 15 individual, actually tearing lines into the reinforced armor we all wore, which was concerning because I knew this armor was high quality and reinforced to withstand most blows from normal weapons. Of course, she didn't have a normal weapon; she'd somehow gotten a magical weapon at the low level of 15.

Her opponent seemed to realize he was outmatched, as his movements and attacks became more erratic and blood poured down his arms and thighs where he'd been hit. I wondered if this was why Sel had given up, because this guy, who had started off with such pep in his step, was now moving to the edge, giving ground, and not looking happy about the fight.

I wondered if he'd be giving up soon, but no, his weapon began to glow and he went in for the attack. Using Quickstep, he appeared inside of her guard and smashed his weapon into her chest, throwing her back as blood sprayed out of her mouth from the attack. He'd used his speed to negate her own speedy guard technique, giving him a single hit that might just be enough to ensure his victory.

He rushed forward to take advantage, his mace glowing and sparking with power as he aimed for her head. A blow like that might just kill her, but he wasn't about to hold back, and I couldn't really blame him.

Moments before the attack would have connected, Fen slipped her head back and slammed her bladed spear forward and into his chest, using his own forward momentum to stab deep past his armor.

The gong was sounded as it was clear the fight was over, and people rushed out with potions ready. Only after he drank one, blood pouring out of his mouth, did she wrench her spear free. Then someone came out with a rare healing wand; it was Velric, I realized. I watched as he cast his magic wand, using one of the rare charges to save this fighter.

He'd only ever used it once or twice in all the time we'd fought in the tower, and it had been during our first few years inside, while we still learned the proper way of fighting monsters. He mumbled something to the fighter as he managed to stand on his own and walk from the arena.

She had literally almost killed the man in the fight. I wasn't so sure I'd have what it took to take her down, but I'd need to try. The next fight was Dawnson and another unknown fighter, the last of the matches.

I watched but learned very little new information about Dawnson. He won with little effort, overpowering his opponent with his class and attribute skills. I honestly wanted to see him fight the spear-wielding girl, Fen, to see if they had it in them to knock each other out. But Ryn and I weren't nothing, so when the new line-ups were announced, I saw that I was going to get my wish.

Ryn was set to fight me, while Fen and Dawnson were set to fight afterward. Then the final two would fight it out for the championship and the reward, which this year was said to be a purse of a golden sun coin. To win that would be quite the reward.

The time between matches was quick, and soon Ryn and I stood beside each other, getting ready for our match against one another. I said very little at first, and it was Ryn who broke the silence.

"No matter what happens," she said, catching my eye. "We won't let it get between us. This is just a friendly competition after all. If I beat you, it doesn't mean you are any less of a fighter."

I cringed a little at her words. Could she beat me so easily? Sure, she was a good fighter and in past years we'd never managed to be pitted against each other, but I was still confident I had what it would take to win the entire competition.

"Either way," I said, holding out a hand. "Friends first."

"Good," Ryn said, a sly smile coming on her face. "So don't be upset when I wipe the floor with you."

"Har har," I said. She was in full boasting mode now, and I was here for it. "I'll win by so many points they'll announce it right after the fight."

"Hah," Ryn said. "You'll be lucky to get a single point on me, slowpoke. Don't be too late on your strikes."

We laughed and boasted some more before going to the opposite ends, ready for the fight. They announced our names, and we both entered the arena, weapons held up and shields at the ready. The crowd cheered, and I could feel the energy in the air; it was intoxicating.

I almost imagined I heard my name being chanted. I turned and saw Tomas shouting my name over and over again, and after a few seconds, he switched to chanting Ryn's name. His voice was loud enough to cut through the din of the crowd and sounded like a dozen men chanting it.

I smiled then, even as I faced off against my friend, and my other close friend cheered us on, I couldn't help but think how lucky I was to have such good friends. They'd do anything for me. I knew I just needed to ask, but I was lucky enough that I didn't need to.

Channeling my energy back to the fight, I focused on Ryn and the tip of her blade. I had to be careful with her; that Quickstep was an easy way to get past my block, and I knew she wouldn't hesitate to use it on me.

Sure enough, and as I expected, she used it to get just behind me, raising her hand to strike, but I used my impressive speed and the fact that I knew this was coming, to dodge to the right just in the nick of time. My sword swiped out, but hit nothing but air. However, it bought me space as she pivoted around me and my blade.

I got my shield up in time to catch a fast blow from her, returning one off her shield a moment later. This fight wore on much like this for several minutes, with each of us scoring only glancing blows on each other, our shields working overtime to keep us safe. It wasn't easy fighting someone you knew all their moves, and vice versa, her knowing all of mine.

It made for a visually exciting fight, constantly moving and striking out, but boring when it came to actual hits. There was less action in this fight than in any of the others, and I could almost feel the crowd's excitement dying off, so I decided to do something drastic.

I slammed my shield against Ryn's, then threw it to the side. Ryn smiled and did the same, both of us pulling out a dagger instead in our off hand. This would make for a much more exciting fight. I was just glad Ryn saw it the same way I did. With only a minute and a half left, we needed to spice things up.

I thrust forward, scoring a hit on Ryn, then taking a dagger to the ribs for my trouble. The armor and my personal Iron Skin kept me safe, but that would still mean she was getting points. My speed had given me an advantage before, but it wasn't huge with our shields in the way. Now that we were double weaponing it, I really leaned into my speed.

Striking out, I got two or even three hits for each of her one. It was clear I'd be pushing ahead in strikes and points, and I saw the moment Ryn realized that, and her tactics changed. Suddenly, she appeared behind me and slammed the end of her dagger's pommel into the back of my head.

If not for my Iron Skin, it might have knocked me right out. Instead, I saw double for a moment, and my vision flashed black, but I recovered in time to slash her chest with my blade. Then I followed it up with another slash and then a poke. The gong sounded only a second after my three-hit combo.

"Damn," Ryn said, shaking her head. "You are just so much faster than you were before. Even with my increased Speed, I can't keep up with you."

"You did pretty damn well yourself," I said, panting and aching from the back of my head. I put my hand up to find it wet with blood; she'd hit so hard just below the helmet line that she'd drawn blood.

"Sorry 'bout that, it was my last-ditch effort to end the fight. Now we leave it to the points," she said, pulling out a smaller, weaker potion that I recognized as one we'd purchased for the group's adventuring. "Better drink this for your head. It's been long enough since your last, I think."

I took it without question and downed it whole. A tingling sensation at the back of my head made me close my eyes for a second. The pain was gone a moment later, and I could focus once more.

"Whoever wins," I said, turning to her. "Promise me you'll win this tourney, and I'll make the same promise."

"I love your enthusiasm," Ryn said, shaking her head. "But I'm not sure we have what it takes to win this fight if Fen wins this next bout. She is just so much more powerful than anything I expected to see in the tournament."

"Second place isn't so bad," Tomas said, appearing from the crowd. "You'll do fine, but I don't see how you beat an impossible foe like that."

"Why are you all assuming it'll be me who faces her? We don't know who won yet," I said, feigning ignorance. I knew I'd won, I could feel it, but what could I do against Fen to win if she was who I faced in the finals? Dawnson was another matter, I could beat him, I just had to be quick, but Fen showed she was as quick as me, and she had the distance required to score loads of points with that spear.

"They just announced the next match, we should watch and learn all we can," Ryn said, seemingly ignoring my comment.

We moved to the edge of the cheering crowd and waited for them to stop circling each other. Dawnson was talking, saying something I couldn't make out to Fen. Meanwhile, Fen remained quiet as a church mouse, swishing her weapon on either side of herself as she prepared to strike.

The silence seemed to anger Dawnson, who charged in with his weapon ready. The massive hammer came down, but Fen was too quick, dodging and striking out at the same moment. She scored a strike on his chest, but it didn't penetrate the armor. That was when I realized Dawnson's armor was more metal plates than enchanted leather.

They had either allowed him to use his own armor or given him an upgrade against Fen, likely the latter. The two Houses sponsoring the Tourney wouldn't want anyone to die, so I guessed that if I faced off against Fen next, I'd be given such armor as well.

Back and forth they fought, and I studied the way Fen fought, always with counter strikes and never the aggressor, at least at first. As Dawnson tired, Fen began to pick at his defenses, scoring point after point before he could recover and strike back. It was like watching a dance when Fen fought, and a drunken stumble of a dance when Dawnson fought back.

However, with his class skills, he scored hit after devastating hit, and I saw Fen begin to limp on her back leg and slow considerably after she took a powerful hit to the leg. They were as close to a match against each other as any of the others I'd seen fight her. This gave me hope, because I did fairly well against Dawnson; if I just had the best fight of my life, then I might stand a chance.

Then I saw through Fen's ruse; she pushed off her 'injured' leg and came around to slash at Dawnson with a red, crackling weapon, hitting him hard in the arm and across the chest, so hard that he was thrown backward and lost grip on his weapon. Then she was atop him, holding her blade against his throat.

The fight was over; he yielded with only a minute to go on the timer. Situations like that, holding an opponent in a death move, were frowned upon, but legal in the tourney. I'd have to watch out for that, because it was as good as a knock-out when you allowed yourself to be disarmed and put into that position.

The winner announcements came shortly after this bout, confirming what I guessed: I'd won mine and would be going on to face Fen in the final match of the tournament. She looked over at me from where she stood, in her armor and sweat on her forehead. Her head inclined just a hair, and I returned the gesture before going to suit up for the upcoming fight.

There would be a half-hour rest so each fighter could regain their stamina, but I wanted to be ready. When I got back to the armor pit, Dawnson was there, and he didn't look happy.

"You don't stand a chance against her; she's a monster," he said, pulling off the armor piece by piece and handing it to me. "If not for this armor, she'd have killed me three times over. Thank your lucky stars they thought to have a more powerful suit on hand."

The armor was scratched, beaten, and dented from her strikes, but nothing had pierced the overlapping metal plates. The inside was the same enchanted leather as before, but covered in a metal laminar akin to what I imagined dragon scales would look like. I gladly pulled the armor on over my clothes, feeling it adjust to my size as I got it into place.

The helmet was a full-sized helm, even offering protection over your face, but making it slightly harder to see through the slits. They weren't taking any chances against Fen; they wanted you dressed to the nines against her. Meanwhile, she wore the same enchanted leather as before.

"I think I'll do fine," I said, finally answering Dawnson's words. I began picking up a shield, but an attendant in House Deymorin colors came by with a black wooden one and handed it to me.

"This is a reinforced Relic of House Deymorin. We don't want you to lose your shield midway in the fight, so they gave me this to give to you or Ryn should either win and make it this far. It is on loan, however, so try not to let it get too damaged. And a message from both heads of the Houses," the attendant said, leaning forward. "Beat that Aether-Touched at her own game."

Was Fen doing something with her Touched heritage that made her stronger? I knew the rumors of Aether-Touched being able to pull more magical use out of items, but surely that was just gossip or legend, not truth. If so, she had a distinct advantage over me with her items that were surely enchanted, giving her an edge.

It didn't matter, I told myself. I had my father's scarf, and I'd use it to its full Speed advantage, destroying her at her own game. The time between the events stretched out, and soon I was just standing with my friends, black shield and metal armor on, waiting to fight against the hardest foe I'd be likely to encounter for some time.

"You nervous?" Tomas asked, crunching on some baked nuts he'd picked up somewhere. "You seem nervous."

"I'm excited to test myself against her," I said. "I'll need to be very lucky and use all my skills if I hope to defeat her, but it's possible."

"What are you going to do with your winnings if you take the purse?" Ashric asked. "Even a single golden sun coin would go a long way to setting you up for the dungeons to come."

I didn't need him to tell me that, I would be on my way to buy an enchanted sword if I won, maybe even a shield if I had enough left over. That alone would give me an edge and see me set up for the next few months at least, if not longer. But before I could cash in on my dreams, I needed to win this fight.

There was no special plan or trick I concocted; rather, I decided to lean the other way. I'd been fighting most every day for five years, so I would stop trying to think too much and just fight. Allow my body to do what I'd trained it to do. With my new Speed and Guard, I had a chance. If only I'd made it to level 10 and been able to pick the Spark ability, it would have given me an edge over her.

So far, I'd noticed her use several Power skills but nothing else, so I didn't have to worry about magic or anything. She moved fast enough to have Quickstep if she wanted, but I had a feeling she'd either taken Fleet Foot or Fast Hands with how she moved and attacked. Regardless, the match was about to start, so I went to my side, saying goodbye to my friends and their well-wishes.

With five minutes on the hourglass, the gong went off, and the fight began in earnest. Immediately, I noticed something different from Fen; she moved more casually and less cautiously. She was even the first one to make a strike at me. I caught it on my shield; her probe was no more than a testing strike. I had no chance to retaliate as she could attack from a distance, where I had to get up closer.

But even though she hit me every few seconds, it was with a bored demeanor of someone who assumed they had the fight in the bag already, not someone facing off an opponent they should fear. I decided it was time to change her mind on that, so as she struck, I let it glance off my shield, and I sort of twirled with speed at her.

My shield caught her off guard as I got within her personal space and smashed my shield against her face and upper torso. It hit with enough force to stagger her, so I caught a few slashes on her before she twirled her spear and forced me back. She smiled through bloody teeth at me and gestured with her spear at my neck.

"I can sense the power in that scarf; it is the only thing putting you even close to my level of power," she said, her voice calm and slightly raspy, not at all what I expected from such a fair-faced Aether-Touched.

"Then stop underestimating me and let's get this fight going already," I said back to her, barely having to raise my voice as she stood only ten paces from me.

"If you wish a quick defeat, I will give it to you," she said, tilting her head to the side and then moving with incredible speed toward me.

Her attacks came faster and faster. I blocked them all, but she was forcing me backward, and eventually I'd run out of room. So I side-stepped the next attack and let the blow glance off my new shield as I struck for her arm, scoring a hit and causing her to curse at me.

Where Dawnson was powerful but left himself open, I was weaker but faster and more guarded. This wasn't the same kind of fight at all, and I think she was starting to realize that as she went from super relaxed to gritting her teeth trying to get past my guard.

It was anyone's guess who was winning by points, but I felt like I was scoring just as many true hits as she was, despite her speed and skills that she continued to use as often as she could. I took a bad hit on the shield, a full, forced Heavy Strike that would have cleaved any normal shield in two, and I felt it in my shoulder. A few more hits like that and I wouldn't be able to lift my shield arm back up, a fact I think she was getting clued in on.

She battered my shield, swiping occasionally for my legs, but I was too quick, matching her speed step for step. The fight was close to its conclusion, and it looked like it would go down to the points, so I kept my guard up and was determined to end the fight with as many strikes as I could manage.

She battered my shield with another powerful strike, practically yelling in frustration at me now, all her calm demeanor shattered. She knew it would come down to points as well, and she didn't like that.

"I'm a proper tank," I said to her as she backed off momentarily to likely think about what to do next. "You won't get past my guard while I have the strength to defend myself."

"Then I'll smash through," she said. Suddenly she was jumping into the air unnaturally high, and her weapon glowed and crackled with red energy.

I braced myself. She'd been too quick, and there was no dodging it now, but at the last second, I smiled, stepped to the side, caught the blow on a glancing angle, and struck out with a piercing blow to her chest. I felt something give in her ribs, just as the gong sounded, and she took a knee after her attack, coughing.

It was up to the judges now, but I felt like I had a fair chance at winning. The fight had been long and hard, but I'd fought better than I'd ever done before, relying on my instincts to get me through.

Putting my sword away in its sheath, I walked over to her, offering a hand, which she took and stood. Then she did something odd, she raised my hand up along with hers, and the crowd went wild. I raised my shielded hand up as much as I could, but she'd done a number on me, and it would still be a few hours before I could take another potion to help it heal.

Hell, I might not even take one. It was just sore after all, which would heal in its own time. We stood there, hand in hand, for several seconds before she turned to me and smiled.

"Winner or not, you held your own better than any of the other fighters. For that, I wish to give you a gift," Fen said, bowing her head to me and slipping a ring from her finger.

"I couldn't," I said, putting my palms up to her.

"Please, it is a mark of my people to give gifts to powerful opponents when death isn't the end result. You earned it," she said, putting the silver ring in my palm and shutting it.

"Thank you," I said, lost at what else to say.

"You are welcome. It is a ring of regeneration, a common item for an adventurer to have. You would have gotten one soon enough, but this will give you an edge over your opponents in the meantime," she said. Then, as I watched, she pulled a golden ring from her pouch and put it in place of her missing ring.

With an awkward glance up at her, she was taller than me by a few inches, I gave her a nod and turned, leaving her in the middle of the arena to go join my friends while the judges compared score cards.

"You were amazing!" Ryn said, slapping my shoulder a bit too hard. I decided to put on the ring I'd been given, and she noticed. "Can I examine it?"

"Go for it," I said, holding out my hand. "It's supposed to be a regeneration ring if that helps you."

"It doesn't, be still so I can see," she said, adjusting the spectacles on her face to get a good look. Then she told me exactly what the read out of it was, and I listened intently.

Name: *Silver Renewal Band*
Rarity: *Uncommon*
Special Properties: *Greatly increases natural health regeneration when out of combat. No effect while actively taking damage.*
Description: *Forged of silver etched with curling vinework, the ring hums with a soft green glow when its wearer is still. The enchantment feeds upon moments of rest, weaving vitality back into the body as if the earth itself were lending its strength. Adventurers often prize this band for shortening recovery between battles, though its magic offers no mercy in the heat of combat.*

"Wow," I said as she finished reading off the detailed description. "That was much more detailed than I thought it would be. Very neat!"

"Yeah, it appears this item is well within the range of what I can identify," Ryn said, pulling off the spectacles and putting them in the hardened leather case they came with.

"They are announcing the winner. Go back to the arena and wait for them to call it out," Tomas said. Fen was still in the middle, waiting eagerly while leaning on her spear, either out of support or boredom, I wasn't sure which.

I rushed to the middle, the ring already working to ease the pain in my shoulder. "I wanted to thank you again, and no matter what happens, you gave me a hell of a fight," I said, standing beside her.

She tilted her head to me but otherwise said nothing.

"And the winner of the weapons tourney for this year goes to..."

The entire place stilled as he drew out the words and paused before announcing the name.

"Kaelric Grimholt, winning by one point! 110 to 109!"

The crowd cheered, Fen lowered her head, and I stood in shock at hearing the news.

CHAPTER 14
PARADE

"I can't believe I won," I said aloud, and Fen looked down at me.

"Neither can I, but I will abide by the decision of the judges. Congratulations, Champion," Fen said, grabbing my hand and raising it up once more. The crowd went wild at that, and I even cheered myself, so enthralled by the fact that I'd won.

The next hour or so passed in a blur. I received a medal and was handed the purse, a single gold sun coin, and my friends surrounded me with kind words. It felt like a dream that didn't end until we were on our way to eat before Tomas's big final eating competition.

I ordered a freshly baked bakery item with a cheese dip, something from the north called a pretzel. Tomas got excited when he saw it and ordered one for himself, even though he needed to be ready for the eating competition in just under an hour.

"You really need to save room," I told him, and he just chuckled.

"Let me explain to you how the human body works. I have to warm my stomach first. Eating this is like stretching for me," Tomas said, and I laughed out loud at the absurdity of it. But he was the food-eating champion, at least for the sugar pies. I wondered how he would handle the thicker, heartier meat pies.

"Whatever works for you," I said, happy to just be hanging out with my friends. "Tell me, Tomas, how are you not like three hundred pounds?"

"I work as hard as I play," Tomas said, shrugging. "Let me ask you something. How'd you pull that win off? She was kicking your ass but still you managed to get in so many hits. I thought for sure she'd shatter your shield and you'd be done."

"I just tried to focus on my instincts and let it rule the fight. It worked, barely, but I can't help but think she was the true winner. She defeated all her opponents until she reached me, and even so, she moved as if she were above level 15. If that were a real fight, like without the enhanced armor and shield, she'd have killed me within a minute out there. I kind of feel like the organizers wanted me to win, giving me more enhanced gear to wear and use," I said, shrugging.

"Well," Ryn said, interjecting and stealing a piece of my pretzel for herself. "I think you won fair and square. They were just being cautious after a contestant nearly died because that Fen girl had a powerful weapon, maybe even an artifact, for how well it cut."

"You think?" I asked, feeling a little better with Ryn on my side. "I'm glad to hear it, because I don't want my victory to feel hollow."

"We all agree you won, right Tomas?" Ryn asked as we sat on a pair of benches and began eating the food we'd gotten. The other three were still out getting food at other vendors, so it was just the three of us right now.

"Yes!" Tomas said with more confidence than was needed.

"And you are going to win your final competition, right?" I asked, nudging him with my elbow.

"Depends on whether or not Gruk is competing," Tomas said, yawning. "If he can get control of how much he drops out of his mouth, then he will beat me for sure. But I don't know if he'll be able to slow down; he practically smashes the food into his mouth. Plus, the meat pie competition is a bit different."

"How so?" I asked. I come to these every year but they always make slight changes, as they did with the weapons tourney, so it wasn't a surprise to me that I didn't know how the meat pie competition worked.

"Instead of a short period of time to eat as many as possible, they are doing a sort of eating marathon race. You get twenty minutes to eat as many meat pies as you possibly can, without leaving any remains, which is where Gruk will get in trouble," Tomas said, chuckling.

"Then you don't need this," Ryn said, stealing a large section of his pretzel and dipping it in my cheese cup.

"Hey," I said. "Use his cheese, mine is almost gone."

The melted cheese was delicious, and I wanted to make sure I could get a little on each bite. Ryn just shot me a teasing look and kept on eating.

"Well," I said, finishing my pretzel up around the same time as the others. "Should we go find the rest of the group and make our way over with Tomas to get his spot in the competition?"

"Let's do it," Ryn said, grinning from ear to ear. "Save me a few meat pies, alright, Tomas? Last year there were only like a dozen left over and I only got like two to save for later."

"They are pretty good, aren't they?" I said, remembering eating one of those pies last year and thinking I needed to find out who provided them, but never actually figuring it out.

"Yeah, they are the best. Worth signing up just to eat a few," Tomas said, grinning as we made our way to find the rest of the group.

They were at a food area with plates and such, so they needed to eat nearby so they could return the dishes to the vendor. They were eating an odd mix of noodles, meat, and veggies, with a dark sauce over it all. Some noodle dish that I forgot the moment they told me, as it was so foreign-sounding to be no more than gibberish to my ears.

The vendor claimed to be from across the seas and just happened to be visiting during the festival. I almost asked him if he knew my landlord, but I figured that would be folly, so I didn't.

They finished their meals, and we headed over for Tomas, letting him lead the way and take off when we got close.

"Good luck," I called out to him.

He turned and patted his stomach. "Don't need it, I've got room."

"He is going to have the meat sweats tonight," Ashric said, shaking his head. "He always gives himself the meat sweats after the meat pie eating contest."

"Oh yeah?" I asked. "Do you think he'll win?"

"I hope so," Ashric said, smiling fondly at his friend.

They were pretty close, Ashric and Tomas. It was only natural; they'd sort of grown up together, and although I considered Tomas and Ryn both my best friends, I wondered if I was Tomas's best friend sometimes, or if Ashric held that spot. But those weren't thoughts worth exploring, so I didn't. Instead, I cheered my friend as they announced his name and the gong went off for them to start.

It was ten competitors, but I only watched Tomas and Gruk, both of whom ate with a speed and efficiency that boggled the mind. Each pie disappeared in four or five bites with Tomas. Meanwhile, Gruk was eating slower than before but keeping pace with Tomas. He was making much less of a mess, but still, pieces fell all around him, and he'd need to eat them before the timer went up.

At ten minutes, Tomas was at twenty pies down, and Gruk had twenty-three, meaning he was pulling ahead. They had cups of water, and Tomas had taken the opportunity to drink some several times, while Gruk ate with single minded fury, not stopping to drink or breathe for that matter.

"You got this, Tomas!" I called out over the cheer of the crowd. "Show him how hungry you really are!"

Tomas grinned and ate the pies in two bites, barely chewing or swallowing. Suddenly, he was catching Gruk, and I wondered why he hadn't done this in the first place.

As the timer fell close to ending, Tomas was tied with Gruk, but Gruk had extras that he was taking time to eat up now that it was almost over. That allowed Tomas to pull ahead by a pie, and he held his lead, though he was sweating profusely now.

"One more pie, you got this!" Ryn yelled, cheering him on.

He took the final pie as Gruk grabbed three and threw them into his massive hog-like face. Then the gong went off, and they had a few seconds to eat what was in their mouths, or they'd have to spit it out.

They both chewed and swallowed with impressive speed, and the judges walked around calling out the number of pies eaten in twenty minutes.

The first person had eaten thirty-four, then twenty-eight, and then much more like that until finally it came to Tomas. He had consumed sixty-two meat pies, a new record, the announcer said. Finally, they got to Gruk and announced a shocking bit of news: he, too, had eaten sixty-two! It was a tie, and both would take home first place, splitting the prize.

Tomas looked like he was ready to hurl. I'd never seen him look so full before, but Gruk reached out and ate another pie, throwing the entire thing in his massive mouth.

Tomas went over to Gruk and shook his hand, then turned and left the stage after receiving his reward and being announced as one of the winners.

"Congratulations!" I said to him the moment he broke through the crowd.

"I feel sick," he said. He was breathing hard and covered in sweat.

"I think it's time to take him home," Ashric said, cutting between us. "Come on, let's get you into bed."

"No celebratory drinks?" I asked, and Tomas just looked at me with that same look of wanting to hurl. For once in my life, I'd seen him get full, and it wasn't a pretty sight.

"Fine, but Ryn will have some drinks with me, right?" I asked, but Ryn bit her lip.

"I was actually going to meet up with an old guard buddy for a few drinks. You are welcome to join us, but I know you aren't his biggest fan," Ryn said, and I sighed.

"I guess I'm heading back home," I said. "We have a big day tomorrow anyway, you know, parade and all."

"See you bright and early," Ryn said, bidding me farewell.

I gave the remaining Sel and Jareth a wave goodbye and departed toward my apartment. Then I had a second thought and turned to head for another place, knowing she'd be there by now with how late it was. Even on festival day, Ana was an early bird, going to sleep early and getting up early.

I made it to her place and was happy to find her awake. She invited me in immediately, and we talked into the night about how I'd done. She said she saw the match, staying up late to see it, but didn't want to bother me with my friends, so she went home after.

It was a good night, me telling all about how it felt to win, and her talking about what she'd gotten up to that day and how excited she was for the parade. We'd get a chance to hang out tomorrow, there would be mostly singing and dancing on parade day, and I promised to take her dancing.

I woke the next morning to Ana getting dressed, and I shot up, realizing I'd be late if I didn't get back to my part of town and change. I thanked her for a lovely night and promised again to dance with her later tonight, and she told me she'd hold me to it. I left after throwing my clothes back on and slipping into my boots.

The air was so fresh, and I had a pep in my step as I moved through town toward the Commons. It was a good walk, and I encountered a few people I knew along the way, saying hello when I could, but keeping it short as I needed to bathe and change clothes. I passed by the nice bathhouse on the way and decided, why not? They could launder clothing fast enough that I could spend a small amount of time bathing and have clean clothes again.

With my two medals handed over to them as well as my sword, I stripped and made my way into the bathhouse. They told me it would be at least twenty minutes before the clothing would be ready, so I relaxed and let the water wash over me. There was some stiff soap nearby, and I scrubbed myself thoroughly before finally relaxing completely in the hot water.

"In a hurry?" someone asked across from the bathhouse. It wasn't someone I knew, just an old fellow enjoying a bath just like me. It was a bit taboo to talk in the bathhouse, but here we were, old folks rarely cared about stuff like that.

"Somewhat," I said, seeing if that would be enough to satisfy him.

"You are one of the newly Unlocked, aren't you? You'd better hurry if you want to make it to the parade in time," he said, guessing my status easily.

"How'd you know that?" I asked, confused by the fount of knowledge he seemed to have.

"Oh, you've got the look about you. Plus, if I were wrong, I'd have guessed you were close to being Unlocked because of your age. Don't mind me, though, carry on, young Kaelric, enjoy your day," he said, further stunning me into silence.

I wondered if I could get up and around him without causing further conversation. Then something hit me as I stood to leave.

"You know my name?" I asked, suddenly very suspicious of him.

"I know much more than that," he said, standing and showing a body marked with scars and time. "I knew your parents, or I knew of them. It's a shame what happened to them. You have my condolences."

"How'd you know my parents?" I asked. What was going on here? I didn't know this man, yet he seemed to know who I was and my parents.

"Nothing too suspicious, trust me," he said. "I was a neighbor when you were young. I only just recognized you after we started speaking. Go on your way, and I'll bother you no more."

More suspicious than ever, I left the bathhouse main room and went to find my clothing. It had just been finished, and I collected my things, including my scarf, which had been pressed and cleaned with my normal clothing. How they managed to clean and dry clothing so fast was anyone's guess; I simply knew it was magical in nature and nothing else.

The attendant smiled kindly at me, and I returned the gesture. She was a cute girl of around my age, but I didn't know her. Sure, I'd seen her around before, but I didn't even have her name. I suddenly thought to ask, but she was already withdrawing, so I let her leave in peace, without bugging her further. I wondered how close she was to being unlocked, or if she had much time to train for a job like this?

I made it out of the bathhouse and into the commons where I lived. My apartment door was secure, so I unlocked it and went inside. I didn't come across my landlord; it was early enough and at the same time late enough that he probably left for the parade by now. I changed my clothes, putting away my clean ones on my bed and dressing in my armor, grabbing my shield.

The parade was a chance to show off what you had, so we'd be armored up with all our equipment and weapons, along with the House representatives from both Deymorin and Ravenlock. Nothing exciting happened while I dressed and hid away my newfound riches. I was up to a small fortune now, and I didn't want to walk around with so much coin at once.

So with my coin purse much lighter than before, I ventured out into the open and cool air of the morning, heading to the start of the parade. Luckily for me, it started in the Forges Quarter, not terribly far from where I lived. Along the way, I grabbed a snack at the local bakery, but this time I didn't get any for anyone else, as I was already late and figured they'd have eaten.

Arriving at the location, I passed by carriages, flags, and all manner of other parade-related stuff. I paid little mind to them; once you saw one parade, you saw them all, but even so, this one was different. This was the one where I was going to be announced to the world as an Unlocked. Well, the others and I, but it felt personal and made me look at the rows of people with new eyes.

There were the carriages up ahead that carried the House Deymorin and then House Ravenlock nobles, and ahead of that, a flat cart with their servants on it, showing off one relic or another. I was surprised to see the blackened shield I'd used up there on display. Had I really used a relic-quality item and not known it? Either way, I let my eyes run over the head of the parade down to the next part, which was where a band would be playing various instruments.

In that group, I saw several musical bard groups; one stood out to me because one member had a squirrel on his shoulder, while another seemed to be half-armored, but under his clothing. As I neared them, I realized that the armored man had replaced his left arm, most of his left side really, with metal gears and springs that appeared to work as well as any old limb.

I marveled a bit too long at him before letting my eyes run over the final two iconic members of the group. One member of the group had shoulder-length brown hair and wore loose-fitting clothing in a darker color. The feature that stood out the most about him was his weapon, which seemed to double as an instrument of some kind. It was unlike any lute I'd seen before, flatter, and the edges were sharpened like an axe.

Then there was the final member of the group, a woman in all black leather using a four stringed version of the axe-like instrument that her fellow bard member used, but without sharpened edges. She seemed more rogue-like than the rest of them, each step she took was careful and precise. They were, all of them, attractive and interesting, which is why they stood out. I found myself having trouble taking my eyes off them as I moved down to the next section, the one that would have all the Unlocked awaiting the start of the parade.

Everyone I knew stood chatting amongst themselves, including Craven and his crew, Ana and hers, and my team, with Tomas looking better than ever after last night's activities. I caught Ana's eye, and she grinned at me. Going up to her and with more bravery than I'd shown during my fight against Fen, I took her in my arms and kissed her for all to see.

She pressed into me and we shared a moment of bliss before I let her go to the hoots and hollers from Tomas and a few from her team. Then they started clapping and it got awkward.

"Sorry, I'm just in a great mood today, and I don't care who knows anymore," I said, and Ana grinned all the wider.

"Glad to hear it," she said, playfully slapping me in the butt as I turned away to go stand with my group.

"Not an item, eh?" Ryn asked, her eyes giving away her jest. "I'd say you are something after all. Unless you go around kissing all the ladies you know like that?"

"Fine," I said, feigning distress. "You caught me."

"Are we telling people now?" Tomas asked; he, of course, knew and had covered for me plenty of times when I wanted to go hang out with Ana instead of the main group of our friends.

"I guess so," I said. It wasn't like I wanted to out us or anything, but with so little time before we all went our separate ways, I couldn't see the point in hiding it any longer.

"Anyone else have a relationship they want to reveal?" Ryn asked jokingly.

Everyone shared glances with each other and others, but no one said anything. I didn't know of any other secret relationships, so I just let it slide as the conversation took a turn toward another direction.

"Did you guys see that armored guy? Half his body seemed to be made of it?" I asked, gesturing forward to the group who were now tuning their instruments, the one with the squirrel on his shoulder somehow had pulled out a four piece drum set that hooked around his back. He had two sticks that he used to drum on them, making for an interesting and exciting beat.

"Oh yeah, that's the Granger Band of traveling bards and adventurers," Ryn said knowingly. Leave it up to her to already know enough about everything to keep us informed.

"Like named after the plant that you smoke?" Tomas asked, and I snorted.

"Yeah seems like an odd name for an adventuring band. Besides that, shouldn't they have six members to be a proper adventuring band?" I asked, watching as they strung their strings and made a chorus of awesome-sounding music even when warming up.

"We should think of a name for our adventuring group," Tomas said, then Ashric laughed before responding.

"I thought we agreed we were called the Lantern Guard," Ashric said. "I always liked the ring of that."

"Oh," Tomas said, scratching at his chin. "I meant Kael, Ryn, and me, because I thought we talked about it, and you guys would be staying around here for a bit longer. We are leaving with the first caravan to depart, so I guess I was thinking about us as a separate unit now."

"Oh," Ashric said, biting his lip and looking away from Tomas. "Right, you're right. Come up with your own name."

"I didn't mean to...," Tomas said, putting a hand on Ashric's back, but he just shook his head, seemingly unaffected by the news.

"I'm fine, it's fine," he said, then added. "I guess I always thought you'd change your mind and stay with me, or uh, I mean us, so that my father could help get us to level 20 before we left."

"I told you," Tomas said, and I felt like I was listening in on a private conversation, but they were having it out in the open, so I couldn't help but listen. "I can't leave Kael and Ryn high and dry. I'll be back eventually. It isn't like we won't see each other again."

They shared a lingering hug, and I felt bad for Ashric. His closest friend was choosing to go with two others instead of him, but at the same time, I was glad, because I couldn't imagine going out into the adventuring world without Tomas at my side.

"So," Ryn said, looking at me with an awkward look in her eyes, like she understood or knew something I didn't. "What should we call our band of three?"

"How about the Red Watch," I suggested. I was taking in my favorite color and adding something from Ryn, her time as a guard, but not including anything from Tomas.

"Or," Ryn said, touching her finger to her chin. "What about Crimson

Lanterns, keeps a bit of the red theme going but calls back to our previous name."

"Names are hard," Tomas said, shaking his head and producing some dried nuts to snack on.

We talked back and forth about names, from Scarlet Blades to Red Hawks, to the Redwatch Company. But we didn't settle on anything just yet. Instead, we decided to sleep on it.

"I'm partial to the Red Hawks," Tomas said. "It has a nice ring to it."

"I like the Redwatch Company or even just Redwatch," I said, giving my two cents.

"And I'm all for the name Scarlet Blades, but Tomas doesn't really use a blade, you know," she said, shrugging.

"What about the Oathbound?" Ashric offered. "I mean, all three of you seem to be taking solitary oaths to go after impossible classes; the Oathbound seems fitting."

"I like that," I said, nodding to Ashric.

"So do I," Tomas said, and then we turned to Ryn.

"Let's sleep on it, but it sounds good to me," she said, licking her lips suddenly as a gong was heard throughout the area, signaling the start of the parade.

Velric stood at the end of us and motioned for us to get into position.

"Remember, my newly Unlocked, you are here to show off what you've become. Don't worry about anything else. Just stand tall and strong, show them that this newest generation of Brackenford's Unlocked is worth the effort the town has put into you! Show them that we are the best to have come out of the tower in five generations of Unlocked!" he said, practically shouting at the end.

A part of me knew what he meant. As a mentor, he only worked with a new group every five years, and we'd been lucky to get him. His students always had some of the greatest potential; their tales of adventure filled the taverns with songs from bards and such.

I took a front position with Sel, the two tanks, flanked by Ryn and Jareth, with Ashric and Tomas taking the rear positions.

Horses neighed in the distance as they pulled forward the carriages, and the march began.

Honestly, it was as boring being a part of the parade as it had been all those years watching them. I didn't understand the point, as I waved my sword and shield at the crowds who cheered in response to our presence. Sure, it was exciting as a child, but that was mostly because of seeing the epic relics, cool music, and fancy-dressed people, not because of the Unlocked, even though it was the main point of the parade.

As was tradition, even the parade goers wore armor and weapons, signifying that they stood with us against the upcoming adventurers we were likely to have. It was pretty amazing seeing so many people in various old-style armor and some in newer gear. Everyone polished up and wore their best on parade day.

It would take at least two hours to circle the city's different districts, including the Commons. Maybe longer if the pace of the bands in front of us was any indication. The Granger Band was popping off with music styles I'd never heard, very rhythmic and raw-sounding. I couldn't hear their lyrics very well from a distance, but their instruments seemed to be magically enhanced to drown out all other sounds in the area.

By the end of the second hour and near the end of the parade, something happened that first brought confusion, then action, from the crowd and the parade. A loud gong was sounded three times, paused, then sounded three times again. That could only mean one thing: our town was under attack by monsters.

"Stay calm," Velric shouted, and then, coming closer to the parties, he said, "Gather together and head for the East wall. I don't know what side is being attacked yet, but we will want each side covered."

"House Deymorin will have the east side well protected from anything short of a monster migration," Craven said, rolling his eyes at Velric.

"Think about what time of year it is, and with the reports I've been getting about early migrations due to bad weather to the north, this very much could be a monster migration we are dealing with. One that will be unchecked by any other central town, as we are the biggest they have likely encountered, being as northern as we are. Get ready, be safe, and work together. You will live through the night!" Velric said, disappearing into the crowds closing in around us.

The town was in chaos right now, but I grabbed hold of Tomas and Ryn's hands, leading them toward the eastern gate. Jareth, Ashric, and Sel followed close behind us, also latching hands together to keep from losing each other.

Once we made it to the center of town, we were pretty close to the end of the parade, so we were more able to walk freely.

"Ready to see what we can do?" I asked the group, and they all nodded, some chuckling. "Time to kill some monsters!"

CHAPTER 15
MONSTER MIGRATIONS

Two truths were clear as we reached the Eastern gate, which was closed fast, and the walls were mounted with dozens of guards shooting arrows down into a mass of what I assumed must be monsters. The first truth was this couldn't have happened at a worse time, with all of House Deymorin in the city, and much of their guards here as well; they likely didn't offer any resistance to the horde of monsters at all, just allowing them to pass and defending their walls as best they could. The second truth became clear as hundreds of armored people with weapons ready gathered at the gates. The truth being, this couldn't have happened at a better time for the town.

With each and every citizen that could fight and some that couldn't, all wearing their armor and weapons, this would be the fastest a horde would be shattered against our walls. I knew from past experience that only a fraction of the monsters stopped to try to get over the walls, with flying ones already moving onward at a faster pace and leaving us alone for now. What remained were roughly a thousand monsters, looking to eat human flesh and grow stronger.

From werewolves to goblins, to hobgoblins to alpha wolves, there were all sorts of monsters out there, and we'd need to drive off or kill them all if we wanted to sleep peacefully tonight.

The guards were arguing with some armored citizens who wanted the doors opened, but we needed to set up a proper defensive line first, so I understood the guards' hesitation. Sure enough, someone began yelling orders, and we found our group put into the third row of rotations to fight the monsters, with enough room for three groups at a time to attack.

Citizens partnered up based on their skills and levels. We were obviously some of the weakest, but we'd still get a chance to fight. Our group was placed on the left edge, meant to catch weaker monsters that tried to sneak by during the main fray. With our lines set up, the guard called out, and the doors opened just enough for a single monster to come in at a time.

They flooded through, one after another, as the fight began in earnest.

The first wave was mostly goblins and hobgoblins. The weaker goblins tried for the edges as they guessed they would, and we stood ready to handle them when our turn came up. I watched in awe as skills were activated and laughter shared as they cut down hobgoblin and goblin alike with the ease that only a higher-level adventurer might deploy.

It was clear that the weaker monsters were at the forefront, with the stronger monsters either moving onward or staying in the back until time came for them to attack. The groups shifted after a minute or so of fighting. We had six lines deep of adventurers, and so there was no point in not switching every few minutes to keep them fresh.

We were one switch from the front when new monsters began to squeeze through, and the dead monsters in front were being moved aside by the adventurers during the small respite from combat that it created.

Skeletons, zombies, and all manner of undead began to rush through, and behind them I thought I saw a robed figure with glowing green lights at the end of a skull-topped staff. But just as I saw him through the gate, the waves of monsters shifted, and he was gone.

The weaker zombies headed for the sides while the stronger weapon-wielding skeletons attacked from the front. Some had bows and shields, were raised as a hail of arrows hit the front line.

A switch was called, and suddenly we were in the middle of the fray, weapons raised and ready.

A zombie came for us, then another and another. They were likely stronger than us, but three against six, they wouldn't get past us. I caught the first one on my shield, slamming my blade point-first into its head, ending it as magic bolts slammed past us and into the second, bringing it down. Tomas, Jareth, and Ryn flanked the sides, killing the final one with a barrage of attacks to its head.

Zombies were all about head damage if you wanted to bring them down quickly. I knew this because the skeleton floor of the tower had zombies as well, so it was a lesson we'd learned over the years of practice.

A group of five goblins made it through, and bee-lined it for our side, so Sel and I separated a little, ready to receive them and allow a few down the middle for our back line to take care of.

The first goblin had a rusty sword, and I caught his blow as he hammered up at me with all his strength. However, I was so much faster as to make his attacks seem like child's play, I swung out and took off his arm, spraying blood all over Sel and my shield. She didn't like that, and I could hear her cursing at me. But I didn't wait for another opening, instead I slammed my shield forward and stabbed the goblin through the chest.

Within seconds, the fight was over and someone was calling for a switch, so we backed off, dragging with us the bodies of the fallen so that they didn't overflow the streets before us. I noticed someone finishing up searching for cores, so we did the same with the kills we took, going back to grab the zombies as well before cutting into them for their cores.

We found cores on all of them and then moved the bodies into a pile being created off to the side. It took several minutes to do this, even with all of us working together, so we found our spots in line and got back into the rotation afterward, bloodied and sweating. The blood on us was all from the monsters, but it made holding our weapons difficult, so we tried our best to wipe our hands off on our armor, making it a tad easier to grip our weapons again.

The monsters got harder to kill as the day wore on, the horde of skeletons and zombies finally ending as someone killed a lich controlling them, a rather weak one by the way it went down when it finally appeared, but still a lich is a lich, so if they hadn't taken him down now, he might become a regional threat later on. Besides that, I was told, by Ryn at the time it got taken down, that it likely wasn't dead forever, as liches had ways of surviving the mundane physical death.

We reached the front of the rotation again, and werewolves and wolves were pouring through the gate. A werewolf made a line for us, then another, and I knew we had our work cut out for us. Already, our experience bars were overflowing, but in the haste to get back into line and watch the battle, I hadn't thought to try and level up.

So instead, I readied my shield, catching the tall werewolf as it clawed at me, and then Tomas appeared, his staff glowing red as he slammed it into the werewolf's legs. A loud crunch sounded, and the thing fell before us, which we quickly stabbed the ever-living hell out of it, killing it just as the other made it to us.

This one hit me with a clawed strike so hard, I felt my shield nearly buckle, and I was pushed back into Ryn, who caught me and held me up as Sel pushed forward with her shield and slammed her mace into the werewolf's rib cage, causing it to howl and turn on her. Which turned out to be a mistake, because Jareth appeared with his curved blade and slashed deep into its spine just as Ashric hit it with a magic bolt.

The combined attack was enough to bring it down to its knees, where Sel hit it with a mace blow so hard its neck snapped at an odd angle, killing it instantly. Tomas and Ryn grabbed the bodies, large as they were, and moved them to the side as wolves filled the spots, biting and snapping their jaws at our ankles.

These, of course, weren't normal wolves, but a monstrous variety, with larger and sharper teeth and nearly as strong as the werewolves we'd just fought, but less tactical in the way they attacked.

We took a little while longer, but we took care of seven of them during our few minutes of fighting, before a switch was called. When we switched, we got their cores and deposited the bodies, but I remembered to check my status this time.

I'd gotten enough essence from our kills and the kills of others that I was level 10 already, an amazing feat after only an hour or so of being in the fighting area. I knew from Ryn that the ones we fought and killed somehow gave us more essence than the ones dying around us, but that didn't mean we got nothing from the dying monsters all around.

I assigned my Attributes and chose my next attribute skill, Spark. Made the selection to slot it into my second skill slot, and instantly my mind filled with the knowledge of the skill and how to employ it. I looked at the others and mentioned they should check their status as well, since we still had two more switches before we hit the front line again.

"Check your status and pick your next skill," I said, looking mostly at Ryn and Tomas as the others already had their level 10 skills.

"We are, just gotta get it all locked in before they call for the switch," Ryn said, her eyes looking somewhere distant, the sign that they were interacting with the unlocked status menus.

"There, got it," Tomas said. "I chose Fast Hands. What'd you pick?"

"Spark, you?" I asked, looking to Ryn.

"Shove," she said, smiling. "This will help tremendously."

"Time to switch," Sel said, catching our attention as we all moved forward, ready to take our place.

During our time not paying attention, the monsters had switched to blue-skinned kobolds by the looks of them. They had ice claws and threw bolts of ice magic from a distance. One such distance attacker raised its claws, and I put my shield up, catching the magical bolt just in time. Then I pointed my sword, not necessary, but I felt like it helped me, and cast Spark on him.

A spark of lightning flung itself from the tip of my blade and struck the monster in the chest, wounding it but not bringing it down. These were higher-level monsters, and we needed to be careful against them. We didn't have the gear to be dealing with these monsters, so my shield would only take so much more before breaking.

Two hopped forward, and Sel and I brought our shields up just as Ryn pushed one with her Shove ability, knocking it into the other one and causing them to almost fall. Then Tomas arrived, smashing one in the head with a strike much faster than his normal, though I knew it would be his new normal speed with how the skill worked that he picked up.

Ashric struck the one I'd zapped, killing it as Jareth appeared and slashed at the other kobold. Blue blood soon wet the ground as we finished off the monsters and awaited another round of them.

This fighting went on for what felt like hours and hours, more people came to the gate, and our time in front began to feel less and less, but still we managed to fight here and there, even killing a zombie swarm that started to rise up from another lich raising our piles of undead. It was quickly dealt with, and the fighting resumed as normal into the night and then into the early morning.

Finally, as the late morning sun began to rise and monster bodies piled all around, it was now our full-time duty to help move corpses and not be in the rotation as monsters got too strong for us as time went on. We had two side streets and three alleys filled with monster bodies, and then, only after the Captain of the Guard showed up, did we break the monsters and make them flee.

He used a sword and called down golden light all around him, walking straight into the monster horde and outside the walls. He fought and slew what looked like a powerful demon waiting in the back of the horde, and when he did, they began to flee from him at all angles.

It was marvelous to watch, and if I weren't so exhausted, I'd check to see if I'd leveled up once more. A cheer rose up, and then the real work began. We had to move the bodies, along with all the others willing to help, outside the wall and begin the burnings. It was nearly dusk again by the time we finished, losing an entire two nights to the monster migration, where we could have been having fun at the festival.

I also knew that each of the gates had the same kind of activity going on, so the entire town had been fighting all night, so it wasn't like anyone had actually enjoyed the festival. I checked my status and was shocked at what I found.

After assigning my spare essence, I was up to level 12, almost 13. This was huge because I knew for a fact that the essence requirements went way up after level 10. I decided to spend my two new points in Power, leaving Speed as my final one to assign five points to. With my new Spark ability and now only 3 points away from getting yet another ability, I was truly on my way to becoming more powerful.

"Wish I'd had this new ability during the fight with Fen, I'd have really gotten ahead of the game then," I said to Tomas as he drew near.

We were all exhausted, but you wouldn't know it by looking at Tomas; he had found someplace to clean off and was snacking while the rest of us finished up the work of moving bodies.

"You did fine without it, but did you see how fast I can attack now?" Tomas said between bites.

"You're right," I said, touching the ring on my finger and glad for its help.

We'd suffered only minor injuries before they pulled us out of the rotation as monsters got too hard for us, but the ring had helped me recover without the use of a potion, like all the others had to take. It just took a little time, and with the horde of people helping now, I had the time.

"So," Ryn said, coming up to the pair of us. "Who is ready to go visit a bathhouse and soak our troubles away?"

I raised my hand, chuckling and turning to Tomas, who also had his hand raised.

"How are you so clean already?" I asked, and he just shrugged.

"Bath house?" Ashric asked. "Count us in, too!"

With that decided, we all migrated away from the burn piles and back into the city. From what I'd been told or overheard, we'd sent riders ahead of the monster swarm, some of our fastest and able-bodied riders, to warn of the early Monster Migration. It would do well to warn everyone, as the migration didn't normally happen for another month or so.

I also overheard that groups were being sent out to fight monsters that might have lingered, as well as to discover the fate of some of the smaller villages that were in the path of the migration.

"We could be one of the monster hunting groups, if we stayed close to home and had a clear path of retreat, even if we encountered something a bit too strong, we could escape," I suggested to the group, but I could tell before anyone spoke that the idea didn't sound good to them.

"Well," Ryn started to say, but Sel cut her off.

"Are you insane?" She asked. "The ones that will be left over will likely be stronger than the ones we faced at the gate. And if they are running in packs of any kind, we won't have time to retreat; we will just be dead."

"I might be able to get a few of us on a group with a more able-bodied group if my father has any say," Ashric said, shrugging. "Maybe we split the group down the middle and see if we can get on board with a more experienced group."

"That could work," I said, ditching my original and obviously risky plan for this new one. "We should hit up the Amber Coin Tavern and see what we can learn."

"After a visit to the bathhouse," Jareth said, and we all chuckled. He'd been hit by the worst of it and was literally covered in drying blood everywhere but his face, which he'd managed to wipe off.

"Yeah," I said. "After a visit to the bathhouse."

We arrived at the closest bathhouse to find it overrun by people, so we went to the one in the Forge Quarter, a lot closer to the commons than people preferred.

My pockets jingled from my portion of the monster cores we'd collected, good as silver moons once we sold them. But there would also be an influx of cores, so prices would drop. We'd be lucky to get a few silver moons per core at the rate I was sure they'd drop.

Either way, as we arrived and stripped down, delivering our items to the washer, I was careful to pull out my coin purse and a handful of cores, setting them aside on a square shelf area where you could leave items for an attendant to watch. It was common practice, and you didn't have to worry about thieves in this part of town, so I let my worry wash away with the filth as I joined my group in the hot waters.

We'd all seen each other naked a hundred times before, from bathing and working in the tower where we'd routinely have to strip one part or another to treat superficial wounds that didn't require a potion or special healing. It was to the point that it was almost mundane seeing Ryn strip bare naked, or Sel glare at everyone as she entered the waters. Jareth was the last to join us, and I kept my distance as he entered the waters because he was filthy with a capital F.

"Catch," I said, throwing him some of the scented hard bar of soap that they kept on the edge of the large pool.

The bathhouses were built to accommodate over a hundred people, at least this one was, with six separate baths, each one large enough that there was plenty of room after the six of us all got inside. Tomas and Ashric were off to the side, close at hand, whispering something to each other, while Ryn and Sel stayed close, helping each other wash.

That left Jareth and me to assist each other to reach the hard-to-find spots, and I didn't want to get close to him at the moment. So I scrubbed all around as best I could, then after about ten minutes, Ryn came over to me. She grabbed the soap roughly out of my hand and physically turned me away from her.

I watched as Sel did something similar with Jareth, helping him reach the hard-to-reach areas on his back. I stood and enjoyed the back scrub, feeling some of the filth being washed away as she worked. Blood was a funny thing; it seemed to get everywhere, even when you were wearing armor and clothes.

If someone could invent some self-cleaning or blood-repellent armor, I'd be all over that in a second.

"There, you are all clean," Ryn said. I turned to see her shaking her head at me. "Just wait till we are out in the wilderness, where our only option to wash ourselves will be streams and rivers, cold as ice."

I let myself sink deeper into the water and sighed. "I don't ever want to lose my hot baths, surely we will be out close to a civilization during our journey?"

"Doubtful. Maybe at first, but if we are going to get you strong enough, we will need to dive dungeons and find rare, hard-to-defeat monsters, making you tough enough to be a Dragon Knight. Then, of course, we will need to find a dragon, a feat no one has accomplished in countless years, at least on the mainland," Ryn said, sitting beside me and leaning on my arm a bit.

"You've heard the rumors, same as me," I said. "The dragons are used as a threat to those who sail still to this day. There are said to be islands infested with them, old and ancient things that have lost their minds to the curse of old age. I'll find and slay one of those, find myself a dragon's egg, and be the next great Dragon Knight."

"Shhh," Ryn said, looking around, but the bathhouse was filled with mostly randoms far enough away not to overhear us.

"No one is here to hear me," I said, remembering well the warning to keep my dreams of being a Dragon Knight to a minimum for my own safety.

"You have to be careful," Ryn said, splashing water at me playfully. "I can't keep you safe all the time. You might find yourself in more trouble than you can handle someday."

"Don't worry," I said, putting an arm around her and pulling her close. "I'll keep you safe."

She laughed and splashed me with more water, then pulled away. She stood fully erect, water dripping down her body, and motioned for me to follow. We all got out of the bath then, eager to get to the next leg of our journey as adventurers.

We were going to try and go hunt some monsters, one way or another.

CHAPTER 16
MONSTER HUNTS

After getting my clothes cleaned and washing off the monster cores, I put them back in my pocket and dressed in my armor. We'd been at the bath, despite how fast it felt, for nearly an hour. Enough time for all our armor and clothing to be cleaned and dried.

"You know it's fascinating how they do the cleaning and the drying," Ryn said, but Sel interrupted her before she could continue.

"Yes, I'm sure it's fascinating, but we need to hurry to the Tavern if we want a chance at a group. Ashric, why don't you go ahead and see if your father had a group we can join, just in case?" Sel said, pushing ahead and jogging toward the Amber Coin Tavern. We quickly followed after her as Ashric ran in a different direction to go find his father.

Because we jogged, we reached the tavern in no time flat, and it was bustling with activity. I saw listings being posted on the board and immediately taken off by group after group.

"At this rate, we will never get an assignment," I said, noticing that there was a line long enough that it nearly snaked out the door.

"Yeah, we are going to go see if Ashric had any luck," Sel said, clearly as confident as I was about finding a group in this mess, which was not at all.

We walked over to where a band was playing, adding a gentle melody to the cacophony of sound vibrating through the room. We were pretty close to them, but it was the only place to stand where people weren't constantly moving about.

"What are we going to do now?" I asked, and Tomas just shrugged, throwing some snacks into his mouth.

"We will find a group, we just have to get in line and wait it out like the rest of them. We don't even need a slip, really, but if we got one it would give us some direction and maybe some leverage to get a group. I'm getting in line," Ryn finally announced, leaving us and getting in line to get a monster hunting slip from the board.

"You need a group, how do you feel about a party of seven?" said a sweet melodic voice from behind me.

I turned to see a familiar group standing on the stage, playing a soft melody that seemed to fight against the harsh exchange of words and shouting in the room. It was almost as if they were calming the room, one note at a time.

"You are adventurers?" I asked, my eyes falling over the dark-haired girl and her sparkling green eyes. She had a mesmerizing way of looking at you, as if she was fully and totally interested in what I had to say.

"We are. The name is Granger, traveling bards and adventurers seeking glory wherever we end up!" she announced in her sweet sing-song voice.

"Yeah," said another behind her with shoulder-length brown hair and dark mysterious brown eyes. "We travel and inspire. But we are willing to take on you pups for a little extra juice when killing the monsters."

"Allow us to introduce ourselves," the woman said, bowing slightly as they continued playing a sweet melody the entire time, unbothered by the conversation and not losing concentration at all. "I am Torwyn, master of the shadows and singer of songs both melodic and terrible for my enemies to behold."

"Well met, Torwyn," I said, bowing slightly back to her, but never taking my eyes off her sparkling green eyes. Tomas cleared his throat and spoke next.

"I am Tomas. This guy here is Kaelric, and our third is Ryn. She's off getting us a mission brief," Tomas said, seemingly unaffected by Torwyn's beauty and the strange hold she had over me.

I bit my lip, hard, to snap myself out of it. I recalled tales of sirens that snared men with their beautiful songs, and I couldn't help but put her in that category, so easily she'd enthralled my mind. But I was back now, just in time for someone else in the band to announce themselves.

"I am Luke of the northern tribes, where we've got the vibes," Luke said, his voice as smooth as Torwyn's, but with a masculine gruff to it. "I bring down my axe just as hard when playing songs as when slaying monsters. That's Hunter, our hunter and tamer of wild beasts. He has currently tamed a squirrel, which he assures us will come in handy."

Luke rolled his eyes as he said this, and I got the impression he wasn't so confident that a squirrel could do much against monsters when the time came. I turned to the final member of the group, who inclined his head and spoke for himself.

"I am Daniel, master crafter," Daniel said, not adding any of the melodic tune to his words or expression in his chosen verbiage.

Hunter was blonde-haired, likely of the northern tribes, similar to

Tomas, but with friendly eyes and an easy smile. As I looked him over, he reached up and fed the squirrel on his shoulder.

Daniel, on the other hand, had a rugged appearance compared with the poise and finery the other three wore. He wore a cutoff shirt that exposed his stomach and arms. One arm was completely covered in metal and gears. I knew his leg was as well, because the left pant leg was cut off right below the crotch, leaving a bare, metallic leg pressing into the stage.

"Are you, uh," I started to say, gesturing to the arm and leg.

"Am I what?" Daniel asked, looking at me with a raised eyebrow. "Not all wounds will heal, as you probably know, but loss of limb can be corrected if you have the right tools and unlimited pain resistance. Not that it always hurts, but it sure isn't a walk in the park."

"So you replaced missing limbs with metal. How does that even work?" I asked, so confused at how he'd been able to pull off such an impressive feat.

"I'm a master craftsman, a master blacksmith, and a master enchanter, truth be told," Daniel said, shrugging as he continued playing the sweet melody on his strange lute that seemed to reverberate with sound much greater than it ought to with strings alone.

"He's our little genius," Torwyn said, shrugging as well. "We joke that someday he will replace his entire body with that metal machinery, but he insists that the head and what's inside is the one thing he hasn't been able to replicate."

"Machinery?" I asked, I'd heard the word before to describe pulleys and other simple mechanisms, but never something so complex as replacing an arm. "How do you attach it to your core? I mean, do your attributes affect your missing limbs anymore, or are you unbalanced?"

"Oh dear," Luke said, chuckling. "He's going to get Daniel on one of his rants; we'd better distract him before we get a full breakdown of how he connects his core with his contraptions."

They changed tempo on the music, and suddenly Daniel looked like he was concentrating to keep up on his lute with Luke's pace of playing. The music was a bit chaotic, really, but it had a nice ring to it that I couldn't get out of my head, even hours later.

Ryn appeared about an hour later with a note from the board.

"We are going to hunt down a lich," Ryn said, then, seeing the bards looking at her, she added. "Who are these guys?"

I did introductions and then asked the important question. "Are we strong enough to challenge a lich?"

"Depends," Torwyn said. "Liches come in all levels of power, from weak enough that you could take it on yourself, to strong enough that it would take a full group or even a raid full of level 40 plus adventurers to take them down, if not stronger. Which are we dealing with?" She posed her question to Ryn, who had a question in return.

"What level are all of you? We are level 12, but I'd like to think we punch above our weight class," Ryn said.

Torwyn smiled down at her from the small stage they stood on. "We are strong enough to help, let's just leave it at that for now," she said, smiling down at us as if she knew a secret we did not.

"Fine," Ryn said. "The lich should be really easy to kill. It was killed once already, but reports are coming in that it is reforming just east of the dungeon, outside of town. Should it be given enough time, it will grow rapidly in power and numbers, so we should hurry and take care of it. At its weakened state, it will have to have its phylactery with it, so it will be killable, but if we don't hurry, it might have time to hide it and then we will have to start over from square one."

"With all the dead monsters around and the additional ones being killed, this lich will have all it needs to build an army. So I agree with this beautiful young lady, we should get moving," Luke said, the music suddenly stopping and the din of the Amber Coin Tavern taking over and washing through us like an angry crowd.

With that, Luke moved some clamps over his lute, and held it by the neck as if it were an axe. Torwyn put her four-stringed odd lute that made much lower sounds than the others, away, and pulled out several daggers that she started placing all about herself. Daniel and Hunter did the same, putting their lutes away and pulling out weapons.

Hunter pulled out a bow and several arrows, as well as a curved sword that he wore around his waist. Meanwhile, Daniel pulled out something I'd never seen before.

It was a tube-like contraption with a downward curved handle. When I gestured to it, he gave me a name for it. "I call it a boomstick, not the most original name, but made of my design and able to use monster cores to shoot out charged energy similar to an Arcana blast."

"Neat," I said, not sure what else to say but fascinated by the weapon. "You must go through a lot of cores. I have some you can buy for cheap if you'd like?"

We haggled over price, and he bought at 3 silver moons a piece, all of our supply, including Ryn's and Tomas's. He fiddled with the nobs on his boomstick saying that he would be able to fire much higher concentrated shots with such a lucrative supply.

With that taken care of, the seven of us left the tavern and started toward the northern gate to seek out this lich.

"Lich's bout to get stitches," Luke said as we walked.

We all chuckled, and Torwyn began to sing as we walked, a slow, haunting melody. Soon Luke joined in, while Hunter tapped his bow in time on the cobblestone road and Daniel hummed low and deep, giving it a mystical sound as they worked together.

"Watch out, Lich, we're coming for you," I said, confident that we had it well in hand.

The scene shifted suddenly as we made our way out of the town and into the open fields surrounding it. Fog, unnatural and eerie, rolled in from the surrounding woods and in the direction we needed to go.

"Seems like someone is working some obscuring magic," Ryn said, looking at me with narrowed eyes.

"This might be a trickier assignment than we thought," Torwyn said, looking to her companions as we walked out and into the fog bank. "Stay close and don't lose each other."

"Take hands and interlock," I said, the fog growing so thick that I could barely see the person in front of me.

We did so, Ryn taking Torwyn's hand, and I took Ryn's and Tomas's. Hunter took the lead, seemingly unaffected by the lack of sight, as he walked sure-footed forward and into the unknown.

I felt the cool sting of the fog on my face, and I wondered how such a fog could be conjured midday with the sun out in full force, but I just put it away as one of the many mysteries of magic I didn't yet understand. Instead, I focused on my other senses as I walked.

My ears picked up movement here and there, but nothing came out to attack us. I felt pressure from the fog pushing in on me, and I smelt the undead stench of zombies nearby.

"I think we are getting close," I called out ahead, and we suddenly stopped dead in our tracks.

"He altered the lich," Hunter said.

"Torwyn, watch over Daniel while he tries to dispel this mess around us," Luke said, giving out commands left and right. "Newbies, get weapons ready and be careful not to attack friends over foes."

We kept our hands interlocked as we moved back-to-back against each other. The three of us knew how to fight well enough in a group, but with such low visibility, we had to rely on a different tactic, staying close enough to touch each other.

Hunter and Luke did something similar, not more than a person's distance from us, and I saw the outline of Torwyn and Daniel working a bit further away. Daniel was on the ground doing something, and Torwyn was in a low, fighter's stance, ready to defend him.

"Incoming!" Luke called out, and I strained my eyes to see what he was seeing, but I didn't manage it until the zombie was shambling right on top of me.

I cut out with my sword, careful not to hit anyone but the zombie, while catching the brunt of it on my shield. It went down from a stab into the eye from Ryn. A moment later, things got interesting as zombie after zombie appeared, surrounding us and slashing out with bone fingers and teeth, looking to sink into human flesh.

I mostly relied on my shield where I could, stabbing out when I could get a clean headshot, but suddenly everything changed mid-battle. The fog was pushed back some twenty paces, and in the center was Daniel fiddling with a little metal box.

"It'll hold for a while, let's clean these weaker mobs up and find ourselves a lich," Luke said, as the slaughter took on a new note since we could finally see.

Torwyn was like a whirlwind of death, her daggers slashing out and taking off heads as easily as stabbing them through the eye, each strike a killing blow. Meanwhile, Luke used his axe/instrument to cleave zombies into two, one strike at a time. I watched in awe when I could, fighting my own desperate battle against the zombie horde.

Hunter had a bow out, and his squirrel was somehow hurling nuts pulled from seemingly nowhere that exploded on contact with the zombies, not doing much damage but staggering a few as Hunter used his bow to kill them one at a time.

Daniel was the most interesting to watch; he didn't fire his boomstick just yet, instead using it as a bludgeoning tool, smashing in heads with his weapon and sometimes with his bare hands. Whatever strength his mechanical limb gave him, it was much greater than what would be considered normal. There was the chance he'd just raised his Power attribute up high enough, but it was more mystical to imagine he just artificially raised his Power level through his new limbs.

Tomas's staff whistled through the air as we fought; his new staff had metal coverings on the end, making it a far more effective bludgeoning weapon than it had been before. I hadn't asked where he'd gotten it or if it was magical, but he sure was having a great time smashing in heads.

Meanwhile, Ryn's daggers flashed out, her most effective weapon against the undead, seeing as she could just stab them in the eye deep enough and they'd die. My sword worked against me with the distance. They kept in so close against my shield that I was having issues getting a proper strike.

Then it hit me, I could strike with my magic now, so I slammed hard with my shield, knocking them back, and aimed as best I could at their heads, unleashing a Spark attack. It leaped off the edge of my blade and struck the closest head, exploding it in a spray of brains and viscera, which my shield only mostly stopped from covering everyone.

"That was gross," Ryn said, her words more indignant than usual. "Maybe don't explode their heads when we still need to try and find monster cores?"

She was right, there would be little chance of getting cores off the undead if I blew off their heads, however a crack of lightning later, and I saw the boomstick had a similar effect on the undead monsters. And they were monsters, I realized, mostly goblin undead zombies, but a mix of others like werewolves and such.

I watched as Daniel leveled his boomstick at the next zombie, an eight-foot-tall something, and exploded its entire head in a single shot.

"Nearly done, keep the momentum!" Luke shouted over the din of battle.

And he was right, of course, with only about five zombies left, the battle was won, it was just going to take a minute or so more. We broke formation, able to see clearly now and needing the space to fully employ our skills, attacking at full speed. We wanted to show these Granger folks that we had what it took, and I made sure to check to see they were watching as I stabbed a zombie full in the face, killing it.

However, my blade stuck fast on the hobgoblin zombie's face, almost knocking me off my feet as it lurched forward, dead as a doornail. With effort, I managed to free my blade, but by the time I did, the remaining four had been put down.

"Very smooth," Ryn said in a low whisper as she passed me by.

"Shut it," I said, not caring who heard me.

They shared a chuckle with Granger, and I just frowned over at them, playfully as I didn't really care that I'd missed the last few, having killed plenty.

"Let's hurry and collect cores before we find the Lich. I'm thinking it'll have only a few stronger undead with it. I'm willing to bet it sent all it had raised at us already," Luke said, taking command once more. His instrument dripped with gore and blood, but with one hardy flick of his wrist, most of it fell clear, and suddenly he was adjusting the neck, releasing the strings to the air once more.

He played a gentle melody while the rest of us worked to collect cores, a dirty and bloody work, but it paid off with almost all of them having cores that could be harvested. It was no wonder, though, from what I understood about undead and raising them, they required cores to be raised, except for undead skeletons, which were raised by the lich's magic in a temporary manner that required nothing but raw material.

It also meant skeletons were the worst kind of monsters to fight, as they didn't drop cores that could be collected and sold. Even so, I heard the shambling of bones nearby and knew we'd be fighting some soon.

Swords didn't work great against skeletons, but we had Tomas with us to break bones with each strike, so I wasn't too worried about being effective. Plus, I could use Spark if I wanted, assuming it didn't create too much shrapnel in the process of them dying.

When the cores were picked up, the music stopped, and Daniel collected his small metal box, stepping forward. I saw the fog stayed exactly twenty paces away from the center of the box he carried. Some sort of enchanted magical box that pushed back the fog? Interesting to say the least.

"How does it work?" I asked, saddling up to Daniel as we walked toward the sound of the undead bones.

"It's complicated and technical, I'm afraid a laymen won't be able to understand," Daniel said, shrugging when I gave him a 'surely you are kidding' look.

"How long have you been enchanting and uh, smithing I guess?" I asked, determined to figure out how this man, who looked no older than me, maybe a few years older, had knowledge so vast on a subject that was guarded and kept secret from most.

"Since I could hold a wrench and a quill," Daniel said. "My father was an engineer and my mother an enchanter, so I had first-class teaching from the moment I could speak and understand."

"Engineer?" I asked, the word was familiar as I'd heard it a few times, but I didn't know its meaning.

"Yeah, basically an advanced blacksmith and crafter all mixed into one," Daniel explained, and I nodded along.

"I'd like to learn," I said, expressing my desire to understand some of the mysteries of magic that normal folks could tap into. If it could do all manner of things like push back fog and explode zombie heads, surely it was worth studying.

"Maybe someday, kid, but right now I'm not taking any apprentices," Daniel said, raising the box as the fog suddenly started to shrink in around us. "I need to change the core; the pressure is getting worse, so we must be close."

Suddenly, the fog slammed in around us, but only for a moment before pushing out roughly fifteen paces as he snapped the top shut on his box, having changed the cores out.

"I can sense it," Hunter said in a low whisper to Luke that we all barely heard. "Due nort,h about a hundred paces, it has a small army of skeletons and two stronger risen monsters. I'd say put the newbies on the skeletons, and we can handle whatever it has risen and the lich."

"We are just as able," Ryn began to say, but I held up a hand.

"It's fine, Ryn, let's kill the skeletons and then we can join them in the fight against the lich. We work together, that is the plan," I said, and everyone nodded.

"Daniel, break a line in the skeletons with your contraption and then provide support by keeping the Lich busy while we deal with whatever it raised to fight us, got it?" Luke said, and Daniel nodded. "Try to keep the attention of all the skeletons, will you? I don't wish to be stabbed in the back."

"We've got it," I said. "Any idea how many skeletons?"

We'd fought a great many in the tower; they tended to swarm in groups of five to ten, but even so, if you handled them right it wasn't too much to worry about. That was with a group of six, and we numbered only three now, but I was still confident that we could take care of it.

"A dozen," Hunter said. "Maybe less, it's hard to tell from this distance."

"Let's move, swift and deadly," Torwyn said, smiling as she cracked her neck to the side.

Her smile was infectious, and soon I realized we were all smiling along with her, ready to do what needed to be done. We ran forward, with Hunter in the lead, approaching the skeletons at speed.

They came into view a moment later, and Daniel fired a powerful shot from his boomstick, killing three skeletons at once and creating a hole through which they ran, leaving us to clean up what remained, nearly fifteen more skeletons.

Luckily, these were the weakest of skeletons, only a couple even having weapons, while the others were just using slightly clawed fingertips. I slammed my shield into a group of three, slashing down hard to try and break bones. Tomas appeared on the flank and shattered two skeletons at once.

Glancing over to the other group, I saw them fighting two strange-looking undead. One was tall and seemed to be wearing a coat of flesh and a top hat. That made its great height seem even more daunting, while the other was a wrinkled, fleshy thing with claws and bug eyes; it moved incredibly fast compared to the other undead.

Both were being cut and battered back, while a cloaked figure of pale flesh and green glowing eyes chanted in the background, undeterred by the fight going on around it.

A skeleton got a lucky slash across my cheek as we fought, and I shifted my attention back to the fight at hand. With five skeletons down, we were already shifting the tide of battle. The biggest advantage here was that only so many skeletons approached us at a time; they weren't mobbing us as I'd expect them to, but were attacking in groups of three.

It made it easy for us to deal with them, killing groups of three in a matter of ten seconds or so. My Spark proved to be effective as well, killing one each time I could cast it. By the time we worked our way through the group, I heard a scream of pain from the other group and saw that Torwyn had her stomach slashed open by the smaller undead and was holding herself together with a bloodied hand.

Her other free hand went to her pouch, and I saw her down a potion in one fluid motion, before grabbing her dagger from where it fell. She was back in the fight, one hand holding her guts together and the other slashing out violently.

We reached them just as she cut the head off the smaller of the two undead, and Luke managed to cleave the legs off the larger undead, with Daniel putting a finishing shot into its face.

"You dare interrupt the powerful Lich of L...," the Lich began to say, but was interrupted as half his face was blown away by Daniel's boomstick. His lower jaw and tongue sort of just hung there as he looked at Daniel and his contraption with wide eyes.

"It's newly formed, so its phylactery will be attached to its center, likely behind the spine or where its heart should be," Luke said, gesturing with his axe to commence the attack.

To say we cut down the Lich with ease would be an understatement. Together, we unleashed so much damage on it that, phylactery or not, I didn't see this thing coming back alive. I used Spark; Hunter unleashed glowing arrows of sparking red; Ryn threw a blade at it; Tomas smashed into its flank with his staff; just as Luke and Torwyn cut into it from the other side.

In a few words, it was a quick death.

We found its core, or what was left of it, after we finished stomping it to a pulp. The lich had transformed its own core, once human and Unlocked, to gain greater power, so its core resembled a fist-sized marble instead of the normal, smaller core most beings had. It was cracked and broken, but Daniel insisted on cracking it apart into dust before he would be satisfied.

"Well, that wasn't too bad," I said, as a sudden howl filled the area.

"Looks like we have company," Luke said. "We'll let you all take care of the wolves, just scream if you need any assistance."

So we readied ourselves as a pack of half a dozen wolves entered the clearing, their eyes glowing red, with a tall werewolf standing in the back, not engaging in the combat at first. We fought the wolves using our new abilities and found that we were much more effective than we'd been before.

Just as we finished the final wolf, the werewolf stepped up, but then its head exploded as Daniel unleashed his weapon one final time for the night.

"Sorry," he said. "He looked like he might give you trouble."

"No worries," I said, checking my status and seeing I'd gotten full essence from it anyway. Whatever level these guys were, they weren't high enough to impede the collection of essence, a real problem when fighting alongside too many or too-high-level individuals.

We returned to the city, eager to collect our reward and pick up a new mission if we could convince Granger to stick around for another go.

CHAPTER 17
LOOKING FOR GEAR

It turned out that no more missions were being listed, so many people got into the action that they were all taken care of, and the area around the city was secured once more. We mentioned that we'd killed an alpha werewolf and a pack of monster wolves, so they threw in an extra silver for each of us.

My wealth was far and above anything I'd ever imagined as an adventurer, but still, I knew I had more coming my way if I kept up the life. Besides that, I needed to find some magical weapons and a shield, if I could, and that would be costly. My entire golden sun coin would likely be eaten up, as well as much of my silver, if I truly wanted magical equipment, which I did.

We bid farewell to Granger, promising to come see them at the festival tonight when they played at the grand pavilion, along with a lineup of many bards, none as cool as Granger, I was willing to wager.

"That was an interesting adventure," Ryn said, watching Granger walk into the distance. "They are an interesting group."

"I think they are epic," I said, wishing I'd gotten more information out of Daniel about how he could do so many impossible things with crafting and enchanting.

"They scare me," Tomas said, snacking on some dried fruit from a bag that I hadn't seen him get. "Like, they are unbelievably powerful, and yet I don't think they are that much higher level than us. By the way, has anyone else hit level 14?"

I checked my status, and sure enough, I had the essence to reach 14, so I did so. Leaving me with only 45 essence to spare. I was surprised at how quickly we appeared to be leveling, but I wasn't complaining. There was nothing quite like a monster migration to fuel your progression. But as the essence requirements rose, I knew greater levels would be even harder to master, since the monster essence you got didn't scale up as fast as the level requirements.

It was common knowledge that even levels 15 to 20 were a hurdle, but 20 to 40 was a year-long endeavor, with each new level introducing harder and more deadly monsters. There was a reason why so many retired before or around level 30 to 40; it just wasn't worth the risk after a certain point. I didn't have that mindset, but I knew many who did, including Ana.

We weren't likely to get much more experience in and around this area, with the average monster level being closer to 25 to 45, so we'd need to do our own little migration. Even the dungeon here was a level 40 dungeon, one that was used by only the more experienced adventurers or clear-out teams from House Deymorin. It would be some time before we could return and benefit from this area.

With that weighing on my mind, I turned to my group and made a suggestion. "Should we go enjoy the rest of the festival? I'm ready to drink and eat until I explode," I said, smiling widely as Tomas and Ryn both nodded along with my words.

"Hell ya," Tomas said. "I wonder if I get any discounts for winning the two food competitions?"

"If anything, I think the food vendors will be afraid of you," Ryn said.

"Why's that?" Tomas asked.

"Because you'll eat them dry," she said, laughing out loud.

"Here's to eating them dry," I said, pulling out my waterskin and taking a deep drink.

We moved toward the middle of town, eager to get our eat and drink on.

Along the way, we bumped into Ashric, Sel, and Jareth, just returning from some hunt or another, still in their armor, like us, but looking much more worn out.

"Find a hunt?" Tomas asked, and Ashric nodded.

"Yeah," Ashric said. "We cleared out a den of werewolves. There were literally like a dozen of them, and twice as many wolves there."

"We killed a lich," Tomas said, a bit of pride in his voice.

"No way?" Sel asked, surprised. "All by yourselves, or did you find a group after all?"

"We found a group," I said. "But we did a lot of the work ourselves."

"We did a fair amount," Ryn said. "But without their help, we never would have found the Lich."

"Whoa," Ashric said. "That's way cooler than what we did. Good job, guys!"

"We are about to go eat and drink ourselves silly. Want to come?" I asked, and they exchanged a look.

"Yeah, we can do that," Sel said. "We were going to clean up some more, but I'm all for just drinking away the night."

"Cool," I said, as they joined us on our walk to the food area and where the music would be played in front of the great tower.

We separated for a bit to grab the food we each wanted most, then gathered and ordered a round of drinks. We sat at one of the community tables and stuffed ourselves full while drinking pint after pint of ale.

I was more than satisfied as the night wore on. Music played, and I forgot my troubles. Sometime during the night, the dancing portion of the evening began, and I found Ana. We danced into the night, having missed the day we wanted to dance, so we made up for it by spending the rest of the night together on the dance floor.

It was a great evening, filled with fun, love, and pure enjoyment. It helped that Granger was playing a large portion of the night; their music had an electrifying sound to it that made you want to move.

The night ended for me when the morning sun reached over the horizon, and the music finally stopped for the night. I went home alone, needing to change and sleep as I was exhausted.

The dreams returned that night, and I slept through the night with images of dragon riders, fire, and mayhem. Besides all that, I woke refreshed and ready for the day.

***

The next few days went by in a blur. We looked for work but found precious little that fit our level. Everything was assigned to the level 25 or above bracket, and Granger sort of disappeared from the festival, missing their last event, so we had no way to contact them to see if they wanted in on the latest challenge. The festival ended, and I didn't find any decent sword or shield during the event, so I decided to go look at a few shops today and see what I could find.

Of course Gallywot's Emporium was the first place I checked, moving through the city toward my destination. Ryn was off with some guard buddies, earning a few extra coin while she could, and Tomas had ditched me to hang out with his friend Ashric. So I was alone, but determined to find something of value.

The shop came into view a few minutes later. It was a strange building, to be sure, with its white and black bricks alternating every other one. I tried not to look too long, as it disturbed my eyes, but soon enough I was through its massive door and into the shop itself.

Mr. Gallywot himself called out greetings to me from the back of his ramshackle store. It truly was a mess, but he seemed to have an order to it, so I decided I'd start by asking him. He waddled up the aisles toward me. I was his only customer this early in the day, or perhaps his store was always empty; I didn't rightly know, as the few times I'd come it had been empty.

"Greetings, Master Grimholt," Gallywot said, bowing a little as he reached me. "What can I assist you with today?"

"I'm actually looking for two specific items," I said, not wasting words. "An enchanted shield and sword, I need something that will take a beating for the shield, I'm tired of getting mine split down the middle, and a sword that could cut just about anything would be a nice addition."

"Oh, very nice, very nice, and where do you think you'll find such rare enchanted items?" he asked, surprising me a little.

"Well, I was hoping from your shop," I said, bewildered.

"Ah, I see," he said, nodding and scratching at his chin. "Well, I think I can help on one of those, but the other, well, I don't have any enchanted blades as of right now."

"But you might have a shield that will interest me?" I asked, my excitement growing. "How much would it cost and what does it do?"

"Unfortunately, it is a bit pricey, at fifty Silver moons, it's a bargain I guarantee you, but as to its effects, I have them written down by the item, give me a moment to fetch them both from the back," he said, waddling back to the place he'd been before behind the counter. Then disappearing to the back a moment later.

He came back with a round shield, painted red and slightly smaller than the one I used now, but still big enough to provide the kind of protection I was looking for. He waddled over to me and set the shield down on the floor, before handing over a sheet of paper with the stats of the item on it.

Name: *Barkiron Shield*
Rarity: *Uncommon*
Special Properties: *Reduces incoming blunt damage by 10%.*
Description: *Crafted from hardened oak layered with iron strips, the shield has a rustic yet reliable sturdiness. Popular among caravan guards and young adventurers, it offers just enough reinforcement to turn aside heavy club strikes without weighing down the arm.*

"Simple yet reliable," he said as I finished reading over it. "You will find it is sturdy enough to take a great many blows and last you well into the lower parts of level 20 or perhaps well into the mid 20s level-wise."

"I'll take it," I said, without any hesitation. "This is just the thing I am looking for!"

"Great!" he said, grabbing the shield and waddling back to the back.

I followed him and he sold me the shield for the requested amount, leaving me without my golden sun coin any longer, but with about sixty-seven silver moons worth of coin. It was much less than I wanted to have, but still a fortune compared to what I'd had before becoming an adventurer.

Moving swiftly, I exited the shop and went in search of a place to buy a decent sword. Not that the one I had wasn't decent, it just lacked any enchantments that I knew of. So as I moved through the Forged Quarter, I found a weapons shop and entered.

They had nothing I could afford. The cheapest enchanted sword was a gold sun and a half, and only the regular weapons were priced low enough that I could spend any coin buying them. I found this to be true at each of the shops I tried to buy from. Only Gallywot's was affordable; the rest expected you to have more gold than I cared to imagine.

I accepted the fact that I wasn't getting a sword today and moved on to other tasks that required my attention, like finding out when the next caravan leaving town would be and where they were off to.

We truly had two options when trying to leave the town. We could take a barge and try to convince them we could serve as protection, getting quickly downstream to one of the more major cities, or we could take a caravan. I was leaning toward the caravan because the barge would take us to cities with higher-level monsters and dungeons, not really what we were looking for.

However, if we got into a caravan heading west, we'd go into what were considered beginner areas for all new adventurers. The monsters were a tad weaker, and the dungeons hadn't developed past level 10 to 25. One town in particular caught my eye when looking over maps in the library with Ryn.

Stonehaven was a town built around a rocky out crop, giving it extreme defensive abilities but also it was near a trio of dungeons each a little more difficult than the last. If we could find a caravan heading that way then we'd truly be able to get our start. The biggest problem with that though, is it was roughly two weeks walk away through monster infested lands, maybe longer if attack slowed you down.

Unsure where to find this information, I went to the Amber Coin Tavern to seek assistance. It didn't take me long to get there, the sun shining and the birds chirping along the way had me in a cheery mood. I entered in and went to the desk where the lady behind the counter looked up at me.

"Serif," I said, recognizing the mousey nosed girl with big eyes. "I wonder if you are the right person to ask."

"About what?" she asked, looking down at a leger in front of her before returning her gaze to me.

"I'm interested in a job of sorts, but specifically I'm looking for any caravans that might be leaving west toward Stonehaven," I said, watching her expression for any signs of hope that it might be something she had information about.

"Hmm, I'd have to check the job postings, but I think I remember something about several dozen guards needed for a westward trip. Give me a few minutes. It might be that I haven't posted them yet because it isn't due to leave for another few weeks," Serif said, disappearing into a book she pulled out from below her desk.

I waited, watching adventurers come and go from the board, but none coming up to Serif to claim the jobs. After about five minutes I excused myself to look at the board while she searched.

There were several listings up, but all still had higher-level suggested requirements. I couldn't find any low level ones at all at first glance, but on my second look through I found a job we might be able to pull off. It was a peculiar job, as it wasn't just a go kill a bunch of monsters per say, but rather a mystery they needed solved that the town guard hadn't gotten around to dealing with.

The job was titled Grain Thieves, and it had to do with just that. Grain was going missing right out of the warehouses on the docks meant to store it between barge runs down the river. They'd posted guards, but they were all younger folk, and down to the last, they were found sleeping instead of keeping watch.

They went to the guards, so the report says, and they said they are working on it. That was weeks ago, and grain continues to go missing. So now they made an adventurer's guild posting, offering six silver if you caught the people responsible, or two silver a day to merely watch over the grain and keep it safe. Either way, it would give us something to do; the only issue was that it was an overnight kind of situation, Tomas and Ryn might not like that.

I could always take on the challenge myself, but if I encountered either monster or man, I might find myself outmatched if they were at any level above 25. Serif caught my eye as I glanced over to her, and I left to go speak with her once more.

"I've found it. I searched through the next few weeks, but nothing turned up. I was planning to post it in three weeks because they intend to leave two weeks after that. So, five weeks from now, there's a caravan heading west, just before Stonehaven, but deep into the newb zones, so you could complete the rest of the journey with your party. You're traveling with a party, right?" Serif asked suddenly, sounding concerned.

"At least three of us, maybe six if I can convince the others to come," I said, and she relaxed a little bit.

"Good, good, any other jobs I can sign you up for?" she asked, before putting a piece of paper before me so I could sign up for the caravan as a guard, giving my level and how far into the trip I'd be willing to stay. I signed up first, but hesitated to sign up the rest of the party, deciding it was worth asking them to sign up themselves.

"The others will be by to sign up. How many guards are they wanting? Do you know?" I asked, seeing that another six people were already signed up, much higher level than us by their own indication.

"They wanted a mix of levels and up to twenty guards, if possible. From what I remember, the caravan will consist of over three dozen wagons and a dozen or so people, none of whom want to be bothered by monsters along the way, so they want a decent contingent of adventurers willing to do the work. The lower your level, the crappier the work you'll get, but it'll get you where you're going," Serif said, her eyes twinkling a little as she spoke.

"Alright, could I also get a copy of the grain thieves job? I want to give it a go," I said, and she nodded, pulling out her book and giving me a copy of the job description.

> *Job: Grain Thieves*
> *Rank: [Common]*
> *Location: Brackenford Docks – Riverside Warehouses*
> *Details: Several grain shipments have gone missing overnight. Warehouse owners report that younger dockhands, tasked with guarding the stores, are always found asleep come morning—unharmed but unable to explain why they dozed off. The city guard is too occupied with larger threats to investigate such "minor matters."*
> *Objective: Discover who or what is behind the thefts and put an end to the grain losses. Return with proof that the culprit has been dealt with.*
> *Reward: 6 Moons (2 Moons for each night you can keep the grain protected and not stolen, even if a culprit isn't found.)*
> *Notes: Merchants are growing restless, claiming their livelihoods are at risk, but they aren't willing to pay out big just yet, which means it's not likely anyone will pick up this job.*

"I'm surprised you think that job is worth your time, but I can imagine being lower level in a town like this offers very few paths to advancement. Too bad the monster migration didn't last longer, you might have been able to grind your way to level 20 and been just low enough to attempt some jobs around here," Serif said, chuckling. "But level 14 isn't a bad haul for having just gotten Unlocked. You'll find it slows down a bit after 20, especially if you just defeat monsters around your level. Have you tried studying for essence yet? I know it's slower, but it does provide a few hundred a day if you have nothing else to do."

"You can earn essence outside of killing monsters?" I asked, confused.

"Sure, tell me you didn't think killing things was the only way to get stronger. You can craft, read, study; it all draws in essence naturally from around you, but at such a slow rate that it's rarely considered a viable option by anyone but the most devoted academics," Serif said, explaining something I'd never heard of.

"How could I have never heard of this?" I asked, confused.

"It's no secret, if that's what you're getting at. It's just common knowledge, something no one talks about because so few people do it or rely on it as their main way to grow stronger," Serif said, shrugging.

I watched her for a second, trying to determine if she was pulling one over on me, and decided that perhaps she was. I'd ask Ryn about it, and I knew she'd give it to me straight.

"Alright," I said, shrugging back at her. "I'll take your word for it. I'm heading off for now."

"See you!" Serif said, her voice bubbly.

CHAPTER 18
WAREHOUSE TROUBLE

I found Ryn in the mid-afternoon and immediately asked her my question.

"Can you earn essence without killing monsters?" I asked, it had been bugging me, so it was literally the first thing to come out of my mouth as she approached me from across the road.

"Yeah, but it's not very effective," Ryn said. "Why do you ask?"

"Because somehow I had no idea, why didn't anyone tell me this? I'd have been studying this entire time or something to try to get more essence," I said, flabbergasted.

"And you'd have gotten jack squat for your efforts. True study of a topic takes many steps and focus before you begin to pull in essence. You'd be better off trying to learn a craft. They pull in at a steady but slow pace just by learning and discovering what to do next with an item or enchantment," Ryn said, giving me a coy look.

"Wonder how much it would cost to try and learn some trade while we wait for the caravan," I said, then remembering I hadn't told her about it, I laid out what I'd learned and how it would be leaving here in roughly a month's time, far longer than we'd hoped, but exactly in the direction we wanted.

"Well, well, well, I'll go sign up right away. Did you find any jobs while you were there? If we have a month left, we really should try to get jobs to keep the essence coming in. That, or we need to start studying how to withdraw essence from monster cores," Ryn said, chuckling at what she said.

"You can do that?" I asked, surprised there was another thing I just didn't seem to know.

"Enchanters can, or so I've read, but most enchantments today use monster core dust or full monster cores. That means the essence is pulled directly from the cores, and none escapes to empower you," Ryn said, shrugging.

"You see what you can learn about that, because that would really come in handy, we could buy our way up to higher levels, why wouldn't everyone do this?" I asked, and she shrugged again.

"I don't have all the answers, but I'm guessing it's a hard process that takes study and commitment, so only those truly committed will take that path," Ryn said, speculating on the nature of it. "I also imagine coin versus amount of essence is pretty low, so it would be the most expensive way possible to level up when you could just go kill monsters with a higher level adventurer, but not too high, and get a majority of the essence."

"I guess that makes sense. I'd still say see what you can learn, but I found a job for us as well. It isn't great, but it'll pay a little, and maybe we will find monsters to kill to level up," I said, looking around the street and noticing Tomas walking our way. "Hey, there's Tomas!"

Pulling out the job posting, I shared it with Ryn and explained the caravan and the job to Tomas, letting him see it next.

"A month?" Tomas asked in a groan. "Talk about a bummer. We would be stagnant for an entire month before we can go level up some more? And this job doesn't seem like it's worth the loss of sleep, does it?"

"Coin is coin," I said, shrugging. "If you both aren't interested, I might try to do it solo, but I'd really appreciate it if at least one of you joined me."

They looked at each other, and Ryn spoke first. "I've got a gig for the next month if I want it, working as a guard. I'd suggest you take the job with him, Tomas. With two Unlocked in place, I doubt the thieves will even come, so you'll get paid a silver a day for your time, which isn't a bad wage at all."

"I wonder how long they'll pay it before assuming the threat is taken care of?" I asked, looking to Tomas to see if he'd be joining me.

He sighed and shook his head. "You are really messing me over with this, but I'll go," he said, stomping a foot as he spoke and rolling his neck to pop it.

I could tell by his actions that he wasn't really feeling it, but I was glad to have him along. If both of us ended up sleeping, then something nefarious was surely going on. But if we stopped the thefts by our mere presence, then all the better for our coin purses.

A cloud bank moved in as we stood there talking, and it made me realize something. If we waited a month, we'd be dealing with storms and perhaps even snow during the caravan. I wondered why they wanted to travel in such bad conditions. It might make more sense to just leave this week.

"You think the caravan will be all right on the road heading west if the storms pick up early? I've even seen snow that early in the year," I said, expressing my doubt about the timing they'd chosen.

"I'm sure they know what they are doing. It is odd timing, though; it almost would have aligned with the normal monster migration if they'd kept to the time and hadn't arrived early. I wonder if that was done on purpose or because of incompetence?" Ryn asked, looking at us with a skeptical expression.

"Who is running the caravan?" Tomas asked, but I hadn't actually looked, so I just shrugged.

"I'm not sure," I said. "But when you go down there to sign up, you should check."

"Sure, sure," Tomas said. "Let's go get some food and drink, I'm starving."

"Alright," I said, and we moved as a single unit to the closest tavern, the Ram's Head Tavern. It was a small place with decent food and very good drinks. A sign of a ram's head on a wooden shield hung over the door. The door was made of dark-stained oak, and the moment we pushed it open, the sound of the patrons inside filled our ears.

The smell of meats and stews filled my nostrils. My eyes adjusted to the dimmer light inside, and we entered just as thunder pealed from outside, speaking of a rainy night. Sure enough, before the door swung closed, rain hammered on the rooftops and the street below. This time of year, such occurrences were common, so I was not even a little surprised as we found a table and sat.

"I'll go to the bar and order for us, you guys want the stew I'm guessing, and to keep the drinks coming?" Tomas asked, then added. "Oh, and I'm going to get the bread rolls too, the kind they serve with the cinnamon butter. So damn good."

Then he went to the bar to place our order and pointed to the table we were at. The barkeep, a burly man with a bushy beard, nodded his head and walked into the back to give the order to the cook, no doubt.

Within minutes, we had warm bread and special butter to melt all over it. The tastes were amazing, and for once, we were all silent as we ate. Then the drinks arrived and we drank our fill, with the stew arriving shortly after.

We joked and spoke of lighter things before our conversation took a turn.

"You think the others will want to go to Stonehaven?" Tomas asked, and I knew he was mostly worried about Ashric not going; they were close friends after all.

"I think we can ask them and try to explain why it is a good idea, but in the end, they'll make whatever decision they want," I said, shrugging.

"I don't know if they will wait that long, with Ashric's family connections, he might be able to get to a town faster and start leveling up," Ryn said, sipping at her drink.

"Maybe I should try to cash in some favor with old Lord Ravenlock,"

Tomas said. "I wonder if he'd bring us with him whenever he takes Ashric to wherever he'll go to train?"

"We can make it on our own," I said, not wanting the help of a House to get on my feet, despite having already received gifts from them. I was no one's fool, and I knew favors like that had strings attached. If we weren't careful, we'd find ourselves forever entangled in their webs.

"I know," Tomas said, shrugging. "It's just, I'm so used to having Ashric around, I can't imagine being without him."

"I'm pretty sure Sel and Jareth are going to go their own way as well, so the Lantern Guard is probably dead. It's time to think about Oathbound and how we will make our mark on this world," Ryn said, her words reverberating with me, not so much Tomas.

"So we are going with that name then?" I asked, and Tomas and Ryn both nodded. "Cool, I like it. I'll toast to that!"

We clinked our glasses together and took a long pull to commemorate our new name and mission. We'd go forth and follow our oaths, becoming the most powerful adventurers this world has ever seen, together.

The rest of the night wore on as the rain filled the streets with water before running off into the sewers. Tomas and I were scheduled to report to the warehouses, so we made our way there, slightly inebriated and ready to work for the next six to eight hours.

***

The warehouses were all lined up in the Commons area between the River Quarter and the Commons. We found, by asking around a bit, the right person to talk to, and, seeing as we were fully geared, he seemed to take us seriously despite our still rather youthful appearances.

"Name's Drew. You the best they got, eh?" he asked upon seeing us. Nodding his head along with his own words, he continued before we could speak. "Very well, let me show you to the string of warehouses. It'll be these six here that have been getting pilfered."

He led us to the front of a massive warehouse filled with boxes of various items and bags of grain. Then pointed down the lane to five other massively built-out warehouses.

"You want us to guard all that?" Tomas asked, a little dumbfounded.

"Sure do," he said. "Remember the deal, if nothing is stolen, I'll pay you two silver, but I'll give you six when you catch whoever is responsible."

He went on to tell us which had been burgled last and how it seemed to be random which one they targeted, but there was only a side door, which was chained shut, and a massive opening door, which had been locked but not chained shut, and was also found open during each of the burglaries.

"We will see what we can do," I said, unsure how the night would go but willing to give it a try. "We can take turns watching the front of the buildings while the other patrols around them. Between the two of us, we ought to catch sight of anything coming or going."

"Don't care how you do it, just get it done," the man said, before turning and leaving us to the job. Drew was a burly and short man, but I couldn't help but think that if one of his crew, all probably retired adventurers, stayed up, they'd be likely to find the culprit. I shared my theory with Tomas, and he disagreed.

"Almost down to the last, dock workers are the younger, not Unlocked folks doing the work. I mean, you know a little bit about that with the work you've done, haven't you ever wondered why everyone was around your age?" Tomas asked, and he was right, if I thought about it I saw maybe one in twenty that wasn't a young man or woman, and even so, they were normally in positions of power over the younger workers.

"I guess I never thought about it," I said. "What do they do if they are working all day, they are missing out on training at the tower."

"Loads of people get unlocked after only barely setting foot into the tower, basically anyone that lives in the Commons," Tomas said, then biting his lip. "Besides you, of course."

"Don't pretend like I don't realize, after all this time, that it was my friendship with you that got me sponsored to join Velric's group. I'm thankful for it, I can't imagine how unprepared I'd have been otherwise," I said, acknowledging his help in my training.

"Enough about that," Tomas said. "Who is taking the first watch and who is patrolling?"

"I'll do first watch if you want to patrol, then we can wait an hour before patrolling again," I said, my plan already laid out. I was sure that if someone was going to steal, it wouldn't be in the early evening, but rather deep into the night when everyone would be asleep.

So Tomas took off at a slow pace, hand on his weapon, walking down each lane and checking the doors were held fast, which they were. I stared out into the water that flowed swiftly and wondered if whoever was stealing was loading it on a barge of their own, or how they managed to empty out enough to get noticed by the dock merchants.

The quiet remained, as this part of town was completely abandoned at night. The closest pub was a hearty five-minute walk away if you hurried. Even so, I thought I could hear something in the wind, a calling of sorts, though I couldn't place it.

Instead, I just watched the water flow by and tried not to get too bored. After about an hour, I felt myself dozing off, and Tomas still hadn't returned, so I shook my head to clear it and decided to go see where he'd gotten off to. But just then, he came around an alley and gave me the scare of my life.

I jumped, more than I cared to admit, and I may have shouted a tiny bit in surprise. All that is to say, I was getting bored and maybe slightly scared of being alone in what felt like an abandoned part of the town. So I was glad to have Tomas back.

"Sorry, I thought I saw something, and I gave chase, but it turned out to be nothing," Tomas said. "So I'm back. Find anything?"

"Not a thing," I said, wishing that we'd have some action so I could get some more essence and not be tempted to fall asleep.

"Well then, I guess it's time to chat it up for an hour before you go off to patrol," Tomas said, and we did just that, chatting about Ana, the caravan, and all manner of other topics. Tomas gave me a hard time about Ana, but I knew he was only teasing. She'd be missing me soon, as I spent every one in three nights over with her, but I'd have to explain that I had a job that took up my time until the time came that we caught whoever was responsible.

The night wore on, and nothing appeared. I did my patrol, saw and heard no one. All the doors remained shut, but I did sneak up on Tomas, who was nearly asleep when I returned, and gave him a good fright.

"I don't know why, but being here alone makes me tired as hell," Tomas said. "I truly almost fell asleep, and I swear I hear some singing out on the river."

"I heard that too," I said. I hadn't mentioned it because I thought it was nothing, but since we both heard it now, perhaps it was time to explore and see what we could find. The lake was covered by a thick blanket of fog, and the rain fell lightly and breezily around us. Not enough to drench us, but my scarf was definitely soaking it all in.

The night wore on, and we decided not to separate again, making for an eventful time of talking and patrolling up and down the front of the warehouses. The soft whisper of song continued on the wind, but where it was coming from was anyone's guess. Daylight came faster than I'd expected, and with it, the dock bustled to life. We collected our 2 silver, gave a brief report that we found nothing, and went our way for the day.

We continued on like this, sleeping a good portion of the day away before returning at night to hear the songs of the river, until finally I'd had enough on the seventh day. We'd managed to find no additional jobs or ways to earn essence the entire week, putting us behind everyone else. Our presence kept whatever had stolen from the warehouses at bay, but I wanted to know why. I told Tomas as much, and we ventured close to the waterline, where the singing seemed to be coming from.

This night in particular was a bad night to make such a choice; the fog had come in hard, and the night washed over us like a blanket, obscuring our view and making it difficult, at best, to see out into the water. However, the singing grew as we neared, and suddenly I felt sleepy, even with Tomas at my side.

I yawned before saying, "You hear that? I think maybe we need to get back to the warehouses," I said, but it was too late; something could be seen in the fog coming right for us.

Fish-like creatures emerged from the fog bank. They were maybe four feet tall, with fish-like heads and fins here and there along their arms and legs. They walked awkwardly up the embankment toward us, but I saw they had claws, so I drew my weapon and readied to fight. This seemed to make them pause, a few turning back, and the song, eerie and still, grew louder, making it harder to keep my eyes open.

"Retreat and fight up on solid ground," I said to Tomas, who looked just as blurry-eyed as I did.

We did as I commanded, fleeing before the water dwellers, and luckily for us, they followed, so we'd be getting some essence after all. The first wave of attackers fell on us, ten at a time. Using the alleyway between two warehouses, we narrowed their attack, forcing them to attack two or three at a time.

I lunged forward, bringing my shield to bear and slashing out with my sword. My attack drew forth green blood, and Tomas cracked one atop the head so hard it stopped moving, making the opening even harder for them to get through. I cast Spark on the one I'd slashed, finishing it off in a spray of magical lightning.

The final one was brave, coming up to us with his brethren pushing him forward. He met the edge of my blade with little resistance, barely raking his claws across my shield. I kicked the dead body to the side and faced the next few. This continued for several minutes, and in the meantime, I heard the creak of the warehouse door opening.

"They are stealing stuff, hurry, we need to slay them faster!" I said, and we grew more reckless, slashing and getting slashed for our trouble. We accumulated a few good wounds, but we defeated the now twenty or so fish monsters that came to attack us. There were another twenty working on bringing items out of the warehouse, and we set upon them with brutal efficiency.

Cutting, smashing, and kicking, we killed them as they came. Then the music suddenly grew louder, and a seven-foot-tall creature emerged from the fog bank toward us, singing some fishy song.

"Focus on the big one, I think it's making us go to sleep," I said, yawning afterward.

"Right," Tomas said, rushing forward only to be slammed by a clawed hand and knocked back and off his feet.

I was there a second later, helping Tomas to his feet as the giant of a fish-beast, basically the same build as the others but with a narrower, longer waist. Its arms were thicker, and the claws more pronounced.

The song cut out suddenly as I reached it and slashed for its legs. It seemed to hiss at me, its song returning in a more rapid and hurried pace. I felt no signs of sleepiness from it this time, but the fish monsters that were still alive suddenly dropped what they had and came running for us.

"Keep them off me while I deal with this one," I said, dodging a strike and slashing again at its feet.

"Got it," Tomas said, twirling his staff expertly and smashing into a fish monster's head, killing it instantly.

I turned my attention back to the fight at hand, catching a glancing blow on my shield just as the monster spewed some odd green bile all over it. Some of it hit my armor, and it sizzled in response. However, for whatever reason, my shield remained unharmed. Slamming forward, I hit the shield against the fish, giving it a taste of its own bile.

Its fleshy scales sizzled and popped when it came into contact with the stuff, but not enough to do any real damage. This would be a fight I'd win by outlasting the monster, not any great show of damage, unless Tomas could rejoin me.

So with that in mind, I fought defensively, using my shield to great effect as I stabbed and slashed at its lower half. This siren fish monster wasn't going to make it back alive, that much I was going to guarantee.

Slashing, cutting, and eventually smashing, as Tomas came to join me, the monster was slowing down immensely. It struck Tomas, seeing as he was likely doing more damage than I with his attribute-unlocked abilities. His attacks were so quick that it was a bit silly, but he was slower on his feet, so I had to get myself in front of the strike to catch it, knocking him aside a little.

He grunted but recovered quickly as the claws raked my shield, and the dead silence of the night was interrupted by the sounds of our battle once more. I slammed my shield forward just as it withdrew its claws, but it wasn't fast enough. I heard a crunch as one of its claws broke free from its body.

It screeched and turned, likely ready to retreat now that we'd dealt so much damage to it, when Tomas rushed forward, activating his Heavy Strike ability, a red aura, and lightning running the length of his staff. He slammed forward with enough force to shatter its spine, which I think it must have done, because it slammed forward unmoving, yet still alive.

The song sputtered to a halt, and I rushed forward, cutting down with a powerful strike and cleaving off its head, ending the monster's attempts to steal from the warehouses.

I wasn't sure if that would be the only attempts these creatures made, but we'd halted this one, and I didn't hear the song on the wind any longer, so I was fairly confident that we'd be able to say we dealt with the threat.

I did wonder why they were interested in grain and other items. My mind turned it over for a few minutes, when I looked up toward the water and saw something. A silhouette of a man in a cloak and burning blue eyes staring toward us.

"I think this might not be over," I said, wiping the blood from my blade.

But just as Tomas turned to look where I was, the eyes blinked and the silhouette disappeared.

"What's that?" Tomas asked, not seeing what I'd seen just moments before.

"I don't know, maybe a trick of the light," I said, but I didn't believe that for a moment.

CHAPTER 19
CARAVAN DEPARTURE

We lined up the heads of the fish monsters, depositing their bodies back into the water to float away, after getting all their cores, of course. Then we did the same with the larger monster, the waters were swift, and the bodies were gone in moments. With our proof of our exploits from the night before, we waited out the last hour for the warehouse foreman, Drew.

He arrived with the first rays of light over the horizon. His form was robust but strong, and the look on his face when he saw the monster heads laid out was priceless. Eyes bulging, hands wringing, and his expression screwed up in general surprise.

"We've caught your thieves," I said as he drew near.

"You killed a good number of sirens, both male and even a singing female, but why'd they want my goods? You sure you didn't just kill some monsters? What proof do you have that they were taking my goods?" Drew asked, his expression now skeptical, eyes narrowed, and mouth in a frown.

"Well, there are the bags of grain and other supplies they tried to carry out while we fought another group. It was like they were desperate to get some, no matter what. These are your culprits, you can bet on it," I said, being as confident as I could when speaking.

"So you saw them take some with your own eyes?" he asked, scratching at his fat chin covered in stubble.

"We did," Tomas said, interjecting his own few words.

"You've got our word," I said, trying to add to the confidence a little bit more.

"Well, no reason to doubt you. I paid the six silver for the job, so you can pick up the reward from that girl, Serif, and I'll give you another two silver for your troubles of keeping most of our grain locked away for the night," Drew said, producing two silver moons and giving each of us one. "Now be gone, I've got work to do, unless you might be interested in loading barges for the day?"

I was seriously considering it, but Tomas answered first.

"Nope, not today at least. We've got a bounty to collect and a celebration to be had," Tomas said, wrapping his arm around me and pulling me away.

With that, we ventured to the Amber Coin Tavern, collected the six silver and searched for any new jobs. It was while doing this that Serif called across the tavern for me to come back.

"Was there a problem with the job?" I asked, confused and not wanting to give back my three silver moon share of it.

"No, not that, but the guy over the caravan came in today, wants me to reach out to all that signed up to say he is leaving tomorrow now, citing the monster migration as his reason. I told him we couldn't guarantee that all those who signed up would be ready, but I'm guessing you and your crew will be ready to go tomorrow?" Serif asked, and I looked down to see that the ledger had about twenty names on it now, including the names of the Granger band.

"I think we can manage that," I said, a burst of adrenaline-fueled excitement coursing through me.

"Good, I'll mark you down," Serif said. "Now to find the rest of the people on this list by tomorrow." She seemed determined, but I didn't know how she'd find them all unless they came into the tavern daily.

"I'll keep an eye out for all the ones I know on the list, and let you know if I talk to any of them by tonight," I said, and Serif gave me a friendly smile.

"Alright, I appreciate that," she said, shooing me away with her hand.

"Guess what just happened," I said the moment I got back to Tomas. I was practically bouncing with excitement.

"You found us a job that will get us to level 15?" Tomas asked, speaking dryly but with a mock excitement.

"We've still got like eleven thousand essence to go, we'd need at least two or three more nights like last night to pull that off," I said, returning his dry way of speaking toward him. Then, switching it back to my excited voic,e I said, "The caravan leaves tomorrow. Gather your things and be ready to depart!"

"Tomorrow!" Tomas said, not as excited as I'd hoped, but more surprised. "I only have one day left? Well, shit I need to find Ashric and uh, the others, and see if I can convince them to go. I thought I had more time. I'll see you first thing in the morning, here at the tavern. I've got loads to do!"

With that, he turned and left, leaving me alone and needing to find as many others as I could from the list, including Ryn and the Granger band.

I found Ryn easily enough; she'd just reported for duty at the Eastern

Gate, the second gate I checked. I knew she preferred gate duty over town patrols, which was good because otherwise it would be damn hard to find her.

"Well, looks like I need to take today off then, I've got a ton to take care of. Meet me for drinks tonight at the Amber Coin Tavern?" Ryn asked, turning to leave and find whoever was in charge, no doubt.

"Sure, I'll meet you tonight," I said, turning and leaving as well.

I made it to my apartment and began packing my meager belongings into my pack and my spare pack, filling both to the brim. When I was finished, I went down to speak with the landlord, Mr. Moroto.

"Let me guess," he said, seeing me approach. "You are leaving, and this will be your last night with me? No refunds for time paid, sorry."

"Good guess, but I don't want a refund, I just wanted to thank you for your kindness for allowing me to stay here for how cheaply you did. I'm sure you can raise the prices now that I'm gone."

"I plan to," Mr. Moroto said. "Too long I have been kind, time to make some money." He rubbed his hands together as he spoke, and I laughed at his show of mock greed.

"Do what you must," I said, chuckling. "I've cleared out the room, but I'll be sleeping there tonight, I think. But either way, I'll be picking my stuff up in the morning, so try not to rent it out until I'm gone at least."

"We will see," Mr. Moroto said, chuckling.

He held out a hand, and I shook it.

It was hard to say goodbye to the life I'd known for nearly ten years, but change was inevitable. I would roll with the punches and come out on top if I just kept fighting. There would always be a way forward.

I found Granger playing at the third pub I visited in the Commons, where I'd heard rumors of a strange kind of music making its way through the Commons recently. I told them of the time change, and they were happy to hear it, saying they were ready to bring their music to different parts of the world.

To the west and to Stonehaven wasn't exactly new world territory, but I just nodded and smiled. With that taken care of, I made it to the baths, laundering my clothes from the night before, then I dropped off my armor and shield, keeping only my blade on me.

I bumped into a few more people on the list just going about my day, ones I'd known, including Ana and her group. Well, her group at least, Ana was off doing something elsewhere, but I invited them to drinks tonight at the Amber Coin Tavern and they agreed to join us.

With all I needed to do taken care of, I hit up a few stores and bought some supplies, including rope, a few potions, and various other useful items.

Finally, by the time I was done, I returned to the tavern and met up with several of my friends.

"Fancy seeing you here," Ana said, smiling widely. "So I hear we are leaving tomorrow. Are you surprised I'm taking the same caravan?"

"Honestly?" I asked, and she nodded. "Yeah, a little bit."

"You aren't upset I'm going, are you?" she asked, my expression neutral.

"Not at all," I said, forcing a smile on my face. I was lost in thought about what the future held, but I forced myself to be present for the last night in town. "Sorry, just distracted."

"I bet. Who knows what we will encounter on the way! I'm sure we will have plenty of opportunities for advancement. I just hit level 15, did I tell you?" she asked, her expression cute as she scrunched her nose together and looked at me.

"You didn't, but congratulations!" I said, happy for her and only slightly annoyed that I wasn't level 15 myself yet.

"Five more levels and I'll have a class already, but I hear it gets harder after that," Ana said, and I realized she'd never told me what class she wanted to choose, so I decided the least I could do was ask.

"What class are you going for?" I asked.

She grinned at me and took a moment to respond.

"I'm going the route of the Arcane Knight, heard of it?" she asked, whispering so as not to give away her secret.

"That one is Power and Arcana-based, right? Ten in each one?" I asked, though I was pretty sure I was right.

"That's right!" Ana said. "I've got ten in Power and five in Arcana now, so just five more to go!"

"That is pretty cool. I hear Arcane Knights are pretty rare too, people prefer the Battlemage combo instead of the magic-infused strikes Arcane Knight offers," I said, trying to remember all I'd learned about the Arcane Knight from Ryn.

"I've been fascinated with the class ever since I read a book on it. It was fictional, but very exciting," Ana said, winking at me for some reason.

"Yeah, that's cool," I said, waving down the bar maiden. "I'll pay for a round for my whole group and keep them coming."

"Yes, sir," she said, turning and returning a few minutes later with over half a dozen ales stacked on top of one another. We drank, and I turned to Ryn.

"You get all your stuff together?" I asked. I knew Ryn had a permanent residence, not one she rented, but I was sure she'd made arrangements for it.

"Yeah, I've got an old guard buddy staying in my place and paying me rent via maintenance on the place and upkeep. It's a raw deal for me, but I'll always have a place to return to when I want it," she said. "Besides, I'm ready to go see the world again. I've been stuck in one place for far too long."

Tomas never made an appearance; however, the rest of us talked and drank into the night. I got to know Ana's team a little better, which was good because I'd be seeing them more often, it seemed.

I spent the night over at Ana's again, the last night we'd have any privacy, we figured, so we made the best of it. Then I left in the middle of the night to sleep in my bed one last time. It turned out to be a mistake. I woke up later than I wanted and didn't have time for a bath, so I rushed straight to the tavern, where the others had already gathered, awaiting our caravan leader.

"I'm Marv, the caravan leader, and this here is Steward. He is in charge of just about everything, so if you have questions, you take them to him," Marv said, waddling over and putting a hand on Steward.

Both men were big, but in very different ways. Where Marv was rotund and round, Steward was buff and muscled. Marv stood about six paces or so high, and Steward was about the same, though slightly taller. Marv had a scraggly beard, glasses, and an overly froglike appearance.

Steward, on the other hand, looked to be carved straight from stone, his appearance that of the ancient demigods so many used to believe in. Beings that walked the planet and had power beyond what was normally granted by the Unlocked ceremony. Of course, such beliefs, mostly religious beliefs, were old news.

Most followed the idea that the god or gods of this realm enacted their will through those with the most power, all of whom had obtained it through the Unlocking ceremony. So it was literally a mindset that the strongest were the will of the gods, and you'd best do your best to get as strong as possible.

Steward reverberating power, and I wouldn't be surprised to learn he was level 40 or higher. When he spoke, his voice seemed to vibrate with how deep and powerful it was.

"Good morning," he said, addressing the crowd of us awaiting directions. "I have a list, but I'm going to do a quick roll call and see who is actually here."

He went on to name and mark all those who were here, including myself. It appeared we were one group short, one of the stronger and first groups to sign up, but he didn't seem worried by it.

"Normally, I could protect this caravan by myself through the lands we are traveling through, but we have many carts, and I can't be everywhere at once. So it will be up to you all to form groups and receive assignments from me, whether that is to venture off the beaten path or stay with the caravan to give warning. You will obey my commands, got it?" he asked, and we all gave our versions of 'yes, sir' and 'alrighty then'.

With that out of the way, it appeared we were going to set off to the West Gate to start our journey.

"Mind teaming up with us again?" Torwyn asked, walking over to greet me with a friendly wave.

"I don't mind at all," I said, returning the wave and looking around for Ryn and Tomas.

I found Tomas, standing in the back alone, and Ryn conversing with the Steward fellow.

"Let me tell my team, I'm sure they'll be fine with it," I told Torwyn, and she smiled at me as I left to talk to Tomas.

He, oddly enough, had no snacks, and his smile, which was almost ever-present, was a frown at the moment.

"What's wrong?" I asked, sensing that he was down about something, and I had a mind about what.

"Just couldn't convince Ashric to come with us. It didn't matter what I said, his father had a plan for him, and he won't go against it," Tomas said, sounding hollow and empty as he spoke.

"We'll see him again," I said, offering up my best reason for him not to be upset. "Besides, think of the adventure that awaits us out there, the foods you'll find and get to sample."

This got a grin on his face, and he punched playfully on my arm. "Yeah, that's true," he said, then pulling out a bag from a pocket, he began to munch again.

With Tomas eating and seeming somewhat normal again, I decided to see if he was down to run with the Granger group again.

"You alright to team up with Granger for the trip?" I asked, and he just nodded between bites.

"Sure," he finally said when I didn't take his nod for enough of an answer.

"Good," I said. Patting him on the arm in a friendly gesture, I went off to find Ryn.

Steward was talking to her, but I didn't listen in fast enough to catch what he'd said, and Ryn laughed, turning and noticing me.

"We can talk later, but I will hear about that fight of yours," she said, turning to me and putting an arm around me, walking me away.

"You alright with us teaming up with Granger during the caravan?" I asked, and she looked at me with a comforting smile on her face.

"What?" she asked a second later but seemed to catch the question before I could ask it again. "Oh, right. Yeah, that's fine."

"Cool, then we are set. Do you want to let Steward know we will be teaming together so we can get our assignment?" I asked, and she almost stumbled.

"S-sure," she said, smiling widely. "I'll go let him now."

With that, she turned and went to find him in the crowd once more, an easy feat since he stood about a pace taller than most in the room.

I found Torwyn with her group and put a friendly hand on her shoulder to get her attention.

"We are all set, and Ryn is letting Steward know so we can get our assignments for the day or week or however they'll do them," I said, and Torwyn just smiled wide.

"That's great! I'm super happy to be working with you all again. We are going to crush it!" she said, and her group all nodded in agreement.

Hunter fed his little squirrel on his shoulder, while Luke talked animatedly with Daniel about something or another. Which left Torwyn and me just looking at each other. It became awkward quickly, and I excused myself as the group moved toward the gate.

"She seems nice," Ana said, catching me as I walked through the crowd.

"Oh, who, Torwyn?" I asked, a bit flustered. "Yeah, she's going to be partnering with my group during the caravan. They are super strong, but I think they aren't too far ahead of us level-wise."

"Too bad you can't team up with our group, I know there are three of you, which would make Stormbreaker a bit too large," Ana said, using the name of their group the Stormbreakers.

"Oathbound is fine teaming up with Granger," I said, smiling over to her.

"Oathbound, I like it much better than your last name. It has weight to it," Ana said, smiling over to me and taking my hand.

I let it happen, even though I knew we ought to keep our relationship a secret if we were going to be traveling together. I feared it might make for an awkward situation in the future, but I set that aside for now. I had the girl I cared most about in that sense at my side; I should be happy that I'd see her a while longer.

We moved as a force through the streets, eventually making it to the West gate, where a dozen or so large covered wagons were laid out in a line, each one drawn by a couple of mules. These crossbred animals weren't fairly common around here, and I wondered where they'd managed to get so many, but Steward called out orders almost immediately to everyone, so I shut up and listened.

Our team, simply mentioned as 'Oathbound and others', was to watch the rear of the caravan for today, making sure none of the wagons got too far behind, and to watch for rear attacks by monsters. I wondered if Ryn hadn't given Granger's name or if Steward just didn't care to mention both groups when one name would do.

I shared a look with Luke, and he nodded, showing his group at least understood they'd be taking the back with us. Meanwhile, Ana and the rest of the Stormbreakers were set to work toward the front of the caravan, fending off monsters and the like.

Kissing Ana with a little peck on the lips, I left her to where she was headed and took position in the back with Granger, Tomas, and Ryn.

"You'd think we'd be put in front with all the flirting I did with him," Ryn said, seeming a bit disappointed by our position.

"Rear duty is actually pretty fun," Torwyn said, addressing her directly. "Last time we had rear duty, we fought like at least a dozen monsters. They like to sneak out behind and get a chance to pick off the weaker wagons, which they assume are at the back."

I cracked my neck to the side. "In that case, they'll have a surprise waiting for them," I said, speaking confidently despite knowing monsters in this area were out of my league. But with Granger at our side, I was sure we'd be fine if we could work together.

Over an hour passed as we waited for the caravan to leave, and in that time, we did little but small talk. Finally, the wagons began to move, and the cloaked drivers spurred the mules forward. Why they wore such large cloaks right now was a mystery, since the weather was fair today, a little overcast but mostly cool and calm.

Regardless, we had a job to do, so we took up position at the end, weapons ready as we departed the city.

Ashric arrived just as we were about to leave, and I had never seen Tomas get so animated as he was when he showed up. They hugged fiercely, but in the end, Ashric stayed behind as we ventured out into the unknown.

CHAPTER 20
CARAVAN LIFE

The first few hours were uneventful and boring. I expected many more monster attacks, so I could gain essence. It wasn't until the sun was truly overhead and breaking from the clouds that we saw our first bit of action.

The road leading out to the west was paved and maintained by the royal family, as were all main roads cutting across the continent, at least the central ones. This led to more traffic than I expected on the main road, since it passes many smaller villages, and it wasn't until we were a good four hours out that we stopped seeing people coming and going to some of the outer villages.

That was when the monsters came out in force. I heard the fights going on toward the front and wished we had a better situation. I was pretty sure we'd missed a goblin raid, not a single one making it to the back of the group.

So when the spiders came, I was surprised, to say the least, to see a few goblins riding atop the larger ones. Casting Spark on the lead goblin, it reared back but didn't leave its perch as it screamed orders to the dozen or so other spider riders and another dozen dog-sized spiders we had to deal with.

Oathbound readied themselves, weapons forward and shield up, while Granger shifted from playing tunes to pulling free weapons in a flash. Daniel took out his boomstick and splattered the lead goblin, doing what I'd tried to do with Spark. Then Luke was there, with Torwyn right behind him, smashing in the fray with his large axe instrument.

"We will focus on the smaller ones," I shouted as they were engaging the goblins just fine, Hunter unleashing arrow after arrow into spider and goblin alike.

I caught two attacks from the spiders on my shield as Tomas smashed one into goo using his special strike and impressive attack speed. He was so fast that he hit the next one just as I turned to catch its attack. Meanwhile, Ryn fought with her sword out, cutting loose legs and bringing forth green ichor with each strike.

This battle of the little spiders lasted only a few minutes, but it was intense, and a number of times they tried to bite me, only to find armor or Iron Skin in the way. I fought more recklessly after realizing they couldn't pierce my skin, at least the smaller spiders.

Given such attacks, we ended them just as the final four or five larger spiders turned to flee. Torwyn moved like lightning, cutting them off and waving her finger at them. "Not so fast." I heard her say as Luke smashed into one of the fleeing ones, just as the boomstick went off for a second time during the fight, exploding a fleeing spider.

We joined the fun, the seven of us making quick work of what was left of the goblin spider attack. We'd lost the caravan ahead, some half mile by now, but we quickly looted and jogged back to the wagons, making it there before any new attack could occur.

This went on like this for a few more hours, with two more waves of spider goblin riders, before we broke to make camp for the night. Each time we'd fought the goblins, I couldn't help but think that these were stronger than the ones we'd fought before, and the spiders were no pushovers either. I hoped Ana and her team would be up to the task, but I'd heard no reports of casualties, just a few injuries, including our team during the final spider goblin attack. Tomas had been bitten in the neck and needed a poison cure-all. Luckily, I had one that I'd purchased, so he took one hit of it, leaving me four more before I'd be out.

Because of how close I was and the events of the day, we'd killed nearly 30 small spiders, half as many big spiders and goblins, I'd leveled up to 15 and could now assign my final attribute into Power and decide what skill I'd take.

It was an easy choice that I'd been waiting for. I took Shove, and now with Spark and Iron Skin, I'd truly be a force to be reckoned with.

I found Ryn and Tomas as the camp was being laid out and the wagons circled.

"You made 15 today, right?" I asked, and Tomas nodded, as did Ryn.

"Barely," Ryn said. "I think you guys got a little ahead of me with that warehouse job you took."

"Well, don't keep me on edge, which attribute have you been increasing and what'd you pick?" I asked, remembering the paths they'd said they'd chosen, but curious to see if they stuck to it.

Ryn answered first. "I got my Arcana up to five and chose the Mana Bolt spell. I know Spark is a bit quicker, but with you covering it, I figure we could use some ranged projectiles occasionally."

"Wonderful!" I said, truly happy with her pick and the path she was on. She'd become a Blade Sage in no time flat!

"I really wanted to go down the Arcana path, but I decided to stick with my plans and went down the Guard attribute, bringing it to five and taking Block to help you out. It seems like a real neat skill, able to create a block anywhere within ten paces of me. I think I might even be able to use it to lift myself or give me a counterweight during attacks. I'm excited to see what it'll do," Tomas said, grinning ear to ear as he snacked on some dried nuts.

"Let's see it in action," I said, pulling out my sword and lifting my shield. "Block my strike."

I cut for his chest, slow enough that I could pull back if he didn't block, but sure enough, a little green flat disc appeared, and it blocked my attack, bouncing my sword away with the same amount of force I'd put into it.

"Check this out," Tomas said, waiting a minute for his skill to come back online before casting it at knee height. He put his foot on it and jumped high into the air, the block disc allowing him to push off before disappearing.

"Damn, maybe I should have taken that skill," I said, shaking my head. Iron Skin was truly powerful, but this supernatural block, with the right amount of focus and skill, might be better.

"We each got what we got, and as a team we are better for it," Ryn said, and I nodded, agreeing. I suddenly wondered what skills Granger had chosen. I knew Luke had Heavy Strike at least, but I hadn't seen any overtly skilled attacks from the others.

Maybe Torwyn had gone Fleet Foot, which would explain her speed, but I couldn't speak for the others. And outside of your personal group, it was considered taboo and even rude to ask such questions, so I kept to myself as we set up a campfire inside the ring of wagons where we could heat up some food.

Ana and the Stormbreakers came over to visit, and I said their names in my head to remember which was which.

Corwyn, Faelon, Raelith, Myrren, and Darian, the five members of Analease Storme's little band of fighters. Corwyn and Darian both used shields, while Faelon focused on more ranged magical means, though they were no slouches with a blade. Leaving Raelith on the bow and Myrren wielding a spear. Together, they were a balanced team, and they'd grown used to fighting together over the last five years. A shame that the rest of our original group didn't want to leave with us, but the old band was dead; it was just Oathbound now.

"So, Corwyn," I said, looking him up and down. He had raven black hair and dark purple eyes that weren't common in the central parts of Vareth, nor anywhere else I'd heard of. "You still using a spear and a shield, eh?"

"Best weapon combo. That, and my belt knife," he said, his sly voice filled with mirth.

"Then why does old Darian use a mace and shield?" I asked, gesturing to the oldest in the group. He was a late start in the program, so he was nearly thirty by the time he finished, holding off all these years so he could advance with his group.

"Because mace and shield are superior," Darian said, his voice a low rumble compared to Corwyn. Darian had thick bushy brown eyebrows and a bald head, by choice, not by hair loss, or so he said.

"Hardly," Corwyn said, cracking his neck to the side. "I'm down to prove it to you in a one-on-one."

"Enough of that, and quit stirring up trouble in my group, you," Ana said, poking me in the side.

"I haven't even gotten started. I wanted to know how Faelon has been doing, going from bow, arrow, and sword to purely magical attacks. Must be a rough change up," I said, looking over to her.

She had long braided hair, all tied up in a loop, and fair features most commonly found in northerners. She had blonde hair like Tomas's, but she sported the brown eyes more commonly found in the central areas of Vareth.

"Honestly?" she asked, and I nodded. "It's been an interesting switch-up. I'm thinking of chasing down the Stormchaser class, which is Speed and Arcana, but I'm still unsure. I might take the Spellblade class, as it has the same requirements and would let me use a sword again, but I kind of like being in the back line during the fights, so we will see. I've taken ten into Arcana and five into Speed so far."

"You'll do fine no matter which path you take," Ana told her, putting a hand on her arm. "Just remember, we support each other no matter the choices we make with our attributes, right Raelith?"

"Hey now," Raelith said, her brown hair up in a tight bun and her expression fierce. "I only suggested that having two archers would be a good idea, maybe even if she took Arcana and Power, meaning she'd have the best of both worlds."

"We don't ask why you think an archer needs Guard and Speed, instead of the more commonly chosen Power and Speed, so you shouldn't try to tell her how to pick," Ana said, and I saw Raelith cringe a little from the remark.

"I've got a plan," she said. "I'm going to be a Wardrunner, fast and durable and able to deal our damage anywhere while taking plenty myself. Not that any of the commonly known classes do well with bow and arrow. It's like the gods want you to be fighting up close with a sword or some large weapon."

"That just leaves Myrren to pick on. How are you today, Myrren?" I asked, looking over at the youthful-faced women with her light brown hair and sparkling green eyes.

"I'm fine," Myrren said. "And if you are wondering, I'll be a Warden, using Magic and Guard to protect and attack. Yeah, we are a pretty heavy Guard group, but we prefer safety over brutish strength."

"What if I told you there were advanced classes you could hold out for if you are willing to make it to level 30 first," I said, grinning widely as I saw their expression.

"Not everyone wants to have a legendary class," Ana was quick to say. "Some of us are happy to take on the more commonly used and trusted classes."

"What other options are there, really?" Torwyn asked, cutting in for the first time during our conversation. I'd almost forgotten they were there with their music playing and carrying us through the night. They played more melodic and calming music right now, which continued without Torwyn's voice for a bit.

"Well, I've discovered several texts that say if you put three attributes to ten, you'll get options beyond just the normal ones. I've also been told by a reliable source that if you wait and do four to ten for each attribute before choosing, you get access to legendary classes, though each is more limited than the more commonly used classes. I for one," I said, looking around to make sure we weren't being overheard. "I'm going to be a Dragon Knight."

"I've heard of the legends," Torwyn said, looking very skeptical. "But even if the attribute layouts were true to unlock the classes, the quests involved would be practically impossible. Are you sure you wouldn't be more comfortable with a core class like the rest of us?"

"Hell no," I said, surprising myself with the vigor with which I said it. "I'm going to reach the top, and when I get there, everyone will see that it was worth it! But also, can we keep this a secret between us? I'm not supposed to be telling everyone."

"Secret's safe with us," Torwyn said. "We are experts at keeping secrets, aren't we, boys?"

"Aye," they said in unison, breaking the melody for a second.

"What are the advanced classes you found? You never said," Torwyn asked.

"Oh well, the ones I know of are Blade Sage, focused on Power, Speed, and Arcana. Then there was War Monk, which was Power, Guard, and Speed. And Battle Priest, which was Guard, Speed, and Arcana," I said, taking a breath.

"What of the Power, Guard, and Arcana mix?" Torwyn asked with a knowing grin on her face. Did she know more than she was letting on, or was I just imagining it?

"That would be the Dragon Vanguard," I said, smiling at the cool naming.

"That seems pretty cool. Why not shoot for that one?" Torwyn asked, with that knowing look still on her face.

"I'm going to be a Dragon Knight, if it's the last thing I do," I said, and she nodded.

"I see. Well, good luck to you, and I hope the quest for the class isn't impossible," she said, returning to her music, strumming her odd lute and singing along to a song I'd never heard before, calm yet with a catchy beat.

"So my shield really proved its weight in silver moons today," I said, turning to Ryn and Tomas. "I can't wait to get into a dungeon and really get some magical loot."

"Or just have him make you something," Ryn said, gesturing to Daniel. "I put my spectacles on around him, and his entire body and everything he wears lights up, down to his shirt. Even his undergarments seem to be enchanted."

Daniel, from a distance, seemed to hear us and chuckled as he played.

"Well, maybe I will," I said, thumbing the hilt of my sword and wishing it too was enchanted in some way.

"I bet Ashric will be on his way to a dungeon soon. He was level 18 already, can you believe that?" Tomas said, shaking his head.

"Forget him for now," I said, but Tomas shot me a look that said he wasn't likely to forget Ashric any time soon. They'd been such close friends, but I was glad Tomas, my best friend, had chosen to stay at my side. He might have other friends, but I almost saw us more as brothers than just friends, same with Ryn, except you know, a sister, I guess.

Chuckling at my own thoughts, I turned to Tomas and gave him a 'forgive me' look, and he just nodded. We didn't need words to communicate most days, and today was one of them. Ryn picked up on it and abruptly changed the topic to something else.

"According to Steward, we will take left side duty tomorrow, moving our way up and around so everyone gets a chance at each position, up to and until he decides who fits into each position best. He even had me give him a report on how well we did, which I was happy to give," Ryn said. I'd never seen her so struck by someone random like this before and it was fairly odd.

"You're a big fan of him, aren't you?" I asked, and her face streaked a little red, before she regained her composure.

"I'm into guys who know all about bringing order from chaos. Why do you think I enjoyed working as a guard all these years?" Ryn asked, giving me a look that said, 'keep it up and lose an eye'.

I decided to back off and not test her. She was easily the most violent out of the three of us, and her knack for standing up against anyone that even remotely seemed threatening to us was legendary.

"Well, I suppose we should think about where we are going to sleep, my bedroll is ready to be laid down, but I don't reckon anyone brought any tents. It doesn't seem like it'll rain tonight, but that is the kind of weather we will be having over the next few weeks," I said, realizing that perhaps I should have gotten a tent or at least a tarp to make a lean-to.

"I brought a tent," Ana said, grinning at me when I gave her a look. Then she added, "It sleeps two."

This got a bunch of eyerolls from her group and mine, as we shared a look that communicated all I needed to know.

"I guess I'll help you set the tent if you're ready to go to sleep?" I asked, and she nodded, grinning like a schoolgirl.

Granger played off into the night, well after I'd gotten the tent set up with Ana's help, and we crawled inside. We didn't fool around, instead we fell asleep in each other's arms, the warmth it provided more than enough to keep us comfortable.

CHAPTER 21
THE WITHERED WARRENS

"For groups level 20 or higher, there is a dungeon nearby, and we've decided to set camp early so those who would like to give it a try can take the time to venture in. Remember, clear out only enough for a night's work because come midafternoon, we will be leaving. That'll give you roughly a full day to clear out as much as possible," Steward announced on the fifth day of our travels.

We'd killed a steady stream of weaker monsters as we traveled, none really as challenging as the first day. But even so, we'd only progressed up a single level, bringing my group to level 16. I put my spare attribute into Speed, ready to get it to five as well as the rest of my build, locking in my choice to go full Dragon Knight.

My Speed was by far my most impressive attribute so far, with an effective 11 in it now, even Torwyn struggled to keep up with me when I hit full speed, which was saying something, because she was fast!

"Did you want to challenge the dungeon?" Torwyn asked, appearing out of nowhere at my side.

"You guys are above level 20?" I asked because we weren't, so this dungeon could be a challenge for us, but I didn't want to say that just yet.

"Aren't you all, you sure fight above your weight class if not," Torwyn said, that knowing look in her eye, like she knew very well we weren't high enough and she was going to ask anyway.

"I'd be willing to give it a try, but as a first dungeon goes, I'm not sure swinging above our level is the best idea," I said, unsure how to handle this.

"Don't worry," Torwyn said. "If things get bad, we will bail you guys out."

"Let me ask Ryn and Tomas, see what they think, and then we can give it a go if they are down," I said, more eager now that it seemed like we might be stepping into our first dungeon today.

I asked Ryn first, and she looked at me oddly. "I'm more than willing, but can't you only bring six into a dungeon run? Someone would have to stay back. Did she mention if that would be from our side or hers?"

"That's a good question, let me ask, but before I do, you are good to try it if we can work it out?" I asked.

Ryn sighed, and her eyes looked up as she thought about it. "I think we can do it, but see about who is getting left behind first," Ryn said. "Then I'll give my final assent."

"Alrighty," I said, wiping a little perspiration off my forehead. It was a random hot day, the kind that showed up even this late in the season, and I was really feeling it with all my armor on.

Finding Torwyn among her group, I approached.

"That was fast," she said. "Are they good to go?"

"A question occurred to me, normal rules state dungeon parties are six members, so who is sitting out?" I asked, and Torwyn chuckled as if she knew something I didn't.

"Doesn't affect our party," she said, shrugging. "Ever since Daniel replaced so much of his body with mechanical parts, the dungeon doesn't count him as a member. So no loot for him, but he still gets essence like the rest of us. He doesn't mind, instead taking any loot we don't need and tinkering with it."

"Oh," I said, surprised by the news. "You know, I don't know how loot works inside a dungeon. Maybe you can explain it to me?"

"Nope," Torwyn said with a grin and a twirl. "I wouldn't dare spoil the fun of learning yourself. If you guys are ready, let's head out."

"I need to ask Tomas real quick, but I don't think he'll have any issues, so I guess we are ready to go once I find him!" I said, turning and finding him easily enough, talking to Ryn.

"So, who is getting left out?" Ryn asked. And Tomas nodded along.

"No one," I said, grinning as she seemed to process that and not have a comment back. I decided to help her out and explain what I meant in more detail. "The dungeon doesn't count Daniel as a person anymore, ever since he replaced parts of himself with, well, gears and whatnot. They say the dungeon doesn't give him loot anymore either, so we are good to seven-man in without any penalty."

"There are no penalties for seven-manning a dungeon," Ryn said, smiling now that she was the one in the know and I was ignorant. "It straight up won't let you enter, so if it lets him enter, it is likely the dungeon sees him as a companion and not a fully Unlocked any longer. Interesting. Even the chests don't give him personalized loot either? That is very interesting."

"Dungeons give personalized loot?" I asked, surprised to learn this fact as I knew very little about dungeons, besides the random book or two I'd skimmed on the topic.

I knew dungeons were of two types, either themed or tiered. If tiered, then they weren't all that different from a Tower challenge, meaning you'd fight monsters, traps, and whatnot before facing a boss monster. Then you'd get to go lower, going as low as you could and eventually defeating the dungeon.

If it were themed, it could literally be anything from a story to a challenge to a race I'd even read about. Themed dungeons were the more magically rich dungeons and would give out the best loot as well. But from the way Steward talked about being able to leave whenever, it seemed this dungeon wasn't likely themed, as you were literally stuck inside those ones unless you were lucky enough to find the hidden exit or defeat the dungeon.

That was the limit on what I knew about dungeons, and neither book had spoken about loot other than to say that it was common enough to find loot on monsters and after bosses. The method of receiving the loot was a mystery to me, and I was excited to see how it turned out.

"Let's gather up with Granger and check out this dungeon," I said. "I bet the first few floors aren't too bad, but I doubt we will full-clear it by this time tomorrow."

"Let's move," Ryn said, and we did so, heading to Granger, stopping off at Steward to inform him, and then off into the woods in the direction of the small town just outside the dungeon.

We didn't enter the town, but it was called Thornwall, named for a wall covered in a thorny plant said to be deadly to the touch, which helped them keep monsters at bay during migrations and such. At about half the size of Brackenford, it was still a bustling place from the looks of it, as we wound around and up to the dungeon it was built next to. I could see the tower at its center and wondered if they had any tower climbers in town. Perhaps we could try that at some point, just for the experience.

"Welcome to Thronwall's Dungeon, The Withered Warrens. Be warned, this dungeon starts off easy enough for those level 10 or higher, but each floor down represents an increase of five levels' worth of attributes for the monsters, meaning the fifth and final floor is level 30 and thereabouts. Make sure you sign in before entering, and remember, we are not responsible for loss of life or limb," the man added as he looked over Daniel. "Also, how do you imagine seven will get inside?"

"He's just a companion of sorts; he doesn't count," Luke said, thumbing over to Daniel and chuckling.

"Thanks," Daniel said, throwing down a few silver moons and walking past the guards.

We followed his example, each giving two silver moons to enter and following him into a large cave mouth. Inside was an obelisk of pure black with blue words carved into it that glowed enough to see by.

"Place your hand on the obelisk, but let Daniel go first so we don't leave him behind. Then we will be inside, be ready because not all dungeons have waiting rooms, some will thrust you right into the action," Torwyn explained, and we did as she requested.

Placing our hands on the obelisk, it was warm to the touch. Finally, when all seven of us touched it, the surface grew hot, and I almost pulled away, but then it was gone, and we were in a room that glowed a faint green, just enough to see by. There was a pedestal in the middle, filled with glistening water.

"Sweet," Luke said, turning to the pool of water and dipping his hands in, drinking some of it up. "Drink up, everyone, this stuff will refresh and energize you for at least an hour. I love it when the dungeon has a proper staging room."

"What is it?" I asked, and Ryn answered before anyone else could, showing off her knowledge despite her lack of experience.

"Mana water, is what they call it," she said. "It will top off all our resource pools and keep them topped off while resting for the next hour at least."

"That's right!" Torwyn said, praising Ryn for her quick knowledge of the mana water. "It also tastes fucking awesome, so there's that."

It did taste pretty awesome, I realized as I took my first drink. The purest and tastiest water I'd ever had the pleasure to drink before. With each drink, I felt lighter, more energized, and, well, whole. It was hard to explain, but it was like someone had hit me with a lightning attack, and that moment of surged awareness and want for movement just lingered on me.

After we'd drunk our fill, the water never seemed to lessen, and we ventured down a steep incline into another part of the warren, an interconnecting path of dirt as round as it was tall. The height had to be at least ten paces, with the width about the same. It looked as if a giant worm had cruised through the area, leaving a perfectly round tunnel.

The first monster to appear wasn't monstrous at all, but rather a white bunny with a slight nub or horn on its head. It rushed us with all speed and no breaks, crashing into my shield as I brought it up. The blow rocked my shield, despite its small size, and I took a step back to balance myself.

"Careful, more are coming!" I yelled as the first one fell to a blow from Tomas's staff.

Sure enough, a literal swarm of bunnies appeared, but we soon turned the hallway red with their blood as we slaughtered them by the tens. Even when they got an attack through, it hurt but did little damage. Perhaps if they got the same location multiple times, a tactic they were sure trying, they might break a bone, but otherwise they were harmless.

We cut, bludgeoned, and smashed our way through them, killing dozens before they stopped appearing. The loot they left behind, when they did, was nothing more than healing ointment or an occasional core. Except that these were dungeon monsters, they sort of faded away after a bit, leaving behind their loot instead of having to dig into it and retrieve it.

Before we knew it, we'd reached an open area with a pathway that led down. The only problem? There was a bunny the size of a mule before us, and it didn't look too happy to see us, red eyes glaring in our direction.

It had a full-on unicorn-style horn, and its white fur was tangled and matted, creating armored sections around its body. This would be a fight for sure, but with the seven of us, it was hardly worth mentioning.

Daniel started it off with his boomstick, likely going for a killing blow, but it turned its massive self to the side, and the attack hit its thick fur, causing it to go up in flames for a second before going out, but doing little damage otherwise.

"Damn," Daniel said. "I was hoping that'd be more effective."

"Right?" Hunter said, unleashing an arrow that flickered with red energy and potential. It sank deep into the same spot, and the large bunny let out a cry of pain.

"Attack!" I yelled as I charged forward with my shield at the ready. All around me, people sprang into action, and the fight was on.

I cast Spark, and it flew from the tip of my sword, crashing not where I aimed but instead on the horn. Similarly, when Ryn cast her magical missile-type attack, it changed course and hit the horn as well.

It swiped out at me with a giant paw attack, my shield catching it as I used Shove to try and push back against its massive bulk. Shove was ineffective, only moving it a few inches, if anything at all. Its horn came down at my shield, but suddenly Tomas was there, flying through the air and slamming his staff into the attacking horn.

His staff shattered under the blow, but not before it knocked a section of the horn apart, surprisingly spilling out red blood from its tip.

It cried out in rage, a sound I never expected to hear from a bunny of any size, before it kicked abruptly with its back legs, sending Luke and Daniel flying backward. I sank my blade in deep, as it was distracted, and it cried out once more. The first was all but over now. We hit it with all we had, and it struggled to fight back from the onslaught of so many fighters.

Slashing, stabbing, and doing massive amounts of damage against it while it kicked randomly and scored an occasional decent hit on us was the way of the battle. It ended when I got off a Spark that didn't go to its horn, and followed up with a stab to its eye.

I could tell, panting and out of breath as we were, that Granger had taken it easy, letting us do most of the work. I felt a rush of essence enter me as we defeated the floor, and a copper chest appeared where the giant bunny had been.

"Oh man, what a bummer, only one chest," Luke said, shaking his head. "It can be up to six, so we really missed out here."

"We pass," Torwyn said. "But you three should roll it out and see who gets the loot. Remember it sort of, but not always, will try and personalize the loot to your needs, something to keep in mind."

"I'll pass," I said. "I have a magical item already. You two roll for it."

"All right," Tomas said, pulling out a set of two six-sided dice.

"Let's roll, you first," Ryn said, gesturing that he should roll.

He did so and got a five and a six, eleven total, and a hard number to beat.

Ryn picked up the dice and rolled them one at a time. The first roll was a six, and she'd need another to beat him. The dice struck the ground and rolled, flipping once, then twice before landing on a three.

"Damn," Ryn said. "You must be using loaded dice. Next time we use mine."

"Fine with me," Tomas said, grinning widely. "Do I just open the lid and look inside?"

"Open it up," Torwyn explained. "Then reach in and pull out what is inside. You won't be able to see it, but you'll be able to grab it and pull it out, no matter the size."

"All right, all right," Tomas said, stepping forward with a hesitant step, before taking a deep breath. He was about to be the first member of Oathbound to get dungeon loot, and I couldn't be happier for him.

He pushed the lid open and reached inside; light, golden, and glorious poured out of the chest. His face screwed up in confusion as he began to pull something out.

It was a staff, or rather it looked like a staff by its length and thickness, but it was twirled similarly to the horn atop the bunnicorn's head. Both sides were blunted with metal caps on the end, similar to his last Bo staff. He looked at it, then at us, then back to it.

"I'll give it a look," Ryn said, coming forward with her spectacles. She read out the exact details of the item moments later.

Name: *Hornwood Staff*

    Rarity: *Rare*

    Special Properties: *Grants +1 to Arcana. Absorbs a small portion of magical energy when struck by spells (up to three charges). Each successful melee strike releases the stored energy as a faint burst, adding minor magical damage. With focus, the user may project magic out of the staff from a distance as well.*

    Description: *Fashioned from the horn of a giant horned hare, the staff's surface is slightly twisted in a spiral, much like a unicorn's horn. Smooth to the touch yet impossibly sturdy, it shimmers faintly under moonlight, hinting at* *the arcane energy woven into its core. While not the weapon of a master mage, it is prized by those who blend martial skill with a touch of magic, turning enemy spells back against them.*

"Holy seven realms of hell," Tomas said, looking about with surprise and elation. "I got a magical staff!"

"Neat spectacles," Torwyn said, eyeing them with a look of wonder on her face. "Could I borrow them and see if I can identify a few items we have lying about?"

Ryn shared a look with Tomas and me, both of us nodded that it was fine, since we were all part owners of the spectacles. She handed over the glasses to Torwyn, who slipped them on and went to Daniel, touching and examining him of all things.

"It says you are a Runeforged, whatever that is," Torwyn said to him in a low whisper, not meant for our ears, but the sound traveled well in this room. "I told you messing with your own core was risky."

"The results have been phenomenal," Daniel said, clear for everyone to hear. "I regret nothing."

Torwyn sighed and went on to look at several other items they had in their unusually large packs. By the time she was done, she seemed satisfied with the glasses and returned them to Ryn.

"Work all right for you?" Ryn asked, and Torwyn merely nodded, lost in her own thoughts most likely.

"Shall we try the next floor? We've only burned, like, what do you think, Daniel, three or four hours?" Torwyn asked, and Daniel stepped forward.

"Five hours, twenty-one minutes, and fourteen seconds have passed since we entered," he said, being more precise than I thought possible. Maybe it had something to do with him being half mechanical or something.

"Let's hurry, then. We can clear most of this dungeon in twenty hours, I think," Torwyn said. We approached the burrow's door, a brown wooden-and-metal thing, pushed it open, and ventured deeper into the warrens.

CHAPTER 22
DEEPER INTO THE WARRENS

We ventured deeper into the group, or it felt that way, the sparse lighting got even dimmer as we walked until Torwyn pulled out a lantern and lit it, holding it high for everyone to see. After an hour of walking and facing no monsters, Luke, probably from boredom more than anything else, began to sing a soft melody, stringing his instrument weapon as we walked.

I didn't know if it was on purpose or what, but almost immediately afterward, a monster came into view before us, a single small thing that I'd never seen before.

"What do the spectacles call that?" I asked, as it nosed around in front of us, as large as a big dog but with the body of a giant rat. It had a very pink nose and massive clawed hands, with tiny, beady eyes that looked closed.

"It's called a Mole Monster, whatever the hell that is," Ryn said, looking at it in disgust.

"Do we just kill it? It doesn't look overly frightening, more sad than anything else," I said, sword at the ready but unsure what actions to take next. "I mean, there is just one of them, maybe we can walk on by?"

"Careful what you wish for," Torwyn said, chuckling as the ground began to rumble around us.

One by one, more moles appeared, falling close by and slashing out with their powerful clawed little arms. I caught one such slash on my shield and was battered backward.

"Don't let them hit you with those claws," I said, as if I needed to state the obvious, but sometimes my mouth moved faster than my brain.

"Copy that," Tomas said, laughing as he batted away a mole and it crunched hard into another one, neither getting up. "They go down pretty easily."

"Yeah, if only there was just one of them," Ryn said, shooting me a look as if it were my fault the dungeon had sent more to attack us right after I said that.

I slashed out, but my blow was caught by a claw and thrust back at me. So I used Spark instea,d and the mole died nearly instantly to magical damage. I remembered that, waiting until I felt ready to cast Spark again, there was a time between each casting where I knew I could, but I shouldn't push myself too far before casting again. Ryn called it a cooldown, but it was merely a mental suggestion to keep yourself from burning out.

With the cooldown up, I cast Spark again, just as I used Shove on another. Two slammed together, and Spark found its target, killing two at a time. The others were having similar success against the targets, until one of them managed to knock Torwyn's lantern aside, spilling the oil and plunging us into near darkness.

The first strike I caught, but the second and third I didn't. These creatures seemed to have no need of light and were doing a number on us all of a sudden. My eyes adjusted quickly, and I saw shapes coming at me. I targeted one with Spark and lit up the room momentarily.

Enough to see that we were being swarmed.

"We need light," I called out, cutting one down and hearing another just in time to avoid having my leg slashed open. I was bleeding from several attacks already; they seemed to have a knack for finding the spots between armor.

Finally, Luke shouted somethin,g and flames covered his weapon, giving us enough light to see by. They were magical flames of some kind, blue and green, and unharming the weapon.

"Let's light them up," Luke called out, and I saw the true power of the Granger band then; they moved with speed and precision, killing all that were left in a matter of seconds. The axe went out a moment later, and Torwyn fumbled with the lantern, getting it back under control and lighting it.

"So moles are terrible," Ryn said, her face bleeding and limping forward to meet me.

"Rest up and take potions if you need," Luke ordered, then he directed Daniela and Hunter to go scout forward with a wave of his hand and two words. "Scout ahead."

"Will they be all right by themselves?" Tomas asked, downing a small potion and joining the rest of us.

"They'll be fine," Luke assured us before looking over himself for injuries, finding none, he began fiddling with his instrument.

"We are a bit stronger than our level suggests," Torwyn said, shrugging. "I bet we could four-man this entire place if we really wanted to, but we don't have the time for that right now."

"Is it your magical items?" I asked, not sure how else one could become stronger than their level suggested.

"Somewhat," Torwyn said. "But I can't give away our secrets, sorry, bud."

"I can't identify anything they are wearing, which means it's much stronger than our level range," Ryn said, not lowering her voice or trying to hide that she'd tried.

"You're right," Torwyn said, looking coyly over at us, and you're wrong. "Let's just say we aren't from around these parts and keep it at that, all right?"

"Fine," I said, tiring of the cloak-and-dagger topics. "Let's get a move on these moles and find the boss."

"Daniel and Hunter will take care of the moles, and we will let you guys take point on the boss, if that's all right with you?" Torwyn asked, and we nodded that it was.

Venturing into the dim tunnels with only the lantern to give us light, we found many dead moles but no signs of Danile and Hunter for a good while. When, finally, we heard signs of life, it was the squeal of death from moles and not humans.

Daniel appeared first, and Hunter emerged from the darkness like a wraith moments later, his form seeming to twist and emerge from the shadows themselves.

"We took care of it. The boss is just ahead, but be warned, we've spent an additional 2 hours on this floor. If we want to clear the entire place, we will want to hurry our pace, as the next floors will start to become difficult," Daniel said.

Hunter nodded, and I noticed the arrow that he had notched was glowing an ethereal purple color, unlike any skill I'd ever seen before. When he saw me looking, it suddenly turned red and crackled like the skills I had seen before. He caught my eye and smirked.

Something was up with this group, but I couldn't understand it, much less come up with an idea of what could be going on. However, it wasn't going to matter much either way if we didn't get moving and clear this dungeon.

"Let's move out," I said, taking command and pushing forward. Everyone followed me, and soon we were passing mole corpses, which we looted, and they disappeared until we reached the boss room, which was a dug-out area twice the size of the hallway, and in the middle sat a huge mole monster.

It had armored plates covering its body, and its claws were much longer than normal, almost needle-like at the ends. It had no eyes to speak of, small or otherwise, but it seemed to hear us approaching, as it moved its large pink nose toward us.

"It can't see, but it can hear. Maybe we can use that," I said, and Torwyn smiled.

"We got this," she said, pulling free her lute, and the others did the same. Before I knew it they were singing and playing a loud but catchy tune.

The mole seemed enraged by this and charged, but I was there, shield up, catching its attack and using a direct Shove skill on it to slow it. It hit hard, my feet sinking a bit into the dirt, but I stayed my ground, ready for a counterattack.

My sword slashed outward and caught a hard plate, bouncing off.

Then Tomas appeared to the side, smashing his staff down and shattering an armored plate like it was nothing. I used that moment to shove the large thing and cast Spark on its exposed flesh.

Then Ryn appeared in a flash right where Tomas had been a moment before, cutting with her dual daggers into the exposed and burnt flesh. The mole monster screeched and slashed harder, its entire body twitching madly.

I was thrown back from the maneuver, knocked off my feet, and my shield flew to the side. Rolling as quickly as possible, I grabbed it just in time for a slash to hit me in the back. My Iron Skin saved me from the brunt of it, but it still hurt as I was slammed against the dirt wall.

"Get up!" Ryn cried; they were fighting it off as best they could, but Tomas's Block skill had its limits, and the mole was clawing right through them with ease.

This was a level 15 boss, and we were only three, so we had to be tactical about this. I was up and back on my feet, my shield and sword in my hands. I cast Spark on its face to get its attention, and it charged me.

The music hit a loud point, and the mole turned toward where they played, but I was ready, striking its face where no plates were and cutting a wide swath of blood. That got its attention, and it slashed out at me, but I ducked the blow, glancing some of it off my shield. Then I uppercut it with my blade right into its tiny pointy mouth.

Tomas was there, and I cast Spark on his staff, empowering it as he slammed down on another plate, shattering it with explosive force. But he followed up, smashing into the raw flesh as Ryn appeared atop the mole, smashing her sword into its head, deeper and deeper, until it finally gave a violent surge forward, then fell still.

The music cut off, and Torwyn clapped for us as we gathered ourselves together. The boss disappeared in a sparkle of light, and a chest awaited us, much like the loot we'd collected from the moles.

"You can take this one as well. We just want a shot at the final floor's loot if we get that far," Torwyn said, and I looked over to Ryn, the only one who hadn't gotten a magical item just yet.

"All you Ryn," I said, and Tomas nodded along.

"You sure?" she asked, looking awkwardly between the two of us.

"Go for it," I said, and she smiled, going forward to open the chest.

She reached down and pulled it open, then, putting her hands inside, seemed surprised when she pulled out a small ring. After showing it to us, she put on her spectacles and identified it for us.

Name: *Ring of Verdant Rest*
Rarity: *Rare*
Special Properties: *Grants +1 to Guard. While outside of combat, the wearer's health regenerates steadily over time.*
Description: *Forged from polished silver and set with a deep green gem flecked with golden motes, the ring carries an aura of quiet vitality. Its magic does not mend wounds in the heat of battle, but once danger has passed, it restores the body as though the wearer were resting on fertile earth. Many adventurers prize this ring for its ability to carry them through long journeys without succumbing to fatigue or minor injury.*

"Hell yes," I said. She'd gotten a regeneration ring, which would be super helpful. Now we just needed to get Tomas one, and we'd be set; all of Oathbound would have one.

"Thank you," Ryn said, catching my eye and grinning. "This will help a ton."

"The dungeons know what we need, and they will provide," Torwyn said, with that knowing look on her face again.

"I've never read anything about that. I thought it was agreed by scholars that it's just random and dungeons have no consciousness," Ryn said, looking at Torwyn with a look that said, 'please tell me more'.

"I don't know about dungeons from around here, but where we come from, dungeons are very much alive, and you have to admit that so far the drops have been tailored to you all. Surely that isn't just blind luck," Torwyn said.

"This next floor is supposed to be level 20, so we will be out-leveled and at a disadvantage," I said, looking over my group. "So let's play it slow and safe."

"Not necessary," Luke said, shrugging. "We are well capable of keeping the pace and making sure you feel challenged enough. Don't worry, we won't just carry you through, but slowing down isn't the answer."

The darkness retreated for some more flat open spaces with many holes in the walls the size of a medium-sized cat. I had a hunch that monsters would be coming out of those holes, but I couldn't really say what kinds, though we heard the slightest squeaks as we walked, so something that would make those sounds.

It turned out we were going to be facing two monster types on this floor, the first of which appeared in the lower light like a flash, exploding before I could really see it.

"Mice," Torwyn said, her dagger piercing a fist-sized little rodent, all of which I didn't see until my eyes stopped pulsing from the bright ass light it had let off.

"So you kill them, and they explode with light, or did it do that, and you killed it?" I asked, and Torwyn gave me a funny smile in response.

"I killed it, and it exploded in light," she finally admitted, and I chuckled.

"Careful then, because those will be annoying to say the least. Incoming!" I shouted as several small mice darted toward us, but something else came as well, shooting from the hole and hitting Tomas full in the chest, easily the size of a medium dog.

It was a crystalized rat; it looked heavy as hell, and Tomas was having trouble batting it off him. So I cast Shove on it, and it tumbled to the side, before Tomas threw up a block, which he used to step on and give himself some height. He slammed his staff down on the crystallized rat and shattered a section of it, but didn't kill it.

I cast Spark on it, and it shattered more of its body, but it still got up and readied to attack again. That was when Ryn appeared before it and cast a point-blank Mana Bolt into the back of its head. It exploded, and Ryn cried out as crystals embedded in her leg, bypassing her armor.

More crystalized rats appeared, and flashes of light filled the space, making it hard to see as Granger tore through the rest of the monsters. They worked like nothing I'd seen before, cutting, smashing, and shooting with such deadly accuracy and power that their foes stood no chance to recover.

We fought and killed another crystallized rat before the others were all down, and Ryn took a minute to pull out the crystal from her legs. We got cores and a few items, a ring and a necklace, from the rats, surprising me because they'd dropped nothing but trash up to this point.

The ring was a common type of regeneration ring that only slightly increased healing factor. We gave it to Tomas, and the necklace was a once-per-hour use skill necklace, which we rolled on. Ryn listed off the status of it, and I smiled at how useful it might be down here.

Name: *Necklace of Moonveil*
   Rarity: *Uncommon*
   Special Properties: *Once per hour, grants night vision for 10 minutes, allowing the wearer to see clearly in complete darkness.*

Description: *A silver chain set with a pale opal, which gleams like moonlight when the ability is invoked.*

"That's a pretty rare drop to get from monster mobs," Torwyn said, looking at it with a small bit of lust. "But go ahead and roll it off, we pass still, but you gotta let us take the final boss rooms' loot no questions asked."

I shared a look with Ryn and Tomas, we shrugged, and I said, "Sure, we can agree to that."

Who knew if we'd make it to the final floor with how powerful the monsters were scaling? One thing I knew for sure was we'd be a liability in the last fight, more likely to get in trouble than do something helpful at our level.

I rolled an eight with the two dice as we split up the rest of the cores between the seven of us. They were as valuable as coins, so we all wanted a piece of that. Ryn rolled her two dice next. She rolled a nine, and I let go of my hope of getting the item, useful as it was; rolls were rolls. Next up was Tomas, who blew on the dice and took his time before rolling.

He rolled a seven, and he cursed at his horrible luck when using someone else's dice. He started to complain about wanting to use his own dice for the roll, but I stopped him with my hands raised.

"She rolled fairly and won it," I said. "Be happy for her and let's move on."

It took another hour before we reached the boss, more of the same fighting, a few Crystal-Fanged Rats while Granger took on the whole mess of them, along with the Lantern Mice that exploded into light when killed. Ryn had given me the names after we finished our second fight, but regardless, it was over faster and faster as we learned to kill them effectively.

The boss was a crystallized rat, but it had many small mice around it, and the boss seemed to shimmer with magical potential.

"You want us to take point, or did you want to give it a try?" Torwyn asked. "We are only eleven hours in, and we are over halfway done, so we have the time if you wanted to give it a go with us playing mild support in the back line."

"Let's just fight it full on, no point in wasting time or effort. We'd normally form a three-versus-three setup and call you in when we need support, but none of you have a shield, so it might be hard for you."

"Daniel is our tank," she said, interrupting me. "We can do the switch tactic. You go first and call a switch when you need us to step in, all right?"

"All right," I said, happy to have things turn back to the normal that I was used to. Sure, we'd done a six vs six switch tactic in the tower, but the bosses were a bit more in the tower, and you almost needed twelve to take them on. Which was odd, considering Tower climbing was considered a solo adventuring endeavor.

I'd need to try to tower climb at some point, but I'd need to find a climber to let me tag along. I wasn't about to go in alone and not learn the tricks of the trade, dying before I had a chance to figure it out.

"Watch when you kill one of the mice, it'll blind us, but I doubt it will affect the boss," I said, turning to my team and getting ready to face off against the horse-sized rat. "We've got this. When I call switch, be ready to retreat. No heroes today, just clean fighting and essence collection."

"Sounds like a plan," Tomas said, cracking his neck to the side and putting away his bag of treats he'd taken out to eat while we all talked.

He was such an easy-going guy, able to relax in almost every situation. I wished he hadn't had to leave Ashric behind, but it was going to happen eventually. Might as well pull off the bandage before it got worst. I often wondered how they'd grown so close, but I knew I couldn't understand, because they'd been almost like brothers, and I'd never had one. The closest I had was Tomas and Ryn, and as much as I wanted it to be the same, it wasn't.

"Let's do this," Ryn said, cutting off my random thoughts and bringing me back to reality.

We shared a look, and I said, "Oathbound, move out!"

Marching forward, I led the charge with my shield, and the rat came to life as we neared. Suddenly, a flash of light went off as I stepped on a mouse, but I managed to keep my run going and slammed into the crystal rat, pieces of it falling off as we clashed.

Tomas was there, high in the air, getting lift from his Block skill, and slamming down his staff on the monster's head. Before he did, though, I cast a quick Spark on it, giving it an extra boom as it hit, and a large chunk flew off.

It suddenly squealed at us, a harmonic sound coming out of a crystalized rat, before turning and slapping Tomas out of the air before he could land with its tail. Ryn was there a moment later, cutting down with her sword, chipping away at the tail. I wasn't idle, joining the attack, and we nearly got the tail cut off before it flipped back and bit at us with enormous teeth.

I brought up my shield and caught the blow, but I felt it in my knees; if not for my Iron Skin skill, I'd have buckled under the load of its single attack. It chomped again, and I stepped to the side and let it glance off before stabbing it in the left eye. It shimmered, and suddenly an explosion of light came off it, throwing us all back.

"Switch!" I yelled over the din of battle, as all three of us had been knocked back.

Granger wasted not a moment, appearing before the rat and tearing it apart with each blow. The fight was over within a minute. While we recovered, we watched Granger's power in awe.

Torwyn cut the tail off easily with her daggers, while Daniel literally grappled with the rat hand-to-hand. Luke took to its neck, slamming his axe down, and arrows filled its eyes from Hunter. In a word, it was devastation. The rat died after less than a minute of that, and I almost wished we hadn't called the switch so fast, or that maybe they'd called a switch so we could finish it off.

"Sorry," Torwyn said, smiling over to me as she saw me watching them. "We can get carried away sometimes."

"No problem," I said, still in awe of how fast they'd taken apart a level 20 dungeon boss. Maybe we'd clear this dungeon after all.

The chest appeared as the body, and the small mice disappeared.

This time, there were three chests, not just the one, and Hunter cheered for us, saying, "There you go! Bonus chests!"

"We still pass them all to you," Torwyn said, and Hunter seemed to deflate a little.

Each of the chests on the side was copper, like before, but the middle one was silver and slightly bigger than the others.

"Should we roll for who gets the middle chest?" I asked. It was pretty clear it would hold better loot than the others, so we should take it into account.

"Sure," Ryn and Tomas said, their eyes never leaving the silver chest.

I took last this time, Ryn rolled an impressive nine, then, rolling with his own dice, Tomas rolled a nine as well, leaving me to either beat them or make them roll again. I took Tomas's dice, and I rolled, smiling at the results: an eleven.

"Damn," Tomas said, frowning. "Shouldn't have let you use my dice."

I walked up to the chest and envisioned what I wanted. It surely couldn't read my mind, but it didn't hurt to try. I even whispered what I wanted as I got closer, my words not loud enough for anyone else to hear.

"A sword worthy of a dragon rider," I whispered the words, hoping against hope I got a decent sword from the chest.

Opening the top, I saw golden light shimmering within, and I reached into the chest, my hand gripping something fast, and pulled it free. A sword, and a pretty freaking sweet looking one at that. It was a long sword, but light enough to wield in a single hand; the blade was darkened steel with a red line down the middle. What it could do and what it was, I didn't know, so I turned to Ryn, who had put her spectacles on and examined the item.

Name: *Emberfang Blade*
  Rarity: *Rare*
  Special Properties: *On a critical hit, the blade releases a spark of fire, dealing minor burn damage over time to the struck enemy.*
  Description: *Forged in heat that never fully cooled, the blade is a dark*

steel longsword with a vivid crimson vein running down its center. It feels faintly warm to the touch, and when drawn, smoke sometimes curls from its edge like rising embers. Balanced and light enough for one-handed use, it is favored by those who want both precision and a touch of flame on the battlefield.

"No freaking way!" Tomas said, rushing forward and looking at the blade more closely. "This is truly awesome. Can you imagine how much this might sell for?"

"I'm not selling this sword," I said, reaching down and into the chest as I thought I saw something else within. I pulled free a sheath of dark, black wood with a web of red. The sword fit perfectly, and as I buckled it on my waist, I then pulled it free, and smoke leaked from the edge, looking freaking amazing.

"You look pretty badass," Ryn said. "You deserve it."

"Well, it isn't over yet, check your chests!" I said, putting my warm blade away and looking eagerly at Tomas as he pulled free his item.

Tomas got a pair of boots that increased his Speed Attribute by one and were said to reduce the sound of his footfalls by a noticeable degree. Ryn got a pair of bracers called Bracers of Sure Grip, which increased grip strength and prevented you from being disarmed by an additional ten percent. Both nice items, but not as cool as what we'd gotten before.

We ventured into the door, an iron door this time around, and went into a darker warren, filled with clicking noises and small insects all around. It was the only hint we had about what we were going to face.

CHAPTER 23
DUNGEON CLEARING

We'd gotten several pieces of pretty impressive loot, and I was happy to say that the sword, staff, necklace, ring, and other items were definitely not going to waste on us, but I did wonder why Granger wasn't interested in anything but the final chest. As we walked through the bug-infested warrens, I hung back a bit and spoke to Ryn in a hushed tone.

"Why do you think they want the final chest and only the final chest?" I asked, curious if Ryn could shed any light on why the final chest would be so important.

"The final chest is said to be the best chest in the entire dungeon; other than that, I know very little else. I'm guessing they are just holding out for the rarest loot," Ryn said, guessing as much as informing me.

"This floor is going to be level twenty-five, nearly ten levels above us, and the final floor is level thirty. We need to stay focused and ready to defend ourselves. Safety first and foremost, all right?" I said, speaking a bit louder so Tomas could hear me as well.

"You guys stay alive," Torwyn said, from up ahead. "And we will take care of the threats."

Just as she said that, a beetle the size of a mule smashed through the side of the wall and charged the front of the group, with Granger taking the brunt of the attack. With oversized mandibles I thought it was going to surprise Daniel and cut him in two, but Daniel bent low and grabbed hold of each side, stopping it from clamping down on him.

"These ones are stronger. Give me a moment to adjust," Daniel said, straining hard against the beetle, and then suddenly he pushed it out with newfound strength, the beetle chittering in response.

It lunged forward with its mandibles again, but Daniel caught them, moving with speed and strength. His Guard must be pretty high to resist the sharp edges of the mandibles, but the fight didn't last long. The others of Granger shot into action arrows, daggers, and a massive axe, finding purchase all within moments of the second attack.

Then something from behind us appeared, making only the slightest noise as it lifted me into the air by my foot and dangled me over rows of sharpened teeth. It was a worm, or rather a snake-like worm with rows and rows of sharp teeth and a head big enough to swallow my head whole.

I heard cries as it dropped me, but I had no intention of being bitten by this thing. Using Shove on myself, I was thrown to the side and missed the head by several feet. Granger had finally turned to help, but then another insect appeared, drawing their attention. This time, large, dog-sized beetles with crazy sharp mandibles.

Looks like this fight was our own for now.

"Take up position," I said, getting to my feet after retrieving my sword and shield.

My sword let off a whiff of smoke as I pulled it free, and I couldn't help but smile. The worm was at least twenty paces long, and besides a narrow tail and rows of teeth, it seemed otherwise unable to attack us. But it used its tail smartly, whipping at my shield and throwing me back with each strike.

Tomas got in and managed a strike to its muscles exterior, but it did very little to damage the worm, as it ignored Tomas and tried its best to get me again. Not until Ryn appeared with her sword out and cut into it did it seem to realize there was more to fight than just me.

As it turned to deal with Ryn and the pain in its side, green ichor coming out of it, I rushed forward and cut into it with my new sword. It cut clean through, effortless as air. The heat and fire damage also left a sizzling burn where it cut; the flesh bubbled and spat where I cut.

It was literally like a hot knife cutting through butter, a very hot knife.

Ryn, passing through the shadows as cleanly as the slight breeze over a pond, appeared before it and struck out again, cutting a large slice into it. This fight wasn't going half bad, I thought, just as the worm tail caught all three of us, swiping away our feet. Then it lunged toward me, teeth and maw open for the kill.

Granger was there, Torwyn burst from the shadows, her daggers sinking deep into the worm, then suddenly releasing in an odd way. The blade tips stayed embedded, but thin wires sprang from the handles, and she ran around the worm before pulling tight and cutting it in two within a moment of its appearance.

"Holy shit," I said, standing finally and getting a good look at her. She wasn't even breathing hard and had that knowing grin on her face.

"You're welcome," she said, bowing slightly in our direction, as the worm bled out.

We recovered our loot, no cool items, but lots of potions and cores.

"You did well, but maybe next time think more defensively," Torwyn said as she passed. "We've got all the offense you'll need for this dungeon, especially this deep."

"I understand," I said, and truly I did. Monsters this deep were just too strong for us; we could fight them, as we'd shown, but it only took one mistake for us to be overwhelmed.

We fought the three types of insects over and over again, until we reached the boss, a giant version of the large armored beetle. It had massive mandibles and sharp feet that could stab you as easily as crush you. The only true advantage we had over it was that it appeared to be very slow, like painfully slow, except for when closing its mandibles.

"Stay back, hit it from a distance if you can, but don't get in front of it. Not even Daniel will be able to stop those mandibles when they come crushing inward," Torwyn said, and Luke nodded as if he agreed but also had something to say. When he didn't after a few moments, the fight started with earnest.

Daniel rushed in, firing his boomstick at its face, and chunking off some of the armor. He was using some of the monster cores from this floor, so they packed a punch; that much was easy to see.

Luke flanked it with his massive axe, scoring hits where he could, but the armor was thick, so it took several hits to break a piece off, and the legs shot out almost as fast as the mandibles when you got too close, a cut scoring Luke's leg showing off how easily you could take damage if you weren't careful.

I cast Spark on cooldown, but I wasn't sure it was doing anything, and Ryn used her Mana Bolt on cooldown as well, which was slightly faster than mine, meaning she pelted it with magic every six seconds or so when I had to wait a solid ten for mine if I wanted to avoid damage to myself.

Tomas, on the other hand, looked sourly at the boss and threw up a Block whenever he thought it would be helpful. He stopped at least one leg from hitting Torwyn, so it wasn't like he wasn't doing anything. Meanwhile, Hunter and his squirrel pelted the giant bug with arrows that exploded on contact and did more damage than even Luke could manage with his axe, due to how fast he could keep firing.

This rapid-fire of attacks and blocks meant the boss was taking a lot of damage really quickly. However, the fight shifted suddenly, with the boss smashing its mandibles together and dust pouring out all around it. Granger moved quickly to back away as a cloud of green dust settled over everything, stopping just shy of us backliners.

"You got that, Daniel?" Luke asked, looking at his friend, who nodded in return.

Daniel did something to his boomstick, twisting the barrel and inserting another monster core. Then the barrel expanded, and it fired the core into the green mist, which settled all around. The core began to shine, then a whirlwind of green dust later, it was all being sucked inside the core.

After a minute of this, the boss stayed dormant the entire time, as if it were afraid to move among the green stuff as well. It finally ended, and the core turned a sickly green color before going black and crumbling to dust.

"Well, that was neat," I said, and Torwyn went up to Daniel and patted him on the back.

"This is why we keep him around," she said jokingly, and Daniel gave her a look that seemed to say, 'tell yourself whatever you want to'. He was a big part of the team, obviously, and they'd be all the weaker without him. With seven people total, we really did have an advantage, but I wasn't about to say that aloud and tempt fate.

The beetle rushed, as fast as it could, back into the action, and Granger was there to meet it. The battle ended much as it began, with arrows and axe strikes, mixed in with an occasional dagger strike, dealing massive amounts of damage altogether.

It was loot time, but only two chests appeared this time, both copper-colored.

"Let's roll, and the top two get to loot the chest," I said, pulling out my dice for once and rolling first this time. I rolled a depressing six and passed my dice to Ryn, but she insisted on using her own. She rolled a ten, giving her one of the spots. Tomas took out his dice, blew on them, and rolled. He rolled a two, snake eyes, not what you want to see on a roll for the highest number, but great if you are gambling.

"I need new dice," Tomas said under his breath as he folded his arms and looked sour. But then his mood shifted as he pulled out some snacks, throwing a handful into his mouth.

"Let's go see what we got," I said, picking the left-most one as Ryn was already approaching the right one.

I reached in and pulled out a charm about the size of a walnut, shaped like a wolf's head, silver and polished. Looking over at Ryn, I saw she'd pulled out a sword with runes etched on its surface, green and sickly-looking in the low light of the warrens.

"Can you give this an identify please?" I said, holding out the emblem to her.

"Sure, just give me a second," Ryn said, reaching back in and pulling out the sheath to go with the sword. She took out her spectacles and looked first at my little emblem before looking at her sword.

Name: *Wolfcaller's Charm*
  Rarity: *Uncommon*
  Special Properties: *Once per day, grants the wearer +5 Power for one minute.*
  Description: *A silver wolf's head that seems to radiate power when*

clutched in your palm. It had a backing that allows you to pin it to yourself on either a cloak or your armor.

Name: *Venomfang Edge*
  Rarity: *Uncommon*
  Special Properties: *Each strike has a minor chance of inflicting a weak poison that damages the enemy over time.*
  Description: *This blackened blade is etched with green runes. The edge glistens faintly as if always freshly oiled.*

"You all good?" Torwyn asked. "We've got roughly four hours to clear the last floor, and it'll be a challenge for us to do it in that time, so we need to hurry. Let's hope it isn't too crazy a floor, right?"

"Yeah, pretty sure it will be," I said, thinking about how level 30 monsters were usually pretty powerful as they had to be strong enough to deal with classed individuals.

Darkness surrounded us as we ventured deeper, but it broke after only a hundred paces or so, leading to an area much different than the warrens we were used to. No, instead it was as if we'd entered ruins of some kind, with massive ceilings above us and rock-shaped pillars all around. What type of building had been here before, I could not tell, as the ruins were much aged by time.

"An interesting shift in scenery, almost like the dungeon is starting on a path to becoming themed," Ryn said, making a parallel between the two types of dungeons.

"Well," I said, shaking my head. "I thought it was either one or the other, not both?"

"She's right, this is the dungeon's first attempt at being a themed dungeon like its brothers. It takes an evolved dungeon core to do such a thing, which means it must be out of its wild stages. This should work, we just have to get to the last boss or challenge," Torwyn said, speaking mostly to her group and looking right at Luke as she spoke.

"What will work?" I asked, wondering about their true intentions.

"Nothing to worry about yet," Torwyn said, winking at me. "Let's clear this floor and then maybe we will tell you."

"Hmm," Daniel said, shaking his head as if he didn't see that as being likely. "We need to hurry if we don't want to be left behind. Let's make haste."

We quickly moved through the room, illuminated by beams of artificial light from the high ceiling. It was so close to shafts of sunlight that I almost felt like I was outside, but it was missing something, perhaps the warmth that came with it?

Mushrooms grew here and there. I noticed them because they were so abundant and consistently around; when one moved, I almost didn't pay attention before it was too late. An undead zombie rose from the ground, clutching a long, gnarled root as a weapon and swinging it at me with a speed I could barely match.

My shield came up, and the blow sent reverberating pain down my arm as I caught it. All around us, zombies appeared, covered in mushrooms and half-skeletal. I played defense, keeping my shield up, but I did manage to get a Spark off between whip-like blows against my shield.

Ryn and Tomas also fought defensively, turning away attacks but taking significant damage from the onslaught. Granger, of course, was on the offensive, taking out zombies every few seconds until they finally reached us and relieved us of the pain of fighting four at a time.

Torwyn arrived first, daggers flashing as she stuck them into a stone pillar of all things, then released her handle's switch to allow the cord to appear. Using the metal cord, she cut down three zombies in a single motion, kicking the fourth in the face for good measure. Then Luke appeared behind her, only a measure slower than her. His axe came down on the fourth, ending it with a bisection down the middle.

"This is actually kind of fun," Torwyn exclaimed as she yanked on her daggers, and the blades came flying back to her and into the hilt.

"If these are the weakest monsters here, we are in for a world of hurt," Tomas said, putting a handful of snacks into his mouth.

"We'll be fine," I assured him, but I wasn't so sure myself.

"As long as we fight defensively, we will recover," Ryn said, holding a sore arm as her ring worked to repair her.

My own aches and pains lessened, so we checked the bodies for loot, finding only a few cores for our trouble.

"I don't know what story or theme this dungeon is going for, but it seems half-formed, so we likely will just kill monsters, then a boss, but give it another ten or so years, and it might have a proper theme," Torwyn explained to me as we walked.

"How do you know so much about dungeons?" Ryn asked, obviously a little jealous at her apparent deep knowledge of things dungeon-related.

"I've been through more than I care to count. You pick up stuff after a while," Torwyn said, smiling kindly over at Ryn, who just huffed a little then sighed.

We continued walking forward, and the buildings transitioned from sturdy pillars of rock to half-formed, melted-looking structures. Soon, we found ourselves on the streets of a town that appeared to be in a state of disarray.

. . .

"It looks so incomplete, like it has an idea of what a building should look like, but it can't quite achieve it yet," I remarked, reaching out to touch the melted stone. It crumbled beneath my fingers, revealing itself to be nothing more than porous, weak rock.

"Eyes forward, we've got a new monster," Luke said, and we all looked forward enough to see a mushroom-covered skeleton appear from behind a building. Then another, and another, until there were five skeletons with shields and rusty swords awaiting us in formation, shields up and swords at the ready.

"Hit them with ranged attacks, see if you can break their shields," Luke ordered, and we answered by casting all the ranged attacks we had.

I had to get a little closer for my Spark to work, but Daniel had the same idea, so I wasn't alone. He pulled free his boomstick, loaded one of the undead cores into it, and fired. My ears hurt from the crack that split the air this time, far more powerful than any shot he'd done before. It split the shield of the lead skeleton into a million pieces as my Spark hit another, doing enough damage to knock it back but not much else.

Then the arrows came, each one exploding on contact, as their shields were broken to bits. The skeletons charged forward, swords raised. However, the arrows never stopped; neither did my Spark and his boomstick, which meant only three got to us alive and mostly in one piece.

Daniel punched through the head of one, bone dust flying up around his fist, and Torwyn and Luke appeared, smashing into the other two before they could reach me. It was all a bit boring, really. Team Granger was kicking ass, and we barely got to do anything.

But alas, the dungeon wasn't about to let half a group do nothing, so zombies appeared in the back line, and I ran to support my friends as they went one-on-one with monsters ten plus levels higher than themselves.

Tomas flipped his special staff around, smashing the jaw of one of the zombies, while Ryn used her daggers to cut into one, before backing off and avoiding a strike. These zombies were markedly slower and had no weapons, but still, we needed to be cautious.

I arrived on scene just as two more zombies appeared before them, slamming my shield into one and stabbing the other through the eye before it could even moan a single syllable. One down, and three to go, I thought as I turned to face the zombie before me.

It had a root, but a fat, gnarled one that was more like a club than anything else, and it swung at me with a slow, deliberate gait. I caught the blow, only partially allowing most of the force to roll off my shield, and countered with a Spark and a Shove, one right after the other.

The zombie went rigid, and when it was shoved, it fell back on its ass, giving me the chance to rush forward and put my blade in its eye, killing it much easier than I would have expected. Turning to help my friends, I saw they had put down their zombies, too.

"Look at us go," I said, smiling. "I wouldn't have thought those were level 30 at all."

"I'm not sure they were," Ryn said, reaching down and looting hers. I looted the ones I killed, getting some potions and a single monster core.

"What do you mean?" I asked, confused how she'd gotten to where she had in her logic. We were obviously on the last floor, and monsters here were level 30; it just made sense.

"I don't know, they were so slow and weak compared to what we'd killed before, it didn't feel the same at all," Ryn said.

"I agree, before I barely could keep up with them, but this time they were slower than me by half," Tomas said, then Torwyn came up and added her two cents.

"I think the dungeon is trying to balance out our experience. It appears it wants you to feel involved as well, so it's sending monsters at your level to fight you since you've been mostly hanging back. Fascinating, dungeons," Torwyn said, shaking her head.

"I'm going to need to take notes of the behaviors I'm seeing here," Ryn said, nodding along with her own words. "I could put out a book on dungeons that could inform and shed so much light on them."

"Yeah, there are precious few scholars in this land; it seems all the deep knowledge is suppressed or something," Torwyn said, nodding as well.

"You think someone or some group is actively making sure knowledge of the unlocked individuals and dungeons and well magic in general is being hidden?" Ryn asked. I could tell her intellectual side was really latching onto this, and it was a mix of excitement and anger for her.

"I wouldn't doubt it, but let's focus up. I see more skeletons forming ranks ahead of us," Torwyn said, turning and leaving to join her group.

The fights were much the same after that, with us hanging back and killing weaker zombies and occasionally a lone skeleton that was a bit tougher to kill, but with each of Tomas's strikes breaking a bone, we managed our way through. Finally, after several hours of this, we reached a colosseum-type building with high, well-formed, and detailed walls.

"This must be where the boss is," Luke said, gesturing forward to the massive building. "It is also where the dungeon core has its most well-formed building. I'd say it's safe to enter, as long as we don't touch anything. All its buildings so far have been very lightweight."

We ventured through one of the many dozen spaces open on the outside. With large pillars running the length of the building, it had door-like openings every few feet and rose at least four stories high. It was all stone, but it looked much more solid than the other stone we'd encountered, so we ventured forward and through to the middle with little fear of collapse.

It wasn't until we reached the middle that we saw the opposite side had actually collapsed, leaving a wide opening.

"Well, at least our side stayed up," Daniel said, as he admired the craftsmanship of the arena.

It was empty, nothing inside, but a distant roar reverberated through the chamber, and I knew it wouldn't stay empty for long. From the crashed out section, something big was coming, only a silhouette in the fake sunlight of the area, but large enough to give us all pause.

"Stay defensive, but attack when you can. I imagine this boss won't be easy, so be ready for a fight," Torwyn said, motioning forward with her daggers before leaving to join the front line.

However, the dungeon had other ideas, because skeletons and zombies appeared from behind and then all around, so much so that Granger looked a little worried in our direction. They did not attack all at once, though; only two came forward for each one facing them, which worked in our favor, as whatever else came was getting closer and closer.

The ones that faced off against us were weaker; that much was for sure, but still, we were outnumbered, so it took some finesse to maneuver the situation.

I blocked the first attack, giving the skeleton a blow to the face for its trouble and staggering it back. My sword grew warm in my grip as I struck out, leaving a charred bone in the wake of my attack. Tomas wasn't idle either, smashing and breaking bones left and right. Before I knew it, we were back on even footing, and we stopped giving ground.

Ryn slashed with her sword, using it more as a club than anything, but the poison of her blade was not doing much against skeletons, and still she swung with enough force to break bones every two strikes. She looked badass, though, with her green glowing sword and perfect stance as she fought back with fire in her eyes.

At one point, she turned and fired off a Mana Bolt into a skeleton only a few feet away, blowing it apart with a single strike, and I remembered that my Spark was also effective on undead, so I used it on the one I was fighting against, splitting the skull down the middle.

More came, but we defeated them with just as much vigor as before, until suddenly they all backed off, the remaining ones, and I turned to see the boss monster had joined the battle, with Granger fighting life and limbs against it.

The monster was an amalgamation of skeletal parts and fleshy bits. It was rotund and at least ten paces wide to its twelve or so paces tall, nearly equally tall as it was fat. It had no fewer than 10 arms, three powerful but stubby legs, and two massive heads.

In a word, it was hideous.

Daniel tried to block it as it ran straight for us, for whatever reason, but he was thrown aside, and it was only Torwyn's quick thinking that kept us from being squashed by its charge. She slammed her daggers into the hard stone ground and extended the line from them, tripping the monstrosity or at least making it stumble.

It seemed to fixate on her then, and she ran while her party attacked it, leaving her daggers behind and pulling out a long, curved blade that was almost long enough to be called a sword. I hated to imagine what would happen to someone if it got a chance to attack; this thing was all bone and muscle, with no shortage of either.

Luckily, Torwyn had the stamina and speed to stay out of its way, only getting into trouble as two skeletons came out to attack her right as the monstrosity decided to focus on Hunter, switching directions and heading his way.

Somehow, Hunter produced a blue glow around his arrows and shot at the legs of the monster, slowing it with some type of ice effect, unlike anything I'd ever seen skill-wise. Who were these people, and how did they have so many unique skills?

It wasn't time to think about that, though, so I used Spark and did my best to keep damage rolling onto the boss while Hunter kited the monster around the room. With every move he made, he led him in circles while we did all we could to burn the boss down. Finally, after like thirty minutes of this, him switching to different targets, including myself at one point, and we got out of whatever locked phase he was in.

Now, with several arms missing and much of his bulk having fallen off while we attacked him, we faced a much more slim monsters. It stood in the middle of the arena and began to screech, not attacking us, but suddenly the remaining zombies and skeletons began to slowly march forward toward it, weapons and arms down.

"I've seen a mechanic like this before," Torwyn yelled. "Kill the weaker monsters, then focus the boss, if he gets any of them he'll likely be buffed by it."

No one answered, but we all moved to obey.

I crashed into a skeleton with my shield held high, but it didn't fight back, so I smashed its head in after two more shield blows. Repeating this method, and occasionally using my sword, I killed another three before we ran out of time. About six reached the boss, and he heaved his arms around them, grabbing them and smashing them against his body.

This had the effect of making him bigger again, even regrowing a few arms. But still, he wasn't as big as he'd been before, so that was good. Suddenly, he focused on Hunter, swinging for him, and the fight started again, with him fixating while we burnt him down as best we could.

The scenario repeated itself three more times. Each time we went down, we killed more monsters; they returned afterward, filling the ring again, but we were making slow progress until finally something changed.

The three-legged monstrosity shifted and changed into something new right before our eyes after absorbing four skeletons. It compacted and changed until we were facing a ten-foot-tall, lean, skeletal monster with a sword and a shield. All the remaining bits of flesh fell free, and it was all skeleton suddenly.

It had only two thick legs, too many bones for it to be natural, and two sets of arms, so four total: two with shields and two with swords. It slammed down its swords on Daniel, who was nearest, but Daniel was able to catch the blades and deflect them with his arms somehow. His entire body seemed to glisten as if metal, and I wondered what ability I was seeing now.

But I had no time to consider, because the fight was on. I used Spark and got up close with my shield, ready to assist Daniel if needed. Luke took that time to jump in and strike, hitting the shield hard before Torwyn appeared behind the skeleton and slashed out at its leg bones, straight up shattering several of them.

It stumbled, and we all mounted attacks while it was unguarded. Mana Bolts, heavy attacks from Tomas's staff, and my own blade cut deep into bone. But the monster recovered soon and, with its massive shield, slammed the three of us all at once, throwing us back several feet and making my very being vibrate with pain.

"Stay back or you'll die," Luke called out as blood trickled down my nose and out of my ears.

Potion, I needed a potion, I vaguely recalled suddenly. Everything was so fuzzy right now that I could barely control myself as I pulled free a vial and took a hit. Then, as the fuzziness began to withdraw, I saw my friends, Tomas with his arm at an unnatural angle, and Ryn knocked out cold. Rushing over to their side as Granger handled the boss, I poured a potion down Ryn's throat before moving over to Tomas.

"It hurts pretty bad," Tomas said.

"Well, here, bite on this," I said, giving him the leather handle of my dagger to bite on. "I need to put your arm back before giving you the potion."

He did as I requested, and I went to work, bending his arm back in a quick and painful move. His screams filled the arena, muffled as they were, but I ripped my dagger free from his teeth and poured the potion down his throat, giving him an instant sense of relief.

"You'll make it, just take it easy, all right?" I said, turning to see Ryn stirring and going back to her side.

"What happened?" Ryn said, her eyes blinking slowly as she took in the room. "Did I die?"

"No," I said quickly. "You just got the snot knocked out of you. It'll be all right now, just relax while Granger cleans up what is left of the boss."

Sure enough, Granger was hard at work, and the boss fight ended only minutes later, with three chests appearing; the middle one was all gold and sparkling. While the other two were just copper chests. I watched as Torwyn went up and kneeled before the middle chest, opening the lid and pulling out a small walnut-sized gem.

Did she just get a freaking monster core as a reward? How cheap is that! I thought, but she seemed thrilled by what she'd gotten.

"It'll work," Torwyn said, holding it up for Daniel to see. "With this, we might be able to get back."

"It'll take time to know if that is true, but we were lucky to encounter a strong enough dungeon to produce a heart stone to the quality we required," Daniel said. Then, seeming to realize that they weren't alone, they turned to us and motioned to the other chests.

"I think you are good to loot these two," Luke said. "We don't need whatever is inside of them, we got what we needed."

CHAPTER 24
PROGRESS

The loot, as it turned out, was all right. I lost the rolls, and Tomas and Ryn got to pick which one they wanted. With Ryn taking out her spectacles, we got to see what the two items could do. First, she told us the item that she got, then Tomas's.

Name: *Torch of Everflame*
> **Rarity:** *Uncommon*
> **Special Properties:** *Burns indefinitely without consuming fuel; cannot be extinguished by water or wind.*
> **Description:** *A wooden torch capped with bronze, its flame steady and bright in all conditions.*

Name: *Belt of Steadfast Guard*
> **Rarity:** *Uncommon*
> **Special Properties:** *Grants +1 to Guard while worn.*
> **Description:** *A wide leather belt with a central brass buckle stamped in the shape of a tower.*

Both items would be nice to have in the group, but neither was groundbreaking, and I didn't need them. So we put them away. The torch had a little switch on the side that put out the flames, and Tomas put on his new belt.

"Let's get back while we still can," Torwyn said. "Touch the obelisk down here, and it will transport us back up."

We did what she asked, a mirror of the obelisk having appeared in the middle of the arena. Touching its warm surface, everything around me shifted, and suddenly we were up top again in the little cave.

"Welcome back, make room for more adventurers coming in," said the door attendant, and we quickly moved out of the way.

With all the monsters slain and us back on our way out of town, I decided to check my status, pulling it up and seeing what had changed. I assigned all of my points that I could into Speed before looking it all over.

Name: Kaelric Grimholt
    Level: 19
    Essence: 995/34,005 Until Next Level
    Attributes:
    Power: 5
    Guard: 5
    Speed: 14(Base 4)
    Arcana: 5
    Equipped Abilities:
    Slot 1: Iron Skin
    Slot 2: Spark
    Slot 3: Shove
    Slot 4: Empty
    Class: Empty
    Class Passive: Empty
    Class Slot Ability: Empty

I'd come a long way in a short period of time. It surprised me more than anything that I was nearly level 20 in a matter of weeks, instead of a year like I'd been led to believe. Experience was getting harder to get, but we'd killed so many monsters in that dungeon that it didn't really matter. Dungeons were the powerhouses of leveling, but they came with great risk and great reward.

We'd come out with magical items that would make our next dungeon trip much easier, but our next one likely wouldn't be with Granger either, so we'd need to be more careful. I didn't want my crew getting used to having such powerful adventurers at our side, but I had a feeling that wouldn't matter.

Granger had been looking for something specific and had now found it. Now I wondered how long they'd stay around. I decided to ask just that of Torwyn as we walked through the forest toward the road.

"Oh, we'll be around for a bit, here and there," she said. "Sur,e we've found a possible method of returning home, but that doesn't mean we don't enjoy what this place has to offer."

"Home?" I asked. "Are you from somewhere distant?"

"You could say that," she said, but gave no further explanation.

"Where is home, on one of the other continents?" I tried to ask, but she pretended not to notice my question. Instea,d she asked one of her own.

"You ever look up in the sky and wonder what is out there?" she asked, it was pitch dark, only Ryn's torch giving us light currently, but the sky was lit up by a thousand stars and a little light from the moons above.

"I guess I've been more concerned about the happenings around me to consider the stars and what mysteries they might hold," I admitted, truly looking and allowing myself to wonder as I looked up at the stars.

"I can't stop gazing up, never have been able to think past the big what if, and it turns out I was right, there is so much out there that we have only just barely begun to scratch the surface of it," she said, but I missed her meaning so I just gazed up for a while until returning my eyes to the party before me.

We were strong, Oathbound, and we would make our mark on this world, and maybe someday, beyond our shores to other worlds, but one thing I hadn't considered was other life out there in the great black sea of stars. Maybe someday we'd be out there as well, fighting among the stars and seeing things we'd never imagined.

"You aren't from around here," I said suddenly, looking up and my brain working to put a few pieces together. "You aren't saying..."

She put a finger to her lips and made a shushing motion. I took the hint, because if this was real, that was mind-blowing, and I had so many questions I wanted to ask. But I kept myself in check, looking around to see if anyone else had made the same conclusion, but Ryn and Tomas were mid-conversation and not paying attention.

"It's a secret I hope you can keep. I can't say more about it, but we are visitors to your land. We've done our best to embrace and mold ourselves as best we can to your culture, but I think we stand out more than we should," she said, speaking in a low whisper.

Daniel appeared at my side, his face stern and his expression that of someone on the edge of anger.

"You will keep our secret, won't you?" Daniel asked, putting a metallic hand on my shoulder and squeezing.

"Stop it," Torwyn said, easily pushing Daniel aside, though the move looked gentle and friendly; he moved a solid three feet, stumbling backward. "He's fine, I vouch for him."

"Check your strength, Torwyn," Daniel said through gritted teeth.

"Sorry," she said, flashing him a quick smile and going on her way.

The conversation ended there, but at the first chance we had alone, I'd be telling the others, because secret or not, I couldn't keep it from them.

The idea that other beings from outside our world could get here and look and act so similar to us, it was mind-boggling at the very least.

We made our way back to camp, and we were just in time for them to leave, meaning we'd get no rest today, but we'd gotten several pieces of gear, and it would be worth trudging forward, tired or not. We were set toward the back again, and made ourselves ready as the caravan rolled onward.

The next few days progressed with little new insight into Granger, who kept to themselves during the night now, Daniel working on something the entire time with the team around him at the edge of camp. We got some decent essence, getting roughly thirty thousand essence over a five-day span, meaning we were averaging six thousand per day. But I was told we were close to leaving the areas where monsters often attacked the roads, so the essence was going to drop a good bit.

That also meant we were close to our destination, the area had weaker monsters, around level 15 to 25, so it would be just perfect for our group, as it tended to lean toward the lower end of that spectrum.

I'd told the group about the Granger Band being from another world, but I wasn't sure they believed me. I mean, they were nice about i,t but that is a lot to take in about a group of people. Especially since they looked so similar to us, it was likely, Ryn said, a practical joke they were playing on me. I wasn't sold on that. Granger had been nothing if not honest and fair with us, so why lie about something so fantastical?

I was determined to get to the bottom of this, and so I went to where they were working at the edge of the camp, and interrupted a conversation that I only caught the tail end of.

"...just switch up the frequency and be done with it," Luke was saying, and Daniel answered, sounding slightly annoyed.

"It isn't that simple. We've already run too many tests on this. We might need a more powerful gem after all," Daniel said, stopping short when he saw me approaching.

"Hey there," I said, waving, and Torwyn appeared before me, blocking my view.

"Hi," she said. "What can we do for you?"

"I was just wanting to see how you guys were doing, is all," I said, leaning to the side to see past her.

She leaned with me.

"It's all a bit technical, even above my understanding, but we don't want to spoil your world by planting seeds of knowledge where they should come naturally. My friends reminded me of that, so if you could just forget what I told you about us being from another world, that'd be great," Torwyn said, offering me a cheesy smile.

"I'm not going to tell anyone, well, anyone else. I told my group, but you can understand that I can't keep secrets from them," I said, and thankfully Torwyn nodded, agreeing with me, I hoped.

"I figured you'd tell them, did they believe you?" Torwyn asked, relaxing a little and letting me see past her as I stood there.

They had a box of some kind, and atop it was the gem they'd gotten. Daniel had his boomstick-looking device out, but it had several small barbs on it now and he was shocking the gem repeatedly while I stood watching.

"They, uhh," I said, getting distracted. "Oh, I mean, no, they didn't, not really. That's part of why I came over here, I wanted to know if you'd tell them so they'll believe me."

"No can do," Luke said, shaking his head. "We need the discretion that secrecy gives us. You understand, don't you?"

"I mean, I do," I sai,d and before I could say more, Hunter interjected a few words.

"See all done, he'll keep our secret, and we will wander the country-side for another few months looking for a powerful enough dungeon," Hunter said, obviously a little frustrated about something or other. His squirrel made a 'cheep-cheep' sound on his shoulder, and he gave it a little nut from his pocket. It munched down, the only sound passing between them other than the occasional zap of Daniel's device on the gem.

"You guys are leaving soon?" I asked, taking Hunter's words for what they were.

"Yeah," Torwyn said. "We can't really grow much stronger off the essence here, it's differen,t and we haven't figured it out just yet. But we need to find stronger dungeons for a better chance of a reward. We'd offer to let you come, but you'll need to grow much stronger before you can help us out."

"I understand," I said, looking at each of them. It had been a magical adventure having them along, and it would be weird having to do a dungeon without these powerful and unique adventurers, but I had a feeling deep in my gut that this wasn't the last I'd heard of them. "I will be seeing you again, maybe after I unlock my class."

"What class are you going for? I can't remember if you told us," Torwyn said, obviously just trying to be nice, but I figured they were all right to tell, hell, they weren't even from around here.

"Dragon Knight," I said, smiling as I did.

"Oh, that sounds interesting. We do find it odd that you guys have to wait so long for classes, when we get ours literally days after we are Awak-ened. It molds our entire skill collection, and don't get me started with how few skills you guys get, it is a wonder you can be as flexible as you seem to be," Torwyn said, and Luke elbowed her for some reason.

"Right, I mean, it seems perfectly normal, and I look forward to seeing you as a Dragon Knight," Luke said, looking sheepish.

"Thanks, I guess," I said, looking between the pair of them. Luke had a perpetual smile on his face, despite the way he sounded or acted. It was a very likable face, but it seemed odd that he always kept a smile on, almost as if it were a mask that hid his true feelings behind it.

I left them to it from there, returning to my friends and telling them of the information I'd learned, not that they believed me.

The caravan would be ending soon, and we'd finally be in a beginner-friendly area, although at level 20, we were on the higher end of what we wanted from this area.

CHAPTER 25
A NEW TOWN

We traveled a distance before passing into Stonehaven, our destination. It was a town of stone and defensive placement. Built on a rocky outcrop and hard to get to from the main road, we found ourselves traveling alone, as all others, including the folk we knew, were going to another town deep to see what lay ahead for them before leaving the caravan.

So, with Tomas and Ryn at my side, we entered through a pair of massive stone gates, looking forward to seeing what the town could offer us.

It was colder here, higher up in elevation, and most people had skins of monsters or animals around them to keep them warm. I met the eye of one or another, hoping to ask them directions, but they immediately turned and didn't speak to me, an oddity, but I carried onward with my friends at my side, looking for any sign of the adventurer's tavern.

It wasn't until I came across the backs of a group of six armored individuals that I took a deep breath and approached them looking for information. But I was stopped dead in my tracks when one of them turned around, and I recognized him.

With a large nose and beady black eyes looking down on me, it could be no one else but Craven Deymorin, the son of the very noble who threatened me when he found out I wanted to be a Dragon Knight. His usual assortment of goons turned to see me as well, but I only recognized two of them from class; the other three were new to me.

"How in the hells are you here and why?" I asked, the words spilling out of my mouth before I could think of a snappier thing to say.

"We've been here for the better part of a week. Caravans are slow, and so are you. Good luck finding anything decent here. We've picked up all the jobs worth doing," Craven said with a smirk on his face.

Light glimmered off a silver ring he wore, and it caught my attention. It had a small fist carved into it, and I felt a pressure from it that indicated it was magical to some extent. I looked away from his ring as he put his hand in a pocket when he saw me looking.

"I'm sure we will find a job," I said, trying to think of a snappy response and failing.

"Besides," Tomas said, smirking right on back. "Any job you lot can do will likely be child's play for us. We are level 20 already."

"Impossible," Craven said, scrunching his brow and looking hard at us. "Even if that were true, I've still got the edge; many of the adventurers out here are fusing jobs because of some spooky monster harassing the area."

"I ain't afraid of no ghosts," Tomas quickly interjected.

"I never said anything about ghosts," Craven said, looking a little confused.

"Is there a posting to take on this monster?" I asked, an idea forming in my head.

"There is, you should check it out so the monster can eat you up," Craven said, laughing to his friends.

That was exactly what we would do, but no monster would get the better of us.

"Any chance you'll tell us where the Adventurer's guild is so we can get that job and die by the monster's hand?" I asked, playing into his own words.

"It's not far, you'll find it soon enough," Craven said, gesturing over his shoulder. "Good riddance, Dragon Knight."

With that, they all laughed, and we pushed past them to where he'd thumbed over his shoulder. Sure enough, there was a group of adventurers outside a large warehouse-like building with high windows, stone construction, and three sets of doors leading inside. With a quick question to an adventurer who didn't want to see us dead, I was told the meaning of the three doors.

The first was for getting new jobs, the second was for turning in, and the third was for administrative purposes only. We went into the first and were surprised by how tavern-like it was inside.

A roaring fire took the bite out of the air, rows of seating, a bar in the back, and plates of hot food and drink being served by cute girls that couldn't be much younger than myself. All this, and I also noted that the design wasn't far off from the Adventurer's Guild back home. So we went up to the job board on the east side of the building and started our search.

"I can't believe that Craven came here too," Ryn said through clenched teeth. "I want nothing more than to knock his teeth out and smash in that enormous nose of his."

"I have a feeling you might get your chance before our time in Stonehaven ends," I said, glancing darkly at the door and imagining what was beyond it—the ever-annoying Craven.

"Let's just focus on getting the levels we need and don't worry about Craven," Tomas said, popping a few snacks into his mouth from a bag he hadn't had just moments before.

"What'd you all choose for your next skills when you hit level 20?" I asked, realizing we hadn't talked about it over the last days of the caravan when we'd made level 20.

"I was waiting to discuss it with the group," Ryn said. "I've assigned the points to Speed, but the options I've been given could go either way. Let's pick out a job then we can discuss it over a pint."

"Right," I said, turning my attention back to the job board and what lay ahead for us.

There were many jobs, all within the level 10 to 25 range. They had a notice marking what level range it was safe for, and a large note with gold fringe and a level thirty mark was the one I was looking for.

Job: Silver Eyes
> *Rank: Rare – High Threat*
> *Location: Stonehaven Countryside, east of Brackenford*
> *Details: A monstrous entity called the Silver Eye has been prowling the rural outskirts of Stonehaven. Witness reports describe a gaunt, towering figure bearing luminescent silver eyes. Two experienced adventuring groups have already perished attempting to eliminate it. Livestock are found grotesquely mutilated, and nightly howls have driven entire farmsteads to evacuate.*
> *Objective: Hunt down and slay the creature with the Silver Eyes. Recover remains or belongings of lost adventurers if feasible.*
> *Reward: 10 Suns*
> *Notes: Travelers are urged to avoid the region after dusk. Survivors report the creature's eye glows brightest under moonlight, often moments before an attack. Only seasoned adventurers need apply.*

"This might be a bit out of our wheelhouse right now," Tomas said as I read over the listing again.

"Yeah, let's tackle a few other smaller jobs and see if we can get a little stronger first. Maybe level 25 or so," Ryn said

"This is the greatest threat to folks and likely the biggest reward we could possibly get. I say we defeat the local dungeon, then take on this threat. Is that a fair compromise?" I asked, and both my friends shared a look before nodding.

I made a note of the job number listed on the bottom corner of the sheet and walked over to the reception desk, just as a group of adventurers left it.

"Welcome to the Stone Inn and adventuring hall. What can I do for three new faces? You are adventurers, are you not? Can I see your coin before we begin?" she asked, her face lined with wrinkles and her voice a sort of whine to it as she spoke.

"Of course," I said, producing the thing that marked us as adventurers and allowing her to look each of them over before returning them to us.

"Alrighty, with that out of the way, which job has caught your interest?" she asked, pulling out a ledger and making ready a feather pen.

"We want to take on job 700140," I said, repeating the six-digit number they'd used on the job posting.

Her eyes went a little wide at first, then she looked us over once more, taking note of our armor, and my scarf, her eye lingering on it longer than the other bits of our equipment.

"I'm afraid I can't, in good conscience, allow you to take this job without knowing your capabilities. Please take on a few other jobs, and once we believe you are strong enough, we will open up high-risk jobs to you and your party. Speaking of which, where is the rest of your party?" she asked, looking at the three of us and undoubtedly expecting to see more.

"Just the three of us for now," I said. "Can you recommend which jobs you'd like to see us complete before taking on the Silver Eyed monster?"

"Sure, we have a goblin infestation. We've got a rogue necromancer somewhere raising the dead at night, and all manner of challenging but doable jobs you can tackle to increase your reputation here in Stonehaven. But I will warn you, the last two groups were six and very capable, but they never returned," she said, her whiny voice intensifying as she spoke.

"We will take that into account, thank you," I said, and we turned and went back to the job board, looking for the jobs she'd mentioned to get more information about each of them.

The goblin one seemed promising, with a description about a ruin nearby said to have been occupied by goblins for a little while now. The quest was ranked uncommon but gave a decent amount of moons, thirty to be exact. The only odd bit about it was the mention of people seeing a "shiny-headed goblin wizard" riding a large cave rat.

The next job posting was about the necromancer and his raising of minions from the graveyard at night. It was odd because no one seemed to be getting harmed, but their livestock had been found with blood drained and such. It rewarded only twenty moons, but otherwise seemed like an open-and-shut case of 'kill the necromancer before he becomes a lich'.

The third option we found was the oddest of the bunch. Livestock were going missing, and talk of a person stepping right out of a puddle and doing it was all over the listing. A hooded figure, one man said, appeared out of a thin puddle and stole his goats, leaving behind a silver shimmering mark on the barn next to where they were taken. This one offered only twenty-five moons, but it was intriguing to say the least.

"I say we take all three, and start with the goblins, then at night we go for the necromancer, and when we finish, we see about the puddle hopper," I said, laying out what I thought for my teammates.

"I agree, but before we start, we need to discuss our new abilities and how we can work together with them," Ryn said.

We all agreed, and we took the job posting numbers to the clerk, got assigned to the case, none had anyone on them yet, and found a table where we could talk.

"So I've put my next five into Speed," I said, starting off the conversation. "Which means I can choose either Quickstep, Fleet Foot, or Fast Hands. You've each chosen one, so do I grab the missing one or double down on Quickstep because it's pretty overpowered, all things considered."

"I think having our tank with slightly more movement Speed is helpful, but I think Quickstep or Fast Hands are the better options," Ryn said, nodding along with her own logic.

"On the other hand, maybe upgrading movement speed would give all your movement speed a kick," Tomas said, throwing more snacks into his mouth.

"I wish I'd studied more about the effects of each one so I could be sure, but knowing what we know now, I think I have to go with Quickstep," I said, locking in my decision and feeling my mind washed over with new knowledge.

"Alrighty, that brings it to me," Ryn said, looking at each of us back and forth. "The three options it's giving me are Double Dash, Evasion Roll, and Spring Burst. Double Dash allows me to Quickstep twice before incurring a cooldown, so it's basically just doubling down on the first choice I made, whereas Evasion Roll gives me temporary invulnerability when using it to avoid strikes. Sprint Burst is what it sounds like, giving me an additional burst of speed when sprinting."

"Oh, interesting. I wonder what choice you'd have if you didn't pick Quickstep, something that further pushes out whatever you chose, maybe?" I asked, my curiosity getting the better of me.

"Evasion Roll seems like the clear winner," Tomas said casually snacking and looking Ryn over. "I mean, come on, how many invulnerable skills are you going to get as an option. Tank or no tank, being in the front lines means there will be unavoidable damage at times, so you'll want to take that one."

"I think he's right," Ryn said, biting her lip. "What do you think, Kael?"

"Logic seems sound enough, I'd go for it," I said, nodding along with Tomas's words.

"So that leaves me," Tomas said. "I've not picked which attribute to add to yet, but I'm so tempted to go Arcana just to round off my build."

"That would lock you out of the class you decided to pick. Are you sure you want that?" I asked, remembering his layout needed to be ten in each attribute except for Arcana.

"I know," Tomas said, groaning. "All right, then maybe I'll go Power, we could always use more damage, right?"

"I think that's the play," I said, nodding my head. "We will rely on you for the huge damage when the time comes, just hope the skills it gives you are worth it."

"I agree," Ryn said, adding her two bits.

"All right, then I'll do it," Tomas said, then a second later, he added, "I've got these three options. Shattering Blow that ignores armor and strikes enemies with a powerful blow, Overhead Smash, an area of effect ability that hits all enemies with two-hundred percent of my weapon damage in a cone in front of me. Or Taunting Roar, an ability that does half my weapon damage and forces all enemies around to attack me for several seconds."

"An area of effect would be nice," I said, letting my thoughts spill out into my words. "But Shattering Blow sounds like it's the heavy hit we were talking about. I'm torn. What do you think, Ryn?"

"I think an aoe would be a great help to us in general, and it does decent damage too, so it's not like you couldn't use it against a single target as well," she said, explaining her point.

"What about Taunting Roar? I could help with tanking if you ever get overwhelmed," Tomas offered.

"I think we need to focus on damage, and I'm leaning toward the aoe ability," I said, then turning to Tomas, I added, "But it's up to you. Obviously, you'll be the one to employ the ability."

"I can go for the aoe," Tomas said. "I think it'll be the best choice."

And just like that, we'd all chosen our newest skills.

We ordered food and drinks next, letting the warmth of the place fill us. The day was young, and we still had work to do, so we asked the waitress about the town's general layout, including where the ruins outside of town, the graveyard, and the final location were, as well as the location of the local dungeon. With all this new information at hand, we ventured out, ready to slay some goblins.

CHAPTER 26
GOBLIN WIZARD

The town was full of life as we walked through street by street, getting our bearings. We found shops of all kinds, many more specifically meant for adventurers than not, and we were halfway tempted to go check a few out, but instead we searched out an area to stow our gear and sleep for the night when the time came. The first place we tried was a bit run-down, and after asking about the price, we determined we could do better, so we left the Goblin's Egg, the oddly named place, to find another better-suited establishment.

Where we landed after that was a quaint little place off the beaten path, but near enough to the wall and the gate that we'd have quick access. It was a mix of cobblestone and wood construction, with a stone foundation and two wooden stories above. It had a light pink, almost white, color to the wood, natural or not, I couldn't tell, but it was worn with age.

A few people were leaving as we approached the dark-stained door, and I caught a bit of what they were saying. Something about how they really enjoyed their stay and would return. They weren't adventurers by their looks, but just average-looking folks.

Entering the inn, which, by the sign outside, was called the Witches' Oven, I saw the words written in black on the pink wooden sign, with the symbol of an oven. I liked the place already from the name, but what I saw inside made me open my eyes wide.

A massive fireplace in the middle of the room heated the place, and tables were spread out on the first floor, a tavern of sorts in full swing, and the thing that gave me pause was the massive woman in a pink dress with bulging muscled arms, and a stern expression on her face as she saw us enter.

"No," she said, waving us toward the door. "No active adventurers can stay here, not on my watch."

"But," I started to say, but she stepped forward, and I felt a spike of fear go down my spine at her size and power that she extruded.

"No buts, just leave," she said, pointing to the door.

"We need a place to stay," Ryn said, obviously getting heated by how we were getting treated by the tone of her voice.

"And I run a no-nonsense business, and adventurers just bring down hell on my establishment. So for all our sakes, just leave all right, little deary," she said, her powerful voice going sort of sweet at the end.

"Can we at least get something to eat?" Tomas asked, his mind always on food.

She looked us up and down for a full ten seconds before answering, the awkward silence stretching to its limits. But finally, she sighed and seemed to let her guard down a bit.

"All right, one meal, but after you leave right away," she said, turning and gesturing to a worn table and chairs close to the fire. "Sit and I will prepare today's special for you."

"We don't get to order?" Tomas said, seeming a bit surprised.

"When you're at the Dragon's Tooth, you eat what I serve or you go elsewhere. I'm not hurting for patrons, so it's your choice," she said, then seeming to realize something, she added. "My name is Gretel, and my brother," she thumbed over to a massive man behind the bar in the back, "is Hansel. He'll bring you a drink, and I'll get your food. No funny business or you'll be tossed into the oven before you can say 'sweet tooth'."

We sat down and waited for our turn to get food, keeping quiet as Hansel approached with a tray of three drinks.

"Some warm hard cider to take the edge off the cold," he said as he approached and set down our drinks. "Don't let Gretel get you down, she's not a fan of adventurers ever since the incident. But I think you look like a fair group of kids. I'll talk to her about getting a room here."

"We appreciate that," I said, looking up to the massive man with a mess of blonde hair on his head and blue eyes. He wore an odd green set of overalls, but I had no doubt he was a match for us three, with his size and the aura of power that came off him, he'd obviously been an adventurer at some point in his life.

He left then and went to the back, leaving us alone with no one else inside the sizeable eating area. A staircase on the eastern wall led to what must be the rooms, and several doors led to the back or to closets of some kind or another.

"So we sure we even want to stay here?" Ryn asked, looking at me with a side glance.

"I mean," I began to say, then sighed. "It looks nice and we are already here. Let's see if we can make it work, and if not we will go back to searching."

"This cider is amazing," Tomas said, his eyes wide. "We are staying here if for no other reason than the drinks are solid."

"Foods on its way," I said, seeing Hansel appear with a tray of food, Gretel nowhere in sight.

"Here we go, three stew specials, with a side of sourdough bread, and candied fruit pies," he said, setting down his tray and giving us our food. Each one a dark, hearty-looking stew and hard exterior bread that was amazingly soft on the inside, we soon found out.

"Any luck?" I asked, looking up to him with a hopeful smile.

He pulled out a single key from his pocket, its pink wooden circle bearing the symbol of a cauldron.

"I got you one room, our suit, it has two rooms and a few beds, it'll accommodate a group of six, but I've got it for you, only two moons a night," he said, causing me to choke on my stew I'd just tried.

"That much?" I asked, but then I thought about it. The price would be for an entire adventuring party, so it wasn't so outlandish to think that it would be so pricey, but even so, I felt like we were being price gouged a bit because Gretel didn't want us here.

"It is the price she set. I know it isn't perfect, but if you accept it I assure you she'll be on your side. We value our guests and their comfort. Once you've paid and lay your heads here, we will protect you while under our walls against any and all threats. We just prefer not to have to dust off the old skills, which is why we stopped renting to adventurers. But let me assure you, once you've laid your head on our pillows, every moon you spend here will be well spent," he said, a gentle look on his massive, muscled face.

A shiver ran down my spine as he spoke of dusting off his old skills, and a part of me knew he was deadly serious. The pair of them could and would protect us while we were here, which was comforting, but still, the price bothered me. I had enough coin to spend, but living so long without coin made wanting to spend any of it very hard.

I shared a look with Ryn and Tomas while I tried to decide, a full dozen seconds going by before I finally let out a sigh and pulled the coin from my coin purse. We had a shared stash for our group, only a few dozen moons so far, but I'd use that to pay, so it would be fair. I placed the coins, several days' worth of rent, on the table in front of him, and he set down the key.

"You won't regret it. The meal is on the house. You get two meals and drinks to go with them per day. If you are out for a few days at a time, the meals stack up, so you can cash them out at any time. If you end your stay with us with active meals, we will give you tokens that you can come and spend here any time you wish. We are fair and protective of our guests, but try not to bring any trouble down on our heads. We are strong, but not invincible," he said with a wink, then left to stand at the bar, a statue of a man, unmoving, keeping a watchful eye on the room.

That is when I noticed the giant axe on the wall behind him. It was two-sided and looked large enough to be able to cleave a man in two easily. Then, as my eyes traveled around the room, I noticed that most of the wall decor, save for the banners and heads of monsters they'd likely killed, was covered in weapons. This place was practically an armory; should something come for us here, they'd have a a hard time getting through these two monsters of people.

I found myself wondering if they had any Touched blood in them. To get so big and strong, it seemed unnatural. I'd heard that Stonebound were large like they were, but they were said to have skin of granite and natural stone plating on their skin. But I knew there were levels of Touched, so perhaps they had a little bit of the blood, because they definitely weren't fully Touched.

I'd ask my friends about it when the time was right, but now wasn't that time, so I enjoyed the food before me, and it was almost intoxicating with how wonderful it tasted. The stew was hearty and filled me up with potatoes, meat, and a variety of root vegetables. Then the pie, or whatever it was, was so sweet but balanced with a touch of salt. It was like a party in my mouth. Not to mention the soft and wonderful flavor of the bread and cinnamon butter that came with it.

No better meal had I had in some time, and I could tell by the quiet expressions on my friends' faces that they were enjoying it just as much as I was in that moment. We ate in silence, and that silence drew out into a thick blanket over the room.

No sound could be heard, but our chewing and the steady beat and clang of dishes being washed somewhere in the back. Finally finishing our food, we tore away the silence with a word.

"Wow," I said, blinking several times as I tried to put words to the tastes I'd experienced.

"I know," Tomas said, nodding. "We are definitely eating here again."

"I had no idea food could taste like that," Ryn said, looking frustrated at the idea.

"Let's get our packs stowed away and check out our room," I said, deciding words just couldn't truly express the beauty of the meal we'd just had. It was a simple meal, but with such elaborate flavors that using the word simple just felt wrong.

We stood, leaving our empty plates behind, our stomachs full of warm stew and cider. It was a great day so far, and I knew it would only get better as we got to go take out some goblins and finish some jobs.

The rooms were up the stairs, as I had thought, and the room we had was at the end of a long hallway on the north side, toward the back of the building, and a bit in the corner. It had a sturdy black door and a heavy lock that the key opened. We entered and locked the door from the inside before looking around.

It was pretty nice, with a sitting room and a small kitchen with a table and chairs. Two doors led to bedrooms with three beds in each, we decided that Tomas and I'd take the left door, and Ryn took the right one for herself. After stowing away our gear, we left in search of some goblins.

Midafternoon was quickly fading to early evening as we ventured out of the gates for a crack at the goblins while there was still sunlight left to search them out. We'd traveled to the most eastern gate that led to a set of ruins just off the main road, roughly two miles out, or so we were told by the guards. Ryn had a way with speaking with guards; they always seemed to just give her any information she requested.

"You'll have to teach me that trick," I said, looking over to her as we walked down the road.

"What's that?" Ryn asked, feigning ignorance.

"How you so easily talk to the guards," I said, elbowing her in her hardened leather armor.

"You mean you want me to teach you to talk to people, because that's all they are, don't treat them any different, and you'll be surprised at how well they treat you back," Ryn said, shaking her head as if I was missing something entirely.

"But they're guards," Tomas said in my support. "They're always looking busy or intimidating, or both. It was one thing in our small town, but these are professional guards; they likely have classes and whatnot. Not to be trifled with."

"And so what?" Ryn said, shaking her head at Tomas now. "We will have classes eventually, does that firmly insert a rod up our asses when that time comes?"

"Well, no," Tomas said, putting a handful of his snacks in his mouth and looking at me for support.

"I guess I get it," I said. "Treat them like the normal people they are, and they'll treat us the same way in return. Seems simple enough."

"I forget how naive you two can be," Ryn said, chuckling. "This is why you need me around to watch after your asses."

"I'm not that naive," I said, while at the same time realizing that I likely was in her eyes, someone well-traveled and wise to much of the dangers of the world. I'd known poverty and want, but I truly was a bit naive to the ways of the world.

"This is the road they mentioned that leads to the ruins," Ryn said, pointing at something that looked to be no more than an old game trail, thin and just enough brush cleared for us to get by.

"You certain?" I asked, but then I saw it too: a road marker indicating an old road in that direction. "Oh, I see it."

"I'm out of snacks," Tomas said, his voice forlorn.

"We'll get you more after we take care of the goblins," I said, reassuring my buddy that his snacks wouldn't go unfilled in the near future.

"I suppose I can wait," Tomas said. We'd left much of our packs behind, and he must have left his backup snacks with them.

We made our way into the brush-filled trail, and I was surprised to find that the road lengthened quite a bit after a quarter of a mile. In the distance, through the trees and high brush, I could almost make out forms in the waning sunlight. Large towers and high gates were before us, but details were lost to the sunlight behind them.

"We should get off the main road as we approach, there is no telling if the goblins have scouts out or how big their party is, we know by experience that the job board doesn't guarantee that the forces we meet are the same as the information we've been given," I said, putting voice to my concern that we might be facing a far greater force than a party of goblins and a goblin mage.

"Gloomspire ruins," Ryn said as we found a spot where the brush was thin and made our way off the road. "We have to be north of Stonehaven with how the road curved, but why they allow a ruin to be so close to the town, when it could easily be home to monsters, surprises me."

"Right," I said, putting a questioning sound to my word. "But more work for us, let's get in and get out, we are to bring the head of the 'shiny-headed goblin wizard,' but ears are fine for any of his compatriots. Let's bring them down and collect our reward."

"I wonder if they have any snacks from the looting they've been doing," Tomas asked, seemingly in his own little world, worrying about snacks still.

"Nothing you'd want to eat, I'm sure," I said, and he laughed.

"I dunno," Tomas said, elbowing me as his stomach gurgled. "I'm getting pretty hungry."

"You've been eating nonstop. I'll never understand how you can always be so hungry," Ryn hissed as we took cover in a bush overlooking the ruins.

Or rather, we ought to be overlooking some ruins, but what we found instead made our eyes go wide. Dozens of goblins worked to reinforce the stone-failing walls all around this once proud city with wooden spikes of all thicknesses. Goblins could be seen manning the walls, holding bows and arrows, while the working goblins had sharp sticks for weapons, and neither had any armor to speak of.

But what was most concerning about it was their numbers. I knew goblins bred quickly, similar to rabbits, where they could reach maturity and breeding age within months instead of years, but how had they gone from a small party to numbering in the dozens? I did a count from what I could see, and I counted roughly thirty-nine goblins, most workers, but still, the sheer number would make this raid difficult for the three of us to execute. We might need to leave and come back after updating the job listing.

"I can't think of a way to do this without more numbers. They have the home field advantage and the fortifications to make our lives hell. We could probably sneak in, but if anything goes wrong and they send up an alert, we will be surrounded on all sides. I vote we return with reinforcements and update them so that the job will be more lucrative," I said, thinking that we had just enough time to get back and see about the suspicious person raising the dead in the western graveyard.

"I'm hungry, so I vote we leave too," Tomas said, turning to Ryn to get her response.

Before she could speak, a gravelly voice spoke behind us, causing us all to jump from our spots and ready weapons that we'd already drawn minutes before.

"I vote you stay for supper," the voice said.

Turning, we caught view of a bald goblin that stood a half taller than the four around it and wore flowing, if a bit ragged, robes and was wielding a staff with a gem that glowed atop it. We'd found the goblin we were looking for, or rather, he'd found us, and I didn't know what to do next, but I followed Ryn's mark as she sprang up and into action.

I cast Quickstep a moment after she did the same, her sword flashing to the side as she readied to strike. We both smashed our weapons into the goblin wizard at the same time, but were met with subpar results. A barrier of some kind slammed into our weapons first, then us as we went bodily into the goblin, knocking us back as it laughed.

But its laughter cut off abruptly as Tomas raised his weapon above him and smashed his staff into the barrier, throwing all of the other goblins off their feet and cracking the barrier all over. I recovered a moment before Ryn, my Speed attribute being slightly faster than hers. I snapped my fingers, not a needed gesture, but it seemed appropriate in the moment, casting Spark at the barrier.

The barrier shattered, making a loud tinkling noise that would surely be heard by some of the closer working goblins. If not, the sound of combat was starting to grow, and soon we'd have more problems than we had answers to, so we had to move fast.

Ryn was anything but sluggish; her sword slashed across the goblin wizard's chest in the same moment it was able to get off a cast of a fireball spell that smashed into me and sent me flying backward. If not for my Iron Skin, I was sure the heat would have done more than just scorch my skin.

Even so, I was sore as I got back to my feet and took a quick moment to survey the field of battle. Reinforcements would be coming for them in our rear direction, with no such advantage coming for us. Tomas was dealing with three goblins at once, these ones armored in rusty metal or leather armor, but he was quickly getting flanked, so I needed to aid him.

Ryn had her full attention on the biggest threat, the goblin wizard, slashing as it conjured shields to block a single attack at a time. A move that made me envies of Tomas's skill 'Block', which I realized he was using with expert skill to keep himself alive against overwhelming numbers. But now wasn't the time to think of such matters, and I flung myself toward Tomas, hoping Ryn had what it took to keep the wizard busy for a time.

I smashed into a pair of goblins to Tomas's left, stabbing one with a thrust and getting a glancing blow on another as a rusty blade bounced off my hardened flesh. It wasn't a direct hit, so it barely broke skin, leaving less than a bruise in its wake. Then I cast Shove, slamming one goblin back that was about to get a successful hit on Tomas's back.

See, I told myself, my choice had benefits too. Spark came off cooldown. I could feel it ease in my mind, so I cast it immediately, targeting the wizard who had his back to me. It slammed into him and lurched him forward, allowing Ryn to get a devastating blow on it, possibly ending that fight, but I had no time to wait and see.

The cry of goblins could be heard from a short distance, and we needed to end this fight so that we could come back and fight another day. I used Quickstep, then appeared before one of the goblins, just as Tomas did his Heavy Strike on another, finishing off our remaining goblin warriors.

Turning just in time to see Ryn take the head off the wizard, I let out a breath of relief, until several more goblins broke through the brush. Reaching down, I had all but ten seconds before they'd reach us, I cut free the ears of the three by me as Tomas did the same to his. Then we all made a mad dash for the road, wizard head safely under Ryn's arm.

When I saw a few new goblins appear, I meant to say, dozens and dozens, with more flowing out of the ruins as we ran. If not for our lucky timing to catch the wizard outside, likely coming back from a raid, then we wouldn't have been successful. But as it was, we spent the better part of an hour running from goblins; only within a mile of the city did they turn and stop the pursuit. Some of them even rode atop giant rats, though they weren't much faster than they could go on foot.

In the end, we'd finished our job, so we made our way to the guild hall to collect our reward and inform them of a bigger goblin problem than they realized. After explaining the circumstances of the job, we were given thirty-five moons, instead of the thirty that was promised, with an assurance that they'd post a new job to take care of the larger, more reinforced goblins soon. Apparently, they'd be dispatching a scout to check it out first, so they could properly gauge the threat level that should be assigned to the job.

I nodded along, happy to get an influx of coin. We split it four ways, each of us getting 8 and giving the party fund 11 moons. With that little adventure out of the way, we made our way to the Witches' Oven Tavern to resupply on a few items, like potions and such that we'd consumed during our fight. On the way, we stopped at several restaurants, and Tomas got snack bags of all kinds, from sugared nuts to dried fruit.

In time, we were ready for what lay ahead, a trip into a graveyard as night descended over the city.

CHAPTER 27
MIDNIGHT ADVENTURE

"Why'd it have to be a graveyard?" Tomas asked, stuffing his face more enthusiastically than normal as we traveled to the west side, where the graveyard was, just outside the walls.

"Oh, that's right," I said, looking to my friend. "You're not a fan of the undead are you?"

"It's not undead, it's graveyards that give me the creeps. I'll smash in a skeleton or zombie without a worry in the world, but thinking about how there are so many people just dead and buried in the ground gives me the creeps," Tomas said, his body shivering from either the onset of the cold night or what lay ahead.

"I would say they can't hurt you, so you shouldn't be afraid, but we all know that the dead rarely stay dead," Ryn said, shrugging off whatever fear Tomas seemed to be holding onto.

"Easy for you to say, what if we go find some giant bats to fight, how'd you feel then?" Tomas asked, his words hitting Ryn like a fireball.

She recoiled and looked right at his words. "Don't you dare," she hissed. "If we somehow end up facing some bats, I am going to kill you."

"Calm down," I said, chuckling as I did so. "We all have fears, and we all know how to face them, so let's just do our job and get it done."

"Easy for you to say, you've got no fears," Tomas said, and I grinned at that.

I had fears, but none that were so overwhelming as these two. For instance I wasn't a fan of fire, not only because it took my parents from me, but every time I was near a fire, I felt a measure of fear from the damage it could cause. I told myself it was a rational fear, but who was I kidding? I did not like the stuff and the idea of being hit by a fireball terrified me.

"Let's focus on what lies ahead," I said, changing the subject.

"So what do we know from this job posting? We are facing a cloaked figure raising the dead and draining the local livestock of blood?" Ryn asked, and I nodded.

"That and the adventurer's guild is worried that it is a necromancer practicing the forbidden arts. Still baffles me that humans can learn magic outside of the skills we learn, like I knew it was possible with items and such, but necromancy seems different," I said, scratching at an itch on my forehead.

"Necromancy is normally done through the combination of blood magic, something I know little about, and a magical item that grants temporary life. Its more a form of alchemic reaction than magic, or at least that is what I read," Ryn said, nodding along to her words Tomas and I waited for her to continue, when she didn't Tomas spoke.

"Then how do Liches come about? I know phylacteries are magical items that hold the soul of a being, but how are so many stumbling on how to craft them and becoming monsters?" Tomas asked.

"That's a secret that we don't know, but I believe it has to do with magical crafting and the alchemic process used to raise the dead. As to how so many are able to figure it out, I'm guessing it's not as difficult as we are assuming. Though, why you'd want to tear your very soul or core out to put it in another object is completely insane to me," Ryn said.

I shrugged, not having much to add to the conversation, until something occurred to me.

"What if we are facing a vampire? I mean, we have drained corpses right, could be the reason?" I asked, smiling at the idea.

"Vampires are more myth and legend than fact," Ryn said. "From what I've read, they are so rare and their condition so debilitating that they don't survive long."

Tomas laughed and asked, "How are vampires created?"

"You know damn well the legends," Ryn snapped.

I did as well.

From the stories I'd heard, vampires are born of hell bats escaped from a place so evil and demonic that their very bite infects someone to their core, making them into a monster that feeds on blood alone as their life force.

"I take it back, I'm sure it isn't a vampire," I said, but Ryn glared at me, obviously not happy with the direction I'd taken the conversation.

Her red tuff of hair seemed to expand as she glared at me, but it must have been a trick of the low light, because when I looked again, it was normal. Just short black hair with a touch of red. Her glare lingered for only a few more seconds before she turned and took the lead just as we crossed the threshold into a nightmarish-looking graveyard.

Duel gargoyles guarded the entrance, made of stone and carved to look like the monsters they represented. Claws, teeth, and stoney thick scaley skin were the features of each. A massive iron gate surrounded the perimeter, and a thick fog covered the entire area, making it impossible to see more than a few feet at a time.

"Well," I said, shaking my head a little. "This might take some time. Let's start by rounding the perimeter, then we can cut through the middle."

"Sure you don't want to split up and cover more ground?" Ryn asked, looking over with a quirky smile.

"Never split the party," Tomas and I said at the same time.

It was a joke we carried, knowing all too well from our times learning in the Tower, that you never split the party if you could help it. Almost always, it resulted in someone getting picked off or injured while the others had to play catch-up, trying to find or save them.

We did as I suggested and skirted the edge for more than an hour, but we found nothing. However, we did hear scratching, scrambling feet, and all manner of other sounds as we walked. There were undead here for sure, but were they what we were looking for, that much I couldn't tell.

The mists rolled in and around us like a cool blanket, but I wanted nothing more than to rip it off and see what surrounded us. With the lingering fear that we were being surrounded, I turned to my party to make a suggestion.

"We should cut through and look to see what we can find," I said, but we'd taken no more than a step toward the middle when something lurched out of the darkness toward us. Not the slow scramble of a newly raised zombie or a skeleton, but something faster, a ghoul.

It was all ravaged flesh, teeth, and claws. Ghouls were attracted to places enriched with the undead presence and fed off their flesh, as well as fresh meat when it was offered to them. I knew from a book that you had to separate the head from the body to kill them, or use silver to inflict lasting wounds on them. Iron worked to cage them, as they were burned by it, but it did no lasting damage.

"Go for the head!" Ryn shouted, drawing her sword in one fluid motion and getting ready to fight. I did the same, and suddenly it was on us, moving faster than Ryn but not quite as fast as me.

I used shove on it just as it clawed at Ryn, smashing it aside and causing it to fall. Which was all good and all, but it made Ryn miss her killing blow. She glared at me, turning to face the ghoul as it got up. That was when I heard scrambling behind me; two zombies and another ghoul entered the picture.

Tomas caught the slower zombie just to the left with his staff, and I raised my sword and shield, ready to catch the ghoul. It slammed into my shield, and I stabbed it, doing minimal damage. Then, using a burst of speed, I slammed my shield into it, staggering it back and slicing out with my sword for its neck.

It dodged, but I took a chunk of its head off in the process, but that didn't seem to slow it, as it clawed my arm, mostly getting my shield but drawing blood all the same. This ghoul must be a decent level to get through my Iron Skin, I thought to myself as I raised my shield and ignored the stinging pain from the wound.

I heard Ryn cry out, and I turned to check on her, giving the ghoul an opportunity to strike. My attention was forced back in that moment, and I saw that Ryn was on her feet, but I couldn't tell much else in that moment.

Claws and teeth bore down on me, but I managed to block most of it on my shield, stabbing again and again before I thought to use my Spark spell.

I stabbed the ghoul and cast Spark on my it at the same time, it arced down my blade, releasing from my hand and giving me temporary immunity to its effects as I zapped the ghoul. It went rigid and suddenly stopped. I knew I'd not have many moments like this again, so I pulled free my blade and sliced for the neck.

Its head rolled free of its body a second later, and I turned just in time to see Ryn relieve her ghoul of its head, blood dripping down the side of her face as she did so. Tomas finished off the zombies a moment later, and we regrouped.

"We need to take a hit of the poison elixir we bought. "These wounds aren't natural," Ryn said, reaching down and pulling out a thick green liquid. It had several uses in it, so she took one first, then passed it to me to do the same. Tomas was uninjured, so we then took a sip of a weaker healing potion, getting us back to one-hundred percent.

"Normally I'd say just wait out the natural healing, but this mist feels toxic, like it might infect our wounds," Ryn said, looking around suspiciously.

"It does have a way of lingering in your gut, doesn't it?" Tomas asked.

"It does," I said, breathing it out and feeling weaker from the effort. "Let's move in deeper, we've got this."

So we did just that, moving deeper into the mist and into the noises we'd heard the entire time. We killed several more zombies, a few skeletons, but no more ghouls over the next hour and a half of searching. It wasn't until we came upon a mausoleum that we saw light inside and came across something of note.

The building was once white stone, but covered in an overgrowth of vines and moss, it looked more earthly than anything else. Four massive pillars held up the front side, and a single door lay out, with light pouring out, but the mist covered whatever was inside enough that I could only make out a silhouette. A deep, sultry voice emanated from within as we approached.

"So you found your way through my spell of concealment. Funny how ineffective true magic is in this world," the voice said. "Please come in and hear my tale. I promise you no harm while we speak, but attack me and I will have to react with deadly force. My name is Drathic, and as to my surname, I left it behind some time ago. Who might you all be?"

We shared a look, each of us skeptical of what trap we might be entering, but no one said anything for a long ten seconds. Finally, I took a deep breath, feeling all the weaker for it, and spoke.

"I'm Kaelric Grimholt, adventurer and slayer of the undead. Are you such a being?" I asked, matching his tone and failing to sound as alluring as his voice.

He laughed, a wicked thing from inside his concealment. "I'm no undead, but I'm far worse, I'm afraid. But it is as I've said, you do not need to fear me, not yet at least. Come in and speak with me. I get so few visitors."

I exchanged a look with my party members, and we shrugged. What were we to do in a situation like this? Ryn got a look of determination on her face, and she stepped forward, weapon drawn, and we followed her lead.

Inside, past the mist, was an interesting sight. A figure stood over a stone casket that had been opened, and the bones thrown to the ground. The rest of the room was lit by candles all over the place, and there were signs of someone living here, but what was most fascinating was the man standing over the casket.

He wore a long black coat with a high collar, his dark hair slicked back and just longer than his ears. His skin was a deathly pale color, except for his hands, which were dripping red blood on the ground. Following the blood from his hands to the casket, I noticed a corpse, fresh it seemed, inside.

"You killed that man," I said, my mouth moving before my better judgment could kick in.

"I did, however, if you will allow me to tell you a tale, you will see it was necessary," Drathic said, and I felt a weight to his words, as if he was somehow weaving magic into them.

"We kill monsters," Ryn said, sword up. "And by the looks of you, I'd say you are a monster."

"Easy there, girl," Drathic said, his words heavy with disdain. "I've lived a thousand lives, and taking care of a small group of adventurers like you wouldn't even make me break a sweat."

With that, something gave way and we felt, for a terrible moment, the true vastness of his power, and I knew that we were more at his mercy than I realized. Monster or not, this thing was powerful, much more than our trio. We all flinched back, and his face seemed to soften, his power fading back to a trickle as it was before.

"I apologize, I only wish to put my point across. I mean you no harm, listen to my tale, and you will know why I've had to do what I did. I will even allow you to take the body with you if you wish; I have no need of it," Drathic said, bowing slightly as he spoke.

"Why would we want the body?" I asked the obvious question.

"Well, I'd wager you are out here on a job from that pesky adventurers guild to collect one of my children, a stray that didn't take to the life as I'd hoped," he said, gesturing to the body. It did have a hooded cloak behind it, so maybe that was the hooded creature after all.

"Your child?" I asked. "I don't understand."

"It isn't terribly important, but I will tell you I am a creature of the night. Some call us vampires, though I always preferred the term strix, as it is closer to the common tongue of my time," he said, pausing for only a moment before continuing.

"You see, I traveled through here roughly a year ago, and I came across a young adventurer, not unlike yourself," he said, looking deeply into my eyes. Only then did I realize they were a dark crimson color. "I took him under my wing as he was struggling to gain the power necessary to reach his dreams. Told him of how great a destiny we 'vampires' had when channeled properly. But after he was turned, he rejected me and my kind. Began to eat of livestock and experiment with our powers to raise the dead."

"Vampires can raise the dead?" Ryn asked, clearly more interested academically than afraid, though we all had reason to worry. If this Drathic wanted us dead, I was sure it would come to pass.

"We are gifted domain over the dead, to a certain extent, but most of that power comes from our blood, and we tend to keep it close to home, as it determines our lifespan, not that blood is hard to come by," he said, wiping his hand on a towel that he pulled out of seemingly nowhere. "In fact, if I were tired enough from my small fight, I'd have three blood bags here waiting for me to drain them. However, I prefer a stronger vintage; your blood would do little to truly satisfy me."

My grip around my weapon tightened, and I felt true fear, pure and strong, for the first time in a very long time. It ate at my resolve, but I held myself together, sweat beading down my face. It was okay to be afraid, I told myself, I just had to be calm and find a way out of here.

"So you killed the vampire that was killing cattle and raising the dead, but you're willing to let us return with the corpse? What's the catch?" I asked, gathering my wits and seeing that there must be something else he wasn't telling us.

"You have a great destiny ahead of you, I can smell it on you," Drathic said. "I fear that I must inform you that I've caught your scent, all three of you, and one day I will surely return to collect on my kindness. I will taste of your blood, but only when you are strong enough to be worth my effort. So count your days and work hard to be worthy of me when I return."

With that, he began to walk toward us, and we moved to the side without even meaning to as he waved his hand for us to part. It was as if my body moved on its own accord. He walked off into the night and disappeared into the mist that surrounded the place, leaving us alone, our spines shivering with cold.

It was a full five minutes before any of us moved, and in that time we said not a word. Instead, I imagined my friends, as I did, stayed, hoping against hope that this Drathic wouldn't return. But somewhere deep inside, I knew he would do as he said. When I was strong enough, I'd have to deal with him, this being who called all vampires his children.

CHAPTER 28
MYSTERIOUS STRANGER

We left the graveyard, finding no monsters to fight, but taking with us the hooded figure's body. Wrapped and covered, it looked no more than a long log, but we knew the truth of it, and it made me uncomfortable. I wasn't sure if it was the fact that we hadn't filled the vampire ourselves or that Drathic promised to return, but something bothered me.

"Are we going to talk about what happened back there?" Ryn asked, breaking the long-held silence.

Having just made the main road and leaving the graveyard behind, it felt like the time to talk, so I answered her.

"What is there to talk about?" I asked back. Before she could respond, I continued. "Drathic is a problem for another day. We finished our job, perhaps in an unconventional way, but it's done. We collect our reward and move on with our lives."

"We just met the self-proclaimed father of all vampires," Ryn said and Tomas continued to munch on his snacks, his head swiveling to watch whoever was speaking in the moment.

"She has a point," Tomas said, nodding and speaking through a mouthful of nuts.

"I know she has a point," I said, looking at them with a touch of exasperation in my voice. "But I also know there isn't much we can do about a threat so far out of our wheelhouse. It is better to ignore it and move forward; the only answer I can think of is get stronger to deal with the threat."

"We should at least report what we were told to the Adventurer's Guild, maybe they can put a job out for a stronger group of adventurers to tackle, taking the threat right off our plate," Ryn said, there was a confidence in her voice that I wish I had in mine but I was still too rattled by the encounter with someone so powerful that I could literally feel it.

"Is that a good idea?" I asked. "If some group comes after him not fully prepared, then we'd just be sending them to their doom. You felt his aura, didn't you? He was so much more powerful than us."

"I felt something from him, yes, but I don't know enough about the aura of power we give off to say much more than that. Sure, I got the distinct impression that he was stronger than us, but that could mean anything, perhaps an ability he has allows him to do that," Ryn said, being much more logical about this situation than myself.

"What do we know about auras and how they work?" Tomas asked, and Ryn brightened up a little as she was about to spill out some of her knowledge.

"Auras are simply a reference to the raw power you carry around yourself. As you grow stronger, you are meant to begin to control and manipulate your aura so that you can hide yourself from monsters and such, but such learning and control doesn't begin until level 50, which is why it's a topic that not many know about, seeing as most don't reach that level before giving up on the life of adventuring."

"So you see," she continued, "It was more likely that he had a skill or something to make his aura appear stronger, maybe a vampire thing, because if he was truly that strong, he'd have to be closer to level 75 or greater to have such control and power behind it. And what would someone so strong be doing here, where monsters in general are weaker?"

"Doing exactly what he said," I said. "Taking care of a loose end so as not to expose his kind further. What do you think he will do if we go to the adventurer's hall and start talking about 'vampire this and vampire that'? I don't want to draw his wrath too quickly; we've got a long path before us if we want to face him."

A roar ripped through the quiet night, and something could be heard running through the brush to our left. We turned, pulling weapons and making ready, as a bear the size of a small wagon appeared on the road, busting through trees and brush as if they weren't there.

It was a grizzly-looking thing, with brown hair and sharp, elongated claws. It stopped short of us and went on its back legs, rearing up some ten feet and roaring. The roar sent a chill down my spine, but I was ready for it, despite the fear it elicited.

Then I saw its eyes, and my fear turned to confusion. It had glowing silver eyes, and now that I looked, tiny silver lines could be seen beneath its fur, tousled by a sudden gust of wind.

"Hit it fast and hard, there is something off about this bear," I yelled to my companions as it came back to all fours and stalked toward us, slow and deliberate.

I put the weight on my back foot, before springing forward with the help of Quickstep, appearing before the massive bear and stabbing for its shoulder, my shield up, ready to catch any attack from claw or teeth.

I felt my blade sink in, but only an inch or two; its hide was so thick as to stop any attempt to go further. Before I could do much else, I felt an enormous pressure on my shield arm, and I was sent tumbling backward.

Blood filled my mouth as I bit my cheek and landed hard on my backside. But I was rolling and moving away before it could maul me, though I saw as I got up that it wasn't needed. It was fighting Tomas as he used his shields and staff to keep it at bay; meanwhile, Ryn stood back, charging a Mana Bolt from the side. I hesitated only a second before rushing back in, watching for where the Mana Bolt hit, then casting my Spark on that location.

The bear roared, this time not in anger or rage, but in pain.

A fist-sized hole had been dug out of its back left leg, and it limped while walking on that side, meaning we'd slowed it down even further. Tomas used this to his advantage, smashing his staff down and backing up as his shield ability kept him safe.

I wasn't so cautious, slamming my shield into its face and getting its full attention as my blade sank back into the same wound as before, but with greater effect. I felt something give a little, be it muscle or tendon, I didn't know, but I earned another smashing blow on my shield for my effort, driving me back.

Then it was on top of me, and I was lucky my shield was up and ready as both claw and maw came for me. Fighting monstrous animals was always different from fighting monsters in general, as they fought with a wild ferocity that not even some monsters could match.

But wild animal or not, it was forgetting that I wasn't alone. Blow after blow rained down on its back as silver eyes pulsed and shimmered only a foot from my face. It snapped and snarled, trying its best to rip my throat out, but I kept my shield in place. Though my arms were being ravaged, my Iron Skin kept the attacks from becoming wounds I'd regret later.

The bear finally seemed to notice the massive damage it was taking and turned to face the threat, but just as it got off me and I rolled to safety, its eyes seemed to pulse and it locked back on me. It charged, bloody and dying, but still with enough power to kill us if we weren't careful.

I hit it with my shield, using Shove on it as it got near, so I could effectively deflect its massive form off of me. It worked, but only barely, and I wouldn't have another Shove ready in time for another charge.

So I did what I thought was best: I charged it instead.

My sword glowed a steady red, and I felt the flame of it ignite as I slashed for its face, scoring a hit on its right eye just as it turned. This cut also carved a burnt line across its head as well, shattering a silver symbol that I'd barely been able to see before, but it surged and became clear as it was destroyed.

It looked like a silver fist with a circle around it. Suddenl,y the other eye went dim, and I couldn't see any silver glow from it anymore. The bear turned toward Tomas, but the,n as he started to run, it ran past him. However, we weren't about to let experience get away when we were so close, so we ran after it.

The remaining bit of the fight wasn't anything exciting. We chased it for a bit before it collapsed from the chase. Ending the fight soon after, we discovered something odd when we tried to harvest its core. Instead of a normal core, we found a lump of malformed silver that turned to dust the moment we pulled it free.

"It must have something to do with the silver eyes," I said, letting the silver dust fall to the ground.

"Didn't we hear something about a silver-eyed monster? We should report in that we took care of it," Ryn said hopefully.

"I thought it was meant to be a greater threat. I know the fight wasn't easy, but it also wasn't the most difficult thing we've come across," I said, shrugging.

"Maybe there are more?" Tomas asked, looking around the dark as we stood back and tried to decide what would be best to do with the remains of the bear.

Ryn had done some hunting and said she could probably harvest some meat and stuff, but I pointed out the silver dust and odd silver veins running through it, suggesting that perhaps it wouldn't be good for consumption. So in the end, we left it to other monsters to consume and made our way back to the road.

First, we recovered the body we'd left behind, then made our way to the gate, where we told the guards why we were bringing in a dead body. They took the news better than I thought, allowing us in and to make our way back to the adventurer's hall.

It was the dead of night, and we moved through the streets with a dead body, yet even with the little activity that still went on, we didn't really draw any attention to ourselves. The streets were filled mostly with random adventuring teams going about their business, and a large wrapped package and a dead body were not so uncommon among our types.

Making it to the inn, we reported our adventure to the clerk and gave a warning about a possible stronger monster at Ryn's request, but we weren't as specific as we could have been. In the end, we got the bounty and left, ready for a good night's sleep and a day of recovery, during which we were going to go shopping, eat out, and generally relax.

The sun poured in from a side window, warming my face as I lay half-conscious on the soft bed. I felt a ripple of air stir and opened an eye to see if someone had entered the room, only to find a strange, dark-haired man sitting in the chair across from the bed, looking right at me with piercing brown eyes.

"Who are you?" I asked, groggily coming to wake and trying to remember where I'd set my sword.

"It's just to your left," the stranger said, gesturing to my sword. "But you won't need it. I come in peace, as it were."

"How'd you?" I began to ask, but then something else caught my attention about the man, and I found myself going silent.

His manner of clothing was unlike anything I'd seen before; he wore a jumpsuit of some kind with emblems on the shoulders and a little silver device of some kind on his waist. I got the oddest impression that this man was lost, but I couldn't place why I was feeling that way.

"I know I should try to adjust my appearance to the places I visit, but I'm still getting the hang of this, so you'll have to pardon my attire," he said, and once more I found myself wondering how this being was able to hear my thoughts before I put voice to them.

"Who are you?" I ended up asking while I sat up in bed and pulled the covers aside.

"I am Mah'kus, a friend here to lend you aid in a time of dire need, but I feel I am too soon," he said, looking around and then glancing at his wrist, where a small metallic device was fastened with a leather band.

I reached for my sword and readied myself to unleash an ability when a wash of power settled over me, startling me so thoroughly that I dropped my blade and gasped for air.

"Sorry, still working that out as well. You don't need to fear me, just hear my warning, and I will be on my way," Mah'kus said. "The path you walk is dangerous, and you must be wary of who you trust. I dare not say much else until your timeline has progressed further, but just be wary, all right. I have to go, but before I do, I'd like to offer you a donut."

He held out a tasty looking donut, and I reached out, took it, and took a bite before I knew what I was doing. The flavors and power that washed over me then had me sit back down and roll my eyes back into my head. When I finished the pastry, I turned to look at my mysterious visitor, but he was gone, and in his place was an empty chair.

If not for the sugar left behind from the donut, I'd have thought I'd imagined it all, but no, that wasn't possible. Someone had visited me, warned me, given me a donut, and left me here. I stood and left to tell my friends of the events as soon as I could stand again.

"You won't believe what just happened to me," I said, getting out of the room and seeing Ryn and Tomas all ready for the day and waiting for me.

"How 'bout you get ready first, then tell us," Ryn suggested, and I sighed, rushing back into my room to clothe and ready myself for the day.

As I dressed, I thought more and more about what the strange man had said. It was advice I'd been given plenty of times over, but who was I trusting that I shouldn't be? No one really came to mind as I finished dressing, but I promised myself I'd think on it later.

Finally ready, I came out and told them of the stranger in my room and how he'd left a pastry for me.

"And you ate it?" Tomas asked, then, grinning, he added, "Should have saved a bite for me."

Ryn, for her credit, rushed into my room and did a quick search. "You sure you weren't dreaming?"

I'd all but lost any sugar or trace of the donut after getting ready, but I was sure, so I nodded, indicating as much to her. "I'm sure," I said for good measure.

"Then perhaps we need to see about getting you warded or something by a magical item. You keep drawing the worst kind of attention, and scrying objects are likely how this stranger found you," Ryn said, getting academic in her response. Tapping at her chin, she nodded, having made up her mind.

"If you say so," I said, chuckling a bit. I was just happy to see that my friends were taking it seriously, and now that we had a day of shopping planned, I would look for a scry-blocking magical item.

We left the room and ventured out.

"So you are seeing strange men now, you sure you didn't hit your head at some point?" Ryn asked, teasing me as we walked through the streets in no particular direction.

"I saw what I saw," I said, ignoring her teasing for the most part as I pointed at a store in the distance. "Let's check that place out."

It was mid-morning, normally I'd feel pretty hungry, but that donut had really done something to me, filling me right up. The streets were cobbled, the sky was clear, and there was a chill in the air. Adventurers, judging by their appearance, walked in and out of the establishment we were heading to in large numbers.

The building in question was a large brick structure with a massive sign reading 'Cal's Curiosities' on the second floor, painted in bright pink with black outlining. I'd heard rumors about this place before; there was said to be one popping up in most towns, as if the owner was expanding and keeping the name in each new establishment.

We entered the flow of people going in, and soon we were passing suits of armor to enter the shop. The armors were curious things; large gaps in the armor showed metal gears and parts inside, almost like a clock.

"Admiring our latest in advancements on golems?" came a sweet voice from the left.

I looked up to see a blonde girl, with odd, almost glowing blue eyes. She must be some kind of Touched, likely an Aether-Touched, with how her eyes contained an inner light. She wore a black dress and her arms were bare, but a crystalline web of veins could be seen under her light pink skin. Then I saw her hair shimmer in the light, and it clenched it; she was Aether-Touched for sure.

"Whoa," Tomas said, catching a look at her. It was rare to come across an Aether-Touched, much less one so beautiful.

"Uh, yeah, what's that?" I asked as the three of us stepped out of the flow of traffic and to the side, where she stood, probably meant to greet people as they entered.

My eyes took a quick look around, and many hundreds of shelves and counters displayed all manner of magical items and potions. It was too much to see, so I turned my gaze back to the woman before she spoke next.

"My name is Angel," she said, introducing herself. "I saw you looking at our latest model, the MXG-012. Are you interested in adding a golem to your party?"

"I'm sure that would be nice, but I doubt we can afford it," Ryn said, side-eying me and elbowing me when I didn't respond, just staring at the exotic beauty of the Touched before us.

"Oh, right, yeah, sorry, we don't have the coin for such an endeavor," I said. "But just for curiosity's sake, how much does one go for?"

"It's actually quite affordable for what they offer, only ten crowns," Angel said, and I nearly swallowed my tongue.

Ten crowns was a ridiculous amount of money, even for an adventurer. There was no way someone would casually just buy one of these to have it join their party.

"Sell many of these lately?" Tomas asked, getting on the same wavelength as me.

"Two today, actually," Angel said, smiling. "If you want to stay competitive, you'll consider buying one as well. We do payment plans. If you can manage a crown a month, we'd love to speak with you about it in more detail."

"We'll pass," Ryn said, taking us by the hand and dragging us away from the eager sales pitch that Angel was likely about to give.

The rest of the store was much more affordable. We found all manner of useful items, including a pole that extended from palm-sized to twice my height. Good for checking traps and pitfalls ahead. We even got some magic rope that lightened your load when you were lifting yourself, so you could climb it even when exhausted.

But it wasn't until we got to the weapons and armor that I really perked up to see what cool items we might be able to find.

First, I found rings; I had room for another, so I decided to treat myself to one. Of the dozens I looked at, these three caught my eye.

. . .

Name: *Draconic Band*
Rarity: *Rare*
Special Properties: *Bestows upon the user the strength of a dragon, periodically increasing Power by 5 when worn in combat.*
Description: *Forged in the fires of actual dragons, this band is perfect for an adventurer seeking strength and glory. While it isn't always active, the scaly band of green metal set with a black stone comes in handy mid-combat and never fails to impress.*
Price: *55 Silver Moons*

Name: *Titan's Grasp Band*
Rarity: *Rare*
Special Properties: *When the wearer of this ring successfully blocks or parries an attack, their Guard increases by 2 for a short period of time. This effect can trigger up to five times and only during active combat.*
Description: *Crafted from the dense, rune-etched iron alloy with earthen-infused mana, this heavy band carries the stubborn resilience of mountain giants. It tightens slightly around the finger when danger approaches, reinforcing the wearer's awareness of potential danger.*
Price: *50 Silver Moons*

Name: *Band of the Crimson Pulse*
Rarity: *Rare*
Special Properties: *When the wearer drops below half health, they gain a temporary +10 to Power for a short period of time. This effect can't occur more than once every two minutes.*
Description: *The dark silver band is set with a pulsing red crystal that beats like a living heart when blood is spilled nearby. Favored by frontline fighters, it rewards aggression and endurance, surging with strength when the wearer is pushed to their limits.*
Price: *65 Silver Moons*

Each ring held such amazing potential, but obviously, I was drawn toward the one that had a kinship with dragons. I could think about how each would help me immensely, but in the end, I selected the Draconic Band, spending a solid one-fourth of my accumulated funds.

"You really going to go for that over the tanking ring?" Tomas said, pointing at the Titan's Grasp Ring. "I would have thought that would be the perfect fit for you."

"He's got a good point. You are still wanting to tank, right?" Ryn asked, a little exasperation in her voice.

"Of course, but you read the plaque, this one was made by dragons," I said, raising my eyebrows to get my point across.

"Oh gods," Ryn said. "That was the deciding factor, the flavor text?"

"It was," I said, grinning. "Now leave me be and buy the rings you want so we can move on."

Both chuckled, but in the end, neither bought a ring; instead, we went to the weapons section to see what they had to offer. We spent the better part of the day exploring nearly every shelf and display case on both floors, finding all manner of cool treasures and items we'd love to have, such as dimensional storage containers, but in the end, we didn't spend any more coin. Deciding to sleep on it, as they grew hungry and despite feeling full, I could eat as well, I'd decided.

We left the establishment, getting another good look at the clockwork golems on the way out, seeing a sign next to them that read, 'Runeforged – Bringing otherworldly power into your hands.'

I had an ominous feeling as I read that, and I thought about Torwyn and her group, wondering whether this was similar or just a marketing gimmick. Either way, my thoughts lingered on Grange,r and I found myself wishing I could check in with them.

CHAPTER 29
MEASURED RESPONSE

The cold was settling down into our skin with a persistency that I didn't care for, but we'd bundled up so it wasn't as bad as it could have been. I pulled my fur-lined jacket closer around my body, the cold fading a touch as I did so. I saw Tomas shiver; his coat was much thinner than Ryn's, and mine was much thicker than hers.

Tomas's 'jacket' was a long black coat of sorts with a high collar that surrounded and shielded his head. Where it failed in thickness, it excelled in coverage.

"It breaks the wind fabulously," he'd said when he got it, but it wasn't a problem of wind today, just a bitter chill that ate to your bone.

"You'll freeze your ass off," Ryn had warned him, but he'd bought it regardless.

Ryn had decided to get a red leather coat, but she also had a heavy cloak over it, providing about as much warmth as my own coat. We'd discussed possibly having the coats enchanted with warning runes of some kind, but we all understood it would be much more expensive than we wanted, so we hadn't sought out someone to do it.

I had no cloak, only my father's scarf, made more for convenience than warmth. It was thin, yet sturdy, and wrapped around my neck, one end billowing in the cold air behind me as I walked.

"I wonder where Granger got off to," I said, then, before they could get suspicious of why I'd say that, I added, "I'd like to hear their music again."

"Music, I'm sure," Ryn said. "Like we couldn't tell you were getting sweet with that entire group. You are far too trusting, Kael; it'll get you in trouble one of these days."

"She's r-right," Tomas said through chattering teeth as he attempted to eat some sugared nuts.

"I think they earned a little trust from us," I said, thinking back on all they'd done for us in that dungeon.

"Aye, he's g-got a point," Tomas said, his face looking bright red from exposure, and I wondered if we should just head inside a tavern for a while to get him to warm up.

Ryn must have thought something similar as she suggested, "Perhaps we ought to get inside for a while. That, or see about pooling some money to get that jacket enchanted. Here, take my cloak, it'll warm you up."

She began to take off her cloak, but Tomas held up a hand, his head gesturing to a trio of shadows heading our way from the crowd.

I turned, putting my feet into a combat-ready position, before tensing when I saw who it was.

Cravin Deymorin.

The last person he wanted to see from Brackenford, yet somehow he'd seen him more than any other, always appearing like a cockroach from some hidden alleyway.

His black hair was tied back, and his large Deymorin nose seemed to point accusingly at me as he approached, a sneer on his face. He had a massive two-handed sword on his back, but he kept it sheathed as he approached. He wore a heavy cloak over his armor, but he let it trail behind him as he walked, leaving him exposed to the cold. Even so, he seemed unphased by it.

The light caught a glint of silver on one hand, and once more I was drawn to a little ring he wore. As he drew nearer, I was still unable to see clearly what the signet ring had on it, other than clearly being a signet and not of his house colors. That ring, a golden and black varnished one, was on his right hand.

"What do we owe the pleasure?" I said, smirking at the trio as they stopped before us.

His thuggish companions both wore heavy cloaks, hiding only the gods knew what under them as they approached, their cloaks closed. One had blonde hair and the other brown. I couldn't remember their names, but I'd seen them before.

"Time to leave town," Craven said, sneering at me as he looked me up and down.

"I don't think so," I said, looking puzzled on purpose. "I mean, we barely got here. Why would we want to leave now?"

"If you don't, you'll regret it. This is my only warning I'll give you," Craven said, his eyes darted to the side as he spoke, as if worried he was being watched.

"I'd like to see you make us," Ryn said, stepping forward and pulling her short blade mostly free, stopping at the edge as she glared down the closest of the goons.

"If that is what it takes, then allow us to show you the true strength of

Brackenford. Get them, but don't kill them, not yet, at least," Craven said, stepping back as his thugs stepped forward, both with cudgels ready and swinging wide for Tomas and Ryn, leaving me alone to face Craven.

I ignored Craven for the moment, casting Shove on one of the goons, then slamming my heel into the back of the knee of the other, moving so fast that they had barely a moment to respond. I saw them both stumble, but not go down, before Craven was on me.

He pulled his sword off his back, yet kept it in its sheath, as he slammed it forward, right for my head. I stepped backward, leaving his strike to hit air, then unclipped my own sword, keeping the sheath on it as well. Our swords slammed together with force, but I didn't allow it to be just an exchange of hits; I slid my blade down the length of his and slammed him in the head a moment after our next exchange finished up.

He stumbled back, dazed, and I took the second opening he gave me. I cast Shove, knocking him back. As he launched forward with the help of some unseen force, I used Quickstep to get around him and his weapon's strike. That gave me an opening, so I struck him hard in the ribs.

He coughed as the wind was knocked out of him, but even so, he moved with haste, swinging his blade wide and forcing me back.

I was trying to have a measured response to his violence, but I could tell it would escalate quickly as Craven grew angrier. His sneer twisted on his face, and he tossed his scabbard off with a quick motion, changing the tempo of the fight.

In the moment that he did this, I spared a glance over to my friends, seeing how their fight was going. Tomas moved quickly, using his shields to block attacks and striking back with force. Meanwhile, Ryn danced around the slower of the two thugs, delivering strike after strike, her blade still sheathed as well.

I didn't immediately unsheath my blade, instead parrying any attack and threw an elbow into Craven's face, but taking a blunted blow from the wide edge of the sword for my trouble. Back and forth we danced, taking small hits, one after another.

He wasn't being deadly with his sword, sheath off or not, and I couldn't understand why. Eventually, my sheath came free, and we both were more cautious in how we attacked, knowing it would take only one good exchange for the fight to be over now.

I heard Ryn scream out in sudden pain, and I turned, giving him an opening that I didn't intend. Pain shot down my shoulder as the large blade cut a line through my armor and into the meat of my shoulder. It wasn't deep, but it was a clear cut, and it hurt like hell.

Using my good arm, I wielded my sword with one hand, danced forward, cut past his guard, and struck his face. I put a line down his cheek, a deep enough wound that it nearly cut through his cheek completely. He screamed in rage, letting his blade drop a touch as he went one-handed, not an easy feat for a blade as large as his, and covering his face.

"This is stupid, just give up and leave us alone!" I yelled to him across the space we'd created. We were drawing a hell of a lot of attention now, and it wouldn't be long before guards came to stop us, but if we weren't careful, it would be too late.

"Stop being so damn thick. Listen to me and leave, or else," Craven said back in a lower-than-normal voice, almost a dark whisper more than anything else.

"You know damn well I'll not be leaving this town or adventuring behind, so give up and leave my friends alone," I said, sparing a glance at the pair. They continued to fight, but Ryn was slowing, and one arm lay still at her side, her dominant side, meaning she was fighting with her off hand. It wasn't as bad as it sounded, since she was proficient with both hands, but still.

In response, Craven growled and rushed forward, his blade no longer tilted to do minimal harm but now point and cutting edge first. It shone in the sunlight, and I had only moments to respond, slamming my blade forward to deflect his blade to the side before striking down the length of his blade.

He spun to avoid the strike, bringing the hilt into my back as he spun, throwing me down to the ground with a sharp pain in my back. Fighting humans was so much different than dumb monsters; I had to remember that. I rolled on the ground and back to my feet, but I'd left my sword on the ground several feet away.

"I have you now," Craven said, sneering as he struck forward with his blade. But if this were life and death, I had more tricks up my sleeve. If my Iron Skin wasn't enough to stop an attack, I'd have to use my other abilities.

I snapped my fingers, and Spark slammed into place right over his exposed chest. The magical strike hit him square in the chest, and he froze momentarily, giving me time to retrieve my blade as he finished his strike where I'd been a second before.

Using Shove, I kept him moving, stumbling forward as I cut down at his back, aiming for his spine. But in a flash of speed and a blur of motion, someone in light-colored armor appeared before my strike, sword out, catching my blow and kicking me hard in the chest. I flew backward, and I noticed at least twelve such knights appearing from all around. The city guard had been called, and they didn't look happy.

"Stand down," came a feminine voice from within the helmet of the one who'd taken me down without much effort.

I let my sword fall from my hands in a show of surrender. I had no desire to fight the city guard, nor was I happy to have let this situation spiral out of my control. All weapons hit the ground and were retrieved by one of the twelve guards, each wearing the same light-colored full plate armor without any recognizable colors, only a raven symbol chiseled into the right shoulder plate.

Whispers from the crowd could be heard, and I caught a few things they said. Something about the White Raven Knights, and something about how they almost never appeared in town.

"If I could only explain," I said as I stood, two knights on each side of me.

"We saw everything," the feminine knight said, her voice almost sweet yet firm. She gestured toward a white bird I hadn't noticed perched on the edge of a nearby building. "You are all being taken in for processing. Punishment will be decided by the judge, so save your pleas for them."

"I understand," I said, taking my sword from one of the knights when it was offered back, surprising me.

"I trust you can control yourself until we get you locked up. If not, you are welcome to challenge us, but you will lose, and we will administer punishment as we see fit. My name is Lady Kay. Heed my words, and you'll be safe."

"I will, Lady Kay, just know that it wasn't my desire for this fight to get so out of hand," I said, hoping that they'd seen enough to know who started the fight.

"It is not our place to judge, only witness and prevent," she said, turning and motioning for us all to follow. Everyone except Craven and I had only one guard, while Craven and I had two.

We moved in a column through the city, and before I knew it, we'd reached a stone building with iron gates surrounding it. Guards in less fine armor stood at attention as the knights arrived.

We were processed through, stripped of our gear and weapons, before being manacled with special irons that made calling upon our magics harder, if not completely impossible. On top of that, there were runes in the cells we were placed in that seemed to drain us even further.

To the guards' credit, the injured were given healing potions, but otherwise we were left feeling very weak, our magic sapped, and our souls stretched as we waited for whoever was meant to judge us.

"This sucks," I said. Ryn, Tomas, and I had been placed in a separate cell from the other three, but even so, I kept my voice down.

"Why did that idiot Craven want to drive us out of town in the first place?" Ryn asked, shaking her head and keeping her voice not quite as low as mine had been.

"Why'd they have to take all my snacks?" Tomas asked, his voice loud enough to carry to the guards.

One of the guards laughed at hearing him, but otherwise said nothing. The knights had left, but there were plenty of guards around, should we find the power to try and escape. Not that we truly could, so deep were the restrictions put on us because of the cell and the cuffs we had on.

"I don't know, but I have a bad feeling about it," I said, being honest as my gut told me there was more to his threats than he was letting on.

We continued our chatter, doing anything to distract from the draining feelings of being in the cell. Time slipped away and no judge appeared to give us any idea of how long we'd be stuck here. Nightfall came, and the guards exchanged shifts, handing off to new faces.

Eventually, we fell asleep in the cells, the stray ground soft enough to slip into sleep. But I didn't sleep long; something pulled me from sleep just as I heard a loud snoring come from outside the cells. Opening my eyes, but remaining on the ground so as not to tip the guards away, I saw something odd.

A cloaked figure, its hood up and face in shadows, with only silver eyes shining through, stood over two sleeping guards. It moved swiftly to the cells where Craven and his goons were kept, opening them with a wave of its hand.

"Come now," said a voice as cold as ice and filled with terrible power.

Craven said nothing, bowing to the creature and waking his two goons. I watched with one eye shut as they left, passing sleeping guards and escaping into the night.

What in the actual hells was that, I thought as I waited a solid ten count before moving. What is the deal with the silver eyes, just like that bear we fought? Now whatever had happened to the bear had been passed to a human?

I woke my friends to tell them what had happened, and we were sitting up when the guards finally awoke. They realized they'd lost a set of prisoners almost a full minute after waking up, so relatively slow.

"Hey there," one of them called to us. "Where'd they go?"

"Someone took them while you both slept," I called back, which seemed to just anger the guards further.

What followed was an hour of more guards, then the knights from before appeared, before it all calmed down and two new guards were put into place as well as an extra one that literally just watched us.

"The judge will be here soon. I suggest you tell us before he arrives how you got your friends out," the guard, looking at us, said.

"They weren't our friends, or have you forgotten we were arrested for fighting them?" I asked him back, and he blinked at me as if I'd said something too far above his intelligence to understand.

Ryn took over, talking sense to him, and he nodded in agreement to her words, even though she was basically saying what I'd said. After a time, the guards all left, and a cloaked figure, this one in silver and gold robes, no hood, and an aged face greeted us with a warm smile.

"I am High Judge William," he said. "I'm here to pass judgment on you.

Before we begin, would you mind telling me all the details behind the lost prisoners? You saw them leave, I was told?"

I told him everything, from the silver eyes to the monster we'd fought with a similar condition. He nodded and took it all in without saying a word.

"We've encountered such beasts before; I'm afraid our area has been plagued by them for some time. This is the first I've heard of a human being infected by it, and how it was able to get past all my guards, I'll never know. But let's get back on track. Your judgment for fighting other adventurers within the walls of our fair city."

"I have lowered your sentence to disturbing the peace, and as you are adventurers, I require you to pay by way of work, not coin. Your punishment is to clear out a warren of monsters just south of town. It has grown into a fairly big issue, but not worth the coin it would take to turn it into a proper adventurer's guild job."

He went through the details, telling us how a small colony of gnolls had appeared to be burrowing far and wide just outside the city, and they needed to be taken care of with extreme prejudice.

"We accept your judgment and will get on it immediately," I said, speaking for the group.

"I'd suggest you find another three to work with, or else you might find yourself a bit overwhelmed," Judge William said, and I nodded.

With that, guards appeared, took us from the cells, returned our gear and weapons, and removed the manacles. I felt the rush of power return to me, but knew it would take a long night's sleep before I felt back to my full power.

We left into the night's cold air, and I felt a shiver run up my spine. Not from the cold but from something far more sinister. I felt like I had silver eyes watching me, but from where, I couldn't tell. So, I walked and kept my eyes peeled for any sign of them.

"What a load of crap," Tomas said, shaking his head.

"What? We did the crime, and now we can repay it by doing some work for the city," Ryn said. "Fair is fair."

"Not that," Tomas said. "They ate most of my snacks."

We laughed, feeling the tension fall away as we did. We'd get a good night's sleep, then start early tomorrow, looking for three people dumb enough to join us for the least amount of coin.

But even so, I felt like eyes were on me the entire time, but nothing I could do helped me locate them. It wasn't until we were inside our own room with the door shut that I finally felt alone.

CHAPTER 30
A DIRTY JOB

Leaving to go out to the street below, we enjoyed the warmth of the sun. It was warmer today than it had been the night before or even the day before. Enough that my coat was warming me a bit too much, and I wished I had something lighter, like what Ryn or even Tomas had.

"Where to go to find people to help us?" I asked, thinking of only one place really, but I wanted to hear what the others thought.

"Adventuring hall, I'd guess," Ryn said, shrugging. Tomas popped snacks into his mouth and nodded his agreement to her words.

We left in that direction and got to the place in no time. We'd already eaten breakfast, but even so, we smelled all manner of delicious foods on our way, making my mouth water.

Going inside, we got in line to talk to the attendant on duty. She was a blonde-haired girl with sharp eyes, and she introduced herself as Nance.

"What can I do for you?" she asked, barely looking up.

"We need to recruit three adventurers for a job assigned to us by the city," I said, smiling a bit as she looked up at us.

"Oh, you must be the adventurers dumb enough to be caught fighting in the city last night. You've been placed on two weeks' leave from the adventurer's guild, so you won't be getting our help until your probationary period ends in two weeks. Sorry," she added at the end as my face dropped.

"How are we supposed to take care of this job if we can't get help?" I asked, confused by the sudden change in the conversation.

"The old-fashioned way, I guess. Just ask around and offer coin," Nance suggested, and I pinched the bridge of my nose.

"All right," I said. "Let's go."

We turned and left, the full implications of what Nance had said sinking in as we did.

"We can't do any jobs for two weeks, that is ridiculous," I said, shaking my head at the annoyance.

"Let's focus on one thing at a time, first we find three others; next, maybe we can go check out the local dungeon," Ryn suggested.

Tomas nodded. "I like that," he said. "That'll take some time, too. Bet we don't even notice our lack of being able to do jobs."

"So, where or how do we find three adventurers without the help of the adventurer's guild?" I asked the obvious question.

"I think I know a few places we can check," Ryn said, smiling as she saw a few guards pass by.

We learned from her conversation with the guards that there was a local drinking establishment where most of them went. Her plan was simple, find some off duty guards and enlist them for a fee. Most guards were also adventurers, especially in a town this big. So we'd be able to find some decent folks, or so that was the plan.

We sat at a table by ourselves, Tomas and I, while Ryn worked the bar for people who might be interested. It worked. She found a group of three who said not only would they like to go clear the warren out for five silver moons each, but they'd also go to the dungeon a day or so later.

Their names were Wyatt, a tall, lean man with a youthful vigor about him and stunning blue eyes. Then there was Goose, whether that was a nickname or his actual name, he never really said, but he had a thick muscled body, a bald head, dark skin, and looked to be in his late thirties. Finally, the last person, and the most important one because he had a wand of healing, was Seth. Seth was athletically built, with dark green eyes and a mess of red hair on his head.

"Well met," I said as they introduced themselves. "If you guys are free now, we will gather our gear and head out immediately."

"Meet us at the South Gate in an hour," Goose said, taking charge. "We've run a few jobs together, so we work decently well together. Just be sure you guys can hold your own."

As they left the bar, Ryn turned to me and said, "Their levels range from 20 to 25, so they should be a good fit with us."

Nodding my head, we left only a minute or two after grabbing our gear and headed to the South Gate.

Goose stood tall and ready in the front of his group, with Wyatt on his left and Seth on his right. They looked much different than before, wearing gear unlike the guard armor they had on before. Seth wore robes, for instance, white and golden ones that looked like they'd seen better days, but for the most part they were clean and well-put-together.

Wyatt, on the other hand, had on light leathers with a thin blade at his side, along with a repeating crossbow hanging from his belt. Then there was Goose, who had a massive shield on his back and a sizable mace with blunted edges, more for crushing than anything else. I saw Seth's wand, a thin, finger-thick thing about the length of a forearm, tucked into his belt.

It would allow him to use his power to heal us to a limited degree, but beyond that, he was said to be going purely down the path of Arcana, meaning he might already have a class. However, if he did, he hadn't said so, and we didn't ask.

Greetings were exchanged, and we followed the intel off the road. The warrens were said to be in a dense forested area, and we wasted no time in tracking down the gnolls.

Gnolls were interesting creatures. Like goblins, they were almost capable of being citizens of this world, not just monsters, but they had the taint of evil within them and acted more like wild animals than people. Most stood about six feet tall and could be of any level, but this warren was said to be filled with weaker ones led by a stronger pack leader.

We encountered our first gnoll patrol after only an hour of searching.

Two shorter gnolls flanked a larger one. They were canine in appearance, with the face of a dog and the body of a man-beast. They had claws, but even so wielded weapons in the form of sharpened stick spears, with the lead one carrying an actual sword, rusted as it was. He also had a shield, believe it or not, and he rushed forward against the six of us with no fear in his eyes.

We'd soon teach him the error of such an attack.

Goose, eager to show off his abilities, rushed forward, blocking an attack with a wave of his hand, meaning he'd taken Block and not Iron Skin. I didn't wait to see what happened next, coming in hard with my shield before me. My sword blazed to life, and as the gnoll attempted to stab me with his wooden spear, I cut the shaft midway through his strike.

It yelped suddenly, and I twisted, digging my hot sword deep into its face and ending the first of the three. The battle didn't last much longer, with Goose's foe going down as he smashed through its shield and shattered its face as well. Then came the final fight, Wyatt versus a stick-spear-goblin. With his light, thin sword, he poked at the gnoll, scoring hit after hit while keeping the spear from finding its mark.

The battle ended with the gnoll dying from so many small wounds.

"Not bad," I said, catching Goose's eyes and then Wyatt's. "Let's loot them and move on. We must be getting close."

So we did so, finding a few crude copper scales, but nothing else worth keeping. Tomas drew the short straw and went digging in for monster cores, finding small ones on each of them.

We cut our way through several more patrols of three to five, never really being challenged, since these were weaker than even the goblins we faced. They had size and strength on their side, but they weren't at a high enough level to make good use of them.

We found the entrance to the warren, a hole in the ground that spread out in three directions.

"Split the party?" Goose asked, his voice a low rumble in the quiet morning light.

"Never," I said. "We pick a path, and go as far as possible, then come back and clear the other paths."

It was easy enough to do; the tunnels had been widened to let six-foot-tall gnolls pass through standing up. It was all dirt, but it had been hard-packed to keep the tunnels open. Even so, I worried about collapse as we ventured into the first tunnel, seeking the gnolls hiding within.

We'd killed roughly three dozen above the ground, which meant we'd have just as many, if not more, to find down in the tunnels. We shared only whispered conversations, but mostly we remained quiet. It took nearly ten minutes of walking before we heard the barking laugh of a gnoll ahead.

The tunnel opened up to a round room, some fifty paces wide from the center of it, and two more tunnels leading elsewhere. But inside this room was a random collection of crates and goods, including a few dead bodies, stripped naked and showing off wounds only a day or so old.

We'd been too late to save them, but we'd avenge them.

Five gnolls, each wielding a sword and wearing some armor, turned to regard us, barking at us in what must be their language. One rushed away, and I thought for sure he'd get away. But at the very last second, Ryn pulled free a dagger and threw it with enhanced strength, catching it in the spine and dropping it.

The armor had been nonexistent on its back, and now we had their full attention. The fight was on.

Goose and I took the front line, going shield to shield and readying our weapons. He happened to be left-handed, which worked out really well. We could attack from the side without getting in each other's way.

"Pepper them," I shouted to Wyatt, who'd drawn his crossbow but had been too slow to end the runner. Luckily, Ryn had been faster to draw her dagger.

Wyatt nodded and released bolt after bolt into them as they charged us, bringing one down before they made it to us, leaving only three to slam into our shields. However, three was enough, because these were stronger than any of the others we'd faced.

Blow after blow, we rained hits down on them as they slammed their bodies against our shields, rocking us back with their sheer weight and strength.

I got a lucky hit on the left-most gnoll, my sword slipping into his head and ending his life. With the numbers finally in our advantage, we quickly cleaned up the rest. I turned to Goose and nodded.

"Good job, we make a decent team," I said, and Goose nodded back.

"Yeah, we do, don't we?" he asked, as a howl echoed through the chamber's back wall.

A newcomer had arrived through one of the tunnels, and now it was sounding the alarm. Wyatt put it down with a bolt to its face, but the damage was done; reinforcements would be coming now, and we needed a decent place to fight them all.

"We have to fight them where we can funnel them into a narrow passage," I said.

"The hallway we came from, it's wide enough to let us fight, let them come, and they will break against our shields," Goose said, his voice vibrating from a sense of excitement.

"Right," I said, turning toward the tunnel. Howls filled the tunnels, and as long as they didn't come up behind us, we'd be fine.

Goose and I positioned ourselves at the head of our party, bracing our shields for impact. The howls reverberated through our very bones, echoing down the long corridor. The anticipation of the gnolls' weapons clashing against our shields was almost too much, so much so that for a brief moment, I wanted to break formation and run headlong into battle and meet them halfway. But I pushed that intrusive thought aside and stood firm alongside Goose, tensing my muscles in preparation for the initial attacks.

I stood steadfast among my team, ready to be the bulwark that defended them in this hour of need. I could taste the bitter tang of fear in the air, but it wasn't coming from me. Looking at Goose, I saw that he was beginning to sweat.

"You doing all right?" I asked. We were seconds away from the attack, and I didn't want Goose to break on me before the wave of monsters hit.

"Just never faced so many at once, feeling it for sure," Goose said, his voice vibrating a touch as he spoke.

"We'll be fine, just keep your shield in front of you and your arm swinging," I said just as the first wave broke against our shields.

The six-foot-tall monsters' initial charge nearly broke us, their weight and visceral charge pushing us back several feet, but in a surge of strength, we held, and the massacre began.

As it turns out, fighting in a hallway has its advantages and disadvantages. We were wide enough to block all but maybe one from getting past us at a time, so the team behind us was not without a job to do. The advantage that kept us alive was the small space, the confinement. The disadvantages were almost enough to stop our killing spree, with bodies piling up high as we killed them and forcing us to move back as we fought.

I almost thought we'd run out of hallway, but they kept coming, one after another, until we must have killed two dozen or more. Then something in the battle shifted, they started clearing out their dead, and a few bow-wielding gnolls peppered us with arrows into our shields.

We were growing tired by then, but our backline had enough sense to return fire, and soon even the bow-wielding gnolls went down. That was when their leader appeared, so large he could barely fit into the tunnel, his silhouette blocking the light from the room beyond.

"Come and face me!" it screamed in a gurgled, almost visceral voice.

He had a shield and a sword. He banged his sword against his shield, stepped back, and awaited us.

"What do we do now?" Goose asked, wiping blood and sweat from his forehead.

We were spent, so much so that I wasn't sure we were ready for a boss fight right now. But we had a duty and a responsibility to attend to, even if it meant it would be hard; we had to fight.

"Nothing left to do but clear out what is likely their leader. Once we kill him, it'll be easy dispatching whatever is left," I said, wiping blood and gore off my shield and sword as I spoke.

"A tactical retreat might be in our best interest if our tanks are out of energy," Ryn said, her voice a resonating sound of reason.

"No," I said, getting my second wind. "We end this now."

Stepping forward, I did my best not to slip on the thickly blood-coated floor. The bodies, most of them at least, had been carried away, but the blood, shit, and piss remained. It sent emotions through me that I dare not dwell on, instead focusing on the sweet smells and tastes I'd have when I returned for a meal after this ordeal.

Everyone had their own ways of coping, and I saw each of them find their resolve as we walked into the flickering torchlight of the room beyond. This would be a fight to remember, I thought to myself as I looked over the nearly eight-foot-tall monster of a gnoll.

"You are really big," Tomas said to it as he twirled his staff around, and he prepared to smash in the gnoll's head.

The plan was simple: surround and destroy. So we executed our plan by surrounding it, or at least Goose, Tomas, Ryn, and I did, while the other two stayed back. Wyatt's job was to keep the healer alive so that he could continue healing us, which he had been doing effectively up to this point.

"You speak our language?" I asked the massive gnoll, taking in his details as I did so.

He was tall and very muscular. Armor of hides and chainmail covered his body, but not so effectively that it would stop us from striking at the right spots. He had a shield that had seen better days, but was as large as a freaking wagon wheel. His sword was clearly meant for two hands, but was being wielded like a mere arming sword.

"I will destroy you!" the gnoll screamed at us, swinging his mighty two-handed sword at me. Goose was at my side instantly, and we raised our shields together and the fight was on. The blow rocked us back, but our shields held.

We had no effective counter, so we relied on our party members to do the damage. To keep the attention of the beast, we hurled curses and unkind words at it like rocks from a sling. The gnoll ate it up, becoming enraged and continuing his assault on us rather than on our team.

I watched as Ryn stepped in close and slashed at its leg, drawing its attention momentarily. This put her in danger, but she rolled out of a swipe, using her special ability that made her immune to damage for a brief window. Good thing too, because it slammed down right on her with its shield.

I cast Spark on it, getting its attention back just as Tomas hit it with an empowered strike over the head. His staff came down, breaking bone and cleaving muscle aside as it did. But the fight was far from over; this gnoll took broken bones and flesh in stride, howling as it was inflicted with wounds.

We took our battle scars as well, twice Tomas got hit and needed a good amount of healing. Ryn took a cut to the chest, but her armor saved her; only her chin was cut, and Seth quickly healed it. Then the gnoll did something unexpected, it raised its shield back and slammed it into us, throwing both Goose and me a great distance back into a hard wall.

The wind was knocked out of my lungs, and I struggled to breath as it advanced on us. The room smelt of blood and pain, my ears rang, and I wondered if I'd be able to get back to my feet, much less fight off this monstrous gnoll.

A warm blanket of power settled over me, and I looked to see Seth casting his heal on us. I coughed a little blood, but otherwise I was fine now, standing and ready to meet the gnoll.

However, Ryn and Tomas had other plans, with Wyatt stepping up as well to give us time to recover. Tomas used his shields so effectively that he battered back blow after blow, fighting very defensively as Ryn and Wyatt moved like wraiths, cutting, slicing, and poking at the monster.

Little by little, they wore down the gnoll, and after a time, we joined the onslaught, with Goose ready to fight by my side once more.

"Stand fast," I shouted, and they made room for Goose and me just as a strike came down, rocking us back but not nearly as much as it had earlier in the fight.

This was a battle we could win; it would just take some time. So we gave it the time it required, biting my lip as I pulled from places I did not know I had to keep me going. The heals helped, but I was so slow on stamina that if the fight went on much longer, my legs might just give out. But nothing would stop me from defending my friends. If the time came that they called for retreat, I might consider it, but until that time, I'd fight on.

"Push it!" Ryn yelled, her attacks redoubling as the gnoll slowed its defenses and attacks.

One minute at a time, I told myself as I raised my shield once more to take a blow from the gnoll. So one minute at a time, we brought the gnoll closer to death. In the end, Tomas delivered the killing blow.

He squared off against the gnoll; its shield lay in pieces from a previous blow, but Tomas seemed to have endless energy to call on. He moved even faster than he had at the start of the fight. Raising his weapon over his head, he jumped off of seemingly nothing to boost himself high enough. It was his shield I realized afterward, a handy trick he could employ with them.

His body flew high into the air, and his staff came crashing down on the ugly, dog-faced monster, a loud crack vibrating through the room. The monster went down and didn't move.

The battle was won, and now we had only to clean up any remaining gnolls before calling it a day.

We moved robotically, collecting cores and hunting down another ten gnolls before the battle was truly won. The fight was over. Now it was time to wash up and celebrate.

"Let's get out of here," I said. "We will tell someone in the city about what we did, and they can clean up the mess here."

"I need a bath," Goose said, wiping more blood off himself, but it was no good; we were practically covered in the stuff and made for a frightening sight to behold.

"Let's clean up and meet up after to celebrate?" I asked, everyone agreed, and soon we were heading for town.

As we entered the forest, I noticed several small glowing silver eyes watching us from a distance. However, I didn't understand what that meant, so we continued walking toward the city. As we grew closer, I realized the silver eyes belonged to a flock of birds, watching us as we walked. But since they didn't attack, we didn't either.

It felt strange, but eventually, as we approached the city walls, the birds flew off, leaving us alone.

CHAPTER 31
BLOWING OFF STEAM

We found a bathhouse just inside the city walls that was open and ready for a big job. They took our armor, clothing, and everything, really, promising to clean it for a fee. I paid the fee for the entire group, and our gear was taken from us, leaving us with nothing but our naked bodies.

As a unit, we went to the baths. Using the soap provided, we cleaned ourselves and relaxed. The nakedness of my team was something I was used to. We often bathed together after big fights, so there was absolutely nothing erotic about the experience.

I did catch Goose checking out Ryn several times, but he was harmless enough about it, and when Ryn caught him looking, she stared at him until he stopped even looking in her direction.

We all sank into the water up to our chins. The water was clear, with bubbles on the surface and a powerful current constantly cleansing the dirty water, so you couldn't see anything but six floating heads. We must have been in there in relative silence for an hour or more before an attendant came to inform us that our gear had been cleaned.

"'Bout time," I said, getting up and out of the water. My body felt like a worn sponge, with wrinkles all over. But I felt refreshed after leaving the warm water.

We collected our gear and clothing, dressed, and got ready to hit the town for some drinks.

Deciding we should stow our armor and gear first, we made plans to meet up at the guard's favorite drinking place, then we'd move to new places as the night wore on.

Dropping off my gear took very little time, as we made our way through the busy city and then to the tavern Goose mentioned. The building was filled with guard activity, most off duty, of course, but still busy all the same.

The outside of the building was mostly brick, with a black sign out front, aptly named the Prancing Guard Shack, in intricate letters.

The blackened oak door swung open for us, and we entered, finding Goose, who was so much larger than your average guard, immediately.

"What's worth drinking here?" I asked as we sat at a table for five, but there were six chairs around it.

"I figured we'd start with something a bit harder to get the day rolling into night, then we can nurse it off with ales," Goose said. Just then, a curly-haired blonde woman brought six small glasses of a clear liquid to the table.

"Shots?" Ryn asked, grinning ear to ear. "Let's do it."

She reached over and took hers, the rest of us following suit. As one, we downed our shots, and Goose ordered another round. Five such rounds happened, alcohol taking a bit longer to affect us at first. But by the fifth, I was feeling the buzz, and more was coming.

"You're a good tank, Goose," I said, patting him on the back.

"Thank you," he said, his words slurring just a touch. "You aren't so bad yourself."

"You guys know much about the dungeon outside of town?" Ryn asked, looking directly at Seth and Wyatt.

"I don't," Wyatt said, but Seth nodded.

"I know a bit," Seth said. I'd seen him discreetly heal himself three shots in, so he wasn't as far gone as we were beginning to be.

A round of ales arrived, and we started sipping on the weak alcoholic drink.

"Tell me all you know," Ryn said, while Tomas snacked on some chips and looked awkwardly up at the ceiling from time to time.

"What are you doing?" I asked him, but he just shrugged.

"Thinking," he finally answered while Ryn listened to Seth's explanation on the dungeon.

"About what?" I asked, then, thinking it over, I amended. "Or about who?"

"I just don't understand why he didn't want to come with us. All this adventure and progress we've made, he could have shared in it," Tomas said, sighing.

I put a hand on his back and met his eyes.

"It'll be alright," I said, wishing he'd snap back already.

"So, despite there being mostly shadow-type monsters, you get a chance to kill a good bit, which increases the essence you can pull out of the dungeon. It's also more of a narrative than anything, so expect that. It changes every few months, and I haven't learned much about the most recent changes," Seth explained. I was only half listening.

"Shadow monsters, like what specifically?" I asked.

"It varies, but they are all made of shadow, so light and fire-based attacks work well against them," Seth said, smiling over to Ryn as he spoke.

"I've got that covered," I said, thinking of my flaming sword and how it would be effective in the dungeon. "How long does it take to get a spot to get into the dungeon?"

"It'll take a week at least," Seth said. "I suggest you go register as soon as possible."

"First thing tomorrow," I said, nodding along with his words.

"I'm hungry," Tomas said, his snacks running out, and looking around for a waitress so he could order.

"There's this great pub down the lane that has the most fantastic pasta dishes, we should go," Goose said, standing and knocking his chair back into someone else. They grumbled and turned only to quiet down when they saw Goose's huge frame staring down at them.

"Let's," I said, scooting my chair back and making my way out of the crowded tavern.

The air was cold, and night had fully descended upon us. Moonlight illuminated the area, while the dim glow from the streetlamps offered little assistance. As we walked in a line toward our next destination, I couldn't help but think what a wonderful night it was. It was almost enough to make me forget the gore and blood we had bathed in earlier that day.

Without the ability to get a job that paid for the next week, we would have to get creative in how we'd keep the essence coming in. There was no way I'd be sitting on my ass for a week when I could grow stronger.

"Any chance we could get the city to inform us of any more monsters they need taken care of that they haven't submitted as jobs to the adventurer's guild yet?" I asked everyone present as we approached our next destination.

"Maybe," Seth answered first. "They might be curious as to why you'd want to help without promise of pay, but it isn't such a stretch."

"Add that to the to-do list for tomorrow," I said, pretending to write a check mark in the air.

The rest of the night was a mix of eating, drinking, and eventually dancing as we went to a dancing hall that Wyatt knew. We had the time of our lives and didn't stop until the sun came up. The three guards had to get to duty, I felt for them, and Ryn, Tomas, and I left to get some sleep.

Waking early in the afternoon, I set about knocking out tasks, one by one. First, I went to the dungeon, just outside the town to the north, and registered a spot under my name. I was told to return in eight days, and we'd be given entry. I agreed and left to find the judge who had sentenced us, if I could.

At the center of the town stood a large stone building that served as the town hall. It featured massive pillars and a statue of a robed figure out front, surrounded by a fountain. I didn't know who the statue represented or why it had been placed there, nor did I inquire to find out.

I went inside and asked to see Judge William, but I was told to wait in an uncomfortable chair for three hours while he would "be right with me." Just as I was about to give up and leave, he finally appeared, his face looking stern.

What brings you here?" he asked. "I got a report that you took care of the warren and that it was a bit more difficult than we were aware it would be. For that I apologize, but you are clean in the sight of the law now, so rejoice."

"I, uh, well, I was actually hoping you might have some leads on additional monsters that need taking care of. We are banned from taking official jobs from the Adventurer's Guild for a week or two, so we have time on our hands, and we want to use it wisely if we can," I said, giving my argument in the best light I could.

"Hmm, an odd request, most of what we learn of is sent to the adventurer's guild to be made a job, so we have very little. But wait here, and I will see what I can scrounge up for you," William said, then pausing, he added. "We won't be able to pay you, you know that, right?"

"Yep," I said, smiling. "We are interested in growth more than anything else, so whatever you can find that involves killing monsters, we are in."

Judge William left, returning to whence he came and leaving me to wait for another hour or so before reappearing.

"I've got three jobs for you, and you can come back for more after you've finished. Here are the files, return these to me as well after you've taken note of the pertinent information," Judge William said, passing over three files.

The jobs weren't much to go off of, one was a report of rats that needed an adventurers touch, the next rumors of travelers being waylaid by forest vine monsters, and finally there was a nearby mountainous area that was a popular hiking destination that was said to be disturbed by a snow monster, though no one could say what exactly it was, either cat, or bear, or something all together different.

It honestly wasn't much, but it was better than nothing. I took note of the info I needed and returned the files to the judge. He smiled in turn and bid me good luck before leaving me alone in the sitting area outside his office.

I left and found my friends where I'd left them in the room above the tavern. Told them what we were up against, and we decided to check out the rats first, as they were the closest and probably the easiest ones to knock out.

"So Jen's Bakery really has no other way to deal with a few rats? She has to call the city about it?" Ryn asked, a little heated that we were doing such a basic job for no pay.

Rats, even monstrous ones, had very little in the way of essence, so they weren't really worth our time. But we'd asked for this work, and I would see all three jobs taken care of.

As we went, I thought I saw one of those silver-eyed birds on the corner of a building, but when I looked back, it was gone. Odd. But I let the thought of it go away as we found the small building where we were meant to kill rats.

"We are from the city, here for a rodent problem," I said, meeting the plump lady's eyes as we entered the establishment.

"About damn time they sent someone. Good, you have weapons; these bastards are large and dangerous. The only reason they haven't left my cellar is their size. I think they are stuck. Be quick 'bout it, and I'll get someone down there to patch the hole when you are finished," the lady said, not even introducing herself as she rushed us to a cellar door set into the ground.

It led down into the dark, and I took the lead, sword at the ready. It was oddly spacious down here, as I slunk into the dark and the only light showing from small windows at the street level high on the walls of the cellar.

We all made it down, and she shut the door above us as we scanned for any sign of monstrous rats. Movement caught my eye in the shadows, and I raised my shield just in time for a horse-sized rat to smash into me, knocking me back.

From the grunts I heard from Ryn and Tomas, they too had found a rat of unusual size. I cut and slashed at the rat, but its hide was thick, and only one in three of my attacks made any progress. It was atop me, thrashing around and ripping at my shield.

Finally, I got lucky. A sword thrust into the eye killed the massive thing, allowing me to push it aside to aid my friends. But I didn't have to. They both finished off their rats at the same time as me.

"That wasn't so bad," I remarked as a screech came from the distant shadows. I followed the sound to a large hole in the stone wall, a five-foot-tall hole leading out into the dirt beyond.

"I think we aren't done here," Ryn said, cleaning her blade and lifting it into a ready position.

Sure enough, more rats could be heard scuttling through the tunnel.

"Well, shit," I said, raising my shield in preparation for what was to come.

"We took care of the rats, although you'll have to talk to someone else about removing the corpses. It's pretty full down there," I said to the lady as we slipped out of the building and into the fresh air of the evening.

"That was awful," Ryn said, folding her arms.

"I'm hungry," Tomas said, twirling his staff aimlessly.

"Let's get some food and call it a night," I said. "Maybe we can catch Goose and the boys before they call it for the night."

And we did, going to hang out and party with Goose, Seth, and Wyatt. It was another night to remember, and I cherished the chance to meet these three. They called it earlier than I would have liked, citing they had guard duty again and hadn't actually slept. I understood, but I also wasn't ready to stop the enjoyment for the night.

Ryn decided to call it, though, so we walked her back before Tomas and I got into some mischief ourselves.

The next day arrived all too soon, and I woke up with a hangover that I wasn't pleased about, but I managed to cope. After a greasy meal and several hot cups of something delicious, I felt much better. We had a busy day ahead, with two jobs left to complete. We decided to take on the vine monsters today and, if time allowed, tackle the snow monster tomorrow.

"So what do you think it is, this vine monster everyone is reporting seeing?" Tomas asked, snacking on something nutty.

"You think it's something more than just a vine monster?" I asked, confused by his question. If so many people reported the same thing, then it was just that, right?

"I just mean, elementals are normally much stronger; this seems like it might be something else," Tomas said, and Ryn joined us at our table.

"I was thinking something similar," she said, digging into the plate of food I'd ordered for her.

"Instead of speculating about something we simply can't know, why don't we go investigate and see what turns up?" I said, and they nodded in agreement with my plan.

We ventured outside the gate toward the general location of the attacks. The cold was ever-present, but as we approached the attack area, it warmed noticeably. The growth of plants and trees here was far more abundant than anywhere else, with trees so close that you could hardly walk between them. That meant we stayed on the road for now, instead of venturing into the brush.

I mused at the idea that the very undergrowth might attack, but just as that thought crossed my mind, motion to the side caught my eye. Turning in time to see a massive vine monster appear, I clenched my fists and pulled my weapons a second later.

"That was easy," Tomas said, twirling his staff and stopping a vine attack from reaching us.

Ryn, on the other hand, did something I didn't expect. She moved behind us and put on glasses that let her identify items and monsters.

"Well?" I asked as she looked at it for several seconds; meanwhile, we blocked or dodged vine strikes as it slowly moved closer.

"It's a summoned elemental; someone is behind its attacks," she shouted, taking the glasses off and cutting a vine as she stepped forward.

"Alrighty then," I said. "Let's dispose of it and get to the bottom of this, shall we?"

It wasn't as easy as I tried to make it sound; the elemental was strong, and the battle was drawn out.

It finally closed the gap, and I rushed forward to meet it, shield raised and sword aflame. It formed a spiky club of vines and slammed my shield to the side. I followed up with a slash to its center, scoring a flaming hit and causing it to screech in pain.

Next, Tomas appeared on its flank and smashed into it with his staff, causing significant bludgeoning damage. However, the plant elemental seemed to recover quickly from his attack, slashing out and throwing Tomas backward.

Ryn was there to close the gap, slashing with her twin blades and making it bleed green ichor as she danced around it, a vision of deathly slashes.

I recovered myself, striking out where Ryn missed, and the battle seemed to turn in our favor. That, of course, was when another appeared, taking me from the side and throwing me down.

I rolled with the blow, feeling myself take many puncture wounds and cuts. I'd heal, but first we needed to focus up and not let this fight get out of our hands. Slashing and cutting, we pruned back the elementals until finally something started to go our way.

I got a lucky strike on the head of the humanoid-shaped elemental of vines and green, taking off what must have been its head and causing it to drop into a heap of vines.

"One more," I said under my breath as I advanced, but the elemental did the oddest thing; it ran from us into the thick brush.

"Follow it!" Ryn yelled, and we were on the chase, barely able to keep up with the trees and brush in the way. We lost it only ten minutes into the chase, but we continued in its general direction, finding a break in the trees some few miles off the road.

A little hut with a chimney and a moss-covered door lay before us. The elemental was nowhere to be seen, but as we approached, the door swung open, and a small man covered in moss appeared before us.

"I take it you are the ones who killed my creation?" the small man asked, his voice unusually deep for someone so small.

"You summoned it and had it attack us, so yes, we destroyed it," I said, keeping my shield at the ready and sword up.

"I was only protecting my territory. If people find themselves to be safe on the road nearby, then they'll explore and find me, but I can't have that; I prefer to be left alone. So I harass but never kill those traveling the road," he said, pulling out a pipe, loading it with some type of weed, and lighting it all in a matter of a few seconds.

"It sure seemed like they were trying to kill us," Tomas said, his neck still bleeding a bit from the attack.

"They can sense power levels and attack with the right power to give you a challenge, not overwhelm you," he answered, waving a hand as he pulled hard on his pipe.

"The attacks must stop, so we must stop you," I said, seeing no other option.

Ryn had her glasses back on, and she was tugging at the end of my sleeve armor.

"What?" I asked, turning to her.

In a whisper, she said, "This guy is high enough level that I can't see it, might not be worth trying to fight."

"Got it," I said, turning back to the grinning short man in his green attire and moss-covered cloak. "We need to come to an agreement then, you can't be attacking random travelers, because eventually the Adventurer's Guild will send out stronger folk to deal with you."

"I suppose you're right. I don't have the power to turn away all attackers, but I was just beginning to like this area. I suppose I could move on further from the road and deeper into the wilds," the man said, rubbing at his chin as he spoke.

I was surprised when he agreed so quickly, so I faltered about what to say next. Instead, Tomas spoke, and I finally got my words together.

"You got any snacks?" Tomas asked him, looking at a few racks of drying berries and an assortment of fruits.

"Sorry, I only prepare what I need, and I need what I prepare," he said, shaking his head.

"So you are in agreement with us, you'll leave and stop attacking the travelers?" I asked.

"Fine, but first I have a few items you might like. My elementals can sometimes have sticky fingers, and I've no use for this loot, but perhaps you do?" he asked, going inside and pulling out a bag of items.

We went through the bag, and most of it was just general armor or non-magical stuff, but there were three items that stuck out to us, and we decided to keep.

Name: *Seashells of Hearing*
   Rarity: *Uncommon*
   Special Properties: *Allows you to speak into one end and hear through the other. The distance is decided by the amount of mana you infuse at the time of speaking; the greater the mana, the greater the distance.*
   Description: *Iridescent shells that curl in on each other, they've got*

magical runes carved into them that seem to amplify the natural ability of the shells. They are fragile but sturdy enough to be stored in your bags without much risk of degradation.

Name*: Ring of Shadows*
   Rarity*: Rare*
   Special Properties*: Allows you to hide in shadows for a short period, several times a day. This will make you extremely hard to spot when you are closed within a shadow.*
   Description*: A silver band with a black line across it, the ring is simple yet elegant.*

Name*: Pocket Watch of Chronos*
   Rarity*: Rare*
   Special Properties*: Slows users' perception of time for three seconds. However, three seconds after the slow, time moves twice as fast, putting the user in potential harm while they remain at their normal speed.*
   Description*: A simple golden and silver pocket watch with an infinity symbol at its center, it tells you the time of day no matter where on the planet you are. It dangles on a silver chain and seems to pulse with power as you look upon it.*

As was normal, we took out some dice to decide who would get first crack at picking the items. I rolled the highest, with Ryn next, and Tomas to get whatever was left over.

Of course, I picked the item that seemed the most powerful out of the bunch. Whether to sell or use, I wasn't sure yet, but I took the pocket watch of Chronos and put it in my pocket. Ryn took the shadow ring and slipped it on, disappearing into a nearby shadow. She was impossible to spot until she stepped out willingly.

Tomas took the shells and shrugged, putting them both in his pack.

With that taken care of, we left the hermit to his packing and made our way back toward town.

CHAPTER 32
MONSTER OF SNOW

We let the rest of the day finish off while we drank in silence. Tomorrow we'd leave early in the morning to check out the snow monster on the nearby mountain, but it would take most of the day to get out there, and we'd likely need to find a place to sleep while out on the mountain. It was said to be a small village of sorts out there, mostly filled with ice workers and such, but I was confident we'd find somewhere to lay our heads.

I didn't know what to expect out in the cold, winter-filled mountain, but we'd find the monster and dispose of it as we were instructed to do. These jobs were turning out to be alright, giving a decent amount of essence and whatnot. We'd made advancements, but I wasn't so much that I'd spent more than a little time looking over my status.

Once I hit 25, which would happen sooner than later, I'd need to look over things in detail, because it would be my first attribute 10 choice and the first time I'd need to unslot an ability if I wanted to use it. But that was a worry for another time, so I pulled hard on my drink and looked about the common room for any familiar faces.

We didn't see the trio we'd met before, so I figured they must still be on duty. So we finished our drinks and meal, then headed in for the night.

It was early morning when a knock came at my door, waking me from my sleep.

"We'd better get a move on now if we want to make it to the mountain at a decent time," Ryn said through the door.

With that, we were up and getting dressed. Our winter attire varied in usefulness, but we also planned to hit a store on the way out for extra gear, because snow and ice were their own kind of monster to deal with.

Snow fell as we left our tavern in search of a store open at this early hour. We found one pretty easily and bought the necessary items before heading to the gate just as the sun began to crest the horizon.

I breathed heavy as I carried the weight of my bag, now twice as heavy as it was before. Ryn had insisted we get a tent made for the snow, and it weighed a fair bit. That and the added rope, chains, and hooks. Hell, we'd even got special snow shoes that made it easier to tread on the soft snow. In all, we'd paid two dozen silver moons, but we took it out of the collection we were keeping for the group, so not a one of us was less well off than we had been.

The trip was going to be long, that much I knew, but what I didn't expect was how many monsters had found their way onto the road as snow made it harder to make out. We fought goblins of all sorts, wolves, and all manner of other monsters on our way, slowing us all the more.

By the time we reached the base of the mountain where the road ventured over and through, we were wet, tired, and more than a little ready for rest.

"I saw we find a place to sleep and take on this monster after a good night's rest," I said, more telling than suggesting, but everyone nodded all the same.

We were in luck, finding the only tavern in the place with a single room left, with two beds. Tomas and I shared one, as uncomfortable as that was, it was better than the floor, while Ryn took the other one by herself. We couldn't have been asleep for more than a few hours when a roar ripped through the air, bringing us all awake.

I was out of bed and sword drawn in moments, rushing downstairs to see what was happening.

"It's fine, it's fine," an older woman said to us, the one who had rented us the room. Her name was Mary, if I remembered right.

"What was that?" I asked, and the roar held power, power I could still feel vibrating through me.

"It's the monster of the northern peaks. Something has brought him down from the mountain, and he's been making it difficult for our ice men, who have been working hard all season. But that's what you're here for, am I right?" Mary asked, looking up at me with hope in her eyes.

"Yeah," I said, then my thoughts churned, and I had a question for her. "Does it come into town and attack? Should I get my party ready?"

"No, he leaves us alone for the most part. Even his attacks are nothing more than warnings to keep us out of the ice lake. He's only hurt one man, old, stubborn Frank, who tried to go get ice despite the trouble with the monster. Lost an arm, Frank did, but no healers around to fix it, so he's out for the season," Mary explained.

I narrowed my eyes and thought it over. "I'm going back to sleep; it'll be easier to hunt the monster in the daylight," I said, turning and making for the stairs.

"Why do you need to hunt the monster at all?" she asked, confusion in her tone.

"What do you mean?" I asked, equally as confused.

"Well, if you go up to the peak, you could find out what drove him from his home and fix that problem. I'm not sure you have what it takes to slay the monster that we face, but perhaps you can get him to return," Mary said, winking at me at the oddest of times.

"I'm going to bed, I'll discuss it with my team tomorrow," I said, walking up the stairs as Ryn and Tomas appeared, geared up from the room. "Back to bed, no monster hunt until we've finished sleeping."

They groaned but turned back to the room to undress and get back into bed.

No further disturbances happened while we slept, and I awoke refreshed and ready for the day a few hours later.

I told my team what Mary had said, and we discussed the best course of action.

"So as I see it, we have two choices. We go after the monster or we go up into the mountain in search of what displaced it, hoping it will return and stop harassing the ice workers," I said, and I knew which I preferred.

"I see it differently," Ryn said. "I bet we could sneak to the lake and get a read on the monster. If it's too strong for us, which might be the case, then we investigate. If not, we kill it and be done with it for now."

"I agree with Ryn," Tomas said, throwing a few snacks into his mouth. "Besides, one course of action means we might not have to travel a bunch, which I'm all for after yesterday's adventures."

"Fair point," I said. "Let's do it that way. We will sneak to the lake and see if we can spot it. Then get a reading on it before deciding what to do next."

With that, we left the tavern and ventured out into the snow with all our supplies. The journey to the lake wasn't far, so we made it there in less than an hour. Putting ourselves in line with the trees, we waited for the monster to show.

We waited for two hours, and nothing appeared.

"I think I'm going to the lake and try to draw it out," I said. "I have the fastest speed, and if I shed most of this gear, it shouldn't be an issue."

To my surprise, no one objected. Instead, they helped me out of most of my heavy winter gear, and I was soon walking toward the edge of the iced-over lake. I'd nearly made it to the edge when a roar split the air, and a ten-foot-tall humanoid shape smashed into view.

It was all long white hair, only its hands and knees, oddly enough, were without hair and showing blue skin. The beast man rushed toward me, and I waited until I got a good judge of its speed before sprinting in a direction away from my group. I'd be able to outrun it, but I also needed to be sure she could get a reading on it before it disappeared again.

The monster, oddly enough again, didn't pursue me; instead, it stopped at the lake's edge and roared as I ran from it. Getting into the trees, I circled back and around to my team, but the monster remained at the lake watching the tree line.

"Good thing we checked," Ryn said. "This thing is strong, but maybe not strong enough for us if we worked together and had a little luck. I'd say our chances are fifty-fifty. What do you want to do?"

"Odds like that aren't exactly in our favor; however, what is to say that the thing we find atop the mountain isn't even stronger to have drawn out this monstrous thing?" I asked, not really expecting an answer.

"Put it to a vote?" Tomas asked, looking from face to face.

"I can live with that," I said. "I vote we slay the monster here and be done with it."

"I agree," Ryn said.

"Well, I guess my vote doesn't matter then, but I was going to say we should kill it anyway, so we are all in agreement," Tomas said cheerfully.

With that decided, we ventured slowly out of our hiding place and into view of the monster.

"What is it called?" I asked Ryn as we approached, it had not yet seen us and remained very still.

"Abominable Yeti," Ryn said, her eyes never leaving our prey. "I didn't see this, but I get the feeling that it has ice attacks, so be ready."

"We will," I said, my sword suddenly surging with fire and catching the monster's attention.

It stared directly at us, but made no motion. Instead, it subtly shifted its body, revealing icy claws extending from its clawed hand. Its expression darkened, and I swear it looked more annoyed than anything else. But even so, we trudged onward toward the fight, ready to put an end to one more monster.

The wind howled, and the icy chill of the morning hit us as we walked. This battle might be tough, but I knew we had it in us to overcome just about any foe. My mind flickered to the one foe we'd encountered so far that I knew we didn't have the strength to kill and a shiver ran down my spine.

Not the time to think about him, I scolded myself. This is just one more hurdle to getting strong enough to deal with threats like that. So with that new mindset in place, I raised my hand and cast Spark, starting off the fight in earnest.

The yeti let out a terrible roar, making us all pause for only a second in our approach to it before it charged forward. My spark had done little more than annoy it, leaving no marks on its tough white fur.

The beast was nearly ten feet tall and half as thick. It had fangs protruding from its mouth, clawed hands with long, icy claws, and large feet that enabled it to run atop the snow. Its fur was mostly white, with patches of blue skin showing here and there. All of this came clearly into view as it charged right at me.

My shield was ready, but I used Shove as well, as it met me, giving me a little more stopping power. Even so, I was rocked back and lost my footing in the wet snow. My sword slashed out, cleaving through icy talons before they could gut me, and my team engaged at that same moment, giving me time to recover.

Tomas used his shield spell to great effect, blocking attack after attack, and giving himself and Ryn openings to attack. For the hundredth time, I thought that perhaps I ought to have taken that ability, but this wasn't the time to worry about such past mistakes. I had skin as hard as iron, and I needed to remember that.

Rushing forward, I let my shield, my armor, and my hardened skin take the brunt of his attacks and found them well-equipped for the task. Claws put grooves into my shield, tore at my armor, but didn't pierce my flesh more than shallow cuts.

But on the opposite side of the attack, my sword bit deep as I cut and slashed from behind my shield. Our combined might seemed enough, but then the battle shifted.

The yeti became enraged, and soon we were on the defensive as it hurled razor-sharp ice bolts at us, forcing us back. I did my best to make space and get back into the melee fight, but he was throwing his attacks with such speed that it was nearly impossible.

Fighting back the urge to panic, I used Quickstep at the same moment Ryn did, then Sparked right into his eyes, before Shoving hard with my last spell aimed right at his knees. It worked, I thought, as Ryn cast a Mana Bolt from mid-range before using Evasion Roll to avoid an unavoidable attack.

Her Venomfang Edge slashed into the leg of the Yeti, adding another application of her poison effect. Meanwhile, Tomas caught attacks on his Hornwood Staff, getting charges he could unleash upon the enemy at any time.

I activated Wolfcaller's Charm, giving me a +5 power bonus for a minute and using the charge for the day. With my increased power and my incredible speed, I was a match for the yeti, at least momentarily.

With one more trinket at my disposal, I waited for the right time, hoping it would give me a chance to give a killing blow before the time ran out on my minute of increased Power. We were drawing blood, soaking its white fur red, but still it didn't seem to weaken or slow, just growing faster and stronger as the fight went on.

I jumped and slashed for its neck, but that left me open to getting hit mid-air and being thrown back. Tomas was there, unleashing a combo of Overhead Smash and releasing the magic he'd stored up in his staff. The air cracked with the power he unleashed, and for once, the yeti slowed and stumbled back from the blow to its head.

The air went still afterward, and I wondered if we'd done it, but no, the yeti recovered and slashed at Tomas. Only his invisible shields saved him. He was so quick with them now that it was almost silly.

Tomas flew past me, hitting hard in the soft snow. Our battlefield of the day was beneficial in that way, but we were staining it with red, and we had no healer to keep us going if we lost too much health.

"Think damnit, we gotta take it out soon!" I yelled more to myself than to them.

Then I saw it, my opening. The yeti turned to face Ryn and put its side to me. I caught Tomas's eye, and he knew what I needed. I held up three fingers, and he nodded, before I sprinted off toward the yeti's exposed back.

I dropped my shield and readied myself. My sword flared in my hands, anticipating my need for heat, and I activated the three-second charm that gave me increased perception just as I dove up, my feet hitting a shield and raising me up higher. Then the next shield appeared beneath my foot, and I stepped even higher, and then the next, putting me high enough up to deal the fatal blow we needed.

Just then, the yeti turned, slow as ever in my perception, and I moved just as slowly, but I had the advantage of knowing where he was going, so my blade was ready. I stabbed it down hard on his spine, just as the three seconds ended, and my perception blurred for a solid three seconds as my mind caught up.

All the while, I held on and pushed down hard with both hands. I had no protection from his claws, and they dug deep into my side, bypassing my armor and Iron Skin with repeated strikes.

I screamed out loud, but never stopped putting my weight into the blade, even casting Spark on it then Shove to make it go deeper. The stabbing suddenly stopped and as blood fell freely from my wounds, the yeti began to sway on its feet.

It was going to fall and crush me in the process, so I released my blade and allowed myself to fall away from it as it crashed down the other direction, narrowly missing Ryn in the process.

We were injured and in poor condition, but the yeti was down. I lay in the snow, allowing my ring to gradually heal my wounds. It took some time, but when I finally got up, Ryn and Tomas were already at work, cutting into the yeti in search of its core.

The core would be powerful and worth a good bit, so I didn't fault them for getting right to it and not checking on me. We all had recovery rings now, Tomas having gotten one from a store for a reasonable price, so we knew that it was only a matter of time before we were back to one hundred percent.

"Find anything?" I asked, and Tomas looked over at me with blue blood covering his arms and a dagger in his grasp.

"I found it, but it's cracked from your killing blow. I'm trying to work around it to keep it intact until we can sell it," Tomas said, wiping sweat from his brow and smearing blue blood over his face. "Oops," he said after realizing what he'd done.

"Move over and give me a chance," Ryn said, and he passed over the dagger he'd obviously borrowed from Ryn in the first place.

We got the monster core out of its head eventually, and then cut the head of the yeti off to show the town. The body would be left out for wolves and other predators to eat. Tomas suggested taking some of the meat, but we had no way to store it and keep it fresh, so we'd leave it to someone else to do that.

Heading back to town, we talked and enjoyed the increased essence we'd gotten from the fight.

"If we keep this up, I'll be level 25 by the end of this week," Tomas said.

"Same," I said, grinning. "That yeti sure had a lot of essence waiting inside of him. Maybe we could go check out where he came from and see if we can kill a few more?"

"I'm not so sure," Ryn said. "We've got to get back for the dungeon run we have planned, remember. We can't take more than a day or two to get back, so we can rest up and stock up before the dungeon starts."

"You're right," I said, remembering that the dungeon wouldn't be much longer now. "The shadow dungeon with a story to tell should be fun."

"I was wondering about that. Maybe we should try to find and question some people who have been inside more recently," Ryn said, raising her eyebrows at me.

"And ruin the surprise?" I asked, laughing. "We know the type of monsters, that'll be enough. Plus, if what they said was right about it, the story changes, so there is no telling if getting intel would even be worth it."

"I'm going to try anyway, I'll just keep it to myself unless it becomes pertinent," she said, shrugging.

I shrugged back. She could do what she wanted, and if it helped, all the better.

We arrived back at the tavern and met with Mary, telling her the task was complete and giving her the yeti's head. She sent out ice workers to fetch the body, saying the meat would be great to use if no wild animals had gotten to it. They knew how to dress and use all parts of the yeti, so she was excited to learn that it was indeed a yeti that had been terrorizing the ice workers.

With that task taken care of, we rested for a couple of hours, eating and drinking our fill. Ice workers came and went, thanking us and buying us drinks, to the point that we decided to stay another night and leave in the morning.

CHAPTER 33
SHADOW DUNGEON PART 1

The travel back to town was as eventful as it was on the way in, which is to say, we were attacked by all manner of monsters and gained a fair bit of essence for our trouble. We made it back into town just after midday and split up the group, Ryn to find intel, Tomas to refill his snacks, and me to take a long, hot bath.

I removed my clothes and joined several others in the bath, sitting beside a cute brunette who seemed to be interested in more than just bathing by the way she locked eyes and kept standing to show off her body. The town baths weren't exactly the place for such interaction, but I talked with her anyway, and we hit it off.

Before I knew it, we were heading to her place, a room she'd rented in a nearby inn. She was an adventurer. She was level 22 and had already chosen a class: Dervish, a whirlwind, fast-attacking class. I told her that I hadn't chosen a class just yet, but that I was near her level as well.

We talked about all manner of things, but mostly we lusted after each other. Before too long, we were in bed together, and I had the evening of my life with a strange new beauty. The lovemaking of two with increased attributes was something different from what I'd ever experienced. With her Speed and Power, she was stronger than me by a fair bit, but I gave as good as I got.

When my evening of fun ended, she asked if I wanted to get a meal and a drink, to which I said yes, but suggested we go check out the guards' favorite tavern, where I knew I'd likely find my friends. She agreed, saying her party was all busy for the night, so she was happy to meet mine.

I took my supplies and armor back to my place before changing into a normal set of clothes and heading off to the tavern, where we met up with my friends and the guards we'd met that joined our party.

The night that followed was filled with laughter, memorable moments, and plenty to drink. The night ended with me sleeping over at her place again, a joyous night indeed.

Waking up, I looked over to her only to find her gone in the morning. She'd said something the night before about having to get an early start, and I must have slept through her getting up. I collected my things, which weren't much as I'd left almost everything at my place, then left with a smile on my face.

I wasn't sure if I'd see her again, but we'd shared a warm bed and experienced each other to the fullest. This was what the life of the adventurer was all about: new experiences and the thrill of living in the moment.

Today was the day we were set to enter the dungeon, so I met with my friends, getting a little heckling from Tomas and a side-eye from Ryn, but in the end, they knew it was what it was, just a night of fun.

"Let's focus up," I said. "Ryn, did you find intel?"

"I did, but I'll keep it to myself as I'm not sure it is going to matter. The guy I spoke with told me it changes so often that you never know which scenario you'll get, and he only knew of three. So I committed them to memory and will help if I can," she said, shrugging.

We were set to meet up with Seth, Goose, and Wyatt at the dungeon, so we left out the gate and headed toward them to start off the adventure. I was just glad the Adventurer's Guild hadn't restricted our dungeon access; otherwise, we'd only be able to take jobs for the city and not gain as much essence as we had the potential to.

We found the three just outside the little settlement where the dungeon lay, greeted them, and headed for the dungeon entrance. We got in without any trouble, and soon our adventure would begin.

"So we are in the middle of the forest, that's original," I said, smirking over to Tomas.

"Be on guard. All the storylines start pretty much the same," Ryn warned. "We will be attacked by waves of shadow creatures until someone finally comes to rescue us when it becomes most dire. They will be the indicator of which story will play out."

"That's right," Seth said, looking over to Ryn with an impressed look.

"Incoming," Goose said, raising his weapon and cracking his neck to the side.

Four wolves, or shadowy monsters in the form of wolves, stalked out of the brush, with only the moonlight showing them as they advanced. Ryn rushed forward, disappearing into the shadows with the help of her ring. I flared the light of my sword, and they shrank back as Ryn appeared behind one, cutting it with her dagger-and-sword combo.

We rushed forward then to give Ryn the support she'd need, but it was hardly necessary; the first wave of shadow wolves went down with one or two strikes, most from Ryn in the first few seconds of the fight.

That wasn't the last wave, not even close. What came next was more of the same, but twice as many. I raised my blade and lowered my shield into position. The first wolves slammed into Goose and me, but we didn't buckle under their strength. Instead, we stabbed and slashed outward, bringing more than a few down.

Back and forth we fought until we finally defeated that wave as well. What came next was fewer in number but much stronger.

Shadow bears.

Lumbering things that roared as they approached and had more than a few of us doing a double-take. They were bears in form, sure, but twice as big as the biggest natural bear I'd ever seen.

Even so, we stood steadfast and attacked with all we had. A clever Shove and a Spark turned one aside, causing it to fall, but the other two hit each of our shields in turn. I almost buckled under the power of it, but I held fast as shadow fire seemed to pour out of the maw of each bear.

The one that had fallen was swiftly dealt with by the others, and Seth made sure to keep us healed as we took shadow burn damage. We had only to wait, as our team flanked the bears and we held fast against them; they were dispatched almost as fast as the wolves.

This continued for another ten minutes, a mixture of bears, wolves, and then foxes—beings of swift speed and sharp claws—but we held fast in the moments of overwhelming power. It wasn't until humanoid creatures began to appear, clad in shadows and throwing bolts of shadow fire at us, that we started taking serious damage and needing to use trees as cover.

It was clear we'd be overwhelmed soon, but not before we defeated at least one more wave, I told myself, activating my wolf's emblem rushing out to bring death to the ranged casters. I made it to the first, cutting him down with my flaming sword. Then the next and the next, as my team joined me.

The final shadow to appear was a giant buck, and it was the only one, with shadow lightning crackling around its horns. It spoke to us, and I readied my weapons in response.

"Not many have the power to reach me, the final entity of this challenge. If you defeat me, you will be rewarded. If you fail, then your adventure ends here," it said, its voice ominous and shaky.

Goose and I took point, just in time for lightning wreathed in shadows to slam into our shields, nearly buckling mine and sending a crack up Goose's. Our team used us as cover as we got closer, but the buck circled us and came behind us before we could reposition.

It's shadow lightning struck Tomas, and he went down, still as I'd ever seen him, and suddenly I saw red. Seth began healing him, and I saw him stir, but a switch had gone off in me, and I was rushing the buck. Lightning struck my shield, but it was a glancing blow and did very little damage.

I reached the tall buck and swiped for its leg with my sword, but it brought its large and many-faceted antlers down to catch my blade and force me back. I cut cleanly through one, using all my strength. Then I took three stabbing wounds to my chest and stumbled back in surprise.

It had been stupid to go in by myself, but here we were, and now Seth would have to heal me, too. I disengaged, dodging lightning strikes as I dove behind a tree. I heard my party attack, but the pain of my stab wounds was greater than they ought to be, almost as if I was poisoned or something.

Seth reached me, dragging an unconscious Tomas along while Ryn, Wyatt, and Goose fought off the shadow buck alone.

"I've stabilized him, but tell me you brought a potion," Seth said, sounding a bit frantic.

"Here," I said, pulling it off my belt and handing it over.

He tipped it into Tomas's mouth, and suddenly his eyes went wide, awake at last.

"Rest here," Seth said, then, turning to me, I felt warmth wash over me. "That should keep you moving."

I still felt weak but much better than I had before, so I stood and bid them farewell with a nod. Along the way, I picked up my shield and rushed into battle.

The buck was working over Goose and keeping Ryn at a distance, but Wyatt was peppering it with one strike after another, black blood leeching into the ground around it. I cast Spark, but its antlers caught the strike, so I turned to Ryn and suggested she use her mana bolt, which she promptly did while Goose and I kept the shadow monster in place.

Attack after attack, we held fast while our shields crumbled. But the ranged attacks were making good progress. The shadow figure slowed, and after what felt like forever, it began to falter.

Then out of nowhere, Tomas appeared behind it, his weapon charged with power and slammed down on its skull with his staff, letting out electric magic power he'd absorbed as he did so. The poor shadow monster didn't know what hit it as it fell down, stunned, but not dead.

We washed over it with blade and magic attack, ending it within a few seconds of it falling down.

We were bloody, our armor and equipment were worked over, but we'd made it through the first part of the dungeon. No one had come to aid us, which was odd, but the six chests that appeared before us were more than enough to make up for it.

"So many rewards," I said, rubbing at my eyes. "Pick a chest and let's see what we got."

Goose and I both got new shields, and Tomas got a better recovery ring than the cheap one we'd gotten from the store. Ryn got another dagger to go with the one she already had, this one dealing shadow damage over time after cutting into something. Meanwhile, Seth got a gauntlet that shot out powerful blasts of white energy, and Wyatt got a case of poisoned bolts that refilled every few hours.

In all, it was a good haul, and no sooner had we gotten them than someone came through the trees, calling out before us.

"Who goes there?" I asked, and they called out a name.

"Jack, just friendly old Jack here. I thought I was coming with my crew to save someone who'd wandered into our shadow-filled forest, but it would appear you killed the guardian already. Good on you!" Jack said as he appeared before us, flanked by several others dressed in greens and browns of the woods.

He was tall, but shorter than me by a handspan or so. He was built much thicker and had a powerful bow out and strung. His companions carried a mix of staves, daggers, bows, and swords.

He wore browns and greens as well, a face covering moved to the side, showing an angular face with a hooked nose and narrowing eyes, dark as the shadows we'd fought. In a word, he looked spooky.

"Well met, Jack," I said, nodding. "We've defeated the guardian, but I'm sure there is more that needs doing?"

"In fact, there is. You have proven yourself most capable. I would warn you that the mission I have for you won't be easy, but the rewards will be great," Jack said, eyeing us all one by one.

"This isn't a narrative I've heard of before," Seth said, and Ryn nodded as well.

"Me neither," Ryn said. "Best just go with it and see what happens."

"I have three tasks for you," Jack said, indicating that we should follow him.

We did so, but kept our guard up as his men surrounded us, weapons still at the ready.

"I'm listening," I said, but Jack just shook his head.

"First, we get to my favorite tavern and share a drink. The shadows have a way of hearing what they should not, best we not tip them off," Jack said, and he led us through the woods toward what I hoped was some sort of village.

Darkness overtook us as the trees thickened, blocking out the moonlight, but they never stopped or slowed their pace, so I trusted they knew the way. Ryn had a way to see in the dark, but I didn't know if she was using it, since I couldn't see in her direction. I could barely make out Jack a few feet ahead of me.

Because of this, I never saw the attackers come, but shadow beasts arrived and were dispatched by Jack and his crew before we could even react. I went to thank him and saw something glint in his eyes as I did; it was almost as if they'd turned a deep red. More than that, his features, for a moment, seemed almost monstrous.

We traveled in silence after that, not even small talk, as we pushed deeper and deeper into the woods. Finally, light appeared ahead, and we walked out into a small village, maybe a dozen buildings, one of which was the biggest of all, with a stone foundation and wooden construction. We entered, and it was brightly lit by several fireplaces, filled with people who continued talking and laughing.

"Welcome to the Shadow's Crest Tavern," Jack said. "I'll fetch us some drinks, and we can talk about what you can do to help us."

"All right," I said, sitting at a long table where the rest all sat along with us. It was just big enough to fit us all, including Jack, and soon we all had ale, and the talks began.

"It all started because of that foul man. His name is lost to time, but he was a sorcerer of great power who chose shadows as his domain. It is his influence that poisons the forest and turns the wildlife against us, even claiming some of our souls from time to time."

"So we need to kill this sorcerer?" I asked, trying to get him to the point.

"Not yet. First, you need to prepare," he said. "His shadowy realm can't be entered except by someone wreathed in the shadows themselves. For this, we can brew a potion to give you all access, but it requires items lost to us, perhaps not outside your reach. One such item is the antler dust of the guardian, which I've already procured from your kill."

"And the others?" I asked, eager to get this dungeon going.

"Well, they are a bit more exotic and rare," he said. "First, you need to find the blood of a being untouched by shadows, but something native to our lands. I know of only a single creature able to keep the shadows at bay, but it is fierce and strong, even stronger than the guardian."

"And the second thing we need?" I asked, figuring he'd tell us more about the blood afterward.

"The tear of the purest one to walk these lands, our princess. She's been captured by the sorcerer and bound to the lake of memories. It won't be easy to get there, and her heart has grown cold, so getting a tear from her won't be easy either," Jack said, then, taking a long drink from his cup, he added, "I'll fill you in on the details of both tasks in the morning. For tonight, we drink and celebrate the freeing of our guardian from the bonds of shadows that held him!"

And celebrate we did. We drank, I flirted with a few pretty girls, and as odd as it was considering they were beings of a dungeon, I took one up to my room, as did most of my party, only Wyatt abstaining. It was a night I'd remember for years to come, and I truly enjoyed myself with these vibrant people.

Sure, it might have been the drink talking, but I still found myself liking them far more than I should the next morning. But it was hard not to like the experience of it all; we ate a greasy breakfast of eggs, sausage, bread, and hot tea. It was wonderful, and I ate my fill before looking for Jack to get the info on the first of the two tasks.

"That was a great night," Tomas said, shaking his head.

I hadn't seen who he'd taken up to the room, but a weight seemed to be off his shoulders, and I saw Ryn eyeing him with a smile. She'd taken up someone as well, but I was too hooked into my own partner that I hadn't noticed.

"I feel a little weird enjoying the flesh of someone that might not technically be real," Ryn said, giving me an awkward smile.

"They seemed pretty real to me," I said, shrugging. "I don't know 'bout you, but that ale was stronger than anything I remember drinking before. Not sure I could have said no if I wanted to."

"Same," Tomas said, then, scratching at the back of his head, he added, "Should we be worried about that?"

Conversation dwindled to nothing after that as we turned and greeted Jack, the man returning from whatever it was he was doing.

"Ready for the first leg of your journey?" he asked, and I nodded.

"Where can we find this being that resists the shadows, as you say?" I asked, sitting where Jack gestured, joining my team at a table.

"She is far south of here, a mighty hunter and a formidable opponent. Though she may merely look like a large cat to your eyes, she is much more than that, and if you can collect her blood without taking her life, our forest will be all the more blessed for your efforts. I'm afraid last I heard she was very aggressive, resisting the shadows will do that to you," Jack said, chuckling. "Get enough blood to fill this vial, and we will have what we require from her."

He held up a vial about the thickness and length of my smallest finger. That shouldn't be too hard, I thought to myself as I took it and nodded.

"What of the second task?" I asked, but Jack shook his head.

"I will tell you more when you return. Let's tackle one issue at a time," he said, making me a little frustrated as he'd promised to reveal all in the morning. "I hear you had a good time last night, all of you but the wiry fellow? Does he not appreciate our hospitality?"

I blushed a little at that and gave Jack a look. "I'm sure he does, but we'd also appreciate it if your hospitality didn't come on so strong. I fear the drink left little question about whether we wanted to enjoy ourselves. Not that we didn't," I added as his face turned sour.

"Of course, of course," Jack said, a twinkle of purple sheen covering his eyes. I felt something stir within me, a pain, the best way I can describe it, but it faded before I could truly lock onto it.

"Well, anyway, we are going to be off soon. Wish us luck, and we will return by nightfall," I said, getting up and looking around the room until I found Seth, Wyatt, and Goose sitting and eating across the room.

"Be sure that you do," Jack said. "The night is a dangerous place for us; we will seek you out if you don't return, but we'd prefer not to."

With that, I gathered up my team, and we ventured out into the woods, following a hastily scrawled map made by Jack to the general direction of our target.

"Anyone else feel a bit icky the longer they think about last night?" Ryn asked, rolling her eyes a bit as I looked over to her.

"Let's focus up and worry about that later," I said, but I was feeling it too, a growing feeling inside that I didn't like.

We traveled through the forest in the shade of the trees, for the first hour of walking, nothing attacked, but then, even in the daytime, the shadows began to appear. Wolf formed ones, moving slower than before, but still a threat if not taken seriously.

I cut down the first to appear, it jumped free of a nearby shadow, before turning and smashing my shield into another that tried to flank me. My team sprang into action, and the dozen shadow wolves that hoped to surprise us went down with very little fight.

What came next was a bit harder to deal with because of the differences in size and shape—shadow spiders. The first few were no bigger than my fist, and we squashed them without much effort, though they were numerous.

Then came the larger ones, and we had to use our weapons to take them down. They were swarming the deeper we got, and our chances weren't looking great, but we continued onward regardless.

Spider after spider emerged from the trees, jumping down on us and casting webs of shadow that slowed and cut at our flesh. I took the lead, jogging forward, as Goose took the bac,k and our other party members fought in the middle. We kept moving, as the spiders' numbers seemed endless, and I had a hunch that we could move out of their territory and be free of most of them.

Sure enough, after ten minutes of moving, the spiders began to back off. But just when I thought we were out, two massive spiders, the size of wagons, appeared before us.

"Goose!" I shouted, and he moved to join me just as the first leg came crashing down on my shield, rocking me backward. I ignited my blade and cut into the spider's leg, but it dug only halfway through, and I almost lost my sword in the process.

Goose's mace was far more effective, crashing into sections of the leg and spraying ichor all around us. The first spider hissed at us and lurched forward, but was met by bolts of steel and magic, followed by a pulse of white energy from Seth's new weapon gauntlet.

The spiders barely seemed to notice the onslaught, with only one backing off while the other pressed its attack. What was the best way to kill a spider? I asked myself and came up blank. Instead, I focused on the one thing I could do: destroy its legs, leaving it defenseless.

My sword came down on the same spot as before, and the first of the eight legs fell before my blade. Back and forth we fought. As the spiders overwhelmed our front line, one of them slipped past Goose and me. My team fought life and limb against one spider while Goose and I dealt with the other.

It was a battle we were slowly losing, but we fought on, waiting for our chance to turn the tide. It came when the second leg fell, and I took a chance, shoving with my power and casting Spark a moment later. I rolled beneath the spider and stabbed upward into its head, killing it with one fatal stab.

However, the weight of it suddenly collapsed onto me, and I was out of the fight, with several bones cracked or completely broken. I only managed to survive because of a hole in the ground where I was saved from the full force of the blow.

Feeling panicked and sick, I struggled against the weight, but it wasn't until a minute later when Goose and the others turned the massive spider off me that I was able to really breathe again.

"That was risky," Ryn said, looking at me and shaking her head.

"You guys get the other one?" I asked, coughing up a little blood as I did so.

"Yeah," Tomas said. "You all right?"

"No," I said, falling to one knee as Seth cast a heal on me, knitting blood, bone, and tissue back together. It took three charges to make me feel like I could walk again, and I took a potion just to be safe. With that out of the way, we made our way out of the spider-infested area and closer to the large cat we needed to bleed.

CHAPTER 34
SHADOW DUNGEON PART 2

The forest opened up around us and we entered the first area that wasn't fully consumed by shadows or shadow creatures. All around, life seemed to be teeming again; insects and all manner of other life were chirping and making noises.

"You nearly ate the dust back there," Tomas said, and I nodded.

"Yeah, that fight wasn't ideal for our team composition, but we made it through," I said, still feeling some phantom pain in my chest, though I was sure I'd healed by now.

"You need to learn to not be the hero," Goose said, elbowing my side as we walked. "A little more time and we'd have had one of them down without the big show of heroics."

"You think so, huh?" I asked, not convinced.

"He's got a point," Ryn said, and I looked behind to see her shaking her head at me.

"Well, I'll remember that in the future," I said, ready to say anything to keep them off my back.

We'd finally entered a larger clearing and I almost didn't notice the enormous yellow cat sitting on a branch until we were right under it.

"Hold up, it's right there!" I said, backing up a few steps.

The cat, for all its troubles, was sleeping in the tree and hadn't seemed to notice us yet. Perhaps we could wound it quickly and quietly, get what we needed from it, and leave before a fight could ensue.

That was a pipe dream, though, and I knew it. Instead I readied my sword and motioned for the team to get ready as well.

"The plan is simple. I'll go and try to wound it and get the blood, you guys hold it down," I said, my words a low whisper.

"Uh, it's looking right at us," Tomas said, gesturing forward with his staff.

I looked and sure enough, it was looking right at us now with both eyes open. It seemed to have a smirk on its face, though that could've been my imagination. With a sudden jerk of my body, I turned to face it, and it lazily got up, yawning and pouncing down before us.

"So you require my blood, do you?" it asked, a feminine voice, very powerful in tone.

"It can talk?" Goose asked, lifting his shield before him and slamming his mace against it in a show of force.

"Appears so," I said. "This could be good, we can reason with it."

"Yes," it said. "Reason with me. Why would I ever give my blood to such delectable meals as yourselves?"

"We are here to stop the spread of shadows. Give me your blood and we can use it to save the forest," I said, getting right to the point.

"No," the beast said flatly. "Or perhaps I should say, not yet. Show me your power, challenge me to one-on-one combat, and if I deem you worthy, I will give you of my lifeblood."

"Don't," Ryn hissed, but I was already walking forward.

"I accept, and I will challenge you one-on-one," I said, ready to put this situation to rest, whether it meant my life or not.

It was probably foolish, but I liked the idea of putting all the risk on myself and keeping my team safe. I felt power coming off this cat in waves, but I was confident that I had what it was going to take to prove myself.

My muscles tensed and I felt the phantom pain from my previous wounds as I stepped forward and raised my shield. No sooner had I done this did the cat pounce forward, knocking me back despite my bracing. I used a quick turn and a Shove to get back on my feet, casting Spark at its head as it neared.

It reeled back a little, but it was ready for a fight and a small Spark wasn't going to stop it. It charged again, but I used Quickstep to move to the side with impossible speed. I slashed down, getting first blood as my sword sunk just enough to piece its flesh.

She growled at me, slashing for my shield, but I caught the blow, a smile appearing on my face. When she charged again at full power, I used Shove to turn it into a glancing blow, then slashed at her again. I could do this, I realized, I could beat the cat and save my team the pain of fighting it.

Then the battle shifted as the cat hissed and growled at me. Suddenly, it was moving with blinding speed, and I barely got my shield up in time; even so, I felt it begin to buckle under the power of the cat's attacks. Back and forth we traded blows, its claws getting past my shield more than once.

My skin was hard as Iron, but its claws still drew blood, weakening me with each strike. I cast Spark again, hopping back to make space, but the cat was on me within a second.

I stabbed and stabbed, but it wasn't going to be enough, the cat was doing far too much damage too quickly. The cries of my team strengthened me and I redoubled my efforts. Slashing out, I dug deep and cast Spark with as much power as I could. This time it left a blackened scorch mark on the cat's side, forcing it to back off.

But doing such a feat made me even more tired, slowly eating away at my reserves.

"You fight well, but I still can't tell if you are worthy," the cat said, panting as she spoke. "I don't want to kill you, but if you don't give it your all, I will."

With that, she pounced back toward me. I used Quickstep, followed by a Shove, throwing the cat off balance and slashing down hard. My sword caught her leg and cut deep into it.

She growled something fierce, but stopped as she slammed into the ground, her front paw unable to support her weight. I rushed forward, ready to take advantage of the moment I'd earned, only to stop dead as her head snapped around, eyes flickering with golden power.

Her foot and all the cuts I'd earned so far healed before my eyes and I swallowed hard.

"Shit," I said, getting my shield in place and raising my sword.

She came at me with speed beyond anything I'd seen a monster do before, knocking my shield right out of my hand and arm. It throbbed from the pain of her blow, but I took my sword into a double grip and focused on sensing her attack.

She came swiftly from my left, and I turned swiping down while casting Spark from the tip of my blade. It struck her full in the face, slowing her momentarily as I slashed deep into her shoulder.

Blood sprayed, and I dove to the side, casting Shove to give me room to avoid her counterattack. I was out of energy, but I had to fight for my friends and that kept me from staying on the ground. Instead, I stood, panting hard, and readied for another attack.

We exchanged blows for what felt like another ten minutes, and I gave it all I had, keeping my sword up and blocking any attacks I could. I was bleeding all over and had a few deeper wounds when the cat finally spoke, surprising me.

"You are a worthy opponent," it said, breathing hard. "For one human to fight me at even half my strength is more than I expected from your kind."

"Are you telling me you aren't even fighting at your full potential?" I asked and the cat chuckled.

It appeared before me as if by teleportation and whispered, "If I wanted you dead, you'd be dead."

I nearly dropped my sword in shock, but I held firm to my weapon and refused to let it overcome me.

"Thank you for pushing me," I said, bowing to the cat and pulling out the vial. "If you don't mind?"

"Please, go ahead," she said, leaning her bleeding shoulder toward me.

I collected the blood and turned to my team, raising it in the air.

They cheered, well, all but Ryn, who looked ready to kill me herself.

With that, I left the cat. It glowed behind me, healing from all the wounds I'd given it. Meanwhile, Seth began casting heals on me, closing up all but the deepest wounds in seconds.

The trip back to the town took considerably less time, and we encountered only a fraction of the monsters we had before. When we finally met up with Jack, nightfall was just beginning to descend on us.

"You got it?" he asked, a hint of surprise in his voice.

"Of course," I said, holding it up. "Now tell us what's next."

Jack took the blood, and it disappeared into one of his pockets. He looked us over, then gestured for us to sit and hear him out. We did so, and the tavern filled with random people, all drinking and filling the place with cheer.

"You are ready to free the princess from the curse that holds her. First, you have to wait for our alchemist to finish the potion. That'll take at least half a day. Then you'll be ready to depart," Jack said, taking a long pull on the ale that had just arrived before him.

The day wore on with much drinking and talk, but nothing like the first night, when we lost ourselves in the drink. The next morning, we were given an antidote and told which direction to go to find a tower where a princess would be locked away at a lake. We were meant to give this to her, then continue onward to the sorcerer to end him after breaking the spell that gave him great power via the princess.

We'd learned this and a bit more over a day of drinking, so we ventured out into the wilds one more time to end this dungeon and reap our rewards.

Moving away from the town and in the direction we were given, we spoke of a little bit of everything, but said nothing of importance. We continued this way for several hours before something finally changed. The woods darkened, and I swear I could sense something watching us just beyond the shadows' edge.

"I feel like we are being watched," I said in a low whisper that reached the ears of everyone present.

"I feel it, too," Ryn said, drawing her weapons.

"Weapons at the ready," I said, following her lead and getting my sword and shield ready.

No sooner had we done this than a howl ripped through the air, and suddenly we were beset on all sides. Wolves, similar to the shadow creatures of before but different all the same.

They were gray wolves with streaks of black shadow running up and down their forms, fangs of pure black, and eyes that glowed the yellow of the moon. It was such a stark difference from the pure shadow creatures we'd faced before that I almost hesitated.

But battle was upon us, and hesitation would only bring death. So I caught the lead wolf on my shield and slashed down, drawing forth red blood in a deadly strike.

They were powerful, rocking me back more than the other shadow wolves, but they seemed more susceptible to wounds, going down almost twice as easily as the shadows. It was clear we outmatched them in strength, and the battle was a foregone conclusion within minutes of starting.

They had numbers, though, and you never let your guard down when you faced superior numbers. It was always better to go into any fight knowing you'd win, but in this case, we needed to be careful.

I took my blade free of a second wolf, putting my back to Goose's as he fought off three at a time. We continued this circle of fighting until we'd finally forced our enemy to retreat, another thing the previous shadow wolves wouldn't do.

It was just strange enough to mention, but instead I turned to tend to any wounded before they returned, only to find our healer finishing up with Tomas, one of the few to sustain a serious injury.

"That was different," I said to Ryn as she approached me, weapon still at the ready in case they returned for a surprise attack.

"It was," she answered, watching the tree line the same as me. "We must be getting to the place where the taint isn't as strong. Remember what Jack said, something about a bubble around the area of the princess that isn't affected so harshly by the shadows. We must be close."

"That tracks," I said. We were close indeed. I was sure of it. "Let's get back to it and stay alert. That isn't the last of the monsters here. I guarantee it."

So we ventured forth back into the woods from the clearing we'd stopped in, heading always to the east as instructed. Some more monsters came upon us, lone things like bears and even what appeared to be a werewolf, a humanoid wolf with sharp claws, but not a single battle was harder than the pack of wolves we'd faced, so we overcame each in turn.

Finally, after hours of traveling, we came upon a clearing that opened up into a small lake, and on the opposite side of us was a single stone tower, looming over the lake like a sentinel of the past. It was old and worn, but light poured out through the topmost window, where a fire must be burning inside.

With the knowledge that we were close, we skirted the edge of the lake until we finally reached the base of the tower. A single wooden door stood ajar, and I exchanged looks with my team before saying, "I'll go up, be ready for anything."

I heard a few grumbles, but no one outright told me not to go, so I drew my weapon and ventured forth. It was just after midday, yet it was dark around the lake, as if moonlight were the only light that could get through. The tower door led into a spiraling staircase, empty of anything else, so I followed it up, ready for anything.

A single door, shut in front of me, greeted me at the top of the stairs. I shrugged, then knocked on it with the pommel of my sword.

Knock, knock, knock.

I heard someone stir within, and then a voice, sweet as sugar and smooth as ice, spoke from within.

"Who is it?" she asked, to which I smiled; we'd found the princess after all.

"I was sent here to rescue you, princess. My name is Kaelric, uh, Kaelric Grimholt," I said, unsure of the proper etiquette when speaking with royalty.

"You may enter Kaelric, but be warned, I am cursed, and only a powerful antidote made of pure blood can free me from what I may do to you," she said. I wasted no time pushing the door open and looking inside.

The room was sparsely decorated, with a bed, an end table, a chest, a large fireplace, and a rug or two on the stone floor. None of that caught my attention as much as the beautiful brunette who sat on the edge of the bed in what appeared to be her nightgown. She had sharp features and a friendly look, with pouty lips that were much too red to be natural and blazing green eyes that shone with power.

"I've brought such an antidote," I said, reaching into my belt and pulling it out. "Take this and be free of the curse that holds you here."

She looked perplexed by that statement, but reached out all the same as I neared, taking the antidote.

"Nothing holds me here. I am here by choice after I was cursed, but I will take your antidote all the same. I feel as if I can trust you, young Kaelric," she said, each word like a spell, drawing me in more and more.

"Jack sent us," I finally said as she hovered over the potion, not drinking it.

"Very well," she said, uncorking the antidote and drinking it down in a single gulp.

Nothing really happened, no big glow or shadows, just the princess, whose name I realized I hadn't even gotten yet, and a slight burp on her end.

"Tell me, Princess, what is your name?" I asked, since neither Jack nor anyone we'd asked had told me, so I remained curious.

"Names are powerful things to give out so freely, Kaelric Grimholt," she said. When she said my name, I felt my back straighten and a power wash over me.

But as soon as it took hold of me, it released, and she gave me a gentle smile.

"What was that?" I asked, my sword hand going to my belt.

"Just a show of power. My name is my own, but you may call me Eliese," she said, bowing her head slightly. "I thank you for your kindness, but I'm afraid I must still wait here unless you have defeated the sorcerer, lest his full fury come upon my kingdom."

"We are going to deal with him next. Please wait here and be safe," I said, turning and hurrying out of the room. That 'show of power' had left me feeling uneasy in her presence, as if she could take hold of me at any moment she wished.

She said nothing as I left, but I felt her eyes on my back. Not until I left her tower did I feel safe again.

"Well?" Ryn said. "You free the princess?"

"Yeah, let's go kill the sorcerer," I said, cracking my neck to the side.

The air outside felt heavy as we pressed forward toward the so-called sorcerer's location. The princess gave us directions to a cave fortress where we'd meet our adversary and get a chance to defeat him. It was said to be guarded by shadow and claw, but that mattered little to us as we were ready for just about anything.

"I'm ready for this dungeon to be over," Ryn said to me as we walked.

"Yeah, its been a strange one," Goose said, shaking his head.

"I've kind of liked it," I said, bemused by my party members' attitudes.

"I'm sure you have," Ryn said, rolling her eyes.

We continued forward, encountering no resistance the entire way, until we finally came upon a cave mouth that was said to be the entrance. Here we saw many shadows lurking about and knew we had a fight on our hands.

"I count at least twenty shadows. We need a plan on how to deal with so many at once," I said, thinking hard about what to do.

"Distraction and destruction," Goose said, stepping forward. "I'll be the distraction, you be the destruction."

With that, he ran forward and slammed on his shield, getting many of the shadows' attention. He ran from them, and over half followed him into the dark of the forest. I looked over to the healer and signaled for him to follow after Goose, while the rest of us rushed into battle.

The fight was in our favor now, slashing and cutting through shadows one at a time. By the time Goose appeared back by us, with Seth on his heel, we'd defeated the last of the shadow monsters. We set upon the other, slightly larger half this time, with our full team and dispatched them in short order.

With the way clear, we entered the cave and searched for the door that was said to be within. We found it with little trouble and made it to the top of the stairs, where we found a single figure waiting for us.

In an otherwise barren room, a tall figure with a long white beard and a cauldron of swirling shadows before him awaited us.

"So, you've found me, have you? Prepare yourself, for I won't go down easy," he said. Suddenly, shadows covered him, making him seem much bigger than he'd been just a minute before.

We attacked as a unit, with Goose and me in the front and our damage dealers flanking us, with Wyatt in the back, ready to unleash hell. Meanwhile, Seth readied his wand to heal us, and the battle was on.

Shadows rose around the sorcerer, and we took formation, shields up, ready to catch the blow that was coming for us like an axe swing meant to split wood. The blow was mighty and rocked both of us back, but neither of us was idle. I cast Shove at the sorcerer, throwing him off balance before he could make another attack, and Goose caught most of the blow, taking it in stride.

I followed up my strike with a Spark, but a cloud of shadows formed around our enemy and absorbed my strike, as well as Ryn's Mana Bolts as they slung one after another at our target. It looked like we'd have to get close after all, so I yelled out, "Charge!" and rushed forward.

Immediately, a shadow struck out for me, but I used Quickstep to dodge to the left, then came in fast on his flank, leaving my Iron Skin to take the blow that was coming as it glanced off my shield. Pain lanced up my arm, but I bore it and struck down with my flaming sword.

The shadows parted, and a look of surprise crossed the sorcerer's face as I gutted him deep into his chest and stomach. But just as I saw blood drawn forth, shadows poured into him, healing him. It all came from the cauldron to his left, so I noted that and readied another strategy.

"Take out the cauldron!" I yelled, and my team shifted their focus midstride, each aiming what they could at the item casting the shadows.

Mana Bolts hit first, doing very little to the cauldron, but then came bolts of magic from Seth and arrows from Wyatt. The combined attacks cracked the cauldron before the sorcerer could react, and suddenly shadows spilled out in a faster rhythm than before.

"You fools, you've unleashed the shadow demon, and now we all die!" the sorcerer said, but suddenly he was engulfed in shadows, his skin turning purple and his eyes glowing an intense black. When he next spoke, it was in a demonic voice that was not his own.

"I will cleave you in two and suck the marrow from your bones," he said, his form shifting and growing into a monstrous amalgamation of a humanoid form.

Suddenly, he was ten feet tall, with claws and a maw of sharp teeth. The battle had changed, but we were still up for the challenge.

Shadows, sharpened to a point, slashed at us, and we raised our shields to block the blows. Goose and I were ready for any attack, but we weren't ready for what came next. The shadow monster shifted and changed, becoming several monsters instead of one.

Two came for me, and I braced myself, swinging my flaming sword with practiced ease. There were several moments of unease as, by sheer numbers, the shadows seemed to be winning, but we fought on and began to stem the tide of battle.

The shadow monster came in quickly, and I raised my shield, catching a blow. Then my teammates did what they had to do, charging in with fierce power to halt its advance.

The fight ended more abruptly than it began, with the shadow creature vanishing in a wisp of smoke and the sorcerer's body, ruined and cut to pieces, falling before us.

"We did it," I said, my breath catching as I struggled to recover from the battle.

We recovered and looked for any sign of loot, but found none. With no loot to be found, we turned and left the tower to see the princess. There, we found our loot.

Six chests of gold lay out before us as we arrived, with the princess standing behind them and a swirling portal behind her that would lead us out of the dungeon.

Everyone went in turn, getting their loot, but I paid attention only to Tomas and Ryn's loot before getting my own.

Tomas got a leather chest piece of armor that, when examined, claimed to provide full-body protection against the elements and physical blows. Ryn got a pair of boots that increased her running speed, while I reached in and pulled out a pair of legging armor that didn't quite go with my outfit but had beneficial attributes.

Name: *Legplates of the Bear*
    Rarity: *Rare*
    Special Properties: *Grants +3 Power and Guard*
    Description: *A furry set of two leg plates that, when worn, increase your attributes.*

I put them on, of course, but I thought I looked rather silly. We thanked the princess and left the dungeon together, ending our dungeon run in the shadow dungeon.

CHAPTER 35
BEARLY SURVIVING

We split the group after leaving the dungeon, saying our goodbyes to the trio who had been instrumental in defeating it. We'd all come out of it with plenty of experience and loot, so we were happy as can be.

The sun was setting on our adventure and our time in this area. But we opted to travel into the waning light to get back to the main city so that we'd have a place to rest. I could feel the tension in the air as we traveled, worried about this monster or that. But we encountered nothing for an entire hour, and my tension began to ease.

"I hit Level 25," I said, eyeing the attributes and deciding to place them in my Power attribute as I had been before.

"Same," Tomas said, and Ryn nodded as well.

"We've come so far," Ryn said, nodding her head as we walked.

"And even so, we have so far to go," I said, pausing in our walk to choose my new ability.

Out of the three, it was an easy choice. Shattering Blow was nice, and so was Overhead Smash, but Taunting Roar was by far the most effective use for a front-line fighter. It allowed me to force nearby enemies to target me for a short while, meaning I could ensure that I was the center of the combat and damage output.

I took the skill and looked over my available slots. I liked all four of my currently active slots, but I needed to replace one, so I looked at each one and thought it through.

Iron Skin was too useful as a tank to get rid of, so I disregarded it immediately. Spark was nice to have, but it was probably the most likely to be replaced for now. Shove was handy as well, and so was Quickstep, but I also had some pretty impressive speed at the moment, so maybe...

After some deliberation, I decided that Quickstep was the one to set aside for now, but I'd switch it in as needed. Focusing on the slot, I cleared it and replaced it with Taunting Roar. No sooner had I done that than a roar split the air, and the hairs on my arm stood up.

"Get your new skills in place; we might have a fight on our hands," I said as the sounds of battle and screams filled the air just ahead of us.

Not one to wait while others were in danger, I ran ahead, my team following. What we found as we entered a clearing was nothing short of a nightmare. A massive brown bear, easily twice as big as the last one we'd fought, was munching on the corpse of an adventurer in robes. His companions fought with steel and bow, but it ignored them, its natural armor deflecting their attacks with ease.

"Form up!" I yelled to them, and they looked over as we entered, a clear sign of relief on their faces. They moved to form up behind us, a ranger-type and a sword-wielding man.

"It killed Joseph, and now it's eating him. He was our healer, and our other two members fled," the older of the two said, his voice uneven but concise.

"Let's get its attention then," I said, using Taunting Roar for the first time and feeling its effects hit the bear as I yelled at it.

The bear dropped the half-eaten corpse and turned to me. My blood was on fire as I breathed in and out, ready for anything. Fire ignited on his sword, and he noticed the white flare in the bear's eyes. This was not unlike the other creature they'd faced, which meant something was definitely wrong with it, but I had no cure other than fire and steel.

With the bear's attention fully on me, I tried to come up with a strategy.

"Flank it, but be wary. Its claws look capable of piercing even the hardest armor," I said as I advanced with my shield raised.

Its first attack came with a casual swipe of its claws. I took the glancing blow and lashed out with my flaming sword, cutting shallowly into its flesh. It didn't seem to expect this, roaring in rage as I delivered it a blow that drew forth blood.

But I had no time to celebrate as its other paw came up and hit me full in the shield with such force that I was thrown back several feet. In that moment of weakness, my team acted with the other two who remained from the party that had been attacked.

Skills activated, and power was unleashed. Meanwhile, the bear ignored them and charged after me as I got to my feet. It hit me headfirst on my shield, but I managed to sidestep it, cast Spark, and Shove shortly after to get to the side. My head hurt from the quick use of skills, but I had to do all I could to keep this monster's attention.

I felt fire on my arm as I took a few scratches from its claw while trying to find my footing. My Iron Skin prevented me from losing a limb, but the cut was deep. Pulling a potion from my belt, I downed it as the muscles and flesh tried to knit themselves back together on the fly.

I rolled, ran, and did all I could to put distance between myself and the bear, but it was quick despite its size. I took another hit, my shield barely holding together under the massive damage I was taking. But it wasn't without some wins. Its singular attempt to kill me meant it was taking hits and bleeding all over. I even thought it seemed to be slowing, but I couldn't be sure.

So I fought on, doing my best to weather blows and keep its attention. I felt my skill fade, and in that moment I tried to do it again, but I was mentally blocked from doing so for another minute or so. Unfortunately, that meant it turned on the nearest fighter and went to bite down hard.

Tomas never saw it coming. His left side and arm were crushed by the bear's massive maw, and, like an angry dog, it began to shake him.

"NO!" I screamed and forced the skill to activate, causing my head to split in pain and my vision to swim red. But it worked. The bear turned to me, dropping Tomas like a rag doll.

His body fell, lifeless, into a heap as Ryn ran up to him, his face a mask of anger. I had no more time to watch, as the bear was on me and I felt like complete shit. I took the first blow, moving myself with Shove to avoid the worst of it, and saw Ryn pour a potion into Tomas's mouth.

She looked over, shaking her head as tears streamed down her face. I didn't understand what she meant, but I could see Tomas move, and she appeared just as shocked as I felt. As I turned, I could swear I saw his eyes turn red. She lowered Tomas and then pulled out her weapons.

She rushed the bear, leaping onto its back and hacking away while I somehow held its attention. Deep, deadly cuts covered both my arms, and I fought on as she dealt devastating damage to the monstrous bear.

The bear slowed, moaned in pain, then collapsed before me, down but not dead.

I rushed forward, not waiting a moment, and stabbed deep into its eye. The blade sank into its brain and ended it.

I turned and rushed toward Tomas, with Ryn joining me while the other two stood at a distance.

"Is he alright?" I asked, but Ryn just shook her head.

"I don't know. I gave him a potion, but we have to get him back to town and to a healer," she said. "He isn't out of the woods just yet. Let's go."

"The loot and the core are yours if you want them. We've got to go," I said, turning to the others and not even getting their names.

"Alright," the deep-voiced older of the two said.

With that, we fled to the city. I held Tomas as gently as I could while Ryn collected his bag and weapons, not complaining about the weight.

About an hour into our run, Tomas woke up and spoke.

"I'm hungry," he said, his face pale and blood dripping from his mouth.

"You'll be fed soon enough," I said through heavy breaths. I wouldn't, no, I couldn't stop until we'd gotten him back to the city.

The run burned my muscles to the point of exhaustion, but I pushed myself further and further. I wouldn't lose Tomas, not him, nothing could happen to us, surely we weren't going to lose him.

He faded back into unconsciousness, and I continued to run.

As I held him, I could feel the warmth leaving his body, and I ran all the faster for it.

We reached the gate after what felt like a century of waiting, and the guards approached as I finally allowed myself to slow.

"We need a healer, and fast," I said. "We've given him as many potions as possible, but he isn't healing."

"That man looks dead," one of the guards said, and Ryn gave him a look that silenced him immediately. Then she came forward and whispered in his ear. He went pale and turned and ran, yelling over his shoulder that he'd find a healer.

I don't know what she said, but within five minutes, he was back, and a robed figure followed after him.

"I can't believe you pulled me out of bed for this," the robed man said. But Ryn's look shut him up too as she spoke in a low whisper to them both.

"Heal him, now," she said, her voice filled with fury and a sense of protectiveness.

"I will try, but that man does not look alive to me," the robed figure said.

The priest pulled out a lantern of sorts with a yellow inner glow and began to chant words that sounded foreign and odd to my ears. The light from the lantern came out like tendrils of smoke and wrapped around Tomas.

At first, it seemed they couldn't enter him, and the priest looked at us with a helpless expression. However, he pressed on when Ryn gave him a nod. Suddenly, it surged into his eyes, ears, and mouth. Tomas's body went rigid and then began to shake.

"I've done what I could," the man said, shaking his head. "It'll be on him if he survives."

"He's breathing!" I said, and felt a small bit of warmth enter his body. "Let's get him back to the inn so he can rest."

"He isn't out of the woods yet," the priest said. "If he is strong enough, he could survive, but I might have just bought him time."

"What do we do then?" I asked, desperate for anything.

"It's in the hands of fate now," the priest said.

I looked at Ryn, and she looked back at me. Together, we nodded. We'd be damned if we left this to fate; there had to be something we could do, and we'd find it. Nothing would stop us from saving Tomas, not even fate.

The end of Book 1 of Call of the Dragon Knight

LEAVE A REVIEW

Thank you for reading. Please leave a review.

Check out my website at AuthorTimothyMcGowen.com

If you really liked the book, please consider reaching out and telling me what you enjoyed about it at, Timothy.mcgowen1@gmail.com.

Join my Facebook group and discuss the books at: https://www.facebook.com/groups/234653175151521/

Join my Patreon at: https://www.patreon.com/TimothyMcGowen

ABOUT THE AUTHOR

Timothy McGowen, a Kansas-based author, cherishes the joys of family life with his wife and two daughters. His journey in the literary world began in grade school, and it's a passion that continues to flourish. Inspired by the imaginative realms of Terry Brooks and Brandon Sanderson, Timothy endeavors to follow in their footsteps, crafting stories that resonate with fantasy and adventure enthusiasts.

Prior to dedicating himself to the art of storytelling, Timothy honed his skills as a Software Developer, an experience that not only enriched his technical knowledge but also subtly influences his narrative style. This unique blend of technology and creativity is evident in his work, where he seamlessly integrates elements of Fantasy with splashes of Sci-Fi and the innovative concepts of LitRPG/Gamelit.

Timothy's passion for both reading and writing books is the lifeblood of his creative journey. For those who share this enthusiasm, he warmly invites you to join his newsletter. Stay updated with the latest news and embark on an exciting journey with each new book release.

facebook.com/timothym.mcgowen

x.com/TimothyMMcGowe1

instagram.com/timothy.mcgowen1

LITRPG GROUP

Check out this group if you want to gather together and hear about new great LitRPG books.

(https://www.facebook.com/groups/LitRPGGroup/)

LEARN MORE ABOUT LITRPG/GAMELIT GENRE

To learn more about LitRPG & GameLit, talk to author and just have an awesome time by joining some LitRPG/Gamelit groups.

Here is another LitRPG group you can join if you are looking for the next great read!

Facebook.com/groups/LitRPG.books

List of LitRPG/Gamelit Facebook Groups:

- https://www.facebook.com/groups/LitRPGReleases/
- https://www.facebook.com/groups/litrpgforum/
- https://www.facebook.com/groups/litrpglegends/
- https://www.facebook.com/groups/LitRPGsociety/
- https://www.facebook.com/groups/AleronKong/

www.ingramcontent.com/pod-product-compliance
Lightning Source LLC
Chambersburg PA
CBHW020911060726
47591CB00004B/1186